# Love on the Byline

# Also From Xio Axelrod

The Girl with Stars in Her Eyes
Frankie and Johnny: Let the Music Play
When Frankie Meets Johnny
Camden
Fast Forward
The Warm Up
The Calum

# Love on the Byline

A Plays and Players Novel

## By Xio Axelrod

BLUE BOX PRESS

Love on the Byline
A Plays and Players Novel
By Xio Axelrod

Copyright 2023 Xio Axelrod
ISBN: 978-1-957568-68-3

Published by Blue Box Press, an imprint of Evil Eye Concepts, Incorporated

# Dedication

For Gabrielle, who didn't need footsteps to follow because she slashed through the weeds and forged her own damned path.

Dedication

*Then*

"It's impossible." Blake Dillon sat back in her chair, dark eyes flashing with irritation as she stared down Professor Crosby. "And, to me, it seems to be rooted in privilege."

Ollie's heart beat hard with unnamed emotion, as it always did when he was near her, especially when she was fired up about something she believed in.

At the front of the room, Professor Crosby leaned against his desk, his arms folded, and regarded Blake with his steely gaze. "Ms. Dillon, a *true* journalist will remain impartial because it is impossible to convey a story fairly and accurately when operating under bias."

"I see," Blake said, sounding not at all convinced. "You're saying reporters need to dehumanize themselves."

Crosby's laugh conveyed his disbelief and his dismissal. He ran a hand through his graying hair. "Of course, not."

"Desensitize, then."

This brought their professor up short, and Ollie found he was deeply invested in the answer. Journalism wasn't his major, but he was glad to have chosen the elective. And not only because it had brought Blake into his life.

"I'm not trying to be challenging for the sake of nuisance," she said.

"I only want to understand your position. You assert that journalists cannot and should not become emotionally involved in the story. Yes?"

"Absolutely correct."

Blake let out a sound that wasn't quite a laugh. "I'm sorry Professor but, unless the reporter is a chatbot, their emotions are going to be involved. If I'm doing a story on, let's say, systemic injustice or reproductive health, it's impossible for me to remain detached from those subjects."

"Then you recuse yourself from those stories."

"I'm sorry?" She squared her shoulders, the movement drawing Ollie's attention to the curve of her neck and the way her hair curled against the shell of her ear.

Then Crosby's words filtered through his distracted brain. Ollie raised his hand.

"Mr. Benjamin, you have thoughts on this?"

"I wanted to clarify," Ollie said. "You believe a journalist shouldn't cover a story that will emotionally compromise them?"

"That's an excellent way of putting it." Crosby smiled as if he'd found an ally.

Ollie could feel Blake's eyes on him. He turned to look at her, hating the frown that creased her brow, and turned back to the professor.

"Forgive me, but I'm not sure that's wise or even possible. Everything affects everyone, even if it's indirectly," Ollie said. "Whether it's the weather, a stray cat in a tree, or war in a foreign country, it's all connected to all of us. I agree with Blake. It's impossible to be completely unbiased, especially if the bias is subconscious."

"Exactly," Blake agreed. Her soft, full lips, which had been pressed into a hard line, pursed. "I would argue that it is a journalist's duty to *become* emotionally involved in certain stories. How else would you get to the heart of a thing? The connection is needed."

"What you are describing, Ms. Blake, is activist journalism," Crosby said. "I believe Professor Johnson's Black issues class covers that. You should enroll."

A hushed murmur filtered its way through the rest of the students.

Beside him, Blake took a deep breath that seemed to lower the temperature of the room.

"Professor Johnson's *African American Studies* course is quite popular, sir," she said calmly, though her hand was curled into a fist under the desk. "I tried to enroll—twice—but there's a waiting list. I had to settle for *your* class."

Several emotions passed over Professor Crosby's face in quick succession before it settled into a mask of indignance. He pushed off the edge of his desk and went to the board, a stretch of green slate that probably dated back fifty years. It might still be considered new in the centuries-old classroom.

"Of the five tenets of journalism, impartiality requires that you maintain a sense of neutrality when reporting a story," he said, scribbling the tenets on the board in hard, quick strokes of the chalk. When he finished, he tossed the chalk down and turned to face them. "And if you can't be impartial, then walk away from the story. Or perhaps consider a different career," he added, glancing at Blake before returning to his desk.

Ollie grit his teeth, biting back the things he wanted to say. Like *fuck off* and *you're the one who needs to rethink his career, you pompous asshole.*

"It isn't on the syllabus, but I'd recommend that you pick up *The Elements of Journalism.* I...think some of you might find it enlightening. See you next Friday."

With that, the class was dismissed.

"Enlightening my ass," Blake muttered as she closed her laptop and shoved it into her bag. "It's easy to be detached when you don't have a soul."

Ollie hadn't meant to laugh, and he shut it down fast when Blake stared daggers at him.

"What's so funny?"

"Nothing." He held up his hands. "Nothing at all, I wasn't laughing at you. I promise."

She'd paused, eyeing him with suspicion before she blew out a breath. Her shoulders sagged. "I know, sorry. That dude is a dick."

"That he is," Ollie agreed.

They stood and made their way to the door.

"Are you still up to working on our final project? I know it's not due for weeks, but I'd love to finish early." *Please say yes,* Ollie prayed silently.

Blake gave him a soft smile. "Of course. I'm all yours."

He wished.

"For the next two hours, anyway," she added with a sigh. "After that, I have to go to work. I have the late shift at the café."

"We'll have to make these two hours count, then."

The quick walk across the University of Philadelphia campus was uneventful. The spring semester had just begun, but everyone already seemed to have their heads down and their routines set. The quad was full of activity. Groups sat gathered under the budding leaves of the oak trees, their books spread out on the sprouting grass. Others tossed Frisbees or simply socialized, enjoying the warming weather.

The library was cool and quiet when they entered, and they walked silently up the stairs to the third floor. The nook in the back corner of the Music and Art section had become their spot.

Ollie loved that he and Blake had a *spot*. He smiled when she set down her bag, sat in the heavy oak chair, and breathed a sigh of relief.

No one ever visited this part of the library, at least not when they had been there, so they could talk without being shushed every ten seconds.

"Don't let Crosby get to you."

"That's great advice." She pulled the tie out of her hair and her curls sprang out in every direction.

He watched her wrestle the coils back into the silk and elastic band, like she was taming a living being, and found her utterly charming.

When she looked up at him, he couldn't hide his grin.

She rolled her eyes. "Sorry. You're right. It's just that he's such a...a..."

"A sanctimonious prick?"

Her smile was blinding. "Come sit and let's crack this assignment wide open."

Helpless, Ollie did as he was told. He sat as close to her as he dared, surprised when she scooted closer and opened her laptop. The warmth of her thigh pressed against his was life-altering.

He scrambled to retrieve his own laptop. Work.

Right.

They had work to do.

"So, I was thinking," she said as she leaned even closer. Her arm brushed his and Ollie felt the contact travel through his body like a current. "What if we approached it by..."

Blake's warm, brown skin was as soft as a petal. He couldn't concentrate on what she was saying.

"...exploration of gender fluidity..."

She smelled like candy.

"...how conventional gender norms..."

He wanted to set her in the middle of his tongue and simply...let her dissolve there.

"... that women were often excluded from literature or portrayed in stereotypical ways..." She trailed off. Blake lifted a hand and wiggled her fingers in front of his face. "Earth to Oliver."

He felt his skin flush, and knew he was red-faced. "Sorry," he stammered, removing his glasses and cleaning them to give his eyes somewhere else to look. His brain needed something else to focus on other than *fuck, she's beautiful.*

She knew. The twinkle in her eyes told him she knew, and that she didn't mind. Maybe even felt a similar pull.

"You with me?"

Ollie nodded because that's the only place he wanted to be. With her.

Replacing his glasses, he swallowed hard and told himself to stop acting like a lovesick idiot. Even if he *was* a lovesick idiot.

"I am with you." He focused on typing up their notes and realized he had no idea what she'd been saying. "The, uh, gender norms."

Blake was staring at him, her dark eyes full of concern. "You okay, bud?"

*Bud. Buddy. Friend.*

Because that's what they were. He really was an idiot.

"Yep, I'm fine." Ollie shook out his shoulders. "I was just...uh...thinking about the party this weekend. Bran asked me to pick up some stuff and I don't know which store carries it."

Blake exhaled harshly, turning her attention back to her screen. "Bran." She made the name sound like a swear word.

It wasn't the first time she'd shown animosity towards Ollie's best friend. He didn't understand why. Everyone loved Bran. Well, everyone except a few of the girls he'd hooked up with.

The thought brought him up short. Had he missed something? No. Nope. He would have known. Right?

Still. "Did you and Bran ever...?"

Blake's head snapped up so fast, Ollie thought she might have hurt herself.

"Me? And *Brandon legacy-golden-boy Peters?* God, no."

The relief that swept over him was swift and definitive. He definitely had it bad for this girl, and he had no clue what to do about it. They were friends and he didn't want to jeopardize that, even if the idea of being *more* than that made his heart tap dance inside his chest.

"I'm actually working on a story about him."

"You are?"

Blake nodded and then seemed to hedge. "Well, not about *him*, per se, but students like him. Legacies, especially those on athletic scholarships."

He frowned. "Bran's not—"

She held up her hand. "Before you say *Bran's not like that*, I know you guys are tight. Though, honestly Ollie, I can't for the life of me understand why."

"Are we really that different? I'm here on an athletic scholarship. Bran and I are on the same soccer team."

She was shaking her head before he even finished. "Yeah, but you two couldn't be more different. You... You're..."

Ollie found himself holding his breath, eager to hear what she had to say about him, while also terrified to know her thoughts.

"I'm...?"

She gave a soft laugh, her eyes warm as she looked at him. "You're you."

Ollie didn't know exactly what she meant by that, but he basked in the glow from her tone and her expression which told him all he needed to know for now.

"Thanks," he said. "I think."

Blake nudged his knee with hers. "One hour and forty-five minutes. Let's get some work done."

He nodded and set his hands back on his keyboard. Before she could say anything else, he asked, "Are you coming to the party? It's Saturday."

She looked up, clearly surprised by the invitation, and seemed to think it over before shrugging one shoulder.

"You know, I might. It depends on whether I can get some work done on my story for the Ledger." She gave him a pointed look and he knew he was pouting. "I'll try."

Ollie tempered his joy. "Cool."

Saturday brought warm weather and sunshine, perfect for Alpha Q's first spring bash.

He wasn't a member of the fraternity but he rented a room in the enormous house, and Bran always included him in their plans as if he were one of them. The brothers didn't seem to mind. There were a number of their teammates in the frat, not to mention other athletes. It had earned them the nickname the *Grocks* or Greek Jocks.

Ollie was a planner, an organizer, so handling the details of the frat's soirees—procuring the kegs, managing the invites, ensuring there was enough food and non-alcoholic beverages to keep anyone from getting alcohol poisoning—those things came naturally. He did it all, happily, as he did many things for Bran. He owed him so much.

"There's my boy," Bran said as he bounded down the curved stairs of the frat's three-story house. "Everything looks great, man. Thanks."

"Not a problem."

"Make sure you actually enjoy yourself, this time. Your work is done. Have a little fun." Bran winked.

"I will, promise." *Especially if Blake actually shows up.*

Ollie wandered through the party, stopping here or there to chat with the brothers and their guests. Two hours in, the rager was in full swing. Music pumped through Bluetooth speakers situated throughout the first and second floors, the pool table at the center of the dining room already had a crowd gathered around it, and the center of the living room had been transformed into a makeshift dance floor.

He made his way into the kitchen, winding around the bodies playing beer pong to get to the fridge where he grabbed his second Corona.

"Oliver!"

He turned to find one of the brothers, Ren, behind him. "Hook me up, man."

He handed Ren the Corona in his hand.

"Sweet! You're, like, *the* best little helper ever. Don't know where *Brando* found you, but we owe that dude some premium bud."

Ollie didn't smoke, so he didn't know how to respond to that. He nodded and smiled, turning back to the fridge to get another beer.

They were out of Corona, so he grabbed the next cold bottle and popped the cap.

Another hour went by, and Ollie's anticipation at seeing Blake turned into resignation that she wasn't going to come. He'd parked himself in a group of people debating whether there was a difference between pro wrestling and the *Real Housewives* of somewhere or other when he heard a commotion in the living room.

His group barely acknowledged the yelling, too engrossed in their own debate, but Ollie excused himself and went to investigate.

He heard a girl's voice, loud and angry over the thumping music. And then Bran's booming baritone cut through the noise.

Pushing past the looky-loos that encircled the altercation, Ollie stopped in his tracks.

Blake and Bran were locked in a face-off, her with her hands on her hips and him with his hands in the air.

"I don't know what you're talking about, Princess."

"*Don't* call me that. I am *not* your princess. Or anyone's. Nor am I buying this Mr. Innocent act. You know perfectly well what you did."

Bran's half smile was for the crowd gathered around them. He shrugged, putting on a show while Ollie tried to assess the situation. "Baby, I wish I did," Bran said, taking a long, languid look at her. "Cause then I could make it right."

There were snickers from the onlookers, but Ollie's focus was on Blake, on the set of her jaw and the vein ticking at her temple. Her expression was murderous, and he stepped between them just as she began to lunge forward.

"What's going on?"

She blinked up at him as if fighting through a red haze. "Oliver. Your *friend* here sabotaged my story."

"He…what?"

"They killed it," she replied, her jaw tight." The Ledger. The editor killed my story on legacies, thanks to your buddy over there."

"I didn't do shit," Bran said over his shoulder.

"Like hell, you didn't." If Blake's eyes could shoot lasers, Bran would have been in pieces on the hardwood floor.

Again, Ollie found himself putting his body between Blake and her target. "Hang on," he said as calmly as he could. "Can we go somewhere else and talk about this?"

"I don't know what's got her panties in a twist, but I'm not gonna take her shit." Bran pushed through the ring of spectators, some of whom followed in his wake.

With the spectacle over, Ollie and Blake stood essentially alone in the center of the room. She was breathing hard and blinking fast.

"Come with me." He led her out to the back porch, where only a few people stood, smoking. They went to the other side.

"Asshole!" She huffed out a frustrated breath. "How are you friends with someone like that?"

"Bran's a good guy."

"He really isn't," Blake spat. "He used his name and h-h-his *weight* to pressure the editor. I know it."

"You have proof?" He didn't want to believe Bran would do something like this.

"No, but—"

Relief and frustration flooded him in equal measure. "Then why did you storm in here accusing him?"

Her eyes flashed dangerously, this time with disbelief. "You think I'm lying? I'm making it up?"

"No, but—"

"Maybe you think I'm too close to the story? Since I have every loan and grant I can possibly get, and I still have to work two part-time jobs to afford this school, I can't be impartial?"

"Can you?" It was the wrong thing to say.

"You sound like Crosby right now."

"Blake," he said, hoping to sound calm. "Be reasonable. I'm only asking if you have some proof that Bran screwed with your story."

"I have my intuition. Of course, there isn't proof. He's dumb but he's still too smart for that, it was something my editor said that makes me sure it's him."

Ollie clenched his jaw. Bran was a goof, and occasionally stuck his foot in his mouth, but he was a little tired of Blake always badmouthing him when she didn't know him at all.

Her eyes narrowed. "You're always so quick to defend him. Why?"

"He's my best friend."

"Yeah, but why? You're so much better than a guy like that, or...I thought you were."

Unease prickled at the back of his neck. "What do you mean?"

Blake took a step back. "Maybe I'm too close to *you* to really see you. Maybe you're more like Brandon Peters than I realized. Why else would you two be so close?"

He couldn't deny it. He and Bran had a lot in common, but none of it made either of them bad people.

"You're jumping to a lot of conclusions," he heard himself say.

"No," she replied in a tone he hadn't heard her use with him before. "Only one. My grandfather always said you could tell a lot about a person by the company they keep."

She took another step backward, and another, until she was standing at the top of the steps.

"Blake, wait." The further she moved away from him, the more it felt like the end of something that hadn't had a chance to start.

The look she gave him was sad. Regretful. "I'm going to have to step away from our project," she said, the words landing like a hammer blow. "It's early in the semester. I'm sure you'll find someone else."

"Blake, I..." He scrambled for the words that would explain how wrong she was, but he couldn't find them. Maybe they didn't exist. Maybe she was right.

She went down the first few steps before turning back to him. "You should really think about what friendship means, Oliver. Because, from where I'm standing, you're more of a friend than he deserves."

Blake took the two remaining steps and walked off into the night.

The following Friday, she didn't show up for class. She'd dropped it.

And him.

*Now*

When her phone rang at you've-got-to-be-kidding o'clock in the morning, Blake fought hard against wakefulness. Sleep had been elusive of late, and she had been running on fumes. She sent up a silent wish for the caller to give up, sighing with relief when her phone went silent. Her lumpy mattress was far more appealing than dealing with a wrong number or a late-night butt dial from one of her roommates, so she remained blissfully starfished.

For about fifteen more seconds.

Whoever it was couldn't seem to take a hint because they called back and kept calling. Awake and grumpy, with her cheek plastered to a sheaf of papers sprawled across her duvet, Blake rolled to her back. She'd surely have creases in her skin, and probably a few ink stains. She had worked late into the night and her laptop lay open beside her, its screen dark.

The house she shared with her two roommates was eerily quiet, which meant they were either still out or sleeping in. She tried rallying herself to grab the phone and see if whoever it was had left a voice mail.

She managed to wriggle towards her nightstand and pick it up before the ringer went off again. Pushing a stray twist of hair from her face, she sat up and looked at the screen.

"Gideon" she answered, frowning. "Why are you calling me at such an unholy hour?"

"There you are, thank fuck," her boss said, sounding equal parts relieved and annoyed. His default. "I need you in the office ASAP. Last night, we got a tip Desiree Stanley was holed up with Brandon Cody."

"Who is where with whom?"

"I sincerely hope you're kidding right now."

Blake yawned, her mind still foggy. "I hate to disappoint you, but I have no idea who those people are."

"Get up, get dressed, and get over here. Right now, before the hounds come sniffing around our story."

"Wait, you want me to come now?" She squinted at her phone and shuddered when she saw the time. She'd been out until three a.m. chasing down a lead on a story she'd been working on for months. One that had real consequences for kids from vulnerable communities in Los Angeles. "Can't it wait a few hours?"

"Didn't you hear what I said?" Gideon's voice got even more nasal the more frustrated he became. "Be here before seven. Desk security will be expecting you."

"But Gid—"

"Dillon, I don't have time for handholding. Do you want the assignment or not?"

No, Blake did not want the assignment. She didn't want anything to do with the whole celebrity beat. But then her stomach growled, reminding her why she couldn't say no. Also, there was her journalistic integrity which she'd somehow managed not to lose entirely, despite spending the last few months digging up dirt on Hollywood puppets. Whenever and wherever the editor said they needed you, you went.

"Can I count on you?" Gideon asked her. For as much grief as she gave him over the assignments, he kept sending them her way. Kept her employed.

She honestly had no right to complain. "Yeah, boss. I'm on my way."

"Good. Thanks." He sounded relieved. "I'd like to scoop TMZ for a change instead of always biting off their content."

"Was that dig aimed at me after you asked *me* to do *you* a favor?" She swung her legs over the side of the bed, her snark booting back up along with her brain, apparently. Gid was a decent boss, and the closest thing to an ally she had at the Los Angeles Gazette—even if he didn't take her career goals as seriously as she'd like.

"I didn't know that asking you to do your job was considered a favor."

Well, touché.

"Yeah, yeah." Blake put the call on speaker, got to her feet, and stretched. Maybe she could sneak in a few minutes of yoga before heading out. "Since you owe me, will you take a look at what I sent you last night?"

"Blake."

"Gideon it's only a few hundred words. Surely you can make time for that. It's only an intro to the story I'm working on, but I think it could be big." She shuffled into the kitchen to make a pot of coffee. She'd need to drink the entire thing if she had any hope of making it through this day.

"You know I love how driven you are, Blake, but Sonya isn't going to let you run with that predatory talent agency or whatever the angle is that you're going for. If there *is* something there, she'll—"

"If?" She set the decanter in the sink and turned on the water to fill it. "What do you mean, if? I'm making enemies all across the city to confirm some of those details about Diamond Moon Enterprises. I'm doing my due diligence."

"That's not what I meant," he said, sounding at least a little contrite. "I know you're thorough. It's just that... Let's be real, that story is too big for a cub reporter."

Well, that was a kick in the teeth.

It cut deep that he still viewed her as green. Blake felt she'd done enough to at least earn the respect of her editor, even if she did grouse a lot.

She thought about her grandfather and what he told her about standing up for the stories he believed in. Was she not allowed to do the same?

"I'm not a kid, Gideon." She yanked open the door to the fridge and rolled her eyes when she was met with mostly empty shelves. Was she the only person in this house share who bought groceries? She poured half a glass of orange juice and grabbed a handful of baby carrots. At least she wouldn't develop scurvy. "And you know I learned from the best."

Gideon cleared his throat, his voice softening. "It has nothing to do with your age. And, yes, you learned a lot from your grandpa. Trent Dillon is a goddamned legend. There's just no way Sonja James will give a story that big to anyone but a senior reporter, no matter what their pedigree. And if you go to her with it now…"

She knew what he was saying, and it stung. She paced around the tiny kitchen.

"You and I both know I'm not cut out for the gossip column. I don't keep up with who's dating who, and I could care less who Delia Stanley—"

"Desiree."

"Whoever! I don't care who some actor is banging in a hotel room in Studio City. If they're consenting adults, I say let people live."

"You better start caring, or at least start faking it. You think I walked out of U of LA, my degree clutched in my hand, and thought to myself, *hell yeah, I'm gonna kill this gossip column game?*" Gid asked, sounding almost as exasperated as she felt. "It's not about what we want, it's about what readers want. They eat these scandals like candy, and we like eating actual food and paying actual rent."

"Yeah, but don't you ever get tired of being the candy man?"

"Sure, I do." She caught the first hint of resignation in his voice. "But stories like these are why we all have jobs. Look, none of us are going to win a Pulitzer."

"Gee, thanks." Deflating, she returned to the sink to find the carafe overflowing. Ugh, she hated wasting water. But, also, he was right.

Thanks to her grandfather, Blake's goals were lofty. She'd grown up at the knee of a great journalist, stealing peeks at the green leather notebook he always had in his pocket that held hints of his process. But maybe that wasn't what the future held for her.

As if reading her thoughts, he said, "Look, if anyone could rise from the muck, it would be you who ends up winning the big prizes. After all, it's in your blood."

She poured the excess water from the carafe into the watering can. "Thanks."

It was a pipe dream, and she knew it. In her head, she did, but her heart grabbed onto Gideon's optimism.

"I mean it," Gideon said. "You're the next Frances Fitzgerald. But for now, get your ass to my office."

At seven on the dot, she knocked on his office door.

"You did good on the Karen K. story, kid," Gideon said as he gestured for her to take the seat across from him. "Stewart said you made friends with the hotel staff."

The bills he pressed into her hands weren't as crisp and new as the ones she'd pulled from the ATM to pay her last source, but she didn't care. It meant she could afford to replenish the pantry, or at least buy a few things to hide from her perpetually ravenous roommates.

"Just the woman at reception." She adjusted her glasses. "Gid, I know you think it's impossible, but if Sonja just—"

He held his hand up, effectively cutting her off, and heaved a sigh. "Before you force me to rehash all the reasons why you will not get the go-ahead from Sonja, I have a proposition for you."

Blake slumped back into the chair. The thing was damned uncomfortable, and she squirmed. "This is the worst chair I've ever sat in."

"Maybe, but it looks cool. Vintage." He steepled his hands on his desk. "How would you like to work on an in-depth exposé on one of Hollywood's rising stars?"

"It sounds like you're trying to dress up a shitpost." She was aware of how whiny she sounded, but come on. "Is this why you dragged me out of bed at Hell o'clock in the morning?"

"This isn't a shitpost, Dillon. I'm trying to give you what you want—a more important story."

"Oh, right, a fluff piece on a talking head is a very important story." Insulted, she was already making a mental grocery list of things that didn't need refrigeration. Pita chips, peanut butter. Lately, she'd been craving Tastykakes. She wondered if she could cajole her mother into sending a case from Philly and dug into her bag for her phone.

"Blake."

"Huh?" When Gideon didn't respond, she sighed and gave her boss her full attention.

Brows drawn together, he stood up and walked over to close the door before turning to lean against it. Arms crossed, he frowned down at her.

"What did you think would happen when you moved out here?"

"What do you mean?" she shifted in her seat.

"I just wonder how you thought this would go. You'd come to town with your expensive Ivy League degree, all your curls and dimples, and L.A. would roll out the red carpet for you?"

She wanted to argue that she'd barely been able to afford the University of Philadelphia, even with scholarships and grants, but she didn't think that was his point.

"I thought I'd come here, pay my dues as a beat reporter, and see where things went from there."

"A beat reporter?" Gideon said brightly. Too brightly. "A beat reporter. Well, damn. If I had known that I would have put you on the celeb beat— Oh, *wait.*" He held his hand to his chest in mock surprise. "I did!"

"Ha. Ha."

Her editor walked over and collapsed into his chair. He tapped on the desk. "Are you familiar with the *Captain Sky* franchise?"

"The one our mark is gunning for, right? Brent?" Gid pursed his lips, and she scrambled to remember the name because she had read something about this. It was a big deal. Branford? Bruce. "Brody...Camden?"

"Brandon Cody," Gideon said, giving Blake a look that wordlessly asked *why am I keeping you employed?*

She sat up straighter and tried to at least appear invested. Blake may have hated the assignments Gideon gave to her, but she was a professional and he was keeping food on her table. "Right. That's who I meant. Brandon Cody. Big star. Huge."

He narrowed his eyes. "Can you even name one of his films?"

She reached for one of the green notebooks in her bag, hoping against hope something in it would jog her memory.

"Without consulting your notes." At her blank stare, he ran a hand over his face. "I swear, sometimes I think you live under a rock."

He wasn't too far off the mark. "I don't have a lot of free time." Or a TV, or any disposable income.

"I know blockbusters aren't good enough for your literary mind, but surely you saw the big ass billboards all over town when the new *Guardians of the Sky* film released last summer?"

"Well, no. I've only been in L.A. for eight months, remember?"

Gideon sat back. "Oh. Right. But still, Cody stole the film. He only had a few scenes, and one memorable line, but it was enough. Rumor has it, they're looking to build an entire franchise around his character. He's got endorsement deals out the wazoo."

"The wazoo?" She laughed.

"Mi abuelo used to say that all the time," he replied, shrugging. "It's what you get when you learn English from watching mid-century, American sitcoms."

"So, Cody has a bad rep he needs to clean up?" At Gideon's nod, Blake continued.

"The last woman he was linked to, a former co-star, is engaged to the actor who played Thor." Gideon said, leaning forward. "And guess how she met her beloved?"

"The Velvet Rope Dating app?" At Gid's headshake, Blake frowned. "I assume you're going to tell me?"

"On set. And he was engaged to someone else at the time."

Blake exhaled, unable to hide her disgust. "Hollywood is so toxic."

"Indeed. So, if Cody is stepping out with a woman engaged to someone else..."

"Right." She wasn't a fan of delving into people's personal lives. After all, who knew what was going on behind closed doors? From what she'd seen since moving to L.A., relationships—real ones, anyway— were as rare as unicorns. Honestly, it was like being back in college. People were either looking to hook up or gossiping about who was hooking up, with the added bonus of everyone chasing fame at any cost.

"This seems pretty shady to me," she said.

Gideon rubbed his hands together. "Oh, it gets better. Cody's people claim the guy in the more...illicit photos we got ahold of isn't him."

"And you think they're telling the truth?"

"I spoke to his publicist directly," he informed her. "Noelia Mokeyane doesn't fuck around. We've agreed to sit on Codygate in exchange for an exclusive, in-depth exposé on the man himself."

"Codygate?"

He grinned. "Awesome name, right?"

"Sometimes, I think you're twelve."

Gideon's grin widened as he picked up his phone. "Only sometimes? Okay, I'm texting you the address. Shadow Cody while he goes about his business. Home, work, whatever access they allow for as long as they allow it."

"You mean shadow him, like, on set?" This time, she didn't need to fake her interest. She hadn't had the opportunity to visit a studio lot yet, and it was on her bucket list.

"Wherever he goes, you'll go. Within reason," Gideon added. "His agent is desperate to clean up Cody's rep. The *Sky* franchise is skittish when it comes to image, and something like this might make them drop him all together."

"If it's true."

"What is truth? You'll write what you see. Get to know the man behind the rumors. Are you in?"

"Okay, yeah." Blake made some mental calculations. It was a lot of fuel, not to mention meals out. She supposed she could pack some PB&J sandwiches and stock up on trail mix.

"What's that face? I thought this would be good for you."

"No, no. I'm grateful, really," she rushed to assure him. "It all sounds…intriguing, but also expensive."

"Ah, right." Gideon opened a drawer and took out his wallet, pulling out a credit card and sliding it over, along with a wad of bills.

"Here's five hundred cash. Don't go crazy with the card, but get what you need," he instructed.

"What if I need something snazzy to wear to one of his events?"

"Just keep track of your expenses."

"Thanks. I will, of course." Blake slipped both the card and the cash into her bag and rose to leave.

"Dillon, you know I think you're a hell of a writer." He folded his hands on the desk and met her surprised gaze. "What? I tell you that all the time."

Not once had he said those words, but she wasn't going to argue. "Thanks, boss."

"I realize this isn't what you signed up for." He paused. "Well, technically, you did sign up for it, but it isn't where your heart is. You want to make a name for yourself. I get that."

"I just want to write stories that matter."

"It's all about perspective. In this case, an actor with a reputation for bad behavior is looking to revamp his image." Gideon smoothed his hands across the desk and sat back. "Either way, look at this as an opportunity. You can write an exclusive portrait of one of Hollywood's brightest stars under thirty. It's not a bad thing to have your name linked to it.

She really hoped that was true.

That afternoon, Blake found herself pulling into the circular drive of a house in Malibu that probably cost more money than she could ever make in five lifetimes. Surprisingly, there was no gate, and no one approached her car when she drove past the front door and parked in the shade of some cypress trees.

She hadn't done her homework on Brandon Cody. Even though she despised the narcissistic nature of his industry, she decided to go into their initial meeting with as little bias as possible. More than once, she'd been warned not to let her personal opinions affect her work, so she was determined to remain neutral. For now. All she knew was that, by all accounts, Cody was a young, handsome actor with a reputation for sleeping around. And that he had a potentially huge franchise on his shoulders. If she learned anything beyond that, for today anyway, it would be first-hand in this preliminary meeting.

The house was modest by Malibu standards, at least from the outside. The two-story, late-century home was white with a terracotta tiled roof, a three-car garage, and about a billion windows. The amount of natural light inside must be incredible.

She was glad she'd chosen the blue silk jumpsuit to wear. Aside from being the most expensive thing in her closest, it made her feel less conspicuous as she walked up to ring the bell. There was a camera, but no disembodied voice asked her who she was and why she was there. Less than a minute passed before the door opened, and a tall, blond man dressed in a tracksuit eyed her up and down.

"Yes?" The amount of impatience suffused in that one syllable would have been impressive had it not been directed at her.

Blake straightened her spine. "I'm here to see Brandon Cody." Assuming she had the right house, she dug in her bag and pulled out her press credentials, holding them up for the man to see. "He should be expecting me."

He squinted at them. "Right. No one mentioned you were coming, but when do they ever tell me anything?" His shoulders slumped as he eyed her again, his head tilting in thought. "You don't look like a reporter."

"Because...?"

"You're a *baby*." He stepped back and gestured Blake inside. "Reporters usually have far more...mileage."

She turned to him as he closed the door behind them. "I can't tell if you're disappointed."

His face broke into a smile. "Oh, not at all. Maybe you'll have a fresh perspective. The media in this town is so jaded. I'm Hans, by the way."

"Blake." She followed Hans as he led her deeper into the house. "Are you Cody's assistant?"

"Me? No, that's a thankless job." He waved his hand in the air as they walked. "Technically, I'm the trainer, but I also handle our boy's nutrition. I was just in the kitchen making smoothies."

As he finished, they turned the corner into an enormous chef's kitchen. It was spotless, except for the island where a blender sat next to a sea of fruits, vegetables, and grasses planted in tiny trays.

"Wow, this is like a personal juice bar."

Hans rounded the island and picked up a knife, slicing the rest of a kiwi and tossing it into the blender. "Only the best for the big guy."

She glanced around. "Speaking of which..."

"He's in a meeting, but they should be done soon. Make yourself comfortable."

Checking her watch, she pondered asking Hans a few questions about his boss. Upon first impression, he seemed like the kind of person who had no qualms spilling tea.

Before she could fish a notebook from her bag, movement from her right drew Blake toward a set of glass doors. They led to a wide balcony overlooking a large patio. The in-ground pool and spa weren't a surprise but, like the rest of the house, they were understated. A small structure, perhaps a pool house, sat in the back corner under a canopy of trees.

"Feel free to go for a dip," Hans said as he stepped up beside her.

"It's tempting."

"Smoothie?" He offered a glass holding a thick, green liquid. It looked like something you'd find at the bottom of a neglected pool.

She recoiled. "Uh, no."

"Not your thing?" he asked, grinning.

"No offense, but it looks like you used that blender to mow the lawn."

Hans let out a sharp bark of laughter. "Well, you're not entirely wrong." He took a sip, smacked his lips together as if judging the taste, and turned back to the counter. "Needs more ginger."

"Mind if I snoop a bit? I see some photos on the mantle in there." She pointed at the fireplace in the great room.

"Be my guest." As he fired up the blender, Blake made her exit from the kitchen.

Again, this room was thoughtfully furnished, with creams and peaches dominating the palette. Natural wood tones kept all the white from feeling too industrial. Over the gas fireplace sat a row of framed photos. An older black and white photo of an African-American couple took her by surprise.

Okay, so maybe she should have done a basic Google search on her subject. She took out her pen and a fresh notebook.

*Cody keeps family photos over the fireplace. Frames look original, mis-matched. Not staged. House is quiet, clean. Fitness and nutrition guy, Hans. Possible interviewee.*

She continued down the line of photos—one of a presumably infant Cody with his parents, another of a tween-aged Cody in a cap and gown. He did look a little familiar, and Blake wondered if she had seen one of his movies or an episode of something. When she moved to the next picture, though, the breath whooshed out of her lungs.

"What the…" Snatching the photo off the mantle, Blake stared hard. She'd never been prone to hallucinations before, but there was a first time for everything.

She moved on to the next and the next, each image more baffling than the last. Maybe her blood sugar was low. Had she forgotten to eat? Because it couldn't possibly be, "Oliver?"

"The only person who calls Ollie that is his mom, and only when she's pissed at him," a booming voice said from across the room.

"I guess this is happening," Bran said as he leaned against his desk.

"What are you really worried about?"

His gaze flicked to Ollie and then away. "I'm not as reckless as people think. I know how to behave or whatever. I don't... I mean, I'm not..." Sighing in frustration, he rounded the glass desk and threw himself into his white leather wingback, swiveling the chair to face the large window on the back wall.

"Do you remember when U of P won the soccer intra-state tournament, and the local paper wanted to interview me?"

Ollie did remember. He winced. "Yeah."

"Not my finest moment," Bran recalled.

"It's probably not something the guy will ever forget."

Bran, in his excitement, had blurted out some embarrassing truths when the reporter asked him how he planned to celebrate the win. "I need to take a shit. Then I'll shower and go get blitzed with my buddies," he'd replied. The university had not been amused, especially when the asshole reporter printed it word-for-uncensored word.

"I'm not good on the fly. You know that," he said. "Give me a script, and I'm golden, but I've never been great at improv."

"I can help." Ollie took the seat across from him. "Give you some talking points to stick to, stuff you can use when you get stuck."

Bran perked up and spun the chair to face him. "Yeah? That would be awesome. Between the two of us, you're definitely the wordsmith. Look at how you fixed those scenes we shot the other day! Lorna is ready to marry you."

All he had done was suggest some tweaks to Bran's dialogue in a few scenes. "That was nothing."

"Are you serious? Even Tim loved the changes. I keep telling you, you have a future as a screenwriter, or at least a script doctor, if you want it."

The back of his neck heated and he adjusted his glasses. "Thanks.

Anyway, like I was saying, I'll be here to help."

"What would I ever do without you?"

"Probably fetch your own drinks?"

Bran chuckled. "Speaking of which, Hans should be making my smoothie. Would you grab it for me? I want to do some prep before the guy from the Gazette gets here." He held his palms together as if to say please?

"Sure." Laughing, Ollie jumped up. "Anything else?"

"Nah, just the smoothie," he replied as he flipped through pages. "Well, maybe one of those multigrain bagels you had the other day?"

"From the farmer's market? It's only held on Sundays."

Bran's eyes were wide and hopeful.

Sighing, Ollie fished out his car keys. "I guess I could track down the bakery. I'll bring your smoothie and go fetch your bagel."

"You're the best, man."

The doorbell rang as Ollie made his way towards the front of the house and he heard Hans speaking to someone.

He swung by the media room to grab the tablet he'd left there the day before, then headed back towards the kitchen. The island was covered with fruits and veggies, some of which were sliced. Chunks of green and yellow filled the blender, and he walked over to grab a glass, stopping in his tracks when a familiar voice floated down the hallway.

"No offense," he heard a woman say, "but it looks like you used that blender to mow the lawn."

Fucking fantastic. One of Bran's hookups was back for another round. He was about to march over to Bran's bedroom and rip him a new one. The last thing they needed was another tale for someone to tattle.

His blood ran cold as he remembered they hadn't settled on a day or time for the Los Angeles Gazette to send someone over for the preliminary Q&A. And then it dawned on him that they'd all been expecting a man when it could very well be a woman—which was disturbingly sexist of all of them. And short-sighted. *Of course*, the Gazette would send a woman. What better way to sneak through Bran's defenses?

Jesus.

And yet, nothing accounted for why the hair stood up on Ollie's arms as she continued talking to Hans.

He *knew* that voice. Had dreamt of it time and time again.

"Mind if I snoop a bit? I see some photos on the mantle in there."

Ollie's heartbeat took off on a sprint. *It couldn't be.*

"Be my guest," Hans replied, and Ollie made a mental note to talk to him about letting strangers have free reign in the house.

His feet carried him down the short hall to the doorway that separated the foyer from the great room where he skidded to a halt.

There was really no reason for him to recognize Blake Dillon, even though she stood in the middle of Bran's house. They were three thousand miles and five years away from the last glimpse he'd had of her, but he had held on to her image somehow. Filed it away in a cabinet at the back of his mind, one he opened only when he was alone and lonely and regretting some of the choices he'd made. Or hadn't made, in her case.

Blake hadn't changed much. Her hair was a couple of inches shorter, and her outfit a little more grown-up than the ripped jeans and band tees he remembered her wearing in college.

He felt a little stalkerish watching her as she perused the photos on the mantle. When she got to the one of Ollie with Bran at his parents' vow renewal ceremony, her shoulders stiffened.

"Oliver?"

"The only person who calls Ollie that is his mom, and only when she's pissed at him."

She turned, shock written all over her face. "Brandon...Peters?"

"Someone's done their homework." Bran walked over to her, his shoulders back and his trademark grin in place. "But, please, let's stick with Cody. Don't want to confuse my fans."

Ollie managed to steady himself, but only barely. Blake. Here. In Bran's house.

It was a nightmare.

It was a dream.

And—yep—she looked like she'd seen a ghost. Her eyes locked on Bran's as she took a tiny step back, her dark eyes narrowed to slits. "Wait, what...? You're...?"

Out of the corner of his eye, he saw Bran's step falter, but he couldn't tear his gaze away from Blake fucking Dillon—standing in Bran's great room—though she didn't seem to notice him.

He guessed some things never changed.

"Is this a joke?" She scowled at Bran.

"Uh, no?" Bran replied, sounding confused. Moving forward, he held out a hand "Brandon Cody, but you can call me Bran. And you are?"

Oh, Jesus. Fuck. Really? Ollie took a step forward, struggling because his muscles were suddenly rigid with tension.

Her expression turned murderous. "Blake." When Bran didn't respond, she added, "Dillon." Her last name was like a single gunshot aimed at his head.

"Nice to meet you, Blake Dillon." Bran continued to hold out his hand, smiling broadly now.

Blake stared at it as if he held a steaming pile of feces. "Nice to meet me? You can't be serious."

"Blake, er... Hi," Ollie finally managed to croak. Clearing his throat, he reminded himself he was an adult and not the gangly teen she'd known in college. Correction, still gangly, just older.

Blake's look of disgust morphed into a smile that put the sun to shame. "Oliver?"

Jesus, he'd forgotten that she did that, how she used his full first name more often than not. It sounded heavenly coming from her lips. With only a few syllables, she had erased years of his practiced composure. Words eluded him.

He waved awkwardly, as if she weren't standing less than three feet away. "Hi," he said again. Closing his eyes, he cursed under his breath. "Good to see you."

"What on earth are you doing here?" She took two steps forward but caught herself, her brows pinching together again in confusion.

"You know her?" Bran asked him.

"Seriously?" she snapped.

"Dude." Ollie shook his head. He loved Bran, but he could be such an ass when it came to remembering things. And people. "This is Blake. From U of P?"

Giving her a onceover, Bran's frown deepened. Zero recognition on his face. Even Ollie was stunned.

"Jesus," she said, spinning away from them both. "This has to be a mistake. I'm calling my editor."

"Wait," Ollie said, remembering there was a reason she was there. "Hang on, you work for the Gazette?"

She turned to him, her expression sheepish. "I... Yeah. I'm supposed to shadow Brandon Cody this week, but—"

"That's me." Bran grinned as he not-so-subtly checked her out, something to which she took clear offense. Or maybe it was the fact that he didn't seem to remember her.

Which, how?

Every interaction Ollie had had with Blake in college, no matter how small, was burned into his memories like tiny brands. Sitting next to her in English Lit, running into her at the library or crossing the quad, he had soaked up every encounter like a sponge. And yet, it was Bran who seems to have left the more visceral impression upon her. Ollie shouldn't have been surprised. Bran was hard to forget, hard to ignore. He was larger than life, even back at school, and their last encounter had taken a wrecking ball to Ollie's friendship with her.

"You really don't remember me, do you?" she asked, her scowl rounding out at the edges, softened by disbelief.

Glancing briefly at Ollie, Bran rubbed the back of his neck. "Uh, well, Ols said I knew you at school. Did we, uh...?"

"Blake was a year behind us at U of P," Ollie rushed to supply. "And you two...met a couple of times. She was a reporter at the university paper. The Ledger."

"The...? Oh!" Bran exclaimed. "The school newspaper, right. Shit, I'm sorry. Sometimes, everything that happened before I moved out here seems like someone else's life. I forget everything all the time. Don't I, Ols?" He turned to Ollie. *Help me out here*, his expression begged.

"Yep. Yeah. All the time," he confirmed. It wasn't even a lie. "Scatterbrain, this one."

"I'm sure you bullied the editor into killing stories all the time back then." Blake crossed her arms and leveled him with a fierce glare. "Seems nothing has changed."

Dawning realization seemed to steal over Bran, and his entire demeanor shifted from panic to embarrassment to—was that regret?—before finally settling on mild irritation.

"Oh, that," was all he said.

An uncomfortable silence descended upon the room, and Ollie idly wondered if the whole interview situation could be salvaged. More than that, he was eager for it to happen. He didn't want Blake to disappear from his life again so soon.

"How...how have you been?" he asked her, going for casual.

Blake's arms dropped to her side, a small smile returning to her lips. "I'm fine. It's..." She exhaled a frustrated breath. "How are you?"

For a moment, it was just the two of them.

"I'm good." He tried not to stare, but he couldn't wrap his mind around the reality of Blake Dillon standing in front of him again.

"What are you doing here?" She stepped closer to him, side-stepping Bran altogether.

Ollie's gaze flicked to his as he watched them. "Well—"

"I asked him to come out here after things took off for me," Bran said, sounding more like himself. "Needed someone on my side."

Her attention slid over to him, her tone icy. "You expected him to drop everything and come running? Of course, you did."

Oh, boy. "To be fair, I'd been looking for something different anyway. My life, such as it was, wasn't going anywhere. And L.A. seemed like the logical choice."

She seemed unconvinced.

"I want a smoothie," Bran announced as he turned and headed towards the kitchen. "Anyone else want a smoothie?"

Hans stood by the island, sipping on some green concoction, and clearly amused by the situation. "So, the three of you were in college together?"

"No." She replied, just as Ollie said, "sort of," and Bran said, "apparently."

"It's a long story."

"I have a large smoothie." Hans took a sip, grinning at Ollie around the bamboo straw.

"This is obviously not going to work," Blake said. She picked up a bag that was hanging from the back of one of the stools at the island. "I'm sure they can assign someone else."

"Why?" Bran asked, giving her the smile that usually had women melting at his feet. All genders, to be fair.

She was unaffected. If anything, her lip curled even more. Not that Ollie could blame her.

"Stop being a dick."

"Me? She's still mad about something that happened, what, six, seven years ago?" Bran snatched the tumbler from Hans, removed the straw, and started chugging it.

"Hey!" Hans cupped his hands under the straw to stop it from dripping all over the white tiled floor.

"There's enough left in the blender for a second one, isn't there?" Bran licked his lips, his eyes on her.

"You're an ogre," Hans muttered.

"I am," Bran's gaze was still locked on Blake's, who shook her head.

"You'd be better off with someone you don't have a history with," she said. "Someone who can write this piece without bias."

"I'd hardly say we have history. You have one incident, not a pattern," Bran countered, straightening to his full height.

"And yet, here I am—sent to clean up your mess." She stood tall. Beautiful. Defiant.

In a way, Ollie thought she and Bran would make a great match. Or they'd end up un-aliving each other. Though, it would make him the ultimate fool to let someone like Blake slip through his fingers again. The truth was, she was far too good for both of them.

"Seems like you still think the world exists to serve you," she nodded at the glass in his hand, "and that everything around you is yours for the taking."

She had a point. "She has a point."

"It was *my* smoothie," Bran argued, tossing a glare Ollie's way.

He should not be enjoying this, but he didn't fight the grin.

"You're still a giant toddler." Blake settled her bag on her shoulder and pulled out her cellphone.

"I'm not the one throwing a tantrum over something that happened years ago."

"Something you didn't even remember, right?" she asked, her voice rising.

"Obviously, it wasn't important enough for me to remember," Bran countered.

Even to Ollie, that sounded petulant. This was like watching a train wreck, and he didn't know how to stop it.

"Guys," he began, "did you know the earliest piece of recorded literature is *The Epic of Gilgamesh?*"

"What?" Blake blinked at him.

"It was written around 2000 BCE," he supplied, happy to have her attention. "In ancient Sumerian."

She seemed to bite back her smile. "Head still full of factoids, eh?"

"Some things never change," he replied, his body flooding with relief.

"Indeed," she said, turning to look at Bran.

Growling, the idiot stalked into the kitchen.

Blake's gaze swept towards the front door, her bag clutched tight to her chest. Despite her threats to leave, she hadn't. Which told Ollie she might need something out of this, too. He took a chance.

"Look, if you don't want to do the story, that's fine," he said. "Maybe the Gazette will send someone else, but I think this could be a good thing."

"Seriously? There's no way he and I could spend a week in the same room without me wanting to strangle him." She waved a hand Bran's way.

"Then go," Bran said from the other side of the island. "Be on your way."

"Fine," she replied, cooly. "I don't need this gig anyway."

That sounded unconvincing. "But—" Ollie tried to interject.

"Nope, I'm out." She turned for the front door. "Good luck with everything."

Shit. He rushed to catch her. "Blake, wait."

She turned to him with a sad smile. "You really moved out here for him? Ollie, you're too nice, and way too good a friend for someone like him. I'd hoped you figured that out by now."

"I know you think you know him, but you don't. He's not the guy he was in college," he said. "I don't even think he was the guy *you* thought he was back then. It was just…unfortunate circumstances."

Blake's smile was bitter. "Yeah, well, this is one set of circumstances I can control. It was good to see you, Oliver. Maybe we can grab a drink or something when the scales fall from your eyes."

With that, she walked out of Ollie's life. Again.

"Are you out of your mind? She'll crucify me." Bran tossed his phone onto the desk.

They were back in the sun-drenched office of his Malibu home. It was a bright and inviting space with large windows facing out onto the vibrant ocean offering a million-dollar view. But all the sunshine in the world couldn't burn away the tension in the room.

"Clark and Noelia believe Blake is perfect for this. She's smart, driven, and doesn't have any industry baggage weighing her down." It had actually taken a bit of convincing on Ollie's part, but they were now fully on board.

He knew Bran. If any other journalist took this on, it would be too easy for him to be evasive or retreat behind his bravado.

"Against my better judgment, I agreed to the interview, but Blake already hates me. Her opinion of me is pretty damn clear."

"She doesn't hate you."

"Well, she sure as shit isn't a fan." Bran was agitated. His hands clutched and unclutched at his sides, his face tight and strained. "Honestly, I don't know what I did to piss her off so badly that she'd hold a grudge all these years later."

"Oh, come on. You totally dicked her over, and you know it."

"And you know why." They stared at each other for a moment. "Besides, it was a lifetime ago."

"I know you did it to protect me and the others on athletic scholarships who were in situations like mine." Ollie bumped shoulders with him. "Okay? I get it. But she doesn't know all of that. Did you ever even apologize?"

"For not wanting the school paper to dick *me* over? Not to mention my friends?"

"For going above her head to the Dean."

Bran's grin was smug. "What can I say? The Dean didn't want to screw with U of P's chance of winning the championship."

"You barely saw time on the pitch."

"We can't all be you, mister thirty-goals-in-a-season MVP." Draping his arm across his shoulders, Bran drew him into a rough, side hug. "When I think of all the panties you could have dropped, I want to cry."

Ollie pushed him away. "I wasn't interested in collecting souvenirs." The one girl who had caught his attention had written him off before anything could develop between them.

There had been a moment, a brief one, when he'd thought things were about to turn a corner. A few tender moments in the library where they'd sat closer than needed, when their gazes had caught, and their touches had bordered on...something else.

He still couldn't believe Blake was in California. Having her conduct the interview would be a challenge, no doubt. For him, it was a matter of control over the situation. Bran needed this to go well, even more than he seemed to realize. Ollie would make sure it did, whatever that took.

He gave Bran a look and the two squared off in a silent stare down that seemed to last an eternity before Bran sighed.

"Fine. It'll only be an afternoon or two, right?"

"After tomorrow, you won't need to be on another set until the second Tuesday of the month," he said as he checked the calendar. "Three weeks shooting, and then you're in New York for two days before we leave for Paris."

A slow smile spread across Bran's face. "Ah, yes. Paris."

"Maybe we should invite Blake to come with us," he joked. Well, half-joked. The idea of roaming the streets of Paris with her was too tempting.

"The woman is a pill."

"A pill? Okay, grandpa."

"Fuck off," Bran said. "I'm serious. It doesn't matter what I do, she'll look for ways to twist my words and make me sound like an entitled asshole. We both know it."

"Brandon, I love you like a brother, but you *are* an entitled asshole."

"Maybe, but I can't have her thinking that when she's writing a fucking article about me, now can I?" He laced his fingers together atop his head. "Fuck, Ols. I'm not sure how to get on her good side. Noelia is up my ass about this fucking Gazette piece. If you believe her, everything is riding on it. Like all the work I've put in over the last six years means nothing."

"You know how this world works," Ollie said. "Build you up just to knock you down."

Bran threw himself onto the sectional, and Ollie sat on the other side. The friction between Blake and his best friend was problematic. He wasn't sure how he'd smooth things out, but if he didn't, they were screwed.

"First, you need to sincerely apologize."

"What do I say?"

Ollie thought about it for a moment. A woman like Blake would see right through Bran's bullshit if he wasn't sincere. "Be honest with her."

"You want me to tell her I don't know why she's so mad about me talking to the Dean?" He huffed out a laugh. "Yeah, that'll go down really well."

"You say *Blake, I was only looking out for people who were less fortunate than me. And I honestly didn't think what I did could make you despise me so much, years later, but now I understand how shitty it was for you. And I deserve whatever punishment you see fit.*"

"That's laying it on a bit thick, isn't it?"

Ollie shrugged. "You treated Blake—and every other person you thought was in your way—like a chess piece to be taken down or manipulated until you got your way."

"Damn," Bran frowned at him. "That's harsh. College was a dog-eat-dog world. You know that. And if that's how you really feel, why are you here? Why stay friends with me?"

"Bran…" Ollie hated the turn this conversation had taken. The last thing he needed was for him to start questioning Ollie's friendship or his loyalty. "You're the best guy I know. Sure, you can be a dick. Most of the time, actually, but dude…" He met his skeptical gaze. "You saved my life."

"Come on. Not that shit again."

"Yes, that shit again."

Backing away and breathing heavily, Bran folded his hands atop his head. "Ols, you have to stop saying that. I didn't save your fucking life. Is *that* why you're working for me? You think you *owe* me?"

*Yes. And...* "I'm here because you need someone in your corner you can trust one hundred percent," he said truthfully. "And, for the record, I wouldn't be standing here if you hadn't—"

Bran threw up a hand. "Stop."

"You know it's true."

Swallowing hard, Bran dropped his arms to his sides. "I still think you should have pressed charges."

A sliver of a memory emerged, the ghost of a pain so acute he could almost feel it. He shook himself.

"They were only kids, I didn't want to ruin anyone's life."

"*You* were a kid, too, Ols. What if your injuries had been more severe? What if you'd hit your head on the concrete, or—"

Ollie held up a hand to stop him. "But they weren't and I didn't. Anyway, it doesn't matter now. What matters is that we make this whole situation work for you. Blake may be a blessing in disguise."

Bran snorted.

"I'm serious. She may not like you, yet, but she seems to still like me. Or at least not hate me on sight."

One corner of Bran's mouth tipped up. "Did you two ever...?"

"No. She... No." The idea that they *could* have—maybe almost had—made it suddenly hard to breathe. "Blake is... She's... Shit, I mean, we were friends. We never..."

"You're the most emo motherfucker I've ever met," Bran said, laughing. "You liked her, didn't you? Now that I think about it, you two were together a lot. Are you sure you didn't hit that?" He ran a hand across his chin. "Blake may be a hard ass, but she's stunning. Smart. Just your type."

"*You're* an ass."

"Never claimed not to be." Bran picked up a stress ball from the corner of the desk and began tossing it in the air. "For real, though. She's...something to you. Isn't she?"

The thing was...he wasn't wrong. Blake *was* the complete package—intelligent, empathetic, in possession of a wicked sense of humor and a steadfast notion of right and wrong. She was just as Ollie remembered her only *more,* somehow.

When they met, he may have been an insecure, mess of a guy, but he wasn't blind. Even now, he was still working through some of his issues, but Ollie had come a long way in six years. He wanted to spend time with Blake, to get to know her again, and to have her know him. For real, this time, and not just in the fantasies born from his sad regrets.

"She's exactly the kind of person you need." Bran's words, spoken softly, ripped through him like a sword.

"What do you mean?"

"You're two nerdy peas in a pod." He scratched his chin. "Hang on, I might be onto something."

Unease made the hair stand up on Ollie's arms. "Something like what?"

Bran sat up and turned to rest his elbows on his knees. "I want her to say nice things about me. But, also, I know I'm not as much of a dick as she thinks I am. I'm not the guy I was in college, at least."

"You're not a dick but you do fuck anything that moves. She can't pretty that up for you."

"Hey! No slut-shaming."

Ollie held up his hands, but he knew that look. It meant Bran had an idea in his head and was determined to see it through. It also meant he was going to help him with whatever it was.

"Right, so…she hates me."

"Hate is a strong word," he argued.

"Severely dislikes me. Whatever." Bran stopped pacing and gave an exaggerated sigh. "I'm not her favorite person. But *you*. You and she were tight, once."

He narrowed his eyes. "I didn't say we were *tight*, but we were friends. So?"

"And she obviously still likes you," Bran continued. "The way she looked when she saw you? We can use that."

"One, she didn't look at me in any particular way, other than…shock. And two, use it how? I won't manipulate her."

"All I need is for her to give me a fair shot." Bran held his hands out. "That's all. And I have a better chance of that if you two are friends again." He paused. "And also, I thought I saw a few sparks."

"There aren't. I lost my chance with her years ago." *Because I'm friends with you*, he didn't say. He stared down at the empty coffee cup in his hand. Remembering what happened with Blake all those years ago was like a bad hangover—once you had it you never wanted to repeat the experience. Too much of this situation felt like déjà vu. Still, it had been amazing to see her.

Ollie had reached out to Noelia to get Blake's contact info, but he hadn't mustered up the courage to use it. Pulling out his phone, he sent her a text before his nerves could get the better of him.

**OLLIE: Blake, it's Ollie. I hope you don't mind me texting. I got your number from Bran's publicist. I just wanted to say it was really good to see you. I'm sorry things went down like that.**

**BLAKE: I'm glad you reached out, Oliver. I'm sorry, too. I shouldn't have lashed out at you. It was really good to see you as well. Maybe we'll run into each other again soon.**

He was grinning at his phone when Bran's voice cut through the warm fuzzy feeling in his chest.

"What really went down between you two?"

He looked up at Bran, the truth on the tip of his tongue. "A difference of opinion."

"Huhn. Well, whatever it was, there's definitely something lingering between you. I saw sparks."

"Again. No sparks."

"You still want her. Admit it."

Setting his phone down, he glared. "What does it matter?"

Bran's face softened with pity, but Ollie ignored that too.

"When did this become about me? We're talking about *your* career. *Your* interview. You want me to, what, cozy up to Blake—a reporter—to make your life easier?" He let out a choked laugh. "What am I asking? Of course, that's how your mind works."

"I don't want to do this fucking interview at all!" Bran snapped. "But if I have to, I'm going to make sure it works in my favor. And if, in the process, I can hook my best friend up with a girl he's been pining after for freaking *years*, then..." He placed his hands on his hips. "So be it."

He stared at him. "You're putting me in an impossible position."

"Because you like her."

"Because *you* need this to go well."

"And because you like her."

Ollie made a sound he'd never made before, a vocalization that was part frustration, part aching desire to be close to Blake again. Fuck. "I won't lie."

Bran's attempt to temper his grin was minimal. He knew he'd won, the asshole. "Would never ask you to."

Against every instinct, he felt himself nodding. This was fine. "Yes!"

Annnd, the volume of his excitement put Ollie right back on edge. "Bran."

"Oh, stop looking at me like I have some nefarious plot up my sleeve." He walked towards the door, a suspicious bounce in his step.

Ollie's second thoughts were having second thoughts, but the idea of spending time with Blake proved irresistible, even if there were a million ways this could go wrong.

"Where are you going?" He got up to follow him down the hall.

"I need a swim," Bran said over his shoulder. "And you need to draft my apology."

"I really think you should do that yourself."

He stopped and turned. "You *really* believe that?"

Okay, no. He didn't, and it must have shown in his face.

"Thought not."

"That's the cheesiest thing I've ever heard." Bran shook his head. "I need another beer. You want one?"

"Yeah, sure." Ollie needed liquid reinforcement to get through tonight. "And it's not cheesy, it's honest." Or it would be if Bran meant any of it, of which Ollie wasn't sure.

"Read it to me again."

**BRAN: Blake, it's Brandon Cody. I want to apologize for my behavior. I haven't been in the best frame of mind, and I projected some of my frustrations onto you. For that, I am sorry.**

"That sounds hella formal," Bran said. "And not like me at all."

"Well, how would we make it sound more like you?"

"I dunno. *Yo, sorry about being a dickhead. Hit me up if you want to hit the red carpet with me and get this exclusive.* Girls love to get dressed up and be photographed."

Wow, this was *not* going to work. At all. "Hit me up? Really?"

Bran's face split with a wide grin. "Yeah, okay. So maybe it's good the text doesn't sound like me, but I don't think your way's gonna work either."

"Only one way to find out."

Bran chewed his bottom lip, took a swig from his beer, and nodded. "Fuck it. Hit send."

"You sure?"

"No." He laughed.

Ollie wasn't sure either, but he sent the message. He put the phone on the coffee table and drank a couple of swallows from his own bottle while they both stared down at the device.

"She won't answer."

"Give her more than thirty seconds. Geez."

Bran shook his head and sank back into the cushions. "She won't. I'm telling you, she hates me."

"She doesn't even know you, not really."

"Tell *her* that."

The phone pinged, startling them both.

"What did she say?"

Jesus, suddenly Ollie was a first-year college student again. He swiped open Bran's messages.

**BLAKE DILLON: Are my eyes deceiving me? Is that an apology from Mr. *I didn't do anything wrong and, if I did, it doesn't count because I don't remember?***

"That woman gets off on busting my balls, I swear."

"This is good," Ollie said. "She's opening the door."

"Ask her to tell her bosses to burn the photos they have."

"It's too soon." He knew Blake's answer would be *go to hell*, and he didn't want to jump the gun.

**BRAN: Yes, it is. And I don't expect you to accept it, I just wanted you to know that I see the error of my ways.**

"What are you typing?" Ollie read him the text and received a frown. "Why apologize if the other person isn't going to forgive you?"

"Apologies are always more about the giver than the receiver," Ollie said. "The receiver owes the giver nothing, and there shouldn't be an expectation of forgiveness. Only an acknowledgment of wrongdoing."

"Sometimes, I forget you majored in English Lit. Then you open your mouth."

Ollie put the phone down. "I don't have to do this, you know?"

Bran laughed, grabbing his knee and squeezing it. "I'm sorry. Alright, alright, we've got her talking to me. Now what?"

When his phone pinged again, he picked it up.

**BLAKE DILLON: That sounds like a line. Probably from one of your scripts. Do you have dialogue in your movies, or do you just grunt and punch people?**

"See?" Bran tossed the phone on the couch between them. "She's not gonna cut me a break. Can't we get someone else to do this interview thing? Someone hot *and* agreeable?"

"I trust Blake to do it right, and so does Noelia."

Bran pushed to his feet. "Yeah, well, we might need a miracle."

"Where are you going? You're in the middle of a conversation with her."

"Correction, *you* are in the middle of a conversation." He stripped off his tee and dropped his shorts to the floor, leaving him in his boxers. "I'm going for a soak in the hot tub. All this shit has me stressed."

Ollie stared after him. Sometimes, he wanted to strangle the guy. Bran was the kind of person anyone would want in their corner. But he was also every bit the entitled asshole Blake believed him to be.

The phone pinged, and he took a deep breath. "I didn't sign up for this."

**BLAKE DILLON: Did I insult your craft?**

**BRAN: I know I should be insulted by that dig, but I think I'm more upset knowing you haven't seen any of my movies.**

**BLAKE DILLON: Don't be. I haven't been to the movies in years, and I don't own a TV.**

Ollie frowned.

**BRAN: Years? That's a crime against fun. Do you not like film or...?**

**BLAKE DILLON:** I did when I was younger.

**BRAN:** And now?

**BLAKE DILLON:** Now it's about choice.

**BRAN:** Between what to see and what to skip?

**BLAKE DILLON:** Between food and rent or blowing it on over-hyped, over-produced rehashes of things I saw when I was a kid.

Well, damn. And okay, she had a point. The projects Bran had done in the beginning of his career weren't exactly examples of cinematic art. He'd become more discerning. Or, rather, Ollie had helped him choose which projects to do. It was a responsibility he considered a privilege.

**BRAN:** There are a lot of good movies out there. You're missing out.

**BLAKE DILLON:** Where should I start then?

It only took Ollie a second to contemplate.

**BRAN:** I Am My Own Country

**BRAN:** Do you know it?

**BLAKE DILLION:** I've heard of it, but I'm surprised you've seen it.

**BRAN:** Why?

**BLAKE DILLON:** No explosions, no one dies, period costumes... Should I go on?

Ollie was about to protest when he remembered who Blake thought she was talking to. Bran would never voluntarily watch something like that unless he was prepping for a role.

**BRAN: It's one of Ollie's favorites.**

There. Not a lie.

**BLAKE DILLON: Ah ha! That makes much more sense.**

**BRAN: Because he's a nerd?**

**BLAKE DILLON: Don't be petty. Oliver is special. You're lucky to have him. He's trying to educate you.**

Ollie stared at the screen, his jaw on the proverbial floor. Blake thought he was special? He had a quadrillion questions, none of which he could ask. Not as Bran. Not without sounding like a creep.

**BLAKE DILLION: I have work to do before bed. Later, Superman.**

His heart thumped hard against his ribcage, his stupid college crush rearing its ugly head. If he weren't careful, it might turn into something much more. Ollie nearly jumped out of his skin when his own phone chimed.

**BLAKE: I think Hell just froze over. Your bestie actually apologized to me.**

**OLLIE: Should I call an ambulance?**

**BLAKE: You might want to check he hasn't been swapped out by aliens.**

He laughed out loud. Despite the ludicrous circumstances, he was thrilled at the chance to get to know Blake all over again. He pictured grabbing coffee with her, spending long afternoons hashing through plot points while she did research for her article. The quiet camaraderie they'd shared in college could blossom into a full-fledged friendship. *Maybe a bit more.*

"Slow down, bud. Gotta walk before you can run."

But he couldn't stop smiling.

# 5

On the drive back to South Pasadena, Blake had made a reluctant call to Gideon. She'd known what he would say, and all of the arguments he would make before he'd even picked up the phone.

"Did he hit on you? Curse you out?" Gid had asked. "Threaten to tank your career if you didn't write what he wanted or something?"

"No, no. Nothing like that."

"Well then, chica, I don't get what the problem is," he'd said. "You're a journalist. Are you telling me you're incapable of setting aside your prejudices about Hollywood for the sake of a story?"

It was a valid question, and one that had cut right through any lingering animosity Blake had towards Brandon Cody. The truth was, Ollie was right. She didn't know either of them, not really. People could change. Even spoiled, entitled, self-centered, *arrogant...*

Blake took a breath. "I already turned the interview down. His agent is probably apoplectic."

"If you're serious, I can fix that. Easy," Gideon promised. She could hear him typing furiously in the background. "And Sonja doesn't even need to know."

"Oh my God, really? I appreciate this so much, Gid. I promise, it'll be the best story I've put on your desk." *Best celebrity beat story, anyway.* "I'll do some research, get some background on—"

"Yeah. Yeah. That's great, but make it fast. You're due on set first thing in the morning."

"*Tomorrow* morning?"

"Is that a complaint?"

"Nope."

Blake had a choice to make. She could either swallow her pride and focus on making this assignment her gateway to better things, or she could hold on to a grudge about something that happened when she was a teenager and Bran was barely in his twenties.

Ambition won in the end.

The next morning, she dug through her closet and realized she hadn't been shopping for anything decent in years.

She tried on a pair of skinny jeans and paired it with a boyfriend shirt. "I look like a slob!" Blake yelled.

"No, you don't!" Enid called back from her room across the hall.

When Blake turned to check how her ass looked in the jeans, her roommate was already standing in the open door. Sizing Blake up, she frowned.

"Hmm. Hang on."

She disappeared for a moment before returning with a jacket Blake had admired when she saw it hanging from the hook behind Enid's bedroom door. "This is my sister's. She left it when she came to visit for Hanukkah last year."

It was a retro-style bomber in gold satin with a black strip that ran across the shoulders and down to each cuff. Blake slipped it on and pushed up the sleeves.

"Is your sister a giant?"

"She's a model."

"Of course she is." Enid was gorgeous, so none of this came as a surprise. "It probably costs more than my car. She won't mind me borrowing it?"

"Nah. I doubt she even misses it. I told her it was here, but she hasn't asked about it since."

"Promise, I'll bring it back in one piece."

"Like I said, don't worry." Enid brushed the shoulders off and helped Blake roll up the cuffs. "There. You look amazing. Smart, no-nonsense, and ready to take over the world. Now, get moving."

"Right." She stepped into a pair of Skechers, hoisted her bag onto her shoulder, and waved goodbye. "Thanks, I owe you."

It had been on Blake's secret bucket list to visit an actual film studio. And not just any studio, one of the venerable grand dames of the industry. Few had the gold-plated legacy of Sterling United, a place that had been at the forefront of every major breakthrough in film, from silent to talkies to 3D and beyond.

Pulling into the lot, she couldn't help but appreciate the history of the place. She accepted her visitor's badge and parked the car in the proper lot before checking herself in the rearview mirror.

"I can't believe I'm going into this blind," she muttered as she applied a little mascara and tinted lip balm. She hadn't even had time to Google Bran's career thus far. Ah, well. Maybe it was for the best. She could walk into this whole situation with a fresh set of eyes and ears. Unbiased. *Right.*

Only, as she approached the stage where Bran was shooting, she realized her first mistake. Okay, maybe her second mistake. Her first had likely been accepting this assignment.

The scope of this production was massive. One moment, she was walking by thirty-foot palm trees, and the next she was in the back alley of some gritty, urban city. She skirted the perimeter until she saw an enormous canopy perched over a line of tables that were covered in food. Next to them, coolers filled with bottles and cans of every size and shape were perched on stands.

On cue, her stomach made its presence known, and Blake wondered if she'd be able to snag a muffin or something without anyone noticing. She made a bee line for the food and had just spied a promising plate of nut-covered rolls glistening with caramel when a figure stepped into her path.

"Take this and get it stitched up," the woman said as she shoved a piece of fabric into Blake's personal space.

"Excuse me?" She took a reflexive step back.

The woman, about Blake's height of five-nine, was curvy. Her pale skin reddened by either the sun or her state of apoplexy. In her right hand, she held onto a forearm crutch. In her left was the garment. She gave Blake a confused look, clearly annoyed. "Wardrobe needs to get this mended before we shoot the next scene. Fucking Cody can't seem to follow directions. Keeps tearing the wrong side."

"Uh, I'm actually looking for him. Mr. Cody."

"Look, you know the rules. Don't hassle the cast. What, are you new?" The woman's head dropped back as she let out an exhausted sigh. "Christ, I can't deal with this today."

She leveled Blake with a look that would have her withering like a dying vine if she'd been under her authority. The woman held up her tablet.

"Name?"

"Uh, I'm Blake Dillon. I—"

"I don't see your name on the crew sheet." She narrowed her eyes at her. "What department are you with?"

"None, actually. I'm with the L.A. Gazette." She pulled out her press credentials, which she rarely had to use and was grateful to have remembered to grab this morning.

The woman's eyes went wide. "Shit. I'm sorry." She tucked the torn garment under her right arm. "Tami Townsend, production assistant. I thought you were... Never mind, you're looking for Cody? Is he expecting you?"

"Yeah, I think so."

"You'll probably need to see his publicist. C'mon, I'll take you to her. Name's Noelia Mokeyane."

She moved to keep up as Tami led her toward a line of trailers just outside the door on the opposite side of the massive sound stage. Blake squinted as they emerged from the relative darkness and back into the bright sunlight.

"Over there, by that two banger." She pointed at a large trailer with two doors. "The stern looking lady in the turquoise shirt."

She thanked Tami and weaved her way past whizzing golf carts and scrambling crew, over to where Bran's publicist paced in a small circle, a phone pressed to her ear.

The cream-colored, linen jumpsuit would have been breezy and casual on anyone else. Crisp on the edges, with not a wrinkle in sight, this woman wore it like armor. Blake had heard stories about PR people in Hollywood, how formidable and ruthless they could be. Some had horrible reputations, spoken about in hushed voices, and referred to only by their surnames. Novak, Clarkson, Windham.

She hadn't heard of Noelia Mokeyane and didn't know what to expect.

"Would you trust me? This will work," the woman said to the person on the other end.

Blake stopped a few feet away and waited, in an attempt to give Ms. Mokeyane as much privacy as she could while letting her know she was being observed.

She took in the scene surrounding her, a buzzing hive of activity the likes of which she'd rarely seen outside of a newsroom on deadline.

Everywhere she looked, people rushed about. Some were in costume, and others obviously crew. Blake hadn't a clue what they were even shooting. Jesus, some reporter she was. She reached into her bag to grab her phone for a quick search.

"Ms. Dillon?" She looked up to find Noelia Mokeyane staring at her expectantly.

She shouldered her bag and stuck out her hand. "Yes. Blake is fine."

The woman's gaze quickly swept over her but then she smiled and accepted the handshake. "Nice to meet you, Blake. You can call me Noelia." She gave her another quick once-over. "You're a lot younger than I expected."

"I could say the same."

Noelia's smile lifted only one corner of her mouth. She nodded. "My family has been in this town a long time."

"Started early?"

Noelia hummed before she turned, her gaze scanning the crowd. "Probably too early. My parents wouldn't win any awards. And you?"

"Following in granddad's footsteps, much to my parents' dismay."

"Way to be a rebel. I spoke at length with your boss," Noelia said, the humor falling away from her voice. "He assured me this wouldn't be a hit piece. Brandon gets enough shit flung at him. We don't want to open the door to his private life just to have it used to try him in the court of public opinion."

Blake chewed on that for a moment. She was there against her better judgement, but she still had journalistic integrity. Noelia seemed like someone who didn't suffer fools, and she found her vehement defense of Bran intriguing.

"I'm not here to dig up dirt," she said truthfully. "But I'm not here to write fluff, either." At least Blake hoped that wasn't what had been promised. No, Gideon wouldn't have agreed to that.

Noelia's gaze sharpened before she gave a quick nod. "Fair enough."

"Is there anything I should know before I dive in?"

"Only that our Brandon can be a lot to take when he's *on*," the publicist confided. "I'm only asking that you give him a chance to show people who he is when he's not."

"If we agree to move forward, I'll write what he shows me." She wondered exactly what Noelia meant by *on* and worked hard to shake her memories of their previous encounters. "That's all I can promise."

"Excellent." Noelia gestured for Blake to follow as she headed to the trailer and reached up to knock. "Most of your time will be spent with his assistant, Ollie. He'll keep you abreast of Bran's schedule, arrange for you to have the access and time you need to do your thing."

Ollie.

She did her best to temper her excitement at seeing him again and tried—once more—to convince herself he had nothing to do with why she'd caved and agreed to this whole thing.

"If there are any problems, Ollie will handle them or inform me if I need to step in."

"What sort of problems do you anticipate?"

Her hand poised to knock on the door, Noelia turned and met her eyes. "I agreed to this exposé because I was guaranteed fair treatment. If I find that's not the case, I'll pull the plug so fast you'll be on the first bus back to Peoria, or wherever you come from. And then I'll do what I can to bring Sonja and the Gazette to its knees, and make sure the only paper that will hire *you* is the supermarket circular back home."

Despite the chill that slid down her spine, Blake admired this woman. She held her gaze, hoping to show her she wasn't the only alpha in the room, so to speak. "Understood."

Noelia barely knocked on the door before opening it, marching up the three steps as she called out. "Brandon, babe, are you in here?"

Blake hesitated a moment before following and closing the door behind her. Steeling herself for her first interview with a bona fide celebrity. Even if it was Brandon Peters, this was a different world. But she almost tripped over her own feet when she came face-to-face with the very naked movie star.

"Hells bells, Brandon," Noelia exclaimed. "Put on some clothes!"

The actor wrapped a towel around his waist and grinned at her, but the corners of his mouth tilted down when he noticed Blake in the doorway. "Sorry, Nellie" he said, grabbing for a t-shirt on the couch. "I thought you were Ols. He went to pick up some analgesic cream from the medic."

He was well-built, it was an undisputable fact. And Blake could see that he worked hard on his physique. She couldn't help but notice the nasty bruise on his abdomen and pointed. "Work-related?"

"Bran does most of his own stunts," his publicist said, brightly. "He's always bruising this or twisting that. Longing to give me a heart attack. Oh, the insurance!"

"I see." She pulled out a fresh notebook to jot down her thoughts.

He winked at her. "I have a rep to maintain."

"Speaking of which, Ms. Dillon here assures me that her article will be fair and unbiased." Noelia gave her a stern look. "And if it isn't, then Mr. Cody's attorneys are on standby."

"I'm sure it won't come to that," he said.

Blake straightened. "I don't have an agenda. I'm here to give the editor what she wants; a rare, behind-the-scenes look at one of Hollywood's fastest-rising stars." She turned to him. "But I won't lie. I'll tell it like I see it."

He nodded. "I'd expect nothing less."

"Excellent. Blake, you'll have full access to Bran's life, and our Ollie will be your guide," Noelia said. "You're in good hands, there."

As if summoned, the door to the trailer opened and Oliver stepped inside. He stopped when he saw the three of them in the center of the living space.

He was even more handsome than she'd remembered—tall and broad-shouldered, with a strong jawline, full lips, and a smoldering gaze. His thick, brown hair was shaggy and unkempt in a way that made him somehow more attractive. She kept her gaze firmly glued to his face.

Cocking his head, Ollie stepped towards her and gestured to a small fridge by her hip. "May I get you something to drink, Blake?"

He smelled of freshly cut grass, sea salt, and sandalwood, a subtle yet tantalizing combination of scents.

A fluttery sensation replaced her stomach's earlier queasiness. "No, I'm fine. Thanks."

He took a small step back. "Am I interrupting anything?"

"No, darling." Noelia kissed both of Ollie's cheeks and stepped around him, heading for the door. "Turning this little circus over to you, Ollie dear. Keep our boy out of trouble, yes?"

"I'll do my best." Ollie smiled after her before turning back and handing a tube of cream to Bran. "Kit said this is the maximum strength you can get over-the-counter."

"It should do the trick," Bran said, inspecting the tube. "Just need something to take the edge off until I get home."

"Ice bath?" Ollie asked him.

"Fuck yeah." Bran let his head drop back. "A sauna after that would be amazing."

"For that, you'll have to wait for your wrap surprise."

"My surprise has a sauna? You're the best, man."

"What's the surprise?" she asked.

Bran straightened as Ollie answered her. "We rent a private retreat on special occasions. We rented a place in San Diego once, for a shoot, and ended up staying a week after. Then we did it again after Bran...wrapped on a project."

"It's become a thing. And it's nice to get away from the scene every once in a while, even if I do have to stay close for work." He and Ollie exchanged a look.

Oh, there was a story there. *The actor lights up like a kid on Christmas morning at the mention of this secret getaway*, she wrote. "The house in Malibu isn't retreat enough?"

Bran narrowed his eyes at her. "Am I not supposed to take vacations?"

"For most of us, living in a place like yours would feel like a vacation," she replied. "The fact that you want to go from one luxurious California home to another, for funsies, is...well..." She shrugged.

Bran snorted. "I remember, now, how judgmental you are. Good thing you won't have to deal with all my *self-indulgence* for long. If we don't finish by the time I wrap here, you'll have to wait until I get back." Bran closed the door to the bedroom behind him.

Fuck. She needed this to go quickly, if not smoothly. Blake wasn't sure how long Sonja would wait before her patience ran out. If another outlet scooped them on this, it wouldn't only mean Blake's job but possibly Gideon's too.

"It may not be *the* job," she muttered, remembering something her granddad had said. "But it's the job you have. Do it well." Ollie frowned, confused, and she waved it off. "Ignore me."

"Never." He said and gestured to the book in her hand. "You still use those, eh? Like your grandfather?"

"I...yeah." A kernel of unexpected warmth filled her chest. "I'm surprised you remember."

"Are you, really?"

A moment passed between them in which he stared at her, she at him. A thousand *what-ifs* that she had thought long-buried began floating to the surface. Finally, she broke the silence.

"I guess I'll have to interview him between takes." She looked around the trailer, through the window to the sound stage and beyond.

"Actually," Ollie said, "it might be good for you to come on the retreat. It's a little removed from...all of this." He gestured around them.

That sounded like a *horrible* idea. "Yeah, I don't know about that."

Forget spending so much time around Bran's insufferable self, she didn't like the math. The commute alone would be unbearable. She wondered if using the company credit card to book a room was permissible when San Diego was only a couple of hours away. It *seemed* like something the paper would be willing to cover, but she'd need to ask. Which meant calling Gideon and explaining the situation but could she even do it?

"What's wrong?" Ollie's bright eyes filled with concern. Going on the retreat with them would also mean spending time with Oliver, a thought that ignited an entirely different feeling inside her. He took a step forward, his long, sweeping gaze making it difficult for Blake to think.

"Logistically, that probably wouldn't work." The words stuttered out of her. "It's better if I do what I can now and…wait until you get back to finish, if necessary." She wanted to be done with this.

Oblivious to her plight, his smile was rich and warm. "I can help."

Another beat of silence passed between them in which Ollie practically vibrated with anticipation, staring at her like she had the power to grant his greatest wish.

Closing her eyes, Blake shook her head. Dammit. She was actually thinking about it. Why did he have this effect on her?

"I'd have to trek all the way down to San Diego to shadow that overgrown child."

Exhaling a breath of what sounded like relief, Ollie chuckled. "You'd mostly be with me. Besides, relaxed Bran is way more fun than work Bran. Trust me."

Unfortunately, Blake did trust Ollie. It made no sense, she barely knew him.

The anticipation and hope in his eyes brought with them a twinge of guilt. She couldn't follow them to Malibu, it would take too long and Sonja would never approve.

Still, she nodded. "I'll think about it—*if* it comes to that—and see what my boss says. But sauna or not, clothing isn't optional. I don't interview naked people."

# 6

It was a reckless, selfish desire, inviting Blake to join them, but Ollie couldn't help himself. The thought of having her with him on a warm sunny beach, a drink in her hand and the wind in her dark curls, had been too tempting. Too much of a fantasy come to life for him to resist blurting out the invitation.

Bran would kill him, but it would be worth it if she'd only agree.

The door to the bedroom opened, and Bran stalked through the trailer to the front door.

"I'm needed in FX." He stopped and turned to Blake, stone-faced.

She hitched her bag up on her shoulder. "I can talk to you there."

"I'll be there for several hours."

"Perfect."

"It's a facial prosthetic." He was glaring and Ollie wanted to punch him in the side of the head.

She frowned.

"He won't be able to talk," Ollie explained.

"Oh." Disappointment creased her brow.

"We'll have to reschedule," Bran said.

Blake lifted her chin, her gaze sharp. "I could observe."

Bran gave Ollie a look.

"It's...proprietary, the process," he said, hoping it was at least a little true. "But, I could show you around the lot. If you want."

Her gaze flicked to his, alight with clear interest, but her voice was steady when she replied. "Sure, I suppose that would be helpful."

He bit back a smile. "No problem."

Bran turned and left, leaving them alone.

Her shoulders, which had been drawn up and back, slumped with something like relief.

Man, she *really* didn't like Bran.

"Have you been on a lot before?"

Blake's expression transformed when she looked at him, a smile curving one corner of her mouth. "I have not, but I've always wanted to."

"Yeah?"

He started for the door, gesturing for her to follow.

"One of Trent's— my grandfather's— favorite movies is *Singin' in the Rain*. I think his parents took him to see it when he was a kid, so we would watch it often."

"That's one of the best of the oldies."

"It really is, and it offers a fantastic glimpse into this whole world," she said. "Or at least the Hollywood of the age. It's remarkably self-aware for, what, the 1950s?"

Ollie closed the door to the trailer behind them. "Anything in particular you want to see?"

"There's a scene in the film when Gene Kelly's character and Debbie Reynold's character are singing on a soundstage with, like, a huge backdrop of open country."

"I haven't seen the film since I was little, but I'm sure we can find something that'll fit the description."

They walked across the lot, passing racks of costumes, actors and crew zooming about, and random props.

As they picked their way through the mayhem, Blake took it all in like a child on her first visit to a zoo full of exotic animals.

Her curious gaze darted back and forth, taking in the details and Ollie couldn't stop marveling at her wide-eyed wonder.

A tram pulled around them and stopped, a tour group alighting as a guide gathered them in front of the door to stage thirty-one.

"This building is used for many of the nature scenes you'd see in our films and shows," the guide explained. She was a short, sturdy woman with copper hair and rosy cheeks. Her pale eyes crinkled behind her glasses, which were attached to a chain around her neck.

Blake drew close as the woman spoke, and he followed behind.

"I have to warn you. Some of the things in here can be a little scary."

"Like what?" Blake asked.

"If you're familiar with *Dem Bones*, our dramedy set in the Jurassic era, then you'll know the family encounters some prehistoric creatures. They all live here." The guide addressed the last part to a young boy at the front of the group.

"There's a T-Rex in there?" he asked, stepping back. An older man put his hand on the boy's shoulder.

"Don't worry," the guide said. "It's only pretend. And all of our creatures are harmless. That said, I have to ask you all to not touch anything and to stay within the red lines on the floor."

He and Blake stood back while the group filed inside. The air filled with the scent of fog juice, sweet and cloying. "Do you want to go in? We can join them."

She shook her head. "No, I'm not a dino girl."

"Come on, then. We're almost there."

"Almost where?"

"You'll see."

The urge to take her hand was overwhelming. He wanted to feel her warmth on his skin, her delicate fingers entwined with his. It was irrational and probably juvenile, but it didn't stop the longing.

Soon enough they arrived at their destination, and Ollie opened the door. "After you."

Building twenty-eight contained a large soundstage that seemed to stretch on forever. In its center were two massive backdrops— one of a verdant forest and another of rolling plains— big enough to make anyone feel tiny in comparison.

Blake gasped as she stepped inside. "Oh, my God."

Her entire face lit up, her eyes sparkling with surprise and delight, and he felt like he'd won the fucking lottery.

"This is amazing!"

Ollie closed the door behind them, blocking out the invading sunlight. On either side of the main stage stood towering trees and other natural elements, carefully crafted out of wood and bark. At the far end of the room, a row of cameras was lined up for filming from different angles.

There was no one there but the two of them, and Ollie followed helplessly as Blake carefully explored the space.

"It's so much bigger than I realized," she said, looking up at the ceiling. At seventy-five feet, this was one of the tallest structures on the lot.

She was still staring up at the rafters as she walked, and he was too busy watching her. Neither of them noticed the enormous black cable on the floor until Blake tripped over it.

Lightning fast, Ollie grabbed her waist and pulled her into him.

"Shit!" Her bag tumbled to the ground, its contents spilling everywhere.

Ollie's heart beat fast and hard in his chest. She was so fucking soft—everywhere—her curls against his cheek, her curves against the hard planes of his own body. He could feel the warmth of her skin through his shirt, and it made him ache for more.

He took a deep breath, inhaling her scent and feeling her tremble in response to his embrace, or maybe to the near-fall. He wanted to stay like this forever, never letting go, but he did let go.

"You okay?" He met her gaze as she turned.

"Yeah, thanks. God, I'm a klutz." She stepped back, reaching down to collect the scattered items. "Those are some reflexes you've got there. Thanks for not letting me faceplant."

"Couldn't allow that," he replied, chuckling as he helped her gather her things.

"I can't believe this place" she said with a smile, gesturing around them when she stood upright. "It just...sits here, empty, waiting for the next scene or whatever?"

He handed her several of the green notebooks that had spilled from her bag. Ollie loved that she still used them. That this little piece of her had remained unchanged.

"They spend a lot of time and money building sets, so they try to get as much use out of things as they can."

"I imagine it's more eco-friendly."

"That's probably a fortunate by-product, rather than by design."

"Probably," she agreed. "Still, it's absolutely incredible," she said in awe, turning back to face him with admiration shining in her eyes. "You have no idea how lucky you are."

"I thought you hated this stuff."

"No, not at all. Movies are great. Well, *good* movies are great. I hate the whole fame and celebrity thing." She blinked, probably realizing what she'd said and to whom. "I mean, it's cool if you're known and admired for your work. Recognized, or whatever, but the worship...it's ridiculous. And the sheer privilege..."

Ollie grinned, remembering a similar rant from years ago. "And yet, you're here. Writing a story on a celebrity. Working for a paper that thrives on gossip and scandal."

"I'm the ultimate hypocrite, I know. But this is a means to an end."

"I figured."

Looking around, she sighed. "Trent would love this."

"Do you see him often?"

The light in her eyes dimmed a little, and Ollie took an involuntary step closer.

"Not as often as I should. He's back East, but he... We had to place him in a home."

"Oh...Blake..."

"Alzheimer's."

"Shit."

"Yeah."

He instinctively ran a hand down her back, grateful when she leaned into his touch. They hadn't regained that level of intimacy. It was a remnant from long ago, but he'd needed to offer comfort with more than his feeble words.

"The hardest thing is watching a mind like his slip away." Her voice wavered in the shadow of the oak tree they'd stopped under. In the quiet of the stage, it almost felt as if they were indeed out in the wild somewhere. Alone.

"If I'm honest," she continued, "I didn't visit often, even when I was still in Philly. I...it was difficult. Sometimes he would remember me, other times..."

Ollie slid his hand up to her shoulder and squeezed. "I've never been through anything similar, but I can imagine how hard it would be to lose someone you love like that. It sounds fucking terrifying, actually."

She looked up. "It is."

"You know he'd be proud of you."

Blake huffed out a sound between disbelief and disdain. "Yeah, I don't know about that."

Ollie gently turned her to face him. "He would. What did you say earlier? Not the job you want, but it's a job. And you're using it as a steppingstone to get to where you want to be, right? There's nothing wrong with that."

Blake's cheeks flushed as she met Ollie's gaze, but instead of looking away she simply smiled before nodding in agreement.

"You're right, I know."

With one last glance around building twenty-eight, Ollie held out his hand to Blake and motioned towards the door leading out onto the lot once again.

"Come on," he said softly. "There's more to see."

They exited into the bright sunlight, hand-in-hand, and Ollie felt like a kid walking with his crush. It was silly. It was simply divine.

"Hungry?" he asked after they'd spent another hour exploring. "The canteen is nearby."

She let out a quick breath. "Food. Yes, *please*."

"Ollie! There you are." Lorna jogged over to them, clutching her tablet to her chest as if it were her offspring. "I texted you."

"Sorry," he replied as he took out his phone. "Weird, I don't have any missed texts from you. What's up?"

"Lorna Vaden." She extended a hand to Blake.

"Lorna's one of the finest writers in L.A.," Ollie said. "She's got two Emmy nominations to her name."

"You flatter me," Lorna said. "Sorry to interrupt."

"Not a problem. Blake Dillon," she replied as they shook. "Should I...?" She hooked a thumb over her shoulder and took a step back.

"No." He exclaimed, resisting the urge to grab her hand again. "I promised to feed you."

Blake grinned. "You did."

"Can you eat and write?" Lorna walked in the direction of the canteen, a few yards away. "I really need you."

"Not happy with the rewrite?"

"This is a whole new *scene*," Lorna said, groaning. "Tim had an *epiphany* after watching the dailies yesterday, and now he wants to add a scene."

"And you're not in the writing room because...?"

She laughed. "Writing room. Two of them quit this morning. Poached by another studio for a prime-time series."

"Ouch."

"Tell me about it. This is what we get for not contracting beyond the pilot phase. Anyway, I need you."

"You want Ollie to write for you?"

"It wouldn't be the first time."

Blake turned to him, delight and surprise in her expression. "You've been holding out on me."

"Not really." The weather was perfect, with a clear sky and a warm summer breeze, and they grabbed a table under one of the canopies.

"I would honestly sell an organ if Ollie would agree to come work for me," Lorna said. "You're wasting your talent. Not that you aren't the best EA I've ever seen—Bran's lucky to have you—but you could do so much more."

"I believe I've told you the same thing," Blake said, looking at him as if seeing him in a new light.

"See? Listen to your friend." Lorna smiled as she looked back and forth between them. "Are you an actress?"

"God, no!" Blake exclaimed before catching herself. "Not that it isn't...an admirable profession."

He snorted before he could stop himself.

She ignored him as she continued. "I'm a journalist."

Lorna's brows rose. "Huhn. I would never have pegged you for a reporter."

"She's doing a piece on Bran."

"Oh! Variety? Esquire?"

"Uh...no." Blake's lips pressed into a thin line.

He hated that she felt shame over her place of employment. Jobs were hard to come by, especially in her field. While the L.A. Gazette wouldn't have been his first choice for her either, he was glad to see her forging her own path.

"What's the new scene about?" he asked, hoping to steer the conversation away from Blake. "I need some context."

Lorna pulled up the script, swiping through the pages. "Right, remember the moment where Aaliyah tells Chris about the hidden passage? Tim wants a flashback of her as a child getting lost in the walls of the house."

"Is this a source of trauma for her?"

"Yes."

"What kind of show is this?" Blake asked.

"Sort of an Agatha Christie whodunit anthology," Lorna explained. "Each episode will be told from the perspective of a different character."

"How interesting!" She seemed genuinely curious. Ollie was inordinately pleased by that.

"How old is Aaliyah when she gets lost?" she asked.

"Tim wasn't specific, but if we go by the timeline, she would have been around nine or ten."

"I have some ideas," he said.

Lorna smiled. "I knew you would."

"When do you need it?" At the look on her face, he laughed softly. "Yesterday. Got it."

Swiping something on her tablet, Lorna stood. "I sent the specs to you and the updated script. Eat. Write. Be the genius that you are."

"I'm not."

"Yes, you are," Lorna and Blake replied at the same time.

He laughed. "Way to make a guy blush."

"Oh, but you're so *cute* when you do," Lorna said as she walked away.

He turned to find Blake grinning at him. "What?"

"There's more to you than meets the eye, Oliver Benjamin."

He rubbed the back of his neck awkwardly, not sure how to respond. He knew he was good at what he did, but it wasn't often that others saw him as more than Bran's go-to guy.

"Lorna obviously values your input— why else would she have asked you to bail her out? And you're writing for a TV series..." She gestured towards the script on the table between them. "...it's amazing!"

"It's not official."

"I hope they're paying you." When he didn't answer, she scowled. "Oliver."

"I've only helped out once or twice." More like four or five times, but she didn't need to know that.

She studied him a moment before leaning close, her arms folded on the table between them.

"Know your worth, Oliver"

"Likewise, Blake."

They gazed at each other, the moment stretching along with the corners of his mouth. The smile he could feel from the bottom of his feet to the top of his head.

"Noted," she said. "Now feed me."

# 7

**GIDEON: I need you in Studio City ASAP. Lead on Karen K. and some boytoy.**

    **BLAKE: I'm changing your name to *alarm clock* in my phone.**

    **GIDEON: A real reporter is up with the dawn.**

Blake groaned, feeling all too real.

"Most people didn't stay up half the night to do research for a story they didn't really want to write while *ignoring* the one that was actually important," she grumbled to her empty bedroom.

She'd fallen asleep in her street clothes. Her bra had dug into her shoulder like a dull knife, and she felt the sharp pain of it as she rolled to her back.

If the Internet was anything to go by, Brandon Cody nee Peters was exactly the vacuous, self-absorbed asshole she'd always thought him to be. The only thing that had her digging a little deeper was Ollie's devotion to him.

Once she swept past the numerous columns and posts on Bran's dating habits, if you could call it dating, she found that he was widely considered to be a decent actor. "A lot of potential" came up frequently, as well as "leading man material."

He had the looks, she could admit that much. Not that he could hold a candle to Oliver Benjamin. Ollie was handsome, but there was more to him than his piercing eyes, dimpled cheeks, or disarming smile.

He was confident without being arrogant, friendly without a hint of pretense. He had a strong moral code and wasn't afraid to stand up for what he believed in, even when it meant standing alone.

She had done a little background on him, too. For the article.

She'd looked up Bran's agent, publicist, and nutritionist as well. So, it had only made sense for her to do a bit of research on Ollie, surprised when she found he had a few writing credits on IMDB.

She smiled now as she had yesterday, thinking of Ollie writing for a hit show or a big blockbuster. Or maybe a quiet, independent film that garnered Oscar buzz.

He deserved the world.

Bran...deserved whatever he got. If he wanted to be taken seriously, he'd have to start behaving as if the head on his shoulders was the one calling the shots.

She was under no illusions about what this interview could mean for Bran's career.

**GIDEON: Tell me you're on your way.**

Shit. She jumped up and stripped out of her clothes, replying *I'm on my way* before she dashed into the shower.

Blake arrived at the La Palma hotel a little before eight a.m., and the only person in the lobby who wasn't hotel staff was Stewart, a photographer for the Gazette.

She peered at him from behind the darkest sunglasses in her meager collection. "Where's your camera?"

"Well, good morning to you, too," he said. The Jamaican lilt in his words making him sound too chipper for so early in the day.

"Is it though?"

His knowing smirk wasn't subtle. "Late night?"

Laughing, Blake rolled her eyes. "Not in the way you think." And not that her dreams hadn't taken interesting, Ollie-shaped turns lately.

"Pity. And how would you know what I think? I'm just the dashing figure behind the lens," he said. "But to answer your first question, the boss said he wanted discretion. I'm using this little point and shoot." He pulled a tiny, silver camera from his pocket.

"Did he say anything more about the guy Karen was with?"

"No, but the one who tipped us off is over there." He nodded toward reception where a pale, petite redhead in designer cats-eye glasses stood behind the counter.

Blake straightened her shoulders and walked over to the desk.

"Good morning, welcome to La Palma. How may I help you?" the woman asked without looking up from the computer screen. Most of her auburn hair was pulled into a stylish bun at her nape, wisps of curls brushing her shoulders as if placed there deliberately. Her bangs were razor sharp. Everything about her appearance seemed deliberate, from her neutral lip color to her French manicure. Classy but non-threatening.

"Hello, I'm from the L.A. Gazette," Blake said, keeping her voice low even though they were essentially alone.

The woman's head snapped up, her eyes widening before she glanced around. "Wow, you got here fast." Her voice had lost some of its polish, taking on a more conspiratorial tone. "Did you bring what we discussed?"

"Money?" she guessed. Correctly, judging by the twinkle in the woman's eyes. Shit. She should've known to ask Gideon if this was pay for play. She made a quick mental assessment of her bank account, wondering if she'd have enough to cover it and how quickly she could get reimbursed. "Uh, sure. You take Venmo?"

The woman—Willow, according to her name tag—sized Blake up before nodding. "I could. Though, there's an ATM down that hallway." She nodded slightly toward a corridor to the left. "That might be better. No digital trail."

Blake almost laughed. Why did they always want cash? This wasn't international espionage. "Thanks, that's probably smart."

Willow nodded, her blunt-cut bangs barely moving. "Coffee?" She rounded the counter and led her to a beverage station in a corner of the lobby. "It's fair-trade, from a small village in Rwanda."

"Wow, um, thanks." She grabbed one of the recycled-paper-brown to-go cups with the La Palma logo.

It was a tasteful setup complete with full coffee and tea service and assorted pastries. Two glass dispensers filled with water, ice, and orange slices stood on an iron stand.

"I heard somewhere this place was—"

"A dump?" Willow supplied.

She gaped at her. "I wasn't going to say that, exactly."

The woman waved her off. "The new owners came through here like a fresh breeze. They updated everything from the bathroom fixtures to the logo and I, for one, am glad."

"How long have you worked here?"

"Five years," she replied. "The previous owners were nice enough, but you could tell they'd sort of...checked out long ago, if you'll pardon the pun. It was a burden they couldn't wait to rid themselves of."

"The updates are nice," Blake observed as she eyed the offerings on the table.

"It's attracted a completely different clientele. Little perks like this," Willow said, pointing at the table. "The cranberry-orange scones are a favorite of mine. Try one."

"I'm fine." But the pastries were temptingly fresh. Rumbling loudly, her stomach decided it was a good time to make its presence known. At Willow's amused expression, she gave in and grabbed one of the scones. "Thanks. It was too early to pick up anything before I rushed over here."

As Blake took a bite of the sinfully delicious breakfast treat, Willow stepped closer.

"Your boss said I could trust you not to name me as a source?"

Chewing, she nodded. "Mmm hmm."

"Good. I don't want to lose my position here over a lousy five hundred dollars."

Five *hundred?* That was a lot of money. She hoped Gid would pay her back right away. "You have my word."

Willow studied her for a moment before she seemed to arrive at a satisfying conclusion. Stepping back, she cleared her throat. "Allow me to show you where the business center is."

Before she could ask why, Willow turned and began walking away. Blake jogged to catch up with her. "The business center?"

"And the ATM."

Right.

She gave Blake privacy as she withdrew the money. The bills were crisp and folded neatly before she slipped them into Willow's hand.

The alcove they stood in was off of the main lobby, but she could see Stewart standing by the door.

He casually drank from his own coffee cup and looked like any other patron waiting for a car to pick them up.

"While I appreciate the coffee and the food, can you tell me what you saw?"

Willow nodded and moved closer. "Karen's makeup assistant and I were in high school together."

Blake already didn't trust how many degrees apart this story began, but she nodded.

"She was here last Friday to brainstorm her look for some awards show," the woman continued, "Karen checked in early last week under a pseudonym."

"She's been here for over a week?"

"Weird, right? She has some big house in Laurel Canyon, and she's staying here? Something is up. Anyway, my friend and I ran into each other in the lobby. My day was over, so I invited her to the bar for a drink or three. Believe me, I wasn't looking for any dirt from her."

"Of course not." Blake didn't buy that for a second. "So, the guy is still here with her?"

"Was. Last night, anyway. I haven't seen him this morning. Trust me, I've been looking." Willow got a dreamy look in her eyes. "He was so hot, I wouldn't blame Karen for cheating on her man. Anyway, Amelia—that's my friend—said this guy showed up wearing a baseball cap and some glasses, and she thinks he's a model."

"And he went to Karen's room?"

"They were having dinner when Amelia left them."

"What time was that?"

"Eight-ish," Willow supplied. "We were at the bar until at least eleven, and we didn't see him leave. Like I said, I haven't seen him at all since then. When I came in this morning, Karen had checked out."

That...didn't sound good for Karen, whoever she was. Blake wasn't a fan of slut-shaming people, especially women, but she'd been paid to get information. She finished off her scone and looked for a place to set her cup down, settling on the ledge of a small window. She pulled out her notepad, preferring to take notes that way. Just because she hated this kind of journalism, if you could call it that, didn't mean she would half-ass it.

"Alright, Willow. What other salacious tidbits did Amelia plate up for you?"

"Oh, salacious," she purred. "That's a great word."

It was too good a word for schlock like this. "Thanks for the info." Blake wrote down the details.

"Thanks for the cash," Willow replied, her eyes bright. "I'm off tonight and the hotel is hosting an event for this hot talent agency. I'm going to see if I can crash it."

"Are you an actress, too?"

"Only aspiring, but I heard from a friend that this company is always looking for fresh faces."

Blake finished up her notes and opened her bag to put them away. "Yeah? Which company is that?"

"They're called Diamond Moon Enterprises."

Blake stilled. "Diamond Moon?"

"You probably haven't heard about them," Willow said in a hushed tone. "My friend Britney said they're very much on the downlow, but that they have deep pockets. She thinks they're backed by the Illuminati."

Biting back a groan, Blake nodded. "Do you happen to have a contact for them?" At Willow's raised eyebrows, she added. "I have a friend looking to break into the business."

"Dillon. My office."

Blake barely had time to step off the elevator and remove her glasses before Sonja barked the order. She was eager to follow up on the info Willow had given her about Diamond Moon but obeyed the summons.

She could count on one hand the number of times she'd been called into the Chief's office where it *hadn't* been to force a course correction or to chastise Blake for not following up on some *juicy* lead.

"Close the door."

Blake did as instructed and turned to face her.

Sonja was of medium height with a slender figure, dark hazel eyes, and blonde hair just this side of snow white. Her sharp features could be at times cold and striking, depending on her mood and her agenda. Right now, her expression was glacial. So was the temperature of her voice.

"I hear you're reluctant to interview Brandon Cody. Care to explain?"

"Actually, I'm scheduled to shadow him again tomorrow."

Sonja looked up from where she'd been signing papers. Blake was surprised to see the relief in her eyes.

"I'm...glad to hear that." Leaning back in her chair, she looked at her. It was an uneasy inventory of Blake's abilities as a reporter, as an employee. As a human being, probably.

Blake didn't squirm.

"I didn't want you on this story, initially."

*I didn't want it*, she didn't reply. "I appreciate the opportunity."

"Do you really?" Sonja crossed her legs. She wore skinny jeans and a billowy, bohemian-style blouse that didn't suit her personality one bit. "Brandon Cody is a hot property. Any number of outlets would kill their own grandmothers for the chance that just landed in your lap. Exclusive," the word sounded foreign in the middle of a familiar language. "One-on-one." It was delivered with more intimacy than was warranted. Her eyes glittered with something that made Blake's spine stiffen.

She cleared her throat. "I'll do my best to represent the Gazette with the utmost professionalism."

The smile she received was as sharp as knives. "I'm sure. Use the opportunity to your advantage. Don't be afraid to get close to him." This time, her gaze swept Blake from head to toe, and it felt like an inventory of a different kind.

"You might find it to your advantage to use *all* of your considerable assets," she said at long last before abruptly returning her attention to her computer screen.

With a wave of Sonja's hand, Blake was dismissed.

Breathing was only possible when she'd cleared the fifty feet from the office door to her cubicle. *What the hell was that about?*

"There you are." Gideon stopped halfway out of the door to his office. "Glad you could make it to work today."

"Sonja wanted to meet as soon as I got in."

His brows drew down and he nodded for her to come to his office.

Once inside, she closed the door and sat down. "Is it me, or does Sonja have a hard-on for Bran?"

"Bran?"

"Brandon Cody, sorry."

"We're on a nickname basis already?" He seemed impressed.

Blake opened her mouth to tell him exactly how she knew Bran, but the words wouldn't come.

What if he thought she was too close to the story? While she and Bran had never been more than casual acquaintances and maybe mutual antagonists, it might have been enough to cause concern. *And then there's Oliver.*

She made a split-second decision.

"It's what his people call him."

"Cute." Gideon pulled the foil off the cup of yogurt on his desk. "What's he like?"

"Arrogant."

He paused, the plastic spoon sticking out of his mouth. Speaking around it, he asked, "And?"

"He's...pretty much what you'd expect. Confident, hyper-masculine... He loves what he does and has a team of people who make his life easy."

"Hunh, well, I'm sure you'll pick up on more as you get stuck in."

Unlike Sonja's office, which offered tons of natural light thanks to a wall of windows overlooking the downtown area, Gideon's space was the kind of beige-y gray she remembered from her granddad's days at the Bulletin.

Even Gideon's hat, jacket and messenger bag—all thrown over the back of his rolling chair—were drab.

"I'll go as far as I'm allowed."

"You think they'll restrict access to certain areas of his life?"

She shrugged. "I'm not sure."

"What did Sonja want to talk to you about?"

"Brandon." Blake opened her notepad and started to write. "She called him a 'hot property.'" Blake hesitated before asking the question that had been niggling at her for the last few minutes. "She seems inordinately invested in this. In him."

"You think so?" Sliding a bit closer to the desk, Gideon looked from his yogurt to Blake as if deciding how much to say.

Interesting.

"It could be that she sees the potential in getting in early."

"Is that what this is?"

He made a non-committal sound. Pushing the cup aside, he sat forward. "You're back at it tomorrow?" She nodded. "Good, good. Let me know when you have some roughs I can look at."

"Will do." Blake rose and started to turn for the door but stopped. "We've run a lot of stories on Cody. More than Pratt, the Hemsworths, and Chalamet combined. Is there...something I should know?"

Gideon met her eyes. "If there is, I haven't figured it out myself," he said. "Let me know when you're ready to compare notes."

The sound of screeching tires cut through the din of the shouted questions and clicking shutters. As soon as the imposing black SUV pulled up, Ollie yanked the door open and shoved his charge inside.

"Does someone want to tell me what the fuck is going on?" After righting himself on the seat, Bran yanked off his sunglasses and glared, his chest heaving.

Ollie's own lungs were screaming. They'd just run the length of two football fields, through a horde of bloodthirsty paparazzi, to get Bran out of a fracas.

Fucking Bran.

"Ols." Bran barked. His whole body shook with rage and something else. Fear, perhaps.

Ollie closed his eyes, needing a moment to organize his thoughts and to rein in his anger.

"Goddamnit, Ollie, start talking."

Ollie's eyes popped open. Whatever expression he wore on his face was enough to make his best friend's jaw snap shut. Swallowing his own outrage and frustration, he cleared his throat.

"Where's your phone?"

Frowning, Bran patted his jacket pocket before producing the offending device. "Right here. Why?"

Without a word, Ollie held out his hand.

After a brief hesitation, Bran handed it over, the lines on his forehead deepening. When he spoke again, his words were calm but laced with annoyance. "What's going on? Why did you pull me out of the pool just when things were getting good?"

"We'll be on the move shortly, Mr. Benjamin," a voice announced through the SUV's speakers. "Club security is clearing a path."

Ollie touched the call button. "Get us the fuck out of here as quickly as you can."

The car lurched forward and to the side, rocking both passengers. Jaw clenched, Bran settled into his corner, his hand on the hold above the door.

Ollie took a deep breath as he scrolled through the contents of Bran's phone. *Jesus fucking Christ*, if the hacker had downloaded even half of what Ollie was seeing, Bran was fucked. He must have made a sound to indicate how pissed off he was because Bran cursed under his breath.

"It's that bad?"

"Someone accessed your personal phone." He spat out every syllable as clearly as he could.

Bran's medium-brown skin went ashen. "*What?*"

"Yeah." He had warned him a million times over never, *ever* to use his main phone for stuff like this. Or any fucking phone, really.

"Jesus, fuck." Bran ran a rough hand over his face and sank back into his seat. "Clark might just lose his shit."

"Might?" On cue, Bran's phone rang in Ollie's hand. "Hi, Clark."

"Oliver." The agent's north London accent turned his name into a full statement. "Where is he?"

"Here with me." He met Bran's wide eyes.

"And where is *here*, exactly?"

"We're en route to the house."

"No!" Clark shouted. "Absofuckinglutely not. Do not take him home. The vultures are already circling outside."

At times like this, Ollie regretted not getting his own place. When he moved to Los Angeles, he couldn't afford anything more than a room in a house share. Working for Bran, he made a decent living and could have found something. It would have been modest, but it would have been his and may have worked to their advantage at a time like this.

"I'd say bring him here," Clark said. "But too many people know where I live."

"There might be an alternative." Ollie navigated to the contacts on his phone. "I'm on it. I'll text you when we arrive."

"Keep him out of sight until I can assess the damage," Clark instructed him.

"That's the plan." Ollie disconnected the call and pulled up his text messages, firing off a note he hoped would solve their immediate problem.

Sighing heavily, Bran stared out the tinted window. "Why is this happening now?"

"Could be a zealous fan, could be a hater. It doesn't matter."

Bran snorted a bitter laugh. "Doesn't matter, he says."

Ollie looked up. "Does it? All of your shit is on this phone. Photos, text messages…all the stuff I specifically told you *not* to leave on your main device. Jesus, you don't even have two-factor authentication on your apps."

"Two factor what? Anyway, I hate carrying multiple phones." His words lacked their usual fire.

"Well, now you don't need to. I'll be carrying your phone from now on."

Alarmed, Bran sat up. "Says who?"

"And we're getting you some personal security."

"No." Bran slashed a hand through the air, as if that actually worked.

"Yes." When the response to his text came through, some of the pressure eased off of his chest. He hit the call button. "Conrad, new address. We're going to 5288 Chelsea Lane. La Jolla."

"We're heading to La Jolla?" Bran's entire demeanor changed. He looked like a kid on Christmas morning.

"No one will think to look for you there." Ollie sent the address to Clark.

**CLARK: I'll meet you there in 2 hours.**

**OLLIE: Text when you're close. I still think it's time Bran had a PSD. Now more than ever.**

**CLARK: I doubt we can get someone within the hour, but I'll make a few calls.**

**OLLIE: To someone we trust?**

**CLARK: You don't trust me?**

He cursed under his breath. Of all the people in Bran's camp, his agent was the *last* person Ollie wanted to piss off. He had a way of making his *suggestions* sound like the only option.

**OLLIE: Of course. Sorry, I'm on edge.**

He also had a contact back in Philly.

**OLLIE: Leave the security to me.**

**CLARK: Look after our asset, I'll take care of the rest.**

Clark's liberal use of the word *asset* made him sick to his stomach. While he understood Bran's value to the agent's bottom line, not to mention those of the studio execs and everyone else who had a stake in his career, it rubbed Ollie the wrong way. Actors, athletes, musicians—they were people, not fucking property.

"How pissed is he?" Bran asked, probably misreading the disgust on Ollie's face for something else.

"Hard to tell via text." He leaned back in the seat, grateful when the ride smoothed out. Resting his head against the cool leather, he closed his eyes. "Clark will meet us in La Jolla. Noelia will probably come, too."

"And...how pissed are you?"

Ollie cracked open one eye. For most of the time he'd known Bran, he had thought of him as larger than life. Even before he was a rising movie star, Bran had occupied a place of honor in Ollie's pantheon. Seeing the look on his face now, hearing the worry in his voice—not about the situation, but about how it affected Ollie—he realized the spot he himself held in Bran's world.

Confidante.

Shield.

Friend.

"We're okay," Ollie said.

Bran visibly relaxed. "Sorry I didn't listen to you before, about the phone security stuff. I never thought..." He trailed off, shaking his head as he returned to look out the window. Cars passed in muted shadows, the occasional glint of sunshine penetrating the dark tint. "I didn't think it would happen to me. I guess I thought I was—"

"Immune?"

Bran shrugged. "Being careful. Guess that was my arrogance. Again," he added bitterly.

"Good thing that's your only flaw," Ollie teased with a half-hearted laugh.

Bran's laugh was equally perfunctory. "Yeah."

The truth was, the breach wasn't his fault. People should be able to store whatever they wanted on their phones without some asshole trolling for compromising photos and texts to use against them.

Despite his bravado, he didn't think Bran understood how fast his star was rising. He was now a target for every jilted lover, jealous upstart, and over-zealous papp looking to make a quick score.

As his executive assistant, one of Ollie's responsibilities was helping to keep Bran's private and public lives separate. He had let their friendship, his love for his best friend, cloud his judgment. From now on, he would insist on locking things up tight.

Ninety minutes later, they pulled into the driveway of a modern, two-story house tucked away on a quiet street near the ocean. Bran had dozed off, drooling a little and looking more like the frat boy he had known in college than the movie star he was quickly becoming.

"We're here." He said it louder than was necessary, and stifled a laugh when Bran jumped.

Yawning, he rubbed a hand over his eyes. "Where is here, again?"

Conrad got out and opened the door for him.

Ollie opened his own door, stretching after he stepped out of the car.

"Holy shit." Bran turned his wide eyes to him.

"Surprise."

"Holy *shit*" A blinding smile split his face before he turned back to look at the wood and concrete structure.

For several months, he had been looking for the sort of showcase home Bran associated with his idols. Heron House had been on a list of properties Ollie had kept in his back pocket.

Personally, he found it to be too much. Too big, too ostentatious, and too damned expensive. But he'd arranged to rent it for a short time, after filming wrapped next week. It was meant to be a retreat after their grueling schedule, and a taste of the kind of lifestyle Bran dreamed of but couldn't quite yet afford.

Bran stood with his jaw hanging open. "I'm afraid to ask what this goes for."

"Trust me, you don't want to know." He led the way across the short bridge that took them over the moat—yes, the place had a moat—and to the front entrance. Keying in the code that unlocked the door, he disarmed the alarm before flicking on the lights.

"Damn," Conrad said as he stood in the doorway. "Is it alright if I use the bathroom?"

Ollie pointed to the right side of a floor-to-ceiling wood panel set seamlessly into a wall of polished concrete. "Push there."

Frowning, the driver followed directions, opening the door to reveal a gleaming glass and travertine powder room. He let out a low whistle as he stepped inside. "I'm afraid to touch anything in here, much less piss in it."

"It's just a bathroom."

"Nothing in this place is *just* anything," Conrad said, shifting uncomfortably on his feet. "I'll, uh, hit the head and then get on the road, unless you need me."

"We're parked here for the night." Ollie waved him off. "But keep your phone handy, just in case."

"Always." Conrad disappeared into the washroom.

Ollie's phone pinged.

**CLARK: Ten minutes out. Noelia will probably beat me there.**

**OLLIE: Roger that.**

He pulled up his contacts and found the one he needed, shooting off a quick text and crossing his fingers. The reply came back almost immediately, and he smiled. One less thing to stress over.

"Bran?" He headed through the atrium and down the hall that led to the back of the house.

"Out here."

He found him standing on the upper deck, overlooking the infinity pool. The sun had begun to set. Everywhere he looked, there was nothing but sky and sea. It was almost enough to settle his jangled nerves.

"I know you think places like this are OTT," Bran said. "But you can't argue with this view."

"You've got me there."

"Brandon. Oliver." The woman's voice startled them both. Turning, Ollie found Noelia standing in the open doorway. Raising her carefully groomed eyebrows, she surveyed the scenery as well. "Well, if this isn't the fanciest hideout I've ever seen."

"Hey, Nellie." Bran moved to hug her but stopped when she gave him a sharp look.

"Don't call me that, especially when I'm pissed at you. What in the fresh hell, Cody?"

"Don't be mad." He gave her his famous cover-worthy grin. "It's just a couple of pics and a naughty text or two. It'll blow over by morning."

"Are you telling me how to do my job now?"

He held his hands up in surrender. "No, ma'am."

She rolled her eyes. In the dying rust of sunset, her dark sepia skin seemed to glow from within. She pointed at the sectional surrounding the rectangular fire pit. "Sit down."

He sat just as the doorbell rang.

"I'll get it. It should be Clark." Ollie jogged to open the door for the agent, who entered with his ear pressed to his phone.

He offered a curt nod. "Where?" Clark whispered, and he directed him towards the back deck.

Clark didn't blink at the opulent surroundings. Given his client roster, Ollie wasn't at all surprised. "I don't care if you have to physically break into their office and rip every hard drive out by hand, I want those photos obliterated. The texts, too. These won't be as easy to deny as the last time we went through this. Bran's *everything* is on full goddamned display."

Before he could close the door, another man stepped across the threshold. Ollie blocked the man's path. "You're not Clark's usual driver."

"You must be Oliver Benjamin," the guy replied, sizing him up.

"And you are?"

"Rory Dunn." He held out a hand. "I'm Mr. Cody's detail. Well, until you find someone permanent."

It was his turn to size Rory up. Ollie was tall, but the guy had three inches and about thirty pounds on him, all of it muscle.

"The Skinner Agency referred me."

He blinked. "I only called a few minutes ago."

"I was finishing a job nearby."

"Lucky us."

"Indeed."

It was hard to pinpoint his age, given his neat, full beard, but Ollie put him somewhere in his late-twenties or early-thirties.

"Glad to have you here," he finally said, relaxing a little. "And thanks for stepping in last-minute."

"Glad I was available. Are you expecting anyone else?" There was a gentle lilt to Rory's English that he couldn't place.

"Hans Visser, the nutritionist-slash-chef will be here later with supplies for the night."

"Description?"

"Uh, well, he's white. About five-eleven, wiry frame, spiky blond hair. Fading Scandinavian accent."

Rory nodded. "Anyone else know you're here?"

"No."

"That's good." He looked around the entranceway. "I'll poke around a bit, get a lay of the land, and then park myself somewhere. I'll need your number."

They exchanged digits. "I assume Pierce filled you in on the situation."

"Not the details," Rory said, his gaze sweeping the space. "I'm on a need-to-know. If I were coming in on a more permanent basis, I'd need everything. For now, I'm good."

Ollie nodded. When he returned to the deck, he felt like he'd waded into a tarpit, the air was so thick. Bran, Noelia, and Clark were huddled around a tablet.

"Jesus Christ," Bran muttered. "This shit was buried really deep, in an archived folder."

"Not deep enough. Thankfully, they haven't been released," Noelia said. "Yet."

He almost didn't want to look, but curiosity got the better of him. He recognized Bran right away, as well as the walls of Bran's bedroom. He also recognized the redhead bent over the edge of Bran's four-poster bed.

"Who is she?" Clark asked.

"Sara Hutchins," he replied. "She's done a few things, small parts, here and there." He remembered her from one of the Malibu parties, eager to ingratiate herself to her host. A little too eager, but then most of that crowd was.

"Well, this would put her on everyone's radar," Clark said.

"And kill her career in the process," Noelia added.

"It's fucking ridiculous." Bran began to pace the patio. "How is this legal? It's an invasion of privacy."

"It's not legal, not the hack. But sex sells, and some outlets will twist themselves into pretzels to claim photos like these were legally obtained from an anonymous source."

"Your college friend, the reporter, do you think she had anything to do with this?" Noelia asked.

The question made his head snap around to her. "No," he said through clenched teeth.

She eyed him before looking at Bran.

"No, Ollie's right. She's too fond of riding her moral high horse to do something this low."

Noelia held up her hands in surrender. "I'll trust you both on this, since you have history. That means Sonja's using the interview as an excuse to run these, or these are her insurance that we'll give her what she wants."

"Which is?"

"Me." Bran's voice was flat. He turned away from them, his hands on his head.

Ollie ran a hand over his face. Sometimes, he hated this business. Most times. "This is so wrong."

"Our Bran is on the mainstage, now," Clark added. "His expectation of privacy is..." Gesturing with his fingers, he made a *poof* sound.

"I don't get why this is acceptable."

"You don't need to," the agent replied, smoothing a hand down the front of his short-sleeved, linen button-down. Clark's hair was a shade of black that could only come from a bottle. "But our main job, from now on, is to stop it from happening again. You're on lockdown, my boy."

Turning, Bran shook his head. "I don't need a goddamned babysitter."

"Don't you?" Clark gave him a pointed look before turning to Noelia. "I can hear your wheels turning. What are you thinking?"

She tapped on her phone as she rose to her feet. "I'm going to call in a favor or three. Give me an hour. I'll be in touch."

Standing, Clark followed her. "I'll keep pressure on the Gazette. Threaten Sonja with a harrassment suit."

"Don't do that," she said, turning abruptly. "We still have the interview. The Gazette is treading on thin ice. If Sonja wants the exclusive, she'll play ball. Bran, you stay put."

"Not a problem, except that none of my things are here. And I'm starving." He gave Ollie a pleading look.

"Hans is on his way with provisions."

"God, he's going to bring me kale. Isn't he? I want real food. Comfort food. Mac and cheese." He sounded every bit like the brat he was at times.

"I'll take care of it, but I need a lift back to my car. I'm teaching this evening." He wasn't about to leave his class in the lurch, and there was nothing more he could do for Bran in the meantime.

"I've got you," Noelia said, gesturing for Ollie to come with her. "Stay here, Brandon. I mean it."

"You're leaving me all by myself? Who knows what kinds of mischief I could get up to?" Bran's tone was light, but Ollie could still hear the tension in his voice.

"Not much, since I have your phone. Besides, Rory will be here."

"Who?" Clark's brow creased.

"That would be me," Rory replied, standing by the edge of the pool.

Everyone turned.

"Shit, who the hell are you?" Bran asked.

The agent gave the bodyguard an assessing look. "Did Russell send you?"

"Rory Skinner, and no. I don't know a Russell." He approached, his hand outstretched to Bran.

"Brandon Cody." He reluctantly shook. "You're my security guy, I take it?"

"For now."

Bran's frown deepened.

"Where are you from? I can't place your accent." Clark glanced at Ollie and back at the newcomer.

"Dublin, by way of Philly." Rory folded his arms, his tattooed biceps on display.

"I called in a favor, and Rory was good enough to jump in," Ollie said.

The guy was a beast, taller than an oak and broader than a boulder. He felt better, knowing Bran would be well covered if anything went down in his absence. Not that he was expecting any more drama.

"He's doing us a huge favor, being here," he said, turning to Bran.

"So, be nice and don't make his job difficult."

"Oh, he won't make my job difficult. Will you, Mr. Cody?" Rory crossed his arms, smiling in a way that said *I won't take any shit from you.*

He liked this guy. "Bran will behave, or you have my permission to kick his ass."

"Fuck you," Bran said without heat.

Ollie grinned as he walked out the door.

# 9

There was something about urban decay that people with money found charming, nostalgic even. There were YouTube channels dedicated to exploring modern ruins—abandoned mansions, dilapidated amusement parks, and vacated neighborhoods—as if those places didn't represent the end of a way of life.

People who struggled to put food on the table were experts at repurposing. Where means were scarce, nothing went to waste. This was why Blake wasn't surprised that Play L.A., a local community center that provided classes for underprivileged kids, was located in an old department store on a once thriving, now barely surviving, stretch of boulevard in south central Los Angeles.

The mid-twentieth-century building had been divided into three storefronts, with Play L.A. nestled between a check cashing shop and a dry cleaner. If her contact hadn't given her such explicit directions, she would have missed the place.

There was plenty of parking and she pulled up right out front, grabbing her bag before she got out of the car. Los Angeles was in the middle of a heat wave, and she knew her seats would be scalding when she came out, but there was no helping it.

She pushed inside and was greeted by a faint combination of a musky scent rising from the painted cement floors and notes of vanilla from a few carefully placed air fresheners.

"Can I help you?" A young woman, no older than seventeen, sat at a desk in the front room. Her eyes were bright against her dark skin, her hair in a million tiny braids that hung past her shoulders. She seemed to be in the middle of doing her math homework.

"I'd ask you the same question, but I suck at that stuff," Blake said, pointing to the book splayed out on the desk.

The girl rolled her eyes and returned to her work. "Well, I just need to pass this class and I'll never have to look at these formulas again."

"That's the spirit. I'm Blake. What's your name?"

There was a long, uncomfortable pause as the girl looked up, assessing her without even raising her head. Finally, she shrugged and straightened in the chair. "Micah. And my pronouns are she and her," she added as if it were a challenge.

"It's nice to meet you, Micah. Same. And you've got the right idea. The only way out is through. Y'know?" Blake offered her most reassuring smile. The young woman was not impressed. "Is Deanna around? Uh, I mean Ms. Lopez?"

"She expecting you?" Micah scribbled something down, erased it, and sucked her teeth.

"Actually, no." She leaned in, lowering her voice as if inviting the girl in on a secret. "But we've been emailing back and forth, and I want to interview her for my paper."

Micah's head popped up, her lip curling. "You're a reporter?"

Sensing imminent defeat, she nodded. "I am. I can show you my—"

The girl smiled, and it managed to be both unnerving and insulting. "I'm so sorry. Ms. Lopez is not available, but you can leave a message," she said overly bright.

She took a step back and tried to think of a new approach. "Look, Micah... I know people in my line of work don't have the best track record around here, but I think Ms. Lopez will want to talk to *me*, if you could just—"

"Hey, Micah."

Blake froze, the hair on the back of her neck standing at attention at the improbable sound of a familiar voice. Turning slowly, she stared at the man who'd come through the door.

"Oliver?"

Eyes the color of storm clouds blinked at her in surprise. "Blake?"

"You two know each other?"

"Yeah, we..," Ollie said, the words barely a whisper before he cleared his throat. "This is...becoming a habit. Hi."

"Hey." For a moment, she forgot where she was. She hadn't expected to find him in a place like this. Years without a sign of him and, suddenly, he was everywhere.

After a beat, they both leaned in for an awkward, one-armed hug. He somehow *smelled* like California, and Blake found herself breathing him in.

"What are you doing here?" Ollie stepped back, and then winced. "Sorry, that's rude. I meant to say what brings you here?"

Blake was glad to know he hadn't changed much. From his shock of untamed hair to his wire-framed glasses to his unfairly symmetrical face and gorgeous smile, Ollie was still...Ollie. Even knowing he worked for Brandon somehow made sense, though she hated the idea of it.

"I'm working on something and had a few questions for Ms. Lopez." Aware that the young girl was watching them, she turned to her. "I'm not having any luck there, though."

Micah gazed at Ollie like he'd hung the moon. Her expression was the very definition of starry eyed, and Blake stifled her smile.

"You've moved on to another story, or..?" his expression dimmed, and the ground beneath her feet seemed to shift. "I wouldn't blame you."

That was cryptic.

"No, I..." God, and now she *had* to make good on her promises. She'd been putting Bran's publicist off for two days, with Gideon breathing down her neck and threatening to give the story to someone else if she didn't get moving on it. She glanced at Micah—"I'm in. But I'm hoping *this* story will help me get my foot in the right door."

"Oh." He perked up a bit. "That's great, about the interview. And I'm sure this will open doors for you. You'll follow in Trent's footsteps."

An inaudible gasp of surprise escaped her. "You always know exactly what to say to me."

Blake didn't know she had the power to make someone blush, but Ollie did. A deep, rich color that stained his cheeks and neck.

"Well... we've talked about him quite a bit. *The great Trent Dillon.*" His smile was teasing, despite his reverent tone.

"What are *you* doing here?"

"Ah, well, I teach a sort of introductory class on scriptwriting." He shoved his hands into his pockets, something he used to do when he was nervous. "To the kids here."

"I gathered." She let her gaze sweep over him and, damn, did he look good. "I wondered, what with...your job, and all, whether you had time for anything else. I thought maybe you'd changed your career goals."

"God, no," he answered too quickly.

She laughed.

"That gig is only for now. I want a career in writing. And I have a few things that aren't ready for public consumption yet."

"The novel you wouldn't show me at school?" He flushed even deeper, and her jaw dropped. "You're still working on it?"

"It'll be finished when it's finished," he said, shutting off that part of the conversation with a shy grin. "As for this place, I'm more than happy to help shape young minds." He glanced at his watch. "Speaking of which..."

"Do you want to meet up when you're done? I could wait for—"

"Yes!" He seemed to catch himself. With a self-deprecating laugh, he shook his head. "I'd like that. I'll be about an hour."

"If I finish before you, I'll wait in my car."

"You're more than welcome to sit in on the class, after you're done talking to Deanna."

"Yeah?"

His smile widened. "Of course."

Of course.

"Alright."

"Okay," he said. They were gazing at one another. He snapped out of it first. "Okay, catch you later."

She watched him walk away and, man. He *really* knew how to wear a pair of jeans.

Tossing her pencil aside, Micah stood up with a long-suffering sigh. "Since you're a friend of Ol...er...*Mr. Benjamin's*, I guess Ms. Lopez wouldn't mind talking to you."

"Yeah?" This day just kept getting better. "You're sure?"

"She's in the mainstage area. I can take you through."

"I'd appreciate it." She followed the young woman through a set of double doors and down a short corridor, passing a few other rooms, before they came to another set of double doors.

The place had seen better days. What had once surely been gleaming chrome accents were now worn or faded, and the wood paneling on the walls was so outdated it was almost back in style.

Still, everything was clean and tidy.

They emerged into a space that had been stripped entirely of its original identity. Gone was the wood and chrome, and in its place a linoleum floor, a set of folding chairs, and a stage that had been painted pitch black. Heavy burgundy curtains hung on either side, framing the black, and an old upright piano sat on the floor beneath the lip. The woman sitting on the piano bench was in her early thirties, with dark olive skin and chestnut hair. A dozen kids, ranging in age from around eight to somewhere around Micah's age sat in a semicircle facing the piano.

"That's her," the girl whispered as she pointed. "They're finishing up, so it won't be long."

"Projection and elocution," Deanna said. She made eye contact with each of the kids before turning back to the piano. "Let's try the last verse and chorus."

The kids launched into a song that sounded vaguely familiar. "Is that from a movie?"

"Yeah, *Encanto*."

"Oh, right."

"I better go finish my homework before my class," Micah said.

"What are you studying here?"

Her face lit up. "Scriptwriting."

"From Mr. Benjamin?"

Her eyes shone with sudden enthusiasm. "It's *so* cool. I love storytelling. It's like Ollie says, you can create your own world with your own rules."

"That does sound like fun."

Micah waved goodbye, and Blake found a chair near a table in the back. She took out her notebook and a pen but found herself scanning the large space for a sign of Ollie. *Stop it.* She focused on her notes.

*Miriam (not her real name) is a beautiful young lady, full of the kind of hope and optimism companies like Diamond Moon Enterprises prey upon. What they offer these kids sounds like a dream because it is. But in a place where dreams rarely come true, every opportunity must seem like the only opportunity.*

"Are you Ms. Dillon?"

She looked up and found Deanna walking towards her. "Yeah, hi. And Blake is fine."

"Sorry to keep you waiting, Blake. I'm Deanna."

"Not a problem at all, Deanna." She got to her feet and offered her hand.

Deanna's grip was firm, her smile inviting. She started to turn, gesturing for Blake to follow her. "To be honest, I was surprised when I got your email. How did you hear about us?"

"There was an article on a Spanish-language site that came across my feed."

Deanna stopped and looked at her, surprised. "You speak Spanish?"

"Not enough to hold a conversation beyond the weather," she admitted. "But I caught the gist of it."

"Enough to reach out," Deanna confirmed. She showed Blake inside a small office, the air inside slightly stale, and took a seat behind an old metal desk covered in stacks of paper, cups of pens, and highlighters. An old flatscreen monitor perched in one corner, a few dead pixels scattered across the screen.

Blake took the chair opposite her. "How many kids, would you say, have been targeted by Diamond Moon?"

"First, tell me why the Gazette is interested in this story." Deanna leaned back and rested her ankle on her knee. She was dressed in a black tank top and black chinos, but wore a gorgeous, multicolored scarf around her neck. Her jewelry was artsy but inexpensive.

Blake figured honesty was probably the best approach. "They're not."

Deanna's eyes went wide, her brows disappearing under the fringe of her bangs. "I wasn't expecting that."

"Look," Blake began as she leaned forward. "You know the reputation of the paper I work for. We're not exactly renowned for hard-nosed journalism. There's a good chance my story will be buried in favor of the scandal of the week. But as my grandfather used to say, you can't bury a blank page."

"I thought it was you can't *edit* a blank page."

"He wasn't above borrowing a thing or two." Blake smiled, glad when Deanna returned it.

"He was a journalist? Like you?"

The question touched a tender bruise, and she must have winced because Deanna's expression filled with sorrow.

"I'm sorry If I-"

"It's okay," Blake assured her. "He was, and I hope to be as accomplished as him someday."

"I'm sure he would be proud of you."

Blake took a deep breath and exhaled, trying to loosen the knot that always formed in her throat when she thought of her granddad. The last time she'd seen him, he'd looked through her like she wasn't even there.

"Thanks." She cleared her throat. "Anyway, as I said, I can't guarantee the story will run. But I want to give it the time and attention it deserves. Give it the best shot."

Deanna nodded slowly. "I would say…seven or eight of my kids have come to me about Diamond Moon. And I know of three who signed with them. One is still active and doing alright, from what I've heard. Videos with a lot of views, and so on. I haven't spoken to Chidi in a year or more, but the kids talk."

She made note of everything. "Does he perform under that name?"

"I think so." Deanna spelled it for her. "He's nineteen now. Used to come here after school, from age twelve until he was sixteen. He stopped coming regularly, and then didn't come at all. I called his mother, to make sure everything was all right, and she told me he'd signed a contract with Diamond Moon. They're an umbrella company with a record label, a talent agency, etcetera. One stop shop."

"I'm aware. And they signed him at sixteen?"

"The mom seemed excited by the idea of having a rap star for a son," the other woman said. "She mentioned moving to a better neighborhood, getting a new car. That sort of thing."

"And did they?"

She nodded. "They did move, but other than that I couldn't say."

"What caused your concern with Diamond Moon?" Blake had her suspicions but didn't want to influence her source.

"I had a young woman in the choir, Belinda." Deanna sighed, her gaze going distant. "She was a stunner. Talented, too. Voice like Amy Winehouse, mixed with a little Fantasia. Anyway, someone from Diamond Moon came to our Fall fundraiser—the kids perform and show off their work for locals and donors. She spoke to Belinda after the show, took her and her parents to dinner."

"Do you remember the woman's name?"

"Taylor. Selina Taylor." The woman's eyes went stormy as she bit the words out.

"What happened?"

Blinking fast, Deanna opened a drawer and pulled out a pack of nicotine gum.

Blake shook her head when she offered some. "I've never smoked."

"You're smarter than me." Deanna popped a piece of gum out of the foil and put it in her mouth, grimacing. "This shit is disgusting." She woke the computer and pulled up a webpage, turning the monitor for Blake to see.

## SEVENTEEN-YEAR-OLD, ARRESTED FOR TRAFFICK-ING, FOUND NOT GUILTY

"*Trafficking?*" Shocked, Blake turned to her. "Is the company a front?"

"I did some digging, but I didn't get far." She reached for Blake's arm, squeezing it with shaky fingers. "Maybe you can ask the questions I couldn't, get the answers. Belinda is a sweet girl, there's no way she did this on her own."

"I'll do what I can."

"I appreciate it." Deanna stood and smoothed her hands over her clothes. "Even if nothing comes of this, it means a lot to me that you're trying."

Blake rose and shook her hand. "Whatever I find, I'll share. And if any of the kids want to talk, with their parents' permission, of course, I'm happy to come back anytime."

"Thank you again. I hate to cut this short, but we have our late afternoon classes soon." The woman rounded the desk and led her through the door. "You're welcome to stick around and watch. Do you sing?"

"God, no." She laughed. "I wouldn't want to inflict that on anyone."

Deanna chuckled. "We have acting classes as well."

She followed her out to the front room, moving aside when a string of kids came in through the door and blew by them. "And scriptwriting."

"Yes." Deanna patted her on the shoulder and pointed to their right. "In fact, there's our new instructor. Oliver—"

"Benjamin," Blake said, fighting the smile that wanted to take over her face as she watched him.

"You know Ollie?"

"Yeah, we went to school together. College. It's surreal to see him again." Not teaching, that seemed to suit what she remembered of him. But L.A., Bran—all of that—did not.

"You're from Philly, too?"

"Born and raised."

Deanna smiled, watching Ollie with his students. "I was so grateful when he agreed to come on-board. We get a lot of actors, musicians, even dancers, but he's our first writing mentor in a long time."

His rich, musical laugh rang out across the room. Blake watched him smile at whatever the kid was saying to him and was transfixed, transported back in time. To the study group, junior year, where he had been team lead.

He'd been so smart and so generous with his time, even then. Gorgeous in a bookish, unassuming way that'd had her daydreaming, in the back of the library, of stolen kisses in the stacks.

Just when she'd gotten up the courage to actually flirt with him, and thought she'd seen interest from him in return...

Brandon Peters happened.

And here they were, the three of them, all over again.

Blake deliberately loosened her shoulders. That was a long time ago.

"He's a good guy," she said. That much hadn't changed either.

"I hope you get a chance to catch up," Deanna looked at her watch. "I'm sorry, my next group is starting soon."

"No need to apologize. Thanks for giving me a bit of your time. I'll be in touch."

The other woman walked away, but Blake found herself watching Ollie.

The way he leaned in, attentive to whomever was speaking was almost hypnotic. His long, elegant fingers moved through the air, expressing whatever point he was making.

He looked up and caught her eyes on him, his hands stilling as he sat up a little straighter.

# 10

He'd found it difficult to concentrate with her eyes on him. The last ten minutes of the class went by in a blur. Ollie could only hope that whatever lesson or advice he'd given to his students made sense and was age-appropriate.

His thoughts, his awareness, had been all about Blake.

"I'm parked just here," she said as they exited the building.

"I'm over there, but it might be simpler if we call a rideshare and leave our cars here."

"You have a place in mind?" She arched one dark brow.

"I do."

He brought her to The Library, a small cafe-slash-bar in the up and coming West Athens area frequented by aspiring writers. He had stumbled across the spot soon after they opened and had come to think of it as his local haunt even though he lived miles away.

"This is very cool," she said as they stepped inside, taking in the dark wood furniture, brocade-covered couches, and leather armchairs in the seating nooks.

The bar's low lighting lent an intimate ambiance to the space, despite the high ceilings, its atmosphere perfect for drinks and long conversations.

Before that moment, Ollie hadn't thought of it as particularly romantic. They were seated at a two-top in a back corner, tucked away from the large central bar. It showcased an array of exquisite glassware and a bottle display that always drew a crowd, and he was glad for their secluded spot.

Blake's warm brown skin glowed in the light from the candelabra over their table.

"That is a lot of books," she said, looking around at the floor-to ceiling bookcases that covered nearly every wall.

They were seated by a bookcase labeled *Western classics*, next to a shelf that held works of American literature from Poe, Wilde, Butler, and others. For a moment, time had rewound itself.

Blake's brows arched as she skimmed the spines. "These bring back memories," she said, her tongue darting out to fold over her plump bottom lip.

She had no idea.

Ollie swallowed tightly, trying to ignore the flicker of heat igniting at the base of his spine.

"I can see why you like this place."

"Yeah?"

"Reminds me of U of P."

*Our spot*, he didn't say. "The library."

"I guess some things never change."

But some things had. "How did you end up at the Gazette?"

There was no humor in her smile this time. "It's a tough industry." Blake picked up the small leather portfolio that held the menu, her gaze scanning the pages as she spoke. "Tougher every day with fewer outlets and AI replacing reporters. I'm on one of the few paths left."

"How much do you hate writing about famous people?"

"So much." Her shoulders slumped. "But I'm working on something that I hope—fingers crossed—will get me out of that racket."

"And that's related to Play L.A.?"

"Yeah." She leaned in, lowering her voice. "Someone is targeting the kids there, and at other organizations like it."

He frowned. "Targeting, how?"

"Deanna confirmed that a couple of the teens have been approached by quote-unquote *talent scouts* and coerced into signing contracts."

"Contracts for...?"

"Recording, modeling, acting... They're not picky," Blake said with obvious distaste. "They prey on the dreams of these kids who have few prospects, and tie them to terms that are extremely unfavorable. It's like...well, it's close to slavery. And..." She hesitated. "In a few cases, I suspect it *is*. One young woman, Belinda—do you know her?"

Ollie frowned. "No, but I have heard her name mentioned a few times. What happened to her?"

"That's what I'm trying to find out. She signed with Diamond Moon Enterprises, that's the company, and not long after she was brought up on trafficking charges. She's seventeen."

"What? Jesus." Shock didn't cover what he felt. Anger, disbelief, and behind that a sense of negligence on his part. "And these people are still after some of the kids?"

"Deanna believes so, and I'm inclined to agree. None of the students will talk to her, and they certainly won't talk to me. And I can't get anyone at the agency to return my calls. I almost crashed an event they were having at a hotel in Studio City."

"What stopped you? I seem to recall you sneaking into a few faculty-only meetings back at school."

She huffed a short laugh. "My sense of self-preservation wasn't too keen back then. I should have been more worried about getting expelled." She sighed. "I can't afford to lose my job, which I would if I were to get caught sneaking into an industry function."

Ollie nodded. "These scouts are harassing students who are still under parental guardianship," he began, thinking aloud. "You have to be eighteen to sign a contract in the U.S., right?"

"Yes." She looked away and began to drum her long fingers on the table next to the green leather notebook she'd placed between them. "Which is why they target the parents as well, promising fame and riches."

"Shit. If there's anything I can do, please ask," he said. "I want to help."

"That would be great." Blake's smile lifted a few of the shadows from her eyes. "I know it's a lot to ask, but could you pass along my info to your kids and tell them they can speak with me if they know or have heard anything? It could be important. And they seem to like you."

"They're great kids."

"With a great mentor."

The server arrived, a slight young woman with light brown skin and a head full of long, thick locs. She smiled at them, the light catching on her lip piercing.

"I'll have Old Forrester 1920, neat."

Surprised, Ollie ordered the same. "And could we get the hummus plate and the Margherita flatbread? If you're okay with that," he added, looking at Blake.

"That sounds perfect. I'm actually starving." Her laugh was a tinkling bell, colored with embarrassment, but she glowed in the low light.

Ollie couldn't stop staring.

"I'll bring over a cup of our spiced pecans from the bar," the server said. "To hold you over."

"Okay, this is officially my favorite spot in Los Angeles." She turned her bright smile towards him.

Pleased, Ollie sat back in the leather wingback, wishing he'd joined her on the bench. "It's a hangout for local writers."

"Is it?" Her gaze swept the room. "You know anyone here?"

He'd noted a few familiar faces when they walked in. "I don't come here as often as I'd like."

"Why not?" Blake's expression hardened as the answer seemed to come to her. "You have to tell me how...why..." She swallowed, taking a deep breath before she met his gaze again. "What's it like working for him?"

"Bran?"

"No, the Pope." Her tone was dry.

For some reason, this made him laugh.

Blake's mouth curved at the corners as if against her will.

Their drinks arrived. The server also set down a bowl of nuts which Blake pounced on, giving Ollie time to get his thoughts together. He'd known the question was coming and cursed himself for not having a better answer than, "Bran needed someone he could trust, now more than ever."

"He has a literal *team* of people working for him."

"It's not the same."

Blake narrowed her eyes. "I get that being in his position, it might be...challenging to find people you can really count on."

"Everyone has an agenda."

"Everyone? Even you?"

"Even me."

He'd surprised her, and he liked that he had.

"Fair enough."

"I'd have come out here to help even if he weren't paying me."

"You're a good friend."

"So is Bran."

This back and forth between them felt familiar. He liked that, too. Loved that they could get back here so quickly.

Blake did not look convinced, and Ollie didn't want to push. Hopefully, she'd get to know Bran on her own. If the interview ever actually happened.

It needed to happen soon. And he needed her to come to La Jolla.

"So, he called, and you came," she said after taking a sip of her bourbon.

"Pretty much." He sampled his own, welcoming the soft burn of the alcohol.

"Just like that?"

"Is this on the record?"

Another aborted smile. "Why me? There are a dozen other reporters who would be better suited for something like this. Why did you want me for it?"

"It goes back to the whole trust issue," he said, leaning back to allow their server to place the hummus between them. The table was small, and he shifted, apologizing when their knees pressed together. Neither of them moved.

"Bran trusts me?" She unfolded a napkin and laid it daintily across her lap.

"Well...no, but I do." He offered her the basket of pita and took a slice after she did.

"And he trusts you. Got it."

"He does. Look, I know it isn't ideal, but... I really think it'll be good for everyone, in the end. Come to La Jolla-"

"La Jolla? I thought you were going after Bran finished filming."

"That was the plan but...something came up."

Her expression was completely without guile. She didn't know about the photos, about the hack. He was ashamed of the relief he felt. Obviously, some small kernel of doubt had impregnated itself in his subconscious.

He brutally snuffed it out.

"Wow, I..."

"I promised to make it easier on you. You can stay in the pool house, or one of the guest rooms. It's a large house. Meals would be on us, of course."

"Of course."

Blake dragged the bread lightly through a pool of olive oil in the center of the dip and brought it to her mouth and he tried—*hard*—not to stare.

Tearing his gaze away from the drop of oil dotting her upper lip, Ollie dipped his bread in the hummus and put it in his suddenly dry mouth. The dip was savory, garlicky, and delicious.

They ate a while in silence, Ollie trying desperately not to notice the way her lips moved as she chewed, or the way she fastidiously licked them after every bite, or—God—the way she moaned softly and let her eyes roll a bit when half the plate had vanished.

"I must have been hungrier than I thought," she said, almost sheepishly. "Sorry. You've barely had a bite."

"No need to apologize. We can always order more. Tonight's on me." It was ridiculous how happy it made him to watch her eat. *What a weirdo*, he thought. How would he get through a week of her sleeping down the hall or across the patio? "You like charcuterie?"

Her eyes lit up at his question before she tried to tamp down her enthusiasm. "What's not to like about salty meat?"

Ollie almost choked on thin air.

"Could I get you anything else?" the server asked, saving him more awkwardness.

"I had a nice time." He said an hour later as they exited the now-packed bar. Ollie had told himself to play it cool, but *I had a nice time? Really, dude?*

"Me, too." Blake's smile was kind as she nudged his shoulder with hers. "Thanks for inviting me along. It was…an experience."

He hadn't realized it, but they'd come on the one night a week local poets came to try out their new works on the patrons.

"I firmly believe any experience is only memorable when it's shared with good people." *Okay, that was better.*

"I'm glad you think of me as good people, Oliver."

He did. And the way she said his name made his steps stutter as they walked along the quiet street. The night air was crisp and clean, with just a hint of wood smoke from the pizzeria they passed.

Above them, the sky was slate gray with wisps of low cloud cover that reflected the glow of the streetlamps.

"You're honestly one of the best people I've ever known."

Oh, he doubted that very much, but it was nice to hear. "We should do this more often."

"What, drinks at a spot so trendy it doesn't have a sign outside?" Blake grinned.

"I meant hanging out. In general."

"Yeah?"

"Absolutely. Whether you still plan to do the interview or not," he added, hoping La Jolla wasn't a dealbreaker. "There are a lot of great places to eat in L.A."

Blake made a face. "I'm sure there are, but I'm on a tight budget. I haven't had the chance to try any. Actually, this is probably my first time eating in a place with tablecloths since I moved out here."

"Don't you ever splurge? Treat yourself when you, I don't know, get an article published? Or some other print milestone. Honestly, I don't know how it works in your world."

"My world?" Blake laughed. "I hope we live in the same world, Ollie. It would be difficult to hang out if we didn't."

"You know what I mean."

"I do, but you're so much fun to tease. You go absolutely pink." Blake poked him in the side and he let out a wholly uncharacteristic sound.

"Okay, enough of that," he said, moving out of her reach. They strolled leisurely down the street. "I'm serious, though. Don't you ever treat yourself to something nice once in a while?"

"My idea of a treat is the occasional tuna on wheat from the convenience store at the gas station near where I live."

"That sounds dire."

"They're actually pretty tasty," Blake said. "Not truffle foam cloud on saffron-infused whats-it tasty, but I try to live within my means."

That drew him up short. He was in a unique position, not only because Bran was surely overpaying him, but working for a celebrity gave Ollie access to things most people didn't get.

They passed a small sitting area, set back from the main pavement. Blake stopped to run her hand over a stalk of bamboo. Square, concrete planters served triple duty as benches and lighting for the space. She shivered. "I should have worn a sweater or something."

"Here."

Ollie took off his jacket and slipped it over her shoulders. His thumb brushed her arm and he fervently wished he had a reason to leave it there. She was petal soft, and the scent she wore was making him lightheaded.

"Thank you."

"It should go without saying," Ollie began as she examined the small garden. "I'm happy to treat you to dinner anywhere you want."

Blake turned to look at him over her shoulder. "Anywhere, huh?"

"Any meal, anywhere, any time."

She turned to face him, looking up at him from under her thick lashes. The low light made her eyes seem dark and fathomless. "How do you feel about tuna sandwiches?"

Twenty minutes and one taxi ride later, Ollie found himself sitting on the concrete curb of a gas station. He stared dubiously as Blake tore into the other half of the tuna sandwich he held in his hand. She didn't appear to stop for breath as she consumed it, making happy little food noises the entire time.

When she finished, Blake looked at Ollie's half of the sandwich and then back at him.

"Have at it," he said and handed it over, content to watch her enjoy it.

"Do you get much free time?" she asked between bites.

"Some."

"I was wondering, because your job seems to keep you busy."

"It does," Ollie admitted. "Bran's job is demanding. Hell, his *life* is demanding. Like I said, I try to help things run more smoothly for him." Somedays he was better at it than others.

"Cooking, running errands, answering his calls," she paused and met his gaze.

*And his texts.*

She knew.

Ollie braced his elbows on his knees. "How did you figure it out? Did Bran say something?"

"No one had to tell me it was you in the texts. You and he are very different people. I know sometimes people talk differently than they text, but your voice is pretty consistent," she said. "I knew it was you." There was no anger in her tone.

"I was going to tell you, I just didn't know how to bring it up."

"I think I knew then, when we were texting."

This surprised him. "Why did you play along?"

After a pause she said, "Because I've always enjoyed talking to you."

There was a question in her words and in the way she stared at him, a slight hint to what she wanted, what they both wanted—more time together.

"Please don't back out," he blurted.

A tiny crease appeared between her brows. "From...?" After a moment, she let out a breath. "Is that what tonight was about? Making sure I'll follow-through? God, it's always about Bran," she muttered as she got to her feet. Disappointment clouded her features.

Ollie took her elbow and gently turned her to face him. "Bran needs this, yes, but I... I just want..."

Her dark eyes widened a little as she looked up at him.

The silence stretched on for a long minute during which Ollie's heart crawled up into his throat and threatened to spill off his tongue in a torrent of begging.

Blake put him out of his misery. "I'm still in."

The wave of relief he felt threatened to buckle his knees.

"On one condition," she added belatedly.

"Anything."

"I can't..." She took a breath. "You and me, we...have unfinished business, I think. And I can't..." Blake stepped back and squared her shoulders. "Am I wrong in thinking you and I... might—?"

"No. You're not wrong."

A little shiver passed through her. Ollie watched it happen, and it took everything in him not to haul her into his arms. He straightened his glasses.

"After," she said. "This—" she paused to gesture between them, "stays inside the bottle until after. I won't compromise myself. We can be friends."

"Understood." He nodded, his heart doing somersaults in his chest. "Friends."

Her eyes said *for now.*

This fucking interview couldn't be over soon enough.

# 11

When Blake got home, she brewed a pot of PG Tips and opened her laptop. Tomorrow, she'd likely be heading down to La Jolla, and she still didn't know how to feel about that. A quick call to Gideon had resulted in her earning carte blanche to get whatever she needed to see this assignment through.

"Whatcha working on?" Enid slid into the chair opposite Blake's and plucked a banana from the fruit bowl between them. "And what's with the bag, you going somewhere?"

"I'm hoping I don't have to, but I have that ready just in case." She flipped her notebook over and angled her laptop away from Enid's wandering eyes.

"In case of what?" When Blake didn't respond, Enid sighed. "Oh, it's like that?"

"Sorry, but yeah. I can't talk about it."

Shrugging, her roomie took a bite of the banana. "What about the other thing, your pet project?"

Blake smiled. "Yeah, that's actually been good." She shuffled through her notebooks until she found the right one. "I went to this place that works with kids, teaching them acting and dance, et cetera, and I found out a few of their students have fallen victim to Diamond Moon."

"Victim how?" Enid finished off the banana, tossing the peel in the general direction of the sink.

Rolling her eyes, Blake got up to retrieve it. "They dangle money or clothes and high-end sneakers in front of them, sometimes chat up the parents, promising to help improve their lives."

"Svengali bullshit," Enid spat.

"Exactly." She tossed the peel into the garbage can before sitting down again. "I have a lead on one of the kids they allegedly signed. The deal went...really far south, and I have reason to believe some really shady things happened."

"And you're writing this for the *Gazette*?"

"Uh huh," she replied, noncommittally. She pulled her laptop close and focused on the open document. When Enid didn't say anything, Blake peeked over the top of the screen. Sighing, she sat back in the uncomfortable kitchen chair. "Fine, I'm *hoping* the Editor-in-Chief will take a look when I'm done."

"And publish it?"

"Of course. Why do you ask like that?"

"Because it's the Gazette," Enid said incredulously. "Why wouldn't you shop it around?"

"Yeah, because that's a thing people do in my position."

"What position is that, exactly?"

"The bottom, Enid," she replied. "I'm on the bottom rung of the ladder. Hell, I'm still on the ground, one foot hovering over that first rung. I'm fighting for the right to ascend those first few inches. Sisyphus looking up the hill."

"You're thinking old school. There are plenty of online outlets." When Blake shook her head, her roommate smirked. "Well, you're definitely a writer. I'll give you that. Sisyphus? Really?"

"Shut up." Laughing, she threw a grape at her nosy, annoying roomie. "Where's Cora?"

"Oh, I forgot to tell you, she moved out."

"What?" Blake hadn't seen her for a few days, but that was normal. Cora was rarely home, but she'd paid her share of the rent and utilities on time every month. "Do you have someone lined up to take her room?"

"Not yet, so I need to ask you to—"

"No, no, no," Blake said, interrupting her. "I can't. I'm barely scraping by."

To her credit, Enid seemed sympathetic. "I know, and same. I'll find someone fast. In the meantime, though, we can split things fifty-

fifty. It's only an extra…six-fifty for each of us."

"Jesus, I don't have that kind of money laying around."

"What about your emergency fund?"

She stared at her. "Emergency fund? I haven't made enough to buy bras that aren't older than this building. You think I make enough to have a rainy-day fund?"

Enid frowned. "No, but I hoped you did. I don't have one either, unless you count the turkey jerky I keep in my underwear drawer."

"You keep turkey jerky in your underwear drawer?" Blake asked, incredulous.

"Hey, don't balk. Jerky has saved me from starving many a night." Enid sank lower in the chair as reality seemed to settle around her. "Shit. What are we going to do? Any chance you could get an advance from your boss?"

"I'd be laughed out of a job I'm barely holding onto." Her gaze landed on her bag, lying open on the chair next to her. She still had the money Gid had advanced to her, and the credit card. She pulled the bag towards her and dug for her wallet.

"Do you have a pot of gold in there somewhere?"

"No, but…" She carefully placed the cash on the table, fanning out the bills.

Enid shot forward in her seat. "What the what?"

"It's petty cash for the assignment I'm on."

Her roommate shot out a hand to grab it but stopped short. "Wait, what kind of assignment is this again?"

It was tempting, but she couldn't betray Bran's privacy. "I can't tell you."

Enid narrowed her eyes. "You working as an escort?"

"Oh my God, no."

"Not that there's anything wrong with sex work, you just seem too…"

"Too, what?" she asked.

"I dunno. Chaste?"

"Chaste."

"Not that there's anything wrong with that either," Enid rushed to say.

"Let me make sure I understand," she replied, unable to contain her laughter any longer. "Either I'm a sex worker or I'm a nun?"

Crossing her legs, her roommate huffed. "Well, I don't know, do I? You've been out here for almost a year, and you haven't dated anyone."

"I've dated!"

Enid seemed surprised by that. "You have?"

"Sure." Hadn't she?

"You haven't brought anyone here, and you're here every night."

Blake pointed to her overnight bag. "I'm going away now."

"For work."

"Yes, for work. Aren't we getting off track?" She pointed at the money on the table. "Take this. I'll give you more when I can, but please try to find someone to replace Cora."

"I will, but are you sure about this?" Frowning, Enid picked the bills up off the table and counted them. "There's five hundred here."

"I might be able to get you another hundred if we're pressed." It would leave her with pennies in the bank, now that she had to cover the advance. *Maybe I could sell a kidney.*

"It's not that, I just don't want you to... Well, I know we're not super close, but I do notice things." Enid wouldn't look at her, and Blake began to squirm.

"Say what you want to say."

Meeting her gaze, Enid squared her shoulders. "You're smart, beautiful, and fun to be around, when you're around."

"Those are all complimentary words, but you somehow made them sound like I should see a doctor."

"You joke, but you're one of those people who kinda forgets they need food and, like, sleep. Sex."

"I eat," she protested. "And I sleep. And..." Thoughts of sex brought thoughts of Oliver Benjamin and she was *not* ready to unpack that yet. "Well, I'm not looking for anything else right now. I'm concentrating on my career."

"And I get that, but you should remember to have some fun every once in a while. All work and no play makes Enid worry about her only viable roommate."

"Very touching." She gently kicked her under the table. "I promise you, I'm fine."

"Eat a banana."

"What?"

"Eat. A. Banana."

She sighed. "Okay, I will have a banana. I promise."

"Right now." Arching a brow, Enid folded her arms and waited.

After a brief stare down, Blake pulled a banana from the bunch in the bowl. It wasn't quite ripe, but she didn't think that would be enough to get Enid to back down. Honestly, it was nice—the attention, the care.

That she noticed Blake's...habits meant more to her than she realized. The banana was mealy and disgusting, but the concern for her well-being was sweet.

When she finished eating, she threw her arms in the air. "Ta da!"

Enid offered her a slow clap. "Well done, princess. Now close your laptop and get some sleep."

"Nah, I have some prep to do. But I promise I'll get to bed by eleven."

Standing, Enid snorted. "Blake, babe. It's almost one a.m."

His heart in his throat, and his nerves on overdrive, Ollie shielded his eyes as he stared up at the platform that kept his best friend from plummeting fifteen feet to the asphalt below.

"That...doesn't look safe," Blake said beside him.

"It's safe. I think."

The way the wind whipped Bran's coat around his large frame, he looked like he was about to take flight. The dodgy looking stunt airbag waiting to catch him after their choreographed fight did not inspire confidence. Accidents happened on set all the damn time.

"You got nowhere to go but down, Slick."

Blake snorted.

He didn't blame her, the guy had delivered with enough extra cheese for a pan pizza.

"No wonder they need you to fix the dialogue."

"I haven't done anything with this scene."

"It shows."

Her compliment warmed him through and through.

On the platform, the other actor waved a prop gun back and forth as if taunting Bran's character. "Let me go and no one else has to get hurt, or..."

"Or, let me guess, I won't live to regret it?" Bran's voice somehow managed to sound both disgusted and amused. It was a gift. But he winced when his scene partner pushed the gun into his temple. Breaking character, he stepped back.

"Dude, what the fuck?"

The other man's eyes went wide. "Shit. Sorry. I got a little carried away."

"A little?" Bran gingerly touched his temple, checking his fingertips as if expecting to see blood there.

"Cut!" The director's voice heralded a flurry of activity and sound as the lot came to life. "Take ten, folks."

"What the fuck?" Ollie growled.

"I take it that wasn't in the script?"

"No."

"Are *you* okay? You look like you're going to kill that guy."

He turned to her, unclenching his hands that had curled into fists. "I'm good. Sorry. I hate guns, even prop ones. Too many goddamned accidents on set."

She nodded. "I read about some of those. You're good though?"

"Yeah." He nodded, conjuring up a smile. "Pissed on Bran's behalf."

"Jesus." The other actor looked terrified as they rode the jig down. "I'm so sorry!"

Even from a distance, Ollie could see the tick in Bran's jaw.

"It's... It's fine."

"Mea culpa!" the guy called out again, this time to the director, who waved him off.

Bran stepped off the lift and headed towards them. "Did you see that?"

"I did."

"Fucking rookie."

"Calm down. We have a guest."

His best friend drew up short. "Oh. Hey, Blake."

"Brandon." Her tone was icy but colored with something else. "I'm surprised to see you here."

"She's agreed to do the interview in La Jolla."

Ollie met Bran's murderous gaze, tossing out a silent challenge of his own. *You want this to work, don't you?*

"That's...great."

"Yep," Blake said, her expression carefully neutral as she stared back at Bran. "Just great."

# 12

*I'm greeted by Rory who, at well over six feet, is more mountain than man. His expression is stoic, his presence palpable, but there's no menace in his dark-eyed stare. I'm allowed into the star's private retreat without much fanfare. I don't know what I was expecting but, as grand as the property is, the atmosphere is serene. I feel as if I'm walking into a day spa and the glittering turquoise pool, visible from the front door, beckons.*

No More Pictures, Please: the Trajectory of a Shooting Star by Blake Dillon for the L.A. Gazette

Blake followed the scent of coffee to a kitchen that belonged in one of Stephen Starr's restaurants. She'd thought the one in Bran's home was impressive, but *that* could have fit inside this one three times over.

This space was outfitted with every amenity a world class chef would want. Gleaming granite countertops, stainless-steel appliances, and designer pendant lights that hung over an island with enough seating for eight people.

Past the island, a set of doors led to an oversized patio and the infinity pool. Beyond that, the vast Pacific stretched out for miles and miles.

Ollie stood in front of the open fridge, his phone to his ear. He turned and smiled over his shoulder. "Hey."

"Good morning." Blake claimed one of the barstools. "Is that orange juice fresh-squeezed?"

"Yeah." Ollie pulled the carafe from the shelf and placed it on the island. Before Blake could ask, he grabbed a glass from a cabinet and moved to pour it for her.

"I've got it."

"Help yourself." He offered a small smile that quickly flattened to a thin line as he returned his attention to the call. "*Allo? Oui, c'est Oliver Benjamin. Oui, à propos du spectacle du dix-huitième, monsieur Cody aura besoin de trois places. Non, non, trois.*"

Blake stared, wide-eyed. Unlike Brandon Peters-slash-Cody, Ollie Benjamin was a mystery she wanted to solve.

Too many of her memories of him from college had been tied up with the incident with Bran. Until recently, she'd filed both men away in her mental yearbook.

In college, Ollie had been a tantalizing combination of hot, shy, brilliant, awkward, and athletic. As well as fiercely loyal to his best friend. He seemed to remain all of those things to varying degrees. If anything, his loyalty to Bran had increased exponentially. Blake found this mentoring kids, French-speaking, expert in organization and people-handling version of Ollie intriguing.

He was also heart-stoppingly beautiful.

"*Bien sûr, si cela n'est pas possible, Monsieur Cody devra malheureusement décliner l'invitation.*" There was a pause, and Ollie looked up at Blake, clearly amused by whatever expression he saw on her face.

Blake realized she'd frozen still, her glass of OJ stuck midway to her lips. Lowering it to the counter, she arched a brow and gestured towards the phone in his hand as if to say *really? French?*

Ollie shrugged one shoulder, the apple of his cheeks turning an adorable shade of pink. Looking away, he blinked a few times before someone on the other end of his call brought back Bossy Oliver. "*Oh? Merci, ce serait merveilleux. Monsieur Cody est impatient d'assister au spectacle. Oui, merci. Merci. Au revoir.*"

When he disconnected the call, Blake raised her glass in a toast. "Impressive."

"What?" Ollie set his phone on a wireless charger underneath one of the kitchen cabinets.

"*What?* he asks, as if he didn't just rattle off his demands in fluent French," she said, teasing.

"Do you speak French?"

"No, I took Spanish. None of it stuck, I'm afraid."

"Then how do you know I was making demands?" Crossing his

arms, he leaned against the counter behind him. They were very nice arms.

"Spanish, French…those romance languages share enough for me to recognize some things," she replied. "But that doesn't answer my question."

"My father is French," he said, casually blowing her tiny mind. "Remember? You met him once."

"I did?"

Ollie visibly deflated, though he tried to cover it by waving away her question. "It was only briefly. Anyway, yeah. I spent every summer in France until I was fifteen."

"Wow, you'd think I'd remember something like that."

"Maybe, maybe not. Back then, people didn't pay much attention to anything I said." He laughed under his breath. "Not much has changed, now that I think of it."

"I think you're severely underestimating yourself," she countered. "My experience with French begins and ends with *Ratatouille*, but I understood enough to know you got what you wanted from that call."

"That has nothing to do with me, and everything to do with Bran. He's at that point in his career that he only needs to ask, and lots of people will bend over backward to give him what he wants."

"Sheesh. I'm not sure that's a good thing."

Thankfully, he laughed. A rich, hearty sound, unguarded and free, that made her insides hum.

"He's not so bad. Believe me, I've heard horror stories from other assistants. At least he's not a diva."

The jury was still out on that. "How did you and he become friends?" It was a curiosity how these two men could have formed such an obviously strong bond. On paper, at least, they were different in almost every possible way. She'd heard of opposites attracting, but still.

"Hey, Ols. Blake." Bran's deep baritone filled the room, and Ollie's entire demeanor changed right before her eyes.

He grabbed a glass from the cabinet and poured Bran some juice.

Bran eyed it suspiciously. "When was this squeezed?"

"Last night. Hans left two pitchers," Ollie replied, opening the fridge.

Bran frowned at the liquid as if it were mud. "Dude, that's not fresh. The vitamin C begins to lose potency as soon as you cut into the orange."

"I'm not sure there's any truth to that. Besides, you prefer it ice cold in the mornings, right? Makes more sense to do it at night."

"Hans makes it in the morning." Bran was sulking, and she wanted to tell him to shut the hell up or squeeze his own damn juice.

But this wasn't a friend doing a friend a favor situation. Ollie worked for Bran, and their working relationship fascinated her. She wondered where the lines were drawn, if any.

"You didn't invite Hans to stay with us on this little…getaway," Ollie said, and, for the first time, she thought she heard irritation creep into his words. "So, I'll be squeezing your orange juice when he's not here, and blending your smoothies, and baking your egg white frittatas with goat cheese and tomatoes. You'll consume them *without* complaint, or you can eat takeout. I really don't care."

"Arugula," Bran said.

"What?"

"Goat cheese, tomatoes, and arugula."

"Fuck." Ollie closed his eyes.

"You forgot the arugula." It wasn't a question. Bran shook his head. "Not a problem. There's a Whole Foods a couple of miles away."

"Yeah, I was there this morning." Ollie ran a hand through his dark hair. "I'll make another run since we're already low on oranges." He turned to her. "Blake, do you want anything specific? Shit! I forgot to ask if you were allergic to anything."

"Nope, and I'm not a picky eater," she assured him. "Trust me, I've had to stretch every dollar since I moved out west. Fresh orange juice, with a view like this, is practically a luxury vacation." Even if the commute was a bitch, it was possibly worth it for the view alone. *You could just take him up on the offer to stay.*

She hadn't spent much time on the actual coast, and it felt almost criminal that she hadn't allowed herself to appreciate its beauty. Then again, she wouldn't have had access to a place like this.

Bran really lived in a different world. By extension, she supposed, Ollie did too.

"You should stay out here with us," Bran offered, and both she and Ollie stared at him as he gulped down his juice. He set the glass on the counter. "What? It doesn't make sense for you to commute all the way out here every day, and there's plenty of space. I know I'm hard to resist, but I promise, I'll be good." He winked.

"I, uh…"

"See? I told you," Ollie said, something moving behind his eyes that she couldn't decipher. "It would be nice to have you around. The pool house is well appointed. Private. Secure." He gestured towards the structure at the edge of the manicured lawn.

She had spotted it earlier. "That thing looks bigger than the apartment I'm in now."

"It's settled then," Bran announced. He stripped off his tee, revealing the sculpted six-pack and well-defined shoulders that had landed him on the covers of fitness magazines. "I'm going for a dip. While you're at the store, could you grab some of those protein bars I like?"

"They're already in the cabinet," Ollie replied.

"And this is why I keep you around." He stepped onto the patio, stretching in the bright sunlight before he stuck his foot in the water, testing the temperature before jumping in and disappearing below the surface.

"I was asking you before. How did you two meet?"

Ollie's brows lifted. "Wow, um, that's a long story."

She picked up the empty glass of orange juice and put it in the sink. "Fortunately, we have to run to the market for arugula, so we have time."

*And apparently, I'll be staying here this week.*

"I guess we do." His smile eased some of the tension in her stomach.

As it turned out, Ollie drove a sporty hatchback that was light years nicer than Blake's old Civic. Not only because it was newer, but because it had air conditioning. Riding shotgun in the heat of the California summer, she was actually chilly. She didn't dare complain, it felt decadent. But once they exited the 5, he killed the AC and put the windows down.

"That's enough of that," he said. "I don't usually run the air when I drive, unless I'm with Bran."

"Why'd you turn it on, then?"

He glanced at her before returning his attention to the road. "Your car, it's the same one from college?"

"Yeah. You remember the car I drove in college?"

He shrugged. "Yeah." She thought he might say more, but he pulled his bottom lip between his teeth and stared resolutely at the crawl of traffic.

As she studied his profile, the wind played through the waves of his longish, dark hair.

"Something on your mind?" he asked.

"You were supposed to tell me how you and Bran got so close."

"Oh."

This was the third time, at least, that she'd asked him. Blake was beginning to think he was hesitant to tell her.

"Did you meet playing soccer for U of P?"

They stopped at a red light, and he turned to look at her. "Is this all part of your profile?"

"Might be," she admitted. "Technically, everything is fair game unless you tell me it's off the record."

"Is that really a thing, *off the record?*"

"Why wouldn't it be?"

He focused on the road, and they were moving again. "In my experience, people like you like to use that phrase to get subjects to spill their secrets."

"People like me?"

"Well, not like *you* but…reporters. In general." Ollie slowed to turn into the parking lot of the market. It took a few minutes to find a space, but soon they'd grabbed a cart and were heading inside.

Blake trailed after him as he made a beeline towards the produce section. He handed her a mesh bag.

"Mind holding this for me?"

"No problem." She held the bag open while he picked through the oranges, inspecting each one carefully. "Does Brandon Cody only eat pretty fruit?"

"What? No," he replied, laughing. "I just thought it would look nice in your photos, to have a bowl of fruit on the counter or whatever." He chose half a dozen picture-perfect oranges, and then a dozen more that he only gave a quick once-over before tossing them in the bag.

Blake tied it off and put the bag in the cart. "Why do I get the feeling you're avoiding the question?"

"What question?"

"The one I've asked you repeatedly." She followed him to a pile of leafy greens.

Sighing, Ollie rolled the cart to a slow stop. "It's not a big mystery, really. I...got into a bit of trouble and he swept in to save the day. That's kind of the story of our friendship," he said as he started walking again.

Something about the tone of his voice suggested there was way more to the story than he was willing to share. She had to tread carefully. "Were you in a fight at one of the frat's parties, or...something happened in the locker room with your team?"

"No, nothing like that. When I was fourteen, Bran's family moved down the block from mine right before sophomore year."

"You went to *high school* together? I had no idea."

"We've been practically inseparable since those days," he said. "I had trouble fitting in, being a quiet kid—being, well...me. I was always kind of a target for loud-mouthed idiots."

Her blood went cold. "You were bullied? God, I'm so sorry."

Ollie gave her a soft smile. "Thanks, but I'm okay. I kept my head down, for the most part. One day, after school, I made the mistake of turning right when I should have turned left. Ran into the very group of loudmouths I'd avoided all year." He inspected a bunch of carrots before laying them in the cart.

"What happened?"

They turned down the dairy aisle and he picked through the selection of aged cheeses. "Earned myself a black eye, among other things. I ate lunch alone most days, sat in the corner and read until the bell rang. Sometimes, someone would say something or chuck a sandwich at my head but, from that day on, things got darker."

"Some kids are dicks."

"Some kids are dicks," he agreed. He picked up a container of olives and stuck it in the cart. "Anyway, I was minding my business when Bran sat down at my empty table. I...well. To be honest, I was fucking terrified. I was shorter then, and even more scrawny than I am now."

"Scrawny? That's not a word I'd use to describe you." Lithe, tall, elegant, handsome as hell. Sexy. Blake had a lot of words to describe Oliver Benjamin. Mysterious was at the top of the list.

"That's because you're kindhearted," Ollie said. "You've always been kind to me."

Blake realized she'd never really talked with him before, not like this. Not about him. She wondered why.

"So, Bran sits down and smiles at me, which I didn't know what to do with. I'm pretty sure I considered running away, but he only said *hi* and asked if I lived in the house down the street from him. We chatted through lunch, and it sort of became our thing for a while."

"Lunch together?"

He nodded. "We started hanging out some weekends, too. Shooting hoops, playing video games, that kind of thing."

"I honestly hadn't realized you were friends before college." It offered a whole new perspective on their friendship.

Ollie's expression grew wistful. "Yeah, for a month or so. And then people started to notice. One day, I was reading under a tree, when a couple of the loudmouths came by asking where my *boyfriend* was."

"Nothing like a little high school homophobia to spice up your day." She stopped walking when he did. They were tucked in a corner by the flower section, bright yellows and reds reflecting in the lenses of Ollie's glasses.

"Racist, too. They said some shit about Bran. But, of course, when he showed up, they were all *hey, man, good match*, like they hadn't just used the N-word to describe him."

"Shit. Did you tell him?"

Shaking his head, he grabbed a tub of Greek yogurt and put it in the cart. "He would have wanted to fuck them up. It wasn't worth him getting suspended."

They wandered over to the bakery section and grabbed a loaf of marble rye, Ollie squeezing it before tossing it in with the rest of the groceries.

"I admit, your friendship fascinates me."

He turned to look at her, one brow raised. "Me and Bran?" He huffed a laugh. "It confuses the hell out of me. When we got to college, I expected him to fall in with a new group of friends and forget all about me. Instead, he talked me into joining the soccer team."

"I seem to recall you two were pretty tight back then," she said, remembering how he always seemed to be wherever Bran was. Or maybe it was the opposite. She wondered if Ollie remembered her flirting with him when they first met, at the campus bookstore. Though, knowing Ollie, he might not have realized she was flirting at the time. He certainly hadn't blinked an eye when she attended one of their house parties with some of her friends. It wasn't until their first class together that he'd spoken to her.

"Bran has always looked out for me," Ollie said as they started walking again. "It's rare to find a friend like that, and I like to think I'm that friend for him."

"He certainly trusts you."

His smile was one of pride. "He does."

"I'm curious about your duties, as they pertain to your position," Blake said, switching gears. "I haven't met many celebrity assistants, but it seems like you do everything but chew Bran's food for him."

He maneuvered the cart down another aisle, stopping to grab a bag of jasmine rice. "From the outside, it probably seems absurd," he began. "Hell, it's absurd from the inside, too. The whole lifestyle is ludicrous. The amount of money people spend on stupid shit, the waste, the sense of entitlement. It's all deeply disturbing."

"Then why be a part of it?"

Ollie met her gaze, his own filled with a gripping determination. "I love Bran like a brother, and my brother decided he wanted to pursue a career that puts him in the spotlight, not to mention the crosshairs of ex-lovers, disgruntled colleagues, tabloid reporters, and Internet trolls. He needed someone by his side, someone not tied to any of this. Who hasn't sold their soul for any of it."

"And that's you?"

"Who else would it be?" He steered them towards the checkout lines. "It's what you do for the people you love."

"It's a privilege to be loved like that. I envy him," Blake admitted, surprising herself.

Ollie's pale blue-grey eyes lowered as he spoke, his tone teasing. "There's plenty to go around."

It took a moment for Blake's brain to command her legs to move again.

# 13

Blake returned early the next morning. After stashing her things in the pool house, her home for at least a few days, she strolled up onto the terrace in a pair of sunglasses rimmed in rhinestones, an orange bikini top under a billowy white shirt, and the tiniest pair of cut off shorts Ollie had ever seen. He stared at her, the script on the table in front of him completely forgotten.

Twice in his lifetime, he had come in contact with someone who had instantly felt like a thread in the tapestry of his life. Like missing puzzle pieces, they'd just fit. The first time, he had avoided him. Bran. A too bright, too loud, too present being for the quiet dark of Ollie's world. Ugly circumstances had brought them together, their friendship forged in a crucible of violence and an all too common (for Bran) act of casual heroism. Ollie had no choice but to love him.

The second time someone crashed through his barriers, there had been no threat. No stress. Only a thirst for knowledge and a search for her place in the world. Blake had sat next to him one Thursday afternoon, and he'd forgotten how to read words. The characters on the pages of the book he'd been studying fluttered like leaves whenever he'd tried to concentrate.

Unlike Bran, Blake was oblivious to her power over the people she caught in her orbit.

"What're you reading?" She took the seat next to his, and he bit back a smile. It was Thursday.

"It's a script for an upcoming project Bran is considering."

She pulled a pen and notebook from her bag before hanging it on the back of her chair. "Is that something you do for him? Part of your duties as his executive assistant?"

He flipped the script over on the table to keep his place. "It's atypical, I think, of the position but he values my opinion."

"On the writing?"

"Ols looks for red flags," Bran said from a lounger by the pool. "I want a role I can sink my teeth into. If it were up to my agent, every film would be a big budget banger, summer blockbuster sort of thing."

"And that's a bad thing?" She scribbled in her book.

"It's not *bad*, per se," Bran replied, stretching his long, muscular frame as he stood. "Damn, girl!" He lowered his shades and gave her a once-over. "Nice to see you getting into the spirit."

"When in La Jolla." She set her notepad on the table and sat back, crossing her long legs. Ollie wasn't mad about being with such pretty people on a gorgeous day in Southern California.

"I swear, the sun is stronger down here than back in Pasadena."

"Is that where you live?" he asked.

"I rent a room in a house in South Pasadena. May I?" Her hand hovered by the bottle of prosecco chilling on the table. When he nodded, she poured some into a flute. "I can see the appeal of this lifestyle. Sparkling wine on a random weekday, renting a multi-million dollar house for the hell of it."

"There's nothing wrong with enjoying the finer things," Bran said as he walked over. He plucked a strawberry out of a bowl, all of them perfectly red and ripe, and popped it into his mouth. "We only get one life, why not splurge on a few little things?"

Blake almost choked on her sparkling wine.

"Forgive the movie star," Ollie said. "He forgets that most of us live in the real world where the finer things are stuff like a night out with friends or dinner in a restaurant that has tablecloths on the tables."

"Vacations to Disneyland," Blake added.

"Wing night at McFadden's." He grinned at the memories.

"Oh, snap!" Bran chuckled. "That place was a vibe."

"It was a disgusting hole in the wall," Blake argued. "You two actually ate the food there?"

"It doesn't surprise me that you didn't." Bran shook his head. "God, even then, you thought you were so much better than the rest of us."

"Bran," he warned. "Don't start."

"No, Bran, please do. Start. Tell me more about my superiority complex while we sit in your thirty-eight million-dollar hideout." She propped her chin in her hand, waiting.

Bran's jaw dropped as he blinked at Ollie. "Fuck. Is this place really thirty-eight mil?"

"At least," he replied. "Why do you think I'm always trying to talk you out of buying something in this area?"

"Why not?"

Confused, he turned to Blake. "Uh, because it's thirty-eight million dollars?"

"You see, Blake—and you might want to write this in your little book—Oliver here is more than my assistant, he's my life coach. He keeps me from doing stupid shit."

"I don't always succeed."

"Obviously," she agreed, grinning.

"Ha fucking ha." Bran walked back over to the lounger and reclined, folding his hands behind his head. "You two should take your act on the road."

"Maybe you missed your calling, Oliver," she said. He loved the teasing tone of her voice, glad that she seemed relaxed. "Ever think about acting?"

"Not for a single moment."

"Ols hates the camera," Bran called over to them.

"He's right, I do."

"But why?" She seemed genuinely perplexed. "You're...a good-looking guy."

Why did it sound like she'd forced the compliment? Ollie tried not to shrink in his seat. He wasn't unattractive, he thought. Of course, standing next to someone like Bran, he probably looked like a troll. But Ollie wasn't blind, he saw the way some people looked at him. Reacted around him. Mostly people who didn't know him well, who didn't know him as Bran's EA.

It was true that he hadn't dated much, but it wasn't for a lack of interested parties. *He* wasn't generally interested most of the time.

It had taken a long time for Ollie to figure out that he needed an emotional connection with someone before any physical attraction would manifest itself. It wasn't something that came up during high school, since he kept pretty much to himself. He'd only known that he was a little different from the people around him. In college, he had no desire to chase after sex the way his classmates did. His friends on the team, the guys in the frat house.

It was one more way he didn't fit in.

He could count on one hand the number of times he'd experienced a pull towards someone in that way and half of those were caused by the two people on this patio.

"I've tried to give him a walk-on role in a couple of my films, but he won't do it," He pointed at Ollie. "He's shy."

"Just because I don't want to slap on spandex and spout lines about some vague, nostalgic notion about truth and freedom doesn't mean I'm shy."

"Hey." Bran sat up. "Don't diss Captain Sky. And no one said anything about lines. I was thinking you'd be in the background." He stood up and planted his feet wide. "Sort of like this, with your arms crossed, looking like a bad ass."

"Were you into theater stuff in college?"

"Bran was a consummate thespian."

"Really?" Blake scribbled furiously in her book.

"Not really." Bran cocked his head. "Hey, why do you take notes like that?"

She stopped writing and looked at him. "Why do I take notes for the article? That I'm writing? About you?" She pursed her lips. "Well, Brandon, it's my job to profile the *real* you. That includes details about your life, your work, and any inside jokes you share with your friends. All of it will help me create a vivid picture of who you really are."

Ollie snickered under his breath. "What you see is what you get."

"I don't doubt it."

"No, no. Why do you write your notes like *that?*" He walked over and picked up Blake's notebook.

"Hey!"

"Dude, give it back."

"God, this thing is tiny." His hand dwarfed the small book. "And your handwriting is atrocious. How can anyone read this?"

Snatching it from him, Ollie handed it back to her. "Sorry about that. He's an idiot."

Blake glared at Bran. "This is not for anyone else's eyes but mine, and I can read it just fine."

"Most of the time," Ollie added.

Her head whipped his way. "What's that supposed to mean?"

He only had to say two words. "Seven tables."

"Oh, my God." Blake's smile was slow. "Jesus," she sputtered as she burst into laughter.

"What?" Bran asked, smiling.

When she seemed unable to answer, laughing so hard there were tears in the corners of her eyes, Ollie tried to explain.

"We had a group assignment in Comparative Literature where each member of your team had to choose a work for you to read. You were supposed to deliver an oral report before the group moved onto the next phase of the assignment. Anyway, we met and discussed our titles and…let's just say Blake's handwriting caused some issues."

Bran grinned wide. "What happened?"

"She was given *The Grey Gables,* this gothic novel about a young, queer boy and his abusive aunt. Deals with some dark stuff. But she read *The Grey Tables* which was a study of a woman developing and living with a violent allergy to spices."

"Sh-she spends the whole book lamenting how bleak the food was," she managed to say between fits.

"It's awful, really," Ollie said. "I think it was some kind of Victorian metaphor for the times. Spices were plentiful but the skies were full of pollution, the world was rapidly changing. Anyway, Blake delivered her oral summary and most of us were confused but went along with it. Then, when she was done, Colin, the guy who chose *Grey Gables* turns to her and says *what the hell book did you read?*"

Bran barked out a laugh. "That's hilarious!"

Having recovered, Blake groaned. "Look, the pencil must have slipped or something. I could've sworn it was a T and not a G."

"Those two letters look nothing alike, if your handwriting didn't look like you held the pen in place and moved the paper around instead."

"We got an A," she protested, feigning outrage.

"How?" Bran asked, laughing more.

Ollie met her eyes. "We made it work."

Wiping her eyes, she smiled. "We did. We were a good team," she added softly.

Suddenly, they were only two people on the patio. He was caught in her gaze again, lost in the teasing light he saw there.

He ducked his head, forcing his attention back to the script. "Bran, when, uh, when did you say you needed to get back to them about this project?" When Bran didn't answer, Ollie looked up to find his best friend's eyes on him. "What?"

"Nothing." His gaze flitted over to Blake as she went over her notes. "Before the 15th."

Ollie frowned. *What?* He mouthed.

Bran shook his head.

"So, Bran," she began. "I'm happy to hang and observe, but I'd like to carve out some time to ask you some real questions."

"Right, but uh…I can't right now. I have a…thing." He started towards the house.

Ollie narrowed his eyes. "You don't have anything on your schedule."

"I planned to go for a drive."

"What?" He stood, but Bran held out his hand.

"Nope, I'm going on my own."

"Rory isn't back yet," he reminded him.

Bran waved him off. "I don't need security to drive along the coast for an hour."

"I could ride with you," Blake offered.

"Nope, you stay. Enjoy yourself. Take a dip in the pool."

While Ollie was tempted by the idea of alone time with Blake, he didn't like Bran going out on his own.

"You should wait for Rory."

"No one knows I'm down here, Ols. I'll be fine. I'll even wear the hat and the sunglasses, the whole incognito special. I promise."

Ollie couldn't think of a valid argument. "Be careful."

"Careful is my middle name." Bran winked at him before turning to Blake. "We'll pick this up later."

She looked skeptical. "Okay, sure."

"Take my car. My keys are on the island," Ollie called after him.

After a moment of silence, he turned to her. "I guess it's just you and me."

But Blake was frowning. "I… If you don't mind, I'm going to go do some work inside."

"Oh." He tried not to read too much into that. Of course, she had stuff to do.

So did he.

"Meet for lunch later?"

Blake rose to her feet. "That sounds great. See you in a bit." She gathered her things and walked down to the pool house.

He watched until she disappeared behind the door and let out the sigh that had been building in his chest.

Flipping the script over, he tried to pick up where he'd left off, but all he could think of was Blake.

She'd been true to her word, giving Bran a chance to show her who he was now. So far, there hadn't been any snide remarks or snap judgements, at least none she'd voiced out loud.

The morning had been nice, with the three of them exchanging stories and banter. He wished it could be like that all the time and could almost imagine it.

Ollie checked his watch. It was half past ten. He had to wait at least ninety minutes to knock on her door.

"Right," he said to no one. "I've got this."

Movement in the front windows of the pool house drew his attention, and he watched as Blake drew back the curtains and opened the windows.

She stood there, stretching, and his breath caught in his throat. The blouse was gone, leaving her in the tiny bikini top and itty, bitty shorts, and... *Christ.* He tried to look away but couldn't tear his gaze away from her curves and—

Blake stopped and gave a little wave which he absently returned, his swim shorts suddenly restricting. Mortified that he'd been caught ogling like a schoolchild, he tried to focus on the script. But his gaze kept drifting to the window, hungry for another glimpse of her honeyed brown skin and unruly curls.

"Fuck."

There was no point in trying to work, his brain was fixated on one thing. One person. One gloriously attractive mind, body, and soul that was tantalizingly close and yet so very far away.

Ollie closed the script and stood, stripping out of his shirt and kicking off his sandals on the way to the pool.

He needed to cool the fuck off before he did something stupid. Blake had put the brakes on anything beyond friendship, and he wasn't about to blow this second chance.

It was too early in the day for the sun to have warmed the water, and it was a shock to the system when he dove in.

But it was just what he needed. Pushing off from the far end of the pool, he began his first lap, pushing hard.

The sound of the water lapping against his skin and the rhythmic motion of his strokes was like a meditation, calming his racing pulse. He pushed away all thoughts of Blake and focused on his breathing, moving through one lap after another.

After several minutes, he stopped at the edge of the pool and looked up towards the pool house window, surprised to find her watching him.

Desire tore through him as their eyes met, but then she offered an adorably nervous smile and a little shrug before disappearing into the shadowy interior.

*She'll be the death of me.*

Defeated, Ollie sank under the water and called on every cell of his being to fucking behave for just a little longer.

# 14

It was official, Blake was a creeper.

She hadn't meant to stand in the window and watch Ollie as he swam, but she'd been passing the window when he stood and whipped off his shirt, revealing a body that made her everything tighten with want.

Holy. Hell. Had he been that delicious in college?

He was cute back then. Sweet. Sexy in his nerdy little way, but this?

This guy was...

Climbing out of the pool, Ollie grabbed a towel from a nearby chair and dried himself off thoroughly before reclining on one of the loungers.

Her gaze wandered the length of his toned, tanned physique.

"Damn." She placed her palm on her chest, over her heart, and could feel it beating as fast as a rabbit.

Her phone pinged, forcing her away from her stalking, and she was grateful for the distraction.

**MOM: Hi baby, call me when you have a moment. Xoxo**

Surprised, she took a seat on the large, cushy sofa and tapped on her mother's icon on her phone.

"Blake, hi." Her tone was careful, which put her on edge.

"Hey, Mom. How are you?"

"Fine, fine. Busy as usual. You know how it is."

"Is everything all right?"

They usually spoke once a week, on Sunday mornings.

Her mother gave a long-suffering sigh. "Things would be a lot better if my child was home where she belongs."

"Mom."

"I know, I know. You're all grown now, and determined to be like your *grandfather*, traipsing all over the globe. You see where that got him."

"I don't think granddad's...condition has anything to do with his job, Mom."

The response was an indignant huff.

"I'm kind of in the middle of something," Blake said. "Did you need—"

"I thought you might want to know we're selling the house."

Blake's mouth dropped open. "What do you mean, selling the house? Why would you do that?"

The line was silent for a moment before her mother finally spoke. "To be frank, we need the money."

"But why the house? You could sell..." Nothing came to mind.

Her mother sighed. "It's for the best, sweetheart. It's too much house for us, now that you and your brothers have moved out, and we think it will be better if we get something smaller."

She felt a knot forming in her stomach as she processed the words.

The house *was* too big for two people and what her mom said made sense, on paper. But it felt like she was losing something—a part of her childhood that she hadn't fully let go of quite yet.

Home was where she'd listened to her granddad's stories, spinning her dreams from the thread of his words. Home was familiar, safe, and steady. She had been feeling untethered since moving to L.A., and losing the touchstone of her family's house...

She felt numb. And childish.

"I understand," she said slowly. "When is this happening?"

"As soon as possible," her mother replied in a soft, cautious voice. "We have to put it on the market before the end of summer. You'll have to come visit and go through your things."

She licked her lips and nodded, even though her mother couldn't see her. "Yeah. What about Granddad's room?"

There was a slight pause. "We...we packed up his things and moved them into storage, until we can figure out what to do with them."

A spike of irrational anger made her breath catch in her throat. Blake hadn't considered the possibility of Trent's room being dismantled and boxed up, his old PC and typewriter put away. All the awards, the plaques, the framed articles...where were they?

"Blake?"

She'd tuned out. "I'm here. Sorry, I'm...on assignment."

The window over the sink was open when she walked into the small kitchen. Through it, she could see white-crested waves undulating as they moved closer to shore, sparkling in the sunlight and casting glimmering reflections on the sand.

"I didn't realize you were at work," her mother said, laughing to herself. "Of course, you are. It's still early in the day out there. I forget, sometimes. How are things at the paper?"

Weird. "Okay. I'm still finding my way."

She'd carefully avoided mentioning the type of stories she'd been writing for the Gazette. Her parents were already iffy on her career choice and her decision to move out West. She didn't need to give them any more ammunition for their guilt trips.

"Is Daddy home?"

"No, he went to take care of some things. I'll tell him you're coming for a visit. Let us know the details when you can."

"Okay, Mom."

"And Blake?"

"Yes?"

"No matter where we end up, there will be space for you if you decide to come home."

For a moment, she couldn't speak around the lump in her throat. "I know, Mom. Thanks."

After she hung up, Blake sat down on the couch and stared at her laptop. She had so much to do, so much to work out regarding Diamond Moon, so much to plan regarding her profile of Bran, but she was suddenly exhausted.

Like someone had cut her strings, her limbs felt heavy. She sank back into the sofa to close her eyes. Just for a moment.

When she opened them again, the sun had moved in the sky and the light in the room had changed dramatically.

"Shit." She sat upright and looked at the time on her phone. It was after one o'clock, and she had two emails. One from Gid asking for roughs, and one from Deanna.

Another former student had signed with Diamond Moon.

No one was on the patio when she went outside, and a quick search of the house found it empty as well.

Had they really left her there alone all day?

She squinted at a figure down on the beach and recognized Ollie's dark waves blowing in the breeze, so she made her way down to him.

"Bran isn't back yet?"

He turned, a lopsided smile turning up the corner of his mouth. "Morning, sleepyhead."

Blake felt herself flush.

"I came by to see if you wanted lunch, but you were out cold."

"I haven't been getting much sleep lately." She walked up to stand beside him at the water's edge, glad she'd removed her sandals and left them on the bottom step. The sand felt glorious between her toes.

Ollie turned back to the water. "I sleep best when I can hear the ocean," he said. "Not sure how I ever slept without that sound."

They were practically shoulder to shoulder, and there was something so intimate and familiar about the moment. Like they'd been there a thousand times before.

She supposed they had, back at school in their little nook in the library. Heads down, voices hushed.

They were hushed now, too.

"I was on the phone with my Mom, earlier."

Out of the corner of her eye, she saw him turn his head to her.

"Is Trent okay?"

"Yeah, he's holding steady," she replied. "My parents are selling the house."

"Oh."

Blake spied a cargo ship in the distance and watched it sail slowly past.

"Do we have…feelings about the house?"

She almost laughed. "Surprisingly, yes."

"Why surprisingly?"

She turned to find his eyes on her, clear and bright and curious.

"Well, I didn't realize what it meant to me until Mom broke the news."

"Isn't that the way of things?" Ollie asked.

"We never know the true meaning until it's gone?"

"Exactly." He nodded. "Or, until it returns."

She frowned but he only smiled and shoved his hands into the pocket of his shorts.

"Lunch?"

"Sure."

"How about a picnic on the beach?"

After a short trip to the kitchen for salad fixings and fresh fruit, they were walking back down the steps to an outcropping of rocks.

Ollie set down the tote full of food and took the throw Blake had snagged from the sectional, spreading it out.

"This feels decadent," she said when he produced two glasses and a bottle of white wine. "And not at all like work."

"Live a little." He poured wine for each of them before putting the bottle back and pulling out the food.

They ate to a soundtrack of waves and birds, with Ollie making contented food noises.

"You know, at some point, I'm going to have to actually ask Bran questions. Real interview questions.

"Are you in a rush?"

"I'm not on a strict deadline, but my editor will expect something sooner rather than later." And she had bigger fish to fry with Diamond Moon.

As if reading her mind, Ollie nodded. "You're anxious to work on your other, more important story."

She opened her mouth to say it wasn't more important but didn't want to lie. "Deanna said another one of the students, well, a former student, signed to them."

His brows dipped. "Shit. Did she say who?"

"His first name was Desmond, but I don't remember his last name."

"Desmond Jiminez?"

"That's it. You know him?"

He shook his head. "No, he was out before I came in, but I've heard some of the kids talk about him. Talented, from what they've said."

"I can't understand how a company with a reputation like theirs is still able to get these families to turn their child's career over to them. No one in the community has raised concerns?"

He handed her one of the salads, taking the other for himself. "It's risk versus reward, and the latter is too tempting a prospect for many."

"They have options. Legitimate agencies and labels."

"Sure, they have options," he agreed. "The option to spend money on headshots, demos, and reels that will sit in a slush pile on someone's desk. The option to spend money on transportation to an audition where they'll be one of hundreds up for the same opportunity," he said, pausing to take a bite. "Companies like Diamond Moon know how desperate the talent is to rise above the rest. They know how hard it is for people from marginalized areas to get their foot in the door. Any door."

"They're using the *we're just like you* schtick to gain trust."

"Exactly," he agreed. "And these kids...they think they're too smart to be taken advantage of, which makes them the easiest targets."

"And the parents?"

"I've met a few, and they're supportive. Hard-working. But few look further than the surface, even with Play L.A."

"That's a terrifying recipe for disaster."

"Which," he said, offering her a slice of freshly baked bread, "is why you need to expose Diamond Moon. Anything I can do to help, I mean it, I'll do."

Smiling, Blake ripped off a piece of the bread and chewed as she went over what she knew so far.

Ollie listened closely, reminding her of the late nights they spent studying. Only, instead of being surrounded by dark wood and books, it was sand, sea, and sunshine.

"Any idea who's behind Diamond Moon?" he asked.

She swallowed a sip of wine. "Whoever set them up was a legal genius. It's a total shell game. I'm hoping the story, if I ever get it published, will smoke out the people behind it."

"You could publish it online. There are dozens of respected portals."

"I want the weight of a legacy paper behind it. It'll give the piece the gravitas it needs to be picked up nationally," she explained. "It wouldn't be as easy to dismiss as a conspiracy theory."

"I'm not so sure about that. Respect for traditional journalism has to be at an all-time low," he said with a sad smile. "You picked a hell of a time to go on a crusade."

"You think I'm in over my head." Just like Gideon and Sonja. Just like her parents. Maybe they were all right, and she was deluding herself.

To her surprise, Ollie shook his head. "I think those kids are lucky to have you on the case."

She smiled. "I think they're lucky to have *you* teaching them."

Laughing softly, he leaned back on hands and turned his face towards the ocean. "I'm still figuring out *my* place in the world. It's probably not the best idea to have me teaching anyone, but I do enjoy it. They get so excited when an idea moves from a thought in their heads to something tangible on the page."

"When are we supposed to have life figured out?"

"Given what I've seen from people two, three times our age, I'm not sure that's a thing."

They both laughed then, falling into a companionable silence. Being with him was easy. Too easy.

"I missed this," he said quietly, and her pulse ticked up a few beats per minute.

When his gaze met hers, Blake was shocked at the emotion in it.

"I don't want to lose it again, so, let's make a pact."

"A pact," she echoed.

"I'm here. You're here. Let's be here...together." The panic she felt must have shown on her face because he sat up, holding up a hand. "I haven't forgotten what you said the other night, at the restaurant. Friends."

"Yes, friends."

"Friends can be together. Can't they?" Slowly, Ollie raised a hand and tucked a lock of her hair behind her ear that had been blowing in and out of her periphery.

"Yeah." It was breathless and she tried desperately to hold on to the thread of the conversation. Because she had severely under-estimated Oliver Benjamin.

"There you two are."

Blake jumped back like a teen caught making out on the couch by her parents.

Bran strolled onto the beach and made himself comfortable on the blanket like he owned it.

Which, to be fair, he kind of did.

Ollie had narrowed his eyes at the newcomer. "How was your *drive?*"

"Fine. Uneventful." Bran popped a grape into his mouth. "Grabbed some real food before heading back, so I'm ready to do this if you are," he said to her.

"Uh, sure."

"Great. Shoot."

"Oh, here?" She looked at Ollie who was still studying Bran closely. "I need my notes."

"Let's head back, then."

"Whatever." Bran got his feet. "Let's get this over with."

Ollie followed, offering her his hand. They gathered everything and trudged up the hill back to the property.

Blake didn't know why the actor was so eager to sit down with her now, but she wasn't going to look a gift horse in the mouth. The sooner she finished here, the sooner she could get back to her life.

# 15

Blake half-expected Bran to don his swim trunks and do the interview in the pool, but he led her back inside. She was grateful. The mid-day sun was stronger than she'd thought, and the interior of the house was cool and welcoming.

They settled in the great room, with him on the sectional and her in an armchair.

"When we take the photos, we could set up in here," she said. "The light is great."

"Sure." Bran was very accomodating.

He also wasn't.

Between the location and the timing, nothing about this situation fit Blake's expectations of how things would go. She'd been so relaxed at lunch, her thoughts settling down after rabbiting between her parents, her granddad, and work. Spending time with Ollie, alone, was her new favorite thing. She'd been tempted to tell Bran they could start fresh in the morning.

But Gideon wanted an update, and Blake had to give him something.

"Tell me one thing you want your...fans...to know," she said, settling back with a notebook in hand.

"I thought part of the interview process was actually asking questions." Bran kept his eyes on her.

She found herself studying his expression, which gave nothing away. "I'm formulating an idea of what to ask."

He nodded as if that made total sense. *Establish a rapport with him and probe away,* Gideon had said.

It struck her how *normal* he seemed. When he wasn't on, in full Hollywood mode, he looked almost like a regular guy in his baseball cap and North Face tee.

"Missing your better half? Why didn't Ollie sit in? I thought he was meant to be stuck to you like glue."

Bran grinned. "I asked him to run some errands for me after he's done reading through that script. Besides, I thought you and I should talk."

"Won't he be concerned about me questioning you without him?"

"Oh, definitely," he confessed, surprising her.

"Sure you don't need him to feed you your lines? How will you know what to say to me?" She held his gaze, daring him to feign ignorance.

"Ah," he said. "The texts."

"The texts."

He sobered quickly and met her gaze. "I'm really sorry for how shitty I was to you back in Philly. If I'm honest, I don't really remember a lot of the stupid shit I got up to back then. But that's no excuse. That whole thing, with the Dean and the paper, must have hurt you or affected you in some way for you to still resent me. I'm truly sorry."

She nodded slowly. "Uh huh. That was actually a decent apology. Is it a monologue from one of your roles?"

His head dropped back onto the cushion. "You aren't gonna cut me a break, are you? I guess I'll have to open a vein." He mimed rolling up his sleeves and picking up a knife.

"Alright, alright. That won't be necessary," she laughed despite herself. "Apology accepted."

He looked at her, surprised. "Really?"

"Yes, Brandon. You are forgiven."

They fell quiet as he stared at her. He always seemed like the type of person who liked to deliver the big reveal, so Blake sat back and waited. Finally, he set the cup down and steepled his fingers on the table.

"Ready to tell me why you wanted to talk to me away from Ollie?"

Smiling, Bran narrowed his eyes. "Don't know what you mean. I thought you might want to actually interview me for this article you're writing. Or is that necessary? Maybe you've already drawn all your conclusions, and everything else—hanging out on set, coming to my house, here to La Jolla—that's just window dressing."

"And here I thought *I* was the cynic."

"Not a cynic, I simply understand how this works."

"How what works, exactly?" Not that he was entirely off-base, but she wasn't sure if Bran was paranoid or merely self-centered. "What do you think is happening here?"

"I think your boss is counting dollar signs and hopes you'll find something to corroborate that ridiculous story about Val," Bran said, sounding angrier by the second. "I think you formed an opinion about me when we were in college and you're either too blind or too stubborn to see I'm not who I was back then. Neither is Ollie, by the way."

"There's a lot to unpack there," she said, frowning. "I literally *just said* I forgave you for what happened at school. Like you said, we were kids. But what story are you talking about? I have no idea who or what Val is. And what does Ollie have to do with any of this?"

"You...you know he's always been into you, right?" At her stunned silence, he went on. "Spring Fling, our junior year, they had that movie night on the quad. With the inflatable screen?"

She remembered. It had been a great night.

"They were showing some kids' movie."

"*The Princess Bride.*"

He frowned. "Huh?"

"It was *The Princess Bride.* It's my favorite, and it's not a kids' movie."

"If you say so. Not my jam. Anyway, Alpha Q had a private rager. With most of the sorors at the movie, it was just going to be the guys and it was...chill. We hung out, played shitty pool, did even shittier shots..."

"I can't imagine Ollie doing shots."

"Oh, Ols wasn't there. He went to the movie." Eyes on hers, Bran took a sip of coffee. "The next morning, he wouldn't shut up about it."

"It's a great film."

"I'm not talking about the film. He wouldn't stop talking about *you.* How amazing you looked, how cool you were, how dumb he was."

Confused, she shook her head. "I... I don't remember seeing him."

"Knowing Ols, that was by design. He was painfully shy. Still is, in some ways."

Hearing such compassion in his voice was disconcerting, she almost missed what came next.

"When he told me you'd dropped that class you had together... Well, the look he gave me is similar to the one you're wearing now," he said, chuckling. "Going to the Dean was not my finest moment, and it took you showing up again to figure it out, but he's into you. He's always been into you, and I feel like an asshole for coming between what you two had."

"I..."

Grinning, he leaned back. "*That's* a look I've never seen on your face."

Stunned, that's what she was. "We weren't...together. We're not."

"I know, but there was potential. Still is, I'd wager."

"He's a good guy."

"The best," he agreed. "Man, you're so hard to read, even more than he is. I would have completely missed it, this thing with you and Ols, but I'm onto it—"

"Wait, wait, wait," Blake said, snapping out of it. She huffed a bitter laugh. "Please tell me you didn't agree to sit down today because you think playing matchmaker will somehow sway me."

"I don't think anything, other than I've never seen my best friend look at anyone the way he looks at you," Bran said as if it were the most casual statement in the world. "I didn't recognize it in college, but I see it now."

"I think you're due for an eye exam," she protested, but damn if her heart rate didn't spike.

"How did it feel, seeing him again?" he asked. "Good, right?"

"Of course."

"And you're open to the idea of more with him?"

"I'm so confused right now. Aren't I supposed to be interviewing you?"

"We'll get to that," Bran crossed his legs and studied her. "You asked me who Val is, you really don't know?"

"Should I?"

"Your paper, the Gazette, is sitting on a story about me having an affair with an actor, Valerie Saunders. She's a friend. A married friend," he added. His gaze was as sharp as knives. One wrong move and he'd cut her to shreds.

"This is the first I'm hearing of it." They may not be friends, but it was important to her that he believe her. "Why haven't they run the story?"

"You tell me."

"I have no idea. I was today years old when I learned anything about it, and you're my source."

Bran nodded but he seemed to remain skeptical. "So, you know nothing about the phone hack? The photos?"

"Your phone was hacked? By whom?"

Shrugging, Bran picked up the mug of coffee he'd made before they began but didn't take a sip. His gaze drifted to the bank of windows, and she fought the urge to write every detail of the conversation into her notebook. His gaze flicked to hers.

"You might want to scribble some of this down," he teased.

Relief flooded her. She grabbed what she needed. "Okay, go on."

Over the next half an hour, Bran laid everything out for her. From the hack to allegations of an affair with Valerie Saunders.

"We're good friends, that's all."

"Then say that. Why all the secrecy? There's nothing to stop you from hanging out whenever or wherever you want."

"It's not a secret," Bran countered quickly. "But we're talking about perception."

"I'm saying why hide if there's nothing to hide?"

"Because," he said, leaning forward. "You can't prove a negative. Once the rumor got out, we'd have no hope of controlling it. I can't let that happen to Val again. There's no truth to it. Zero. It's just the product of a sick imagination."

Either he was the best actor Blake had ever seen, or someone had it out for him. Could be Sonja, Sonja's bosses, or a powerful studio exec. If she had to put her money on a safe bet, it would be Sonja. Something about the way she had spoken about Bran in her office, her insistence… Something wasn't right.

"You've given me a lot to think about," she said, her thoughts in a whirl.

"I'm trusting you because Ols trusts you. And I trust him. Though, he'd probably murder me if he knew I'd shared all that stuff with you."

"Really? Wouldn't he think I'd need background for this article?"

"Oh, I'm not talking about the shit with the Gazette, I'm talking about him. And you. I believe you when you say nothing happened between you two in college, but this could be your big second chance."

"You seem a little too invested in this, if I'm being honest."

Bran's smile was genuine, and different from the ones she'd seen him use on set and in photos. "Ols would never say anything to you. He'd just pine in private like something out of Jane Austen."

She laughed, thinking of how clear Ollie had been with his intentions.

"He's shy, our Oliver. If you're interested, you might need to make the first move. That's all I'm saying."

What an odd turn of events this was. She couldn't deny the warm, fuzzy feeling she got whenever she looked at Ollie. But it would be beyond unprofessional to pursue anything, at least while she was on this assignment.

"I can see the debate going on inside that head of yours, but you know I'm right."

"Frankly, it's none of your business."

Something in his expression changed, the smile on his face sharpening into something bordering on unpleasant.

"Actually, it is. Ols is more than my friend, he's my brother. You work for a newspaper that's been out for my blood since the first moment I stepped onto a red carpet."

"Why is that?"

He tilted his head, as if the answer was self-evident. "You'll have to ask your boss."

Oh, she would. Gideon hadn't mentioned anything about Valerie to her, and she wondered if Bran's ramblings had any basis in truth or if it was all his inflated sense of self-importance. Only, when she looked at him, she didn't see narcissism or ego, she saw...irritation. He was angry.

"What do you want out of this?"

Her question seemed to catch him off-guard.

"What do *I* want?" he repeated, his voice quiet.

"Yes. You're clearly using me for something."

Bran's mouth twisted. "I don't want anything from *you*, Blake. Except maybe for you to consider giving Ols a chance. He's a good guy, and he deserves someone who can appreciate him."

It was her turn to be surprised. "And you think that's me?"

Bran gave her a long look, and she felt like he was seeing right through her. "I think you're the only one who's ever made him truly happy," he said finally.

It was an odd thing to say, but the sincerity in his voice made her believe it. She'd always thought Ollie was happy-go-lucky, but maybe she'd missed something beneath the surface.

"As for this article, interview, whatever," he continued, resting his ankle on the opposite knee— a casual pose, though he was anything but, his whole demeanor practically sang with tension—"my agent, publicist, and executive assistant all believe it will clear up some of the preconceptions about me. That it will give the public more to go on than what the, no offense, gossip rags write. No offense," he repeated, spreading his hands.

"None taken. And you think I'm the right person for *that*?"

"You're the only reason I agreed to let this move forward."

Blake chewed on that for a few moments, while they sized each other up. Something about this whole thing—not being told about the *other* story the paper had on Bran, Sonja's insistence on Blake taking the assignment, getting close to her subject—it was shady as fuck. And she didn't like being used. If Sonja thought having her do this profile on Bran, knowing how much she despises celebrity culture, would result in a character assassination, then she really didn't know Blake at all.

"I promise to be fair, if you promise to take this seriously."

He offered a single nod, his eyes full of intent. "Deal."

Later, back in the pool house, she called Gideon who picked up on the first ring.

"Dillon, how goes?"

It was late, and the sky was nearly dark. Outside, the lights had come on surrounding the pool and patio, and it looked like something from a magazine.

"Just had my first real sit-down with Cody. It was...interesting."

"Oh? Interesting how? And please tell me you'll have something for me to look at tonight."

She winced. "I, uh... I'll send five hundred words your way by midnight. Promise. But, listen..."

She took a breath, wondering how to approach this. She trusted Gideon, but her spidey senses were tingling.

"Bran mentioned another story we have about him. Do you know anything about that?"

"Geez, we've probably run a dozen over the last year and a half. Which one is he talking about?"

"This...would be one we *haven't* run," she said. "I get the feeling it's being held."

A heavy sigh came through the phone. "I did hear something about his phone getting hacked, and you know how I feel about private photos," he said, indignant. "I wouldn't run those if they landed on my desk."

"No, I know." She knew he would never. "He also mentioned Val Saunders."

"Hmmm, I'm not aware of anything we have on her," he said. She could hear him typing away in the background. "Nothing recent, anyway. Did he say what it might be about? I'm assuming, he doesn't want whatever it is to go to print."

Torn between revealing too much and needing to know if what Bran said was true, she hedged.

"Only that this interview was in exchange for the Gazette not running those pics."

Gideon whistled low. "Now you've got me curious to see them."

"Don't ask Sonja," she said, quickly. "But if you can find out anything more, I really want to know."

"You and me both," he replied. "And I won't ask Sonja."

There was a long pause during which Blake could hear Gideon humming while he clicked, likely searching the network.

"Gid?"

"Sorry, I was looking through the pool's files. There's...an awfully large reference folder on Cody. Nothing new about Val Saunders here, though. I'll keep digging."

"Discreetly."

"I'm sorry, did you really just tell me how to do *my* job? Concentrate on your own, smartass, and get me five hundred words by midnight," he groused. "How long do you think you'll need on this, anyway?"

"I don't know. Three days? A week? A year? This isn't going the way I thought it would."

"You're staying at the rental with him?"

"Not *with* him, but yeah. I'm in the pool house And, yes, before you make a joke, it is nicer than my place."

"That's not hard." She could hear the grin in his voice. "Enjoy your working vacation and stay safe. Let me know if he steps out of line."

"Aww, you care."

"Nope," Gideon replied. "If he tried anything, and you got arrested for breaking his nose, I'd have to fill out a shit ton of paperwork."

# 16

Blake had been sequestered in the pool house when Ollie returned from his outing. He tried not to read too much into that, nor into the smug grin that Bran had thrown his way before taking off for his evening run.

"Take your phone with you," he yelled after him.

Bran waved the device in the air in response, before pocketing it.

Ollie had been about to go down and knock on Blake's door when a call came through from Noelia.

"Hey. Bran's not here."

She paused before saying carefully, "I need you to use better words, Oliver Benjamin."

"Hello, Noelia. How are you?" he asked, speaking with deliberate care. "If you're looking for Bran, he went for a run on the beach. His car is parked at the house in Malibu, and we are still holed up in La Jolla. As planned."

He could feel her relief through the phone. "Next time, please lead with that. What's up with the reporter? Has she been down there yet?"

"She has. In fact, Blake is staying here."

"Alright, before I react to your words, I'm going to give you a chance to elaborate."

"Did you know we all went to school together? Bran, Blake and me?"

"I...did not know that, no." She sighed. "Do I need to worry?"

"About?"

"I'm assuming there's some sort of…relationship drama? With Blake and Brandon? Or *you* and Blake? Or…?"

"God, no. Nothing like that," he rushed to tell her. "Not then, and not now. Everything's been completely professional. We've reminisced a little, but mostly she's asked about his work, my role, his upcoming projects. That sort of thing."

"I see." She was quiet for some time. "Well, I was calling because there's an event tomorrow night that I think Brandon should attend."

Ollie put her on speaker and opened his calendar. "Where and when?"

"Seven o'clock at the Beverly Wilshire."

"I'll make the arrangements. What's it for?" He texted Rory to give him a heads-up that they would need him.

"Azure Studios is celebrating its newest indie darling. Rumor has it, they're in talks with Sam Newman about his debut."

"Really? I thought he'd signed with Sterling." He typed in the appointment and began firing off instructions for Bran's stylist and driver.

"Not a done deal, apparently," Noelia said. "And I can't guarantee it, but I would be surprised if Tiersen doesn't attend."

"You think so?" Bran had been trying to set up a meeting with Mikkel Tiersen for months, hoping to set up an audition for an epic drama he was rumored to be casting.

"It's highly probable, but try to manage Brandon's expectations."

"That I can do," he replied, mentally crossing all of his fingers and toes that tomorrow night would set things back on track.

"Alright, keep me posted."

"Thanks, Noelia." He sent a text to Bran's new cell phone.

"Was that Bran's publicist?"

Ollie turned to find Blake standing in the patio doors.

"Yeah."

Ollie couldn't help but smile as she walked over and settled into the armchair across from his. He shoved some of his things aside on the coffee table so she could set down her laptop. It was chunky and had seen many long days by the looks of it.

"Duct tape?" He pointed to the top corner of the lid.

"Oh, yeah. I dropped it and some of the plastic casing came off." She inspected the tape around the damaged area. "It's not pretty but it still works. For the most part," she added. "Where's Bran?"

"Went for a run."

"Ah, well, that's fine. I can ask you some questions instead."

"About?"

"Your boss, of course." She smiled as she propped her knee on her ankle and opened her notebook. The green leather holder was worn but in good shape, the entire book small enough to fit in a pocket or the palm of a hand.

He laughed softly. "Your laptop is right there."

"What?"

"How many of those notebook inserts do you go through in a month?"

She ran a thumb over the leather cover. "I'm not sure. Five or six?"

"You carry that around with you everywhere?"

"Yep, for the most part."

He settled back into his seat. "Do you have something against technology?"

"Not at all," she said. Smiling, she gestured towards her closed laptop. "Clearly. Why?"

"Well, you have a perfectly good phone. A functioning laptop, I just wonder why you use notebooks."

A small crease appeared in her forehead.

"Or...," he looked more closely at the leather case. "Wait, is that his? Your grandfather's?"

She nodded quickly. "Yeah."

"May I?" Ollie held out his hand, and she leaned forward to give it to him. Their fingers brushed, sending a spark of electricity traveling up his arm. The leather was warm and soft, but so was her skin.

Clearing his throat, he examined the book more closely. It was a rich, verdant green. Like a forest floor. All of the little scratches and marks only enhanced its appearance. Considering how old it was, the little portfolio was in remarkable shape.

"I buy the inserts by the case," she said, watching him closely as if he were handling something precious. And he supposed it was. "I guess I'm worried they're going to stop making them."

"The company's been around a long time, haven't they?" He handed it back.

"That's not a guarantee anymore."

"True."

A note of melancholy hung in the air, one he wanted to dispel. He'd no doubt conjured memories of her grandfather, and knew she'd get lost in them as she ran her hands over the leather.

"Hey, are you hungry?"

"I am, actually. I was going to run out and grab a taco somewhere."

He frowned. "Why would you do that? We have plenty of food here."

She laughed nervously. "It's not... I mean, that's Bran's food. I mean *your* food. Whatever. I didn't want to presume."

He had to laugh. "Blake, I know we lost touch for a while, but I thought... Well, we're friends. Right? That's what you said."

"Yes, of course. We're friends."

He loved the twinkle in her eyes that said she was curious about what that friendship could lead to later. Loved that he'd been able to push away the sadness she wore like a veil around her, at least for a few minutes.

"Great. Well, then, *friend*," he said as he got to his feet, "what's mine—uh, Bran's—is yours, at least in the kitchen. Use the hot tub, watch TV, go for a swim. You have the run of the house while you're here."

"I'd only planned to be here for a day or two."

"You have a deadline?"

"I...no, but—"

"Then live a little." He gestured for Blake to follow him to the kitchen and was unreasonably pleased when she took a seat at the counter.

The whole scenario was entirely too domestic, and he liked it. A lot.

"Are you allergic to shrimp?"

"No."

"And what's your stance on garlic? Yea or nay?" He pulled a cutting board out of the cupboard and opened the fridge to grab the shrimp.

"The more the better, unless I'm planning to kiss someone."

He nearly dropped the open bag of shellfish and ice on the floor, which would have been a smelly mess to clean up.

She peered over the counter. "You okay?"

"Yep. It's slippery." He got his shit together and grabbed a colander, placing it in the farmhouse sink. "Hans insists that Bran's seafood be really fresh, so I grabbed these while I was out."

"I thought Hans was the cook?"

"Sometimes. He's the nutritionist, and he isn't able to stay with us all week." He filled a bowl with ice water and removed a small paring knife from the block. "Hans runs a catering company. That's his main job, actually."

"Not celebrity chef to the stars and their executive assistants?"

He turned to smile at her over his shoulder. "Hardly. He catered a party for us once. Bran loved the food so much, he asked Hans to cook for him a few times a month. That turned into a few times a week, and then into him preparing reheatable meals on a weekly basis."

"Does Bran always get what Bran wants?"

"I feel like that's a *gotcha* question."

"It's not. I'm genuinely curious," Blake said. "Hollywood is still something of a myth to me. I've lived here for almost nine months, and I've yet to see the truth of it."

"What truth are you hoping to find?"

"The *why* of it, I suppose. Why people are willing to give up their privacy, their hometowns, their families in some cases, their dignity in others, in order to be famous."

Ollie carefully cleaned the shrimp and placed them in the bowl to keep them cold.

"Do you need any help?"

"If you want, you can take the pasta dough out of the fridge. I need it to warm up before I extrude it."

She slid off the stool and walked to the fridge. "God, this thing is huge," she said, looking up at it.

"It is."

She opened the door and emerged with the ball of dough he had made earlier. "Is this it?"

"Yeah, put it next to the Kitchen Aid."

"You're actually making fresh pasta?" She resumed her seat at the counter.

"It's not hard." He washed and dried his hands before pulling a head of garlic from the strand he'd picked up on their trip to the store. He moved the cutting board to the island so he wouldn't have his back to her as they chatted.

The whole scenario—her sitting there while he cooked for her—was beginning to put ideas into Ollie's head that he hadn't entertained in a long time. Probably since college.

He didn't know why things had felt so comfortable with Blake. From the moment they'd met, he'd been drawn to her. He wanted to hold onto the feeling. Hold onto her, their friendship, their...possibility.

"Don't cut yourself."

He looked down at the knife in his hand. "Right." Forcing himself to concentrate, he sliced the cloves into paper thin wafers. The sharp smell of garlic filled the air, creating a fragrant aroma.

"Where did you learn to cook, from Hans?"

"*Ma grand mère*," he replied, exaggerating the accent and pleased when he glanced up and saw her eyes on him.

He wanted to keep them there.

"That's my father's mother. She was a big deal in her village. Her family ran a small restaurant that she worked in from a young age. That's how she met my grandfather, actually."

"She served him a meal, and he fell in love?" She rested her chin on her hand and smiled up at him.

"That's not far from the truth." He filled a small bowl with ice and water before tossing the garlic in for sixty seconds.

"What does that do?" she asked, pointing at the bowl.

"I don't know that it actually *does* anything," he admitted. "But my grandma swears it keeps the garlic from becoming bitter when it cooks."

"I thought that was onions."

"It could be, but her mother told her to do it and her mother's mother told *her*, so…"

"Never wise to break a family tradition, at least when it comes to food."

"Or journalism," he said, winking at her. It earned a melodious laugh and, damn, if that didn't make his heart do a little dance inside his chest.

"I've observed all sorts of new things about you, Oliver Benjamin."

After straining the garlic, he dried the slices on a paper towel. "Like what?"

"Let's see, you speak French."

"I feel like you should have known that already."

"Maybe, but it feels like new information," she countered. "Let's call it a *rediscovery*."

"I'll allow it."

"You cook, you're very detail oriented," she said, ticking the list off on her fingers.

"That's new information?" he asked as he prepped the counter with flour.

"Okay, it's not. But watching you apply it to your…work…as Bran's executive assistant puts it in a new perspective."

"I see." He hadn't missed her slight hesitation over his occupation.

He thought he'd picked up on some disapproval, beyond the whole

Bran was an asshole in college thing, and wondered what she thought about his position.

"What else have you learned?"

"That you underestimate yourself. But then you've always done that."

"Have I?" Surprised, Ollie stopped to look at her.

"You have." Blake held his gaze, and there was so much unspoken between them, he had to swallow and turn away.

"I'll, uh, just text Bran to see if he still wants dinner at eight." He washed his hands and went back to the living room to retrieve his phone. There was a text from Bran's private line.

**BPL: Ran into Adam Mac (literally) down the beach. Going to eat at his place.**

**OLLIE: Secure?**

**BPL: It's just him and me.**

**OLLIE: Did you get my text about tomorrow night?**

**BPL: I did and I'll be back before curfew, dad. [winking emoji]**

Ollie thought about informing Clark or Noelia, but put his phone in his pocket. At the end of the day, Bran was an adult. Free to make his own choices, good or bad. He knew what was at stake.

He turned for the kitchen but couldn't stop himself from taking out his phone and looking up Adam McKenna.

There didn't seem to be much online about the guy, save his screen credits and his charity work. There was nothing on TMZ, nothing in a search on the Gazette's website.

"Huh."

"Everything alright?" Blake appeared in the doorway.

"Looks like it's just you and me for dinner."

Three emotions crossed her features in quick succession. First, surprise, followed by concern, and finally one that he didn't recognize. But it had brought a shy smile to her full lips, so he wasn't about to complain.

# 17

"Is there such a thing as a foodgasm?"

Blake moaned around her fork as the flavors exploded across her tongue. Garlic, olive oil, cherry tomatoes, a hint of white truffle oil, and freshly grated pepper weren't things she'd never tasted before. Somehow, though, Ollie had alchemized those simple ingredients into a masterpiece. The shrimp were so fresh, they still tasted like the ocean. And the pasta!

She opened her eyes to find him watching her with amusement. "It's good?"

"Dude, it's friggin' amazing!" She wiped her mouth and forced herself not to scarf down the entire bowl of pasta at once. "Please tell your grandma *merci* from me for teaching you how to make this."

When he smiled, *really* smiled, his eyes practically disappeared. He was all white teeth and dimples, and utterly adorable. And he was blushing, though he picked up his glass of white wine to try and hide it.

They were sitting on the patio as the sun set over the water. The temperature had dropped and, though it wasn't exactly cool, he had turned on the fire pit. For such an opulent property, he seemed right at home there.

"I'm curious," she began. "When we were in school, what did you think you'd be doing in five years? For work, I mean. It couldn't have been this."

His hand slowed as he set the glass down. "No, obviously not."

"You were an English major, minoring in communication. Right?"

"I was."

"So, either you wanted to write the next Great American Novel, or you wanted to teach."

"After we graduated, I went to Peck."

"The film school?" That surprised her. She had a hard time picturing Oliver Benjamin in charge of a cast, a crew, and whomever else was involved in the making of a movie. Then again, she'd only recently come to understand how little she knew about him. "I don't recall you wanting to be in film."

"I didn't. But Dr. Danish—you remember him?" She nodded. "A few months before graduation, he told me about the MFA in film and media, about the scriptwriting program, and something clicked."

"Wow, Ollie. You've been holding out on me. It's a pretty competitive program, from what I've heard."

He shrugged. "I'm lucky, I guess."

"Lucky? No one gets into a program like that because of luck." She put her fork down and studied him. "I don't know why you do that."

"Do what?"

"Attribute everything you accomplish to luck or to someone else's hard work."

"I don't."

"You do," she argued. "You did it in college, though I'm only now recognizing the pattern."

"Name one time," he said, chuckling as he refilled her glass and then his.

"Your essay, the something, something of forgotten words."

"*The Secret History of Misplaced Nouns.*" He blinked with surprise. "You remember that?"

"Of course, I do," she said, tossing his own words back at him. "You won top prize for that essay, and you said it was because your sources had all been exceptionally researched."

"It's true. They were."

She laughed, incredulous. "God, Ollie. I'm sure they were, but those researchers didn't write your goddamned essay. *You* did. And you couldn't even take credit for it. Couldn't accept the praise."

His face was one big flame, now, and she fought hard not to find it cute. She lost the battle when he lowered his eyes and smiled. Christ, this guy.

She needed to focus, needed to stay on task. It was hard to do with Bran off somewhere cavorting and leaving them alone in this romantic as hell setting.

"I've missed this," he said quietly. "I didn't realize how much until now."

"Missed what?" They hadn't done this sort of thing back in college.

"I guess *missed* isn't the right word," he mused, looking out over the dark mass of the ocean. "No, it *is*, but it's not so much missing something I had as missing something I never had."

Maybe it was the wine, but Blake had trouble following. "I think I need you to explain."

He smiled. "At school, I was focused on doing the best I could. Focused on figuring out what I wanted to do with my life. I had friends. Well, one friend."

"Bran?"

"Bran. I mean, there were other people—like with study group—but they came and went each semester. Bran was my constant. Still is."

"It could have been different. We could have—" This was definitely the wine talking. But the things Bran had said earlier wouldn't leave her alone. "I had a crush on you."

Ollie jumped, turning to her as his hand knocked over the glass. Wine spilled across the table and into her lap.

"Oh, fuck!" He scrambled out of his chair and grabbed their napkins. They were linen, and the cloth did absolutely nothing to soak up the liquid. "Jesus, I'm sorry."

Laughing, she stood up as he bent down and tried to wipe the front of her shirt. "Ollie, it's fine. I'll go change."

He looked up, his storm cloud eyes going even more stormy, and Blake forgot how to breathe. She pulled her bottom lip into her mouth and bit it to keep from asking for the impossible.

He sucked in a quick breath before he took a slow step back. "Sure. Okay, I'll, uh…get some fresh... Yeah."

But neither of them moved. His feet seemed planted to the ground, and she couldn't stop staring at the way the firelight played in the highlights of his hair. The way it danced across his features.

Without her permission, Blake's hand drifted up to push a lock of hair out of his eyes.

"Why didn't you ask me out? Back then?"

"What…?" His eyes were wide, the word barely a breath.

"Why didn't we at least stay in touch?"

"I..." She watched him swallow hard and followed the dip of his Adam's apple. "After what happened with the paper and Bran, you made it clear you didn't want to be friends. And, honestly, I didn't know if *I* could be friends. With *you*."

"Like it would betray Bran?"

"Sounds silly."

"It would have then, yeah. But now? I get it."

His gaze roamed over her face. It wasn't the first time he'd looked at her like that, and Blake remembered all the times in the library when she'd caught him watching her. God, she wished he'd made a move then. Wished *she* had. And as improbable and inappropriate as it was, she wished one of them would make a move now.

"Something smells amazing!" Bran's voice floated up from the stairs leading to the beach.

"I'm going to go change." She announced loudly before darting around Ollie and heading for the pool house. Her heart was pounding so hard, it beat out the sound of the crashing waves.

When she returned, Ollie had cleaned up and refilled their wine glasses. Bran had grabbed a plate of food and was sitting at the head of the table scarfing it down like he hadn't eaten in years. There was something different about his meal, though.

"Why is this pasta orange?"

"It's spaghetti squash," Ollie replied.

"I don't really do carbs," Bran said. "Not when I'm training, anyway."

"No carbs?" She took her seat, horrified. "Like, at all?"

"Well, I drink them," Bran replied after swallowing a huge bite. "Wine, the occasional beer."

"Smoothies," she supplied.

Bran smiled. "Complex carbs are fuel. The rest is garbage and I try to stay away from garbage."

"You're training for a new role?"

"Yeah. It'll be even more physically demanding." He stabbed a shrimp and popped it into his mouth. "They'll probably have me out of my shirt for half of it."

"You do that a lot? Structure your diet and exercise around whatever role you have at the time?"

"Once an actor signs on, they're required to do what's necessary for the character," Ollie supplied. "If it's an action role, like most of Bran's, they're sometimes assigned trainers."

"I prefer to work with my guy." Bran had opened another bottle of wine. He indicated Blake's glass, and she nodded.

"Doesn't it seem a bit...excessive, though?"

"What do you mean?" Ollie asked.

"Watching what you eat, working out for hours every day, and not for your health but for a character. From the outside, it seems weird."

"If I were...a ballet dancer or an athlete, would you think it was strange?"

She cocked her head at Bran, surprised she hadn't made the correlation herself. "No, I guess I wouldn't."

"Why do you think it would be different for actors?" He took a sip from his glass and waited, but Blake didn't know what else to say. He had a very valid point. "See, people who aren't in this business—hell, in this town—can't really wrap their heads around everything it takes to make a movie like the ones I make."

"Here we go," Ollie said, shaking his head.

"I'm serious," Bran continued. "Do you have any idea how many people worked on my last film?"

She shrugged. "I don't know. A hundred?"

"More than two thousand," Ollie said, sounding proud.

As her jaw dropped, Bran added. "And franchise properties, like the Marvel films, can employ even more."

"I think the *Black Panther* crew was more than three thousand," Ollie said.

"Wow, that's...a whole ass village."

"More like a small town," he replied. "The village where my grandparents were born had around fifteen hundred residents."

"Each person has a specific job, from the make-up girl..." Bran held up his hand. "Person, sorry...to the grip to the caterer to the stunt double. We all train to be the best at what we do, or at least be what the film needs. It's more than, how did you put it? Shrugging on a pair of tights and swinging from cables on the ceiling."

*What the hell?* "Were you reading my notes?"

"You left them sitting on the table."

"Bran," Ollie warned.

"What?" He speared another shrimp.

"It's...fine."

She reigned in her kneejerk reaction, which was to lay into Bran for invading her privacy. But it was her fault for leaving her stuff laying around. This wasn't her home. She was a guest. More than that, she was on assignment. All the scenery and the food and the wine and the...Ollie...had gone to her head.

"What drew you to acting?" she asked Bran. "And be honest."

His jaw flexed a few times, and he looked at Ollie.

"Don't look at me, I'm curious, too."

"Traitor," Bran muttered. "Fine. I read an article, an interview with Ryan Reynolds, and it made me think *yeah, I can do what he does*."

She frowned. "Own a team in a sport he doesn't follow?"

"Oi!" Ollie said. "Ryan and Rob have done a fantastic job in Wrexham."

"He's got a similar sense of humor, similar laid-back style," Bran said, cutting Ollie off.

"Laid back?" She glanced around the expansive, expensive house.

"This is different," Bran argued. "A place like this is the dream, right? At least, it's supposed to be."

"Am I hearing you right?" Ollie asked him. "Are you no longer set on owning one of these Pacific palaces?"

Bran laughed. "Never say never. But what I mean is that... Like, Reynolds has a nice home and a gorgeous wife, all that. But it's real. It's not a fantasy. This place, it's a fantasy."

They fell silent as she took a sip from her glass, both men glancing between her and each other.

"How did you end up at the L.A. Gazette?" Bran asked. "I don't remember much from college, but I do remember how serious you were about being a journalist. The Gazette is a rag."

"It is," she agreed.

"You couldn't find anything on the East Coast?" Ollie met her eyes. There was sympathy there, and she wasn't sure how to take it.

"There were a couple of outlets I could have gone to, thanks to my granddad."

"He's a reporter?"

"He used to be, yeah. And he cast a long shadow."

"You want to make a name for yourself. I get that," Bran said. "In school, I wasn't good at anything but playing soccer and talking shit. My dad, his dad, they were both businesspeople. Corporate life is *not* for me. So, I did everything to avoid that."

"Can't get much further from corporate life than this," she agreed. "What about you, Oliver?"

"What about me? I'm not the subject of your profile."

"Ols doesn't like to talk about his life plans."

"You have some, though?"

"Course he does," Bran replied. "Our Oliver is going to be a screenwriter."

Ollie's laugh was self-deprecating. "You think finding a position at a respectable news outlet is hard? Try getting someone to read your script."

"How would you know? It's not like you let anyone read your stuff, other than the doctoring you've done for me and the odd job for Lorna. She'd kill to have you full time, and you know it," Bran added.

"Have you shopped anything?" She asked Ollie.

"No, he hasn't."

"Will you stop answering for me?"

"Turnabout is fair play, and all that," Bran said, laughing. "He won't even let me read his stuff. You know what I think? I think he's got this cushy gig, looking after my dumb ass, and he's in no hurry to move on."

The look Ollie gave him, if it had been a weapon, would have split the man's head in two.

Bran frowned. "Hey, I'm kidding."

Ollie nodded, but the storm clouds didn't leave his expression.

"Blake," Bran said a little too loudly. "What're you doing tomorrow night?"

"I guess I'm doing whatever you're doing."

"Fantastic! I hope you packed a party dress, 'cause we're taking you to a premiere. Isn't that right, Ols?"

"Me?" Ollie gaped at him. "You want *me* to go?"

"Don't you usually?"

"No."

"Well, this time you are. You wouldn't want Blake to sit all by herself while I work the room, would you?" Bran winked at her, and she felt her cheeks heat. Not from his wink, never that. But the idea of spending an evening like that with Ollie...it was too tempting.

She glared at Bran. What was he playing at? His attempts to play matchmaker were even more suspicious, now. She was about to decline his invitation, but when Ollie turned to look at her, the hope in his eyes was undeniable.

"I need to drive home in the morning anyway."

Bran grinned like he'd won a hand of poker. "Grab something shiny. We'll be on the red carpet."

# 18

*If nothing else, Brandon Cody knows what he is and doesn't pretend to be what he's not unless someone is paying him to do so. When asked why he chose a career that puts such a strain on his fitness, diet, and personal life, Cody likened himself to an athlete. It's an apt comparison, and one I hadn't thought of. The more I pull back the curtains, the more I realize they're sheer. With Cody, what you see is what you get.*

*No More Pictures, Please: the Trajectory of a Shooting Star by Blake Dillon for the L.A. Gazette*

Blake sat across from Gideon, her leg bouncing as he read over the rough she'd sent that morning.

"I know it's thin at the moment, but I promise I'm making headway."

He sat back in his chair and looked at her, his expression unreadable.

"Gid," she begged. "Come on, you're killing me."

One corner of his mouth lifted. "You know, I give you a lot of shit for the school you attended and your...pedigree, or whatnot, but I have to say. You're good, Dillon. You're really good."

The bubble of anxiety that had settled in her chest popped, leaving behind blessed relief.

"You're right, it's thin, but I can see where you're going with it," her editor continued. "I think it'll be a really good piece when you're done, if you can dive deeper into his psyche."

"I will," she said eagerly. "I'll dive so deep I'll need an oxygen tank, I promise."

They both winced.

"That sounded better in my head," she said.

"I'm sure."

"Hey," she leaned in, lowering her voice to almost a whisper. "Did you find out anything else about...what we talked about on the phone?"

Gideon glanced behind her. "Close the door."

She scrambled to do so before returning to her seat.

"I'm only telling you this because you might be able to shed some light on it, while you're trailing Cody," he began. "You were right about there being a second story. For some reason, Sonja's keeping it close to the vest."

"It has to do with Valerie Saunders?"

He nodded. "The allegation is that Cody and Saunders are having an affair."

Blake frowned. "That's it? I mean, I don't condone extra-marital relations, unless both spouses agree, but this seems like a lot of cloak and dagger for an affair."

"Cody would likely lose his chance at the *Captain Sky* franchise."

"He's a dude. He'd bounce back, but Valerie?"

"She wouldn't," Gideon agreed. "And she met her husband, Sam, on set. When he was married."

"Oh. Shit."

"Yeah," he said, nodding. "Granted, that was an ugly situation. Sam's ex was...well, to put it nicely, unstable and highly dangerous. The public was all for him getting out of that situation. And yet, Val was vilified by certain factions."

"I see." She needed to read up on this whole thing, and fast.

"Young, Black actress, older, white, *married* man. I'm sure you can imagine the comments."

"And now people think she's stepping out with Bran?"

He shrugged. "Honestly, this is the first I've heard of any rumor like that. After we spoke, I did a casual search of some of the more well-known blogs and found nothing about any alleged affair."

"So, where is this coming from?"

"Us, as far as I can tell," he replied. "And it bugs the hell out of me." His face had scrunched up like he'd taken a bite out of a lemon.

"Bran mentioned something about the Gazette being out to get him," she said. "I didn't think anything of it, but if this affair story originated with us and *no* one else has wind of it?"

"And we're sitting on it for this exclusive."

"Plus, the hack? Gid, something weird is going on here."

He was nodding, deep in thought. "Okay, look. I maintain that this feature will do wonders for you. Stay the course, write what you see and learn, and don't worry about any of this."

"Uh, that's kind of impossible. If I'm being used as a pawn in someone's game—

"I'll deal with it," he stated firmly. "*I'm* your firewall. Nothing gets to you but through me. Okay? Trust me. I've got your back."

She nodded. "Thanks."

"It's my job. Now, you mentioned something about a premiere?"

"Oh, yeah. Tonight. I'm invited."

He smiled. "Baby's first premiere, I'm so proud."

"Ha ha, funny. I'm only going because I think it'll be good to see him in that environment. See how he's perceived by others."

"You plan on interviewing people there?" His brow lifted.

"No, not exactly. I'll chat with people. Observe."

"Alright, good. I don't want to get a call from so-and-so's publicist chewing me out because you took something their client said out of context.

"Strictly information gathering on my subject," she promised.

"Though, if you *happen* across any juicy tidbits..."

"I'll be sure to text you so that you can get someone else on it."

He grinned. "There's my team player."

That afternoon, Blake was back in South Pasadena, trying on outfits for the party.

The current dress was entirely too tight, too short and left little to the imagination, but she could admit, to herself at least, that red was definitely her color. She'd been so overwhelmed by the idea of a red-carpet event that she'd accepted before remembering she had nothing to wear.

Enid's best friend, Lucy, worked in the wardrobe department of a studio in Toluca Lake and often brought over discarded or unused clothing for them to try on.

"How much did this cost?" The garment itself was off-the-rack but still exorbitantly expensive, easily worth as much as half of her combined wardrobe.

Lucy waved her off. "You never ask a lady a question like that. Didn't your mama teach you any manners at all?"

"Are you sure wardrobe doesn't mind?"

"I liberated it from the shuttered wardrobe of a cancelled cable network series." Lucy fussed with the side zipper. "You should thank me. It could have ended up in a landfill somewhere."

"Aww, Luce. I had no idea you were a conservationist," she said, gasping when Lucy closed the last inch of the zipper. "Ooof. It's tight."

"Too tight?"

Draping low in the front, it showed off more cleavage than she had ever dared. The back was almost identical, dipping low with the sides held together by a rhinestone chain. The hem fell mid-thigh and made her legs look longer than they were.

"A little?"

"Take shallow breaths and don't eat a morsel," she was instructed. "I have to say, you wear it well."

A pair of black Louboutin knockoffs, complete with red soles, and crystal drop earrings finished the look. For an extra touch, she'd adorned her right wrist with her mother's rose gold bangles.

"I can't believe you're going to one of the hottest events of the season," Enid said as she leaned against the doorframe. "Are you at least going to tell me who invited you? Is it for work?"

"I really can't say who, but yes. It's for work."

"A story?" Enid's dark eyes went wide. "Are you going undercover to snoop on the rich and beautiful so you can eviscerate them in the paper?"

"Wow, bloodlust much?"

"I admit, I get a perverse thrill out of what you do," Lucy said. "And that makes me sound like a horrible human being."

"I don't know about horrible. There's something about watching the people we put on pedestals come crashing down that fulfills some dark need in people." She stepped into the bathroom to apply her mascara.

"Babes," Lucy called out. "Your phone is pinging like a slot machine. Please, make it stop."

"Oh, thanks. Sorry!" She slipped off the shoes and sprinted to where she'd left the phone charging on the kitchen counter. She'd expected a call from Ollie, but it was an unknown number. "Hello?"

"Is this Blake Dillon?" The teen girl's voice sounded shaky.

"Yes."

"It's Micah."

It took a moment for her brain to pull up a memory of the young girl from Play L.A. "Micah, hi. Is everything okay?"

"I'm okay, but…um… Are you busy? Can you come meet me?"

Blake looked down at her outfit and rushed back to her room to grab her shoes. "Actually, I have to go to—"

"Please, Miss Dillon."

She stopped, shoes in hand. "Are you hurt? What happened?" She shook her head at Enid's quizzical look.

"No, ma'am, but I, um…"

She could hear her heavy breathing on the other end of the call. Waving Lucy over to help her, she unzipped the dress and shoved it into a bag, along with her shoes. "It's okay, tell me where you are, and I'll be there as soon as I can."

She found Micah standing in the parking lot of the twenty-four-hour diner, just where she said she'd be. The area was well lit, and the restaurant seemed to have a steady stream of patrons.

"Why didn't you wait inside?"

"They don't let you have a table unless you're ordering, and I ain't got no money to spare." Micah folded her arms around herself. She was dressed in an old school Raiders jersey, baggy jeans, and white tennis shoes.

"Are you hungry?"

"Your make-up looks nice," the girl replied, skirting the question. "Were you going somewhere? I'm sorry."

"Don't worry about that." In her bag, her phone buzzed but she ignored it. "I can get you something to eat, if you want."

"I ate at home." Micah glanced around. "I just didn't want you coming there, in case someone saw you. You asked me if I knew anyone else who worked with that company. The talent agency."

"Yeah, do you?"

"This pop singer out east. I don't know her, but my friend does. Says she signed with them in New York," Micah said. "They used a different name then, but it's the same people. If you find her, she can probably tell you what you want to know."

"That's great!" She pulled out her notebook. "What's the singer's name?"

"Yara. Yara Bujold." That definitely rang a bell, and she made a mental note to Google her in the morning.

Blake smiled. "Thank you, Micah. I'll try to reach out to her first thing tomorrow."

Micah glanced around, flinching when someone honked their horn at the two women.

"You should get home. You want a lift?"

"No, no. I'm good."

"Need some money? I don't have much, but—"

"Nah, miss. I don't need your money." Micah shook her head. "I just want you to tell the world who these assholes are that hurt my girl."

"I'll do whatever I can," she said, knowing she couldn't promise justice for these kids.

Micah nodded and Blake watched her duck around the side of the restaurant. Her phone vibrated in her hand.

**OLLIE: The car will be there in 10 to pick you up.**

"Shit." She jumped back into her car and typed out a quick reply, telling him she was running late and would meet him at the venue.

**OLLIE: No worries. I'll be waiting.**

She refused to entertain the idea of why those three words gave her butterflies.

# 19

"It's cute that you're so nervous," Bran said, casually.

Ollie spun in his seat. "Why would I be nervous?" He was met by a knowing smirk. "Okay, fine. I'm nervous. Blake is... She's..."

"A beautiful, smart, single woman into whose pants you wish to get?"

"God, you're an idiot." Rolling his eyes, he went back to looking out the window.

Bran's low chuckle filled the back of the SUV. "It's too easy to bust your balls."

"Try resisting sometime."

"Oh, I do," Bran said, laughing louder. "All the time. Listen, Ols... I was skeptical about this whole profile thing, even with Blake writing it, but she's solid. I like her. And she's nice to look at," he added, casually.

Alarm bells went off in his head, and he turned to face him.

"Oh my God, look at your face!" Bran cackled.

"What the fuck is so funny?"

"H-hang on." When he regained control of himself, he wiped his eyes. "Jesus, I've never seen you like this. You dolt, I said she was nice to look at, not that I wanted to get with her. This isn't high school where we talk about like and *like* like. Okay?"

"Okay, fine."

"What I meant was, I like this for you. When this whole profile thing is done, I think you should go for it," he said. "I'd tell you to go for it now, but I figure she wouldn't want to cross any professional lines."

"That's...surprisingly astute of you."

"Ooo! Astute. I got one of the big words, so I must have done something right." He winked.

Ollie shoved his knee. "Like I said, you're an idiot."

"Yeah, well, I have my own agenda tonight, but I want you to relax and hang out with your future girlfriend."

He pretended the jolt of possessiveness he got from hearing those words didn't occur. "What is on your agenda tonight?"

"Hang with Val, for one thing."

"Is that smart?"

Bran frowned. "I'm not allowed to spend time with my oldest friend at a public event?"

"Of course you are. Just..." He searched for words that wouldn't piss off his oldest friend. "Keep a cool distance when you interact with her. I think she'll understand."

"She doesn't understand this anymore than I do, but she said this isn't her first rodeo." Bran grit his teeth. "People still give her shit for the way she and Sam came together. I mean, he gets it too, he was married at the time, as toxic as that relationship was. But it's nothing like the things people say about Val."

"She's the woman," he agreed.

"She's a *Black* woman," Bran corrected him. "And I'm a Black man."

"Your mom is white, so doesn't that mean you're mixed?"

"Dude, this is America. Besides, I'm proud of my skin just like Val is proud of hers, but they sure do love to make it a liability when they can."

"And by they, you mean...?"

Bran shrugged. "Everyone. Sam gets a pass from people because he was bewitched by the sexy, Black seductress." He lifted his hand to make air quotes around the phrase.

"Jesus, do people really believe that shit?"

"Yes. And now I'm the baddie because someone thinks I'm stabbing Sam in the back. It's ridiculous."

"Well, it'll blow over. In the meantime, don't give anyone more fuel to throw onto the fire. Maybe Rory should stick closer to you. I'm sure we could have them issue him security credentials."

He met Rory's gaze in the rear-view mirror.

"If I'm inside, you'll need someone on standby with the car."

Bran shook his head. "I don't think anything will pop off at a high-profile event."

Ollie wasn't convinced, but he acquiesced.

"Don't worry about me, you stick close to Blake." Bran gave him a knowing smirk.

"Shut up."

"I didn't say a word!" He was laughing again.

"Fucking idiot."

About half a block from the Beverly Wilshire, Ollie got out of the SUV. He hated the whole red-carpet experience and had managed to avoid walking it, except for a few times when Bran had needed an entourage around him to act as a shield from adoring fans and pushy paparazzi.

He flashed his credentials at the checkpoint and waited a safe distance away while Rory inched the SUV up the line.

When Bran emerged, wearing sunglasses for some reason, Ollie made his way through the back line and towards the door, where he'd wait for him. It wasn't a major motion picture, so it didn't take long.

"Where's Blake?"

"Still running late, I expect." He'd checked his phone but there was no update from her.

"You don't think she's going to bail on us, do you? Change her mind?"

He narrowed his eyes. "Why do you want her here so badly?"

Ignoring him, Bran walked on ahead.

It took a moment for Ollie to catch up, and he reached him just as the line through the door began to flow.

"Put the glasses away," he said, motioning for Bran to remove them.

"Right, because I look like such an ass in sunglasses at night."

"You always look like an ass. Those make you look like a *pretentious* ass."

"Shit, really? Fuck that." He tucked the shades away.

With a glance around, Ollie ushered him towards the main ballroom.

"There are way more people here than I was expecting." He spoke to Bran's back as they moved through the crowd.

They were stopped by a Latinx woman in a striking gold lamé gown. She looked up at Bran from under feathered lashes too long and thick to be real.

"And who is this?"

Bran put a hand on his shoulder. "This is Oliver Benjamin. Ols, this is Viviana Lopez."

"A pleasure." He gave a polite nod of greeting but didn't extend his hand out of fear of being judged for his sweaty palms. Where the hell was Blake? He was starting to worry. Had her car broken down somewhere? Was her cellphone out of juice?

"I'm *so* glad you came, Brandon. Let me introduce you to my friend, Dakota Fink."

He hung back while Bran charmed the two women. And he was not at all watching the doors for a particular reporter with an hourglass figure, silky black curls, and eyes that could cut through him with one glance.

After a few minutes, Bran excused himself and they continued into the ballroom.

"That's us," he said, pointing to their assigned table. He scanned the room as they reached it, but there was no sign of Blake. Frowning, he wondered if maybe she had changed her mind after all.

"Sit down." Bran grabbed him by the arm and gently pulled. "Nothing from her yet?"

"Not since before we arrived." He pulled out his chair and sat.

"Text her and let her know where we are. Maybe her signal is weak."

When he didn't respond, Bran clasped his shoulder.

"She'll find a way to reach out."

"I hope so." He shook his head, feeling uneasy.

"Did you see Val or Sam while you were scoping out the room?"

"Not yet. You think they'll show up?"

"I don't know." Bran sat back in his chair, drumming his fingers against the table as he looked around at the crowd. "I came here to see Val. You came to hang out with Blake. The night couldn't be a bust for both of us. Could it?"

After a few minutes, Bran left the table and Ollie watched him mingle, making note of the people in attendance. It was a veritable who's who of independent film, and a good place for Bran to be seen.

"Excuse me," a voice said from over his shoulder.

He turned to find a tall, Asian man in his mid-thirties smiling at him. He had glossy black hair swept back from his forehead and bright eyes that seemed to miss nothing.

"You're Oliver Benjamin, right?"

"Yes." He frowned at the man, trying to place him. "Sorry. Have we met?"

"Not yet," he replied, extending his hand. "Vincent Park."

"Ah, it's so nice to finally meet you." He took the man's hand, giving it a firm shake. "You work with Lorna Verden."

"On *Blackbird*, yes. And I've been wanting to meet you." He smiled, his gaze intense and inquisitive. He wore the air of someone who could launch or kill a career with a flick of his wrist. Which, of course, he could. "I have to say, I'm very impressed with the work you've done with Lorna."

He frowned. "The work I've done?"

"The rewrite on episode three really tightened it up, especially Aaliyah's dialogue. You captured exactly what I was hoping for."

"I..." Ollie was a little stunned. "Honestly, it was only a few lines."

Park smiled. "She said you would say that. Listen," he reached into his jacket and pulled out his phone. "Could I give you my info?"

"Of course." Ollie retrieved his phone from the table and held it out. One tap later, the other man's contact information appeared on his screen. "I'm happy to help anytime."

"I'd like you to do more than help, but I'll let Lorna twist your arm on that."

"Well, I look forward to it, Mr. Park."

"Vincent, please," he held his hand up. "Do you prefer Ollie or Oliver?"

"Either."

The man surveyed Ollie from head to toe, taking in every detail as his lips curved into an amused grin. "You're either the most affable man in Hollywood, or the most cunning."

"Neither," he replied, laughing softly. "I promise, what you get is what you see."

"How refreshing. Are you here alone?" He gestured behind him. "I have a table over there."

"I'm here with...friends." Ollie wasn't sure why he'd hesitated, but Vincent didn't seem to notice.

"Well, enjoy yourself. I'd love to get your thoughts on tonight's film, sometime."

"I guess I'll be in touch," he said, his head spinning. He was genuinely surprised that the man seemed so interested in his work.

"Was that Vincent Park?" Bran walked up beside him, gesturing with the whiskey glass in his hand.

"You know him?"

"Mostly by reputation," he replied. "Lorna introduced me to him once when he came by the set."

"Seems like a decent guy."

"By all accounts he is, for someone in his position." Bran turned to him. "Did he offer you a job?"

He laughed. "No, of course not."

Bran's eyebrows lifted. "Why'd you say it like that? Lorna hasn't been subtle about it."

"About what?"

The room was filling quickly, bodies jostling for space between the tables, so they took their seats.

"About wanting you to write for her new show."

"I've helped her out a few times, that's all."

He was met with narrowed eyes.

"What?"

"*What?* He asks. Dude, why do you do that? Drives me fucking crazy."

"Do what?"

"Downplay everything when it comes to you."

Why did he sound like Blake? Had they been talking about him? "I don't."

"You sure as hell do, and I don't understand why."

If he didn't know any better, Ollie would think Bran was angry. It was there in the stiff set of his shoulders and the furrow of his brow.

"I'm good where I am."

"Working for me, you mean?"

Confused by his tone, he nodded. "Well, yeah. Where else?"

Bran leaned his elbows on the table. "You won't be with me forever, Ols."

He knew that. Of course, he knew that. This gig was temporary. He'd only planned to work for Bran until...

The dawning realization that he *didn't* have a timeline for all of this was startling. It must have shown on his face because Bran sat back with a knowing smile.

"Are you planning to fire me?"

"No," he replied. "But I will if you keep turning away opportunities I *know*, somewhere deep down, you really want."

He had to smile at that, however misguided it was. "I'm the one who's supposed to be looking out for you."

Bran's smile brightened. "Nothing says it can't go both ways, little brother."

# 20

The Beverly Wilshire was a grand dame of old Hollywood. As a teenager, Blake would spend hours in the library reading old issues of Glamour and Life magazines and pouring over books about Hollywood. It never occurred to her that she would one day attend one of the most glamorous and exclusive events in the country. After parking in a nearby garage, she changed into her party clothes and texted Ollie to let him know she'd arrived. She hoped she would find him quickly. The idea of being alone at an event like this was overwhelming.

Flash bulbs popped all around her, but she couldn't see who was drawing all the attention. She quickly walked through the crowded lobby and made her way down to the main ballroom. The winding staircase to the bottom floor seemed daunting in her heels, so she opted for the elevator. Its mirrored interior would be a bonus, one last chance to check her hair and make-up before making a discreet entrance. She waited until the doors were closed and then gave her lips a touch-up before checking her phone. No response from Ollie. She thought about trying Bran's phone but realized, even if he had it on him, he probably wouldn't hear it.

The space outside of the ballroom was set up for cocktail hour. Several dozen people were clumped around, drinks in hand, taking full advantage of the open bar. In the eight months since she'd moved to

L.A. and began reporting on the rich and famous, Blake had learned the more money people had, the more they loved free stuff.

She made her way to the furthest bar, situated by one of the arched windows. It was the perfect place to watch the comings and goings and, hopefully, spot Bran and Ollie when they arrived.

"Champagne, miss?"

"Yes, thanks."

Blake didn't know much about champagne, but it was delicious and went down too easily. With each sip, she let the tartness roll around her tongue for a few moments before swallowing. She scanned the room, fascinated by the dynamics at play.

"Ms. Dillon." The sound of her name startled her. Blake turned to the source, even more surprised to find Lowan Farrell smiling down at her.

"Mr. Farrell."

The CEO of the corporation that owned the Los Angeles Gazette, among other news outlets, had sidled up next to her.

"Lovely to see you again." He leaned in and kissed her on the cheek, and Blake struggled not to flinch.

Some people wore money well. Farrell was not one of those people. His tux was at least a size too small, and his aftershave was pungent.

She stifled a cough.

He held a tumbler of golden liquid in his right hand and cupped her shoulder in his left. The touch was cold and a little clammy. A shiver of unease trickled over her skin. "And you. You...look well, sir."

"Thank you, dear. I feel great. Spent the holiday week in Vermont. I do love the East Coast."

"Me too." She glanced around the room, hoping Farrell would take the hint.

"Your family is back East, isn't it?" he asked, leaning in too close for comfort.

"Uh, yes." She met his eyes briefly and put some distance between them. "Philadelphia."

"Ah, yes. Philadelphia. The Bulletin, right?"

"Yes, that's right," she replied, hoping the group of people heading their way were looking for him.

"Sorry, if you'll excuse me..."

He met the on-comers, and Blake took the opportunity to move to a nearby cocktail table and set down her drink. She opened her clutch and grabbed her phone to text Ollie again.

"As I was about to say, I've never been there," Farrell said from over her shoulder. "But I know the University of Philadelphia turns out some of the best and brightest. You attended, didn't you?"

"Yes." Blake had run out of real estate in her tiny pocket of patience. She looked up and forced a smile. "I graduated a few years ago."

"Indeed. Oh, excuse me dear, Evelyn Tyne is here, and I need to speak to her." He was already walking away, much to her relief. "Have a lovely time."

"Thank you, Mr. Farrell."

He stopped, offering her a sly smile. "Lowan, honey. Call me Lowan."

Blake nodded. *Honey?* She downed her champagne and went to the sidebar for another. Where the hell were Bran and Ollie? In her hand, her phone vibrated. Then again. And again.

**O. BENJAMIN: Have you arrived?**

**O. BENJAMIN: Grand Ballroom, table #18 near the far left entrance.**

**O. BENJAMIN: If you've decided not to come just let me know so I can stop imagining the worst. Hope you're okay.**

Oh, no. Stupid phone must have lost the signal at some point.

Blake fired off to let Ollie know she was on her way to their table. She spotted him as she approached the door, waving when he ushered her over.

"Hey!"

"Hi," he stepped aside to let her pass. "Wow," he breathed, making her glad she at least looked somewhat presentable.

"Not too much? Or too little?" She grinned at his wide eyes as he took her in, preening under his hungry perusal of her outfit.

He cleared his throat. "Uh, yes. I mean no! I mean...*fuck*."

"You, sir, are excellent for my ego."

He chuckled. "Glad I can be of service. You look...incredible."

"Thank you." She ignored the warmth his words ignited in her belly. He led her to a table near the stage but against a wall. The sightlines weren't ideal. Ollie pulled out a chair for her and they sat down. There were four other people at the table already. The six of them exchanged pleasantries.

"I'm surprised Bran isn't sitting at one of the center tables."

Ollie turned to her. "Oh, he is. For now, anyway." He pointed to a full table at the center of the room.

She recognized a few of the people seated there, though she was terrible at connecting actors' faces to their names. God, she really was in the wrong town. It only took a moment for her to spot Bran, deep in conversation.

"Who is he talking to?"

Ollie gave her an odd look. "That's Valerie Saunders-Newman."

"Oh!" That would explain why so many people were staring at them and why so many photographers had huddled nearby. She didn't recognize any of the cameramen and wondered if the Gazette had anyone there. Besides her.

"Is it a good idea for them to be around each other in public right now?"

"It was your idea," Ollie said.

"Mine?"

"You told Bran if he didn't have anything to hide then he shouldn't hide." He looked back at Bran and Val. "They're friends and they've known one another forever. It would only look suspicious if they avoided each other at an event as big as this one. And Bran thought, if he was gonna play it that way, he may as well go all in."

"Some people will see this as proof."

He nodded and accepted a couple of flutes of champagne from a passing tray, handing one to her, which she set down next to her half-empty glass.

"Some will, but you can't control everything. Anyway, enough about Bran. I never asked. How do you like L.A.? To be honest, I never pictured you out here."

"Where did you picture me?"

She loved the way his Adam's apple bobbed and the way color spilled into his face and up his throat. "I, uh... I assumed you were a four seasons girl. Isn't autumn your jam?"

"Yeah. How...?"

"Oh, well, you mentioned it once back at U of P." He scratched his temple and turned away, as if she'd caught him out.

"You remember that, too? I barely remember anything about college," she said, omitting the *except you* that sat on her tongue. "It's a blur of books and assignments and working two part-time jobs so I could afford the good packages of ramen."

"The spicy ones." He looked back at her, one side of his mouth curving up, and tapped his temple.

She laughed, utterly delighted. "The only way to go if you can't get hand-drawn."

She smiled at him and was rewarded with another deep flush of his skin. Blake took the opportunity to admire Ollie in his tux. "You clean up well."

"Why, thank you." He lifted his glass. "If I didn't say it before, I'm glad you're here."

"I am, too." She touched her glass to his and realized she meant it. She was glad she'd come. It was a rare glimpse into a world that, while it didn't mean much to her, was still fascinating to observe, if not a little disturbing.

Blake had never been self-conscious about her curves until she'd moved to Hollywood. Everywhere she looked people were toned and sculpted in search of an almost frightening perfection. It was as if the town had been populated with genetically engineered, hand-crafted people of extraordinary, horrific beauty. Even the receptionist at the Gazette was tall and thin, with platinum blond hair that hung down to her waist and a wardrobe that wouldn't look out of place on a runway.

Blake shook her head. That wasn't a world she wanted to live in. She turned her attention back to Ollie, who was watching the band on stage. He seemed, if not exactly comfortable, accustomed to the lights and the glamour.

"What's it been like living out here around all this?" she asked, eyeing him over the rim of her champagne glass.

"Exhausting," he said with a rueful smile. "But it has its own rewards. L.A.'s a unique place. One minute you can be at a launch party at the mansion of some hot, new director and the next you're getting coffee from a place that serves breakfast twenty-four-seven with last year's Oscar winner."

"It sounds amazing."

"It is." He ran his hand over the fine linen tablecloth. "This suits some people, like Bran."

"But not you?"

"No, but I realized pretty quickly that if I ever wanted to take a crack at writing, I needed to be where the action is."

She only recognized a handful of people in the room, but she knew many of those gathered had the power to make or break a career. Whether it was someone like Lowan Farrell or the white-haired man holding court three tables over from theirs, the seconds on the clock were precious. There were aspirants everywhere hoping to spend them wisely in the company of the right person.

"I respect that," she said

His eyes warmed as he smiled, the expression erasing the ever-present worry from his face. "It's nice to be around someone who isn't trying to hustle or find their next...whatever."

She grinned. "Who says I'm not? I am here on assignment, remember."

"Indeed." His lips curved into a grin that made his eyes twinkle and made her only dimly aware of the people around them.

The band started up a familiar song and Ollie stood gracefully, holding out his hand.

"Come on. You need to dance."

She hesitated, glancing around. "My boss's boss's boss is here."

"Everyone here is too busy plotting their next move to pay any attention." He grabbed her hand and pulled her from the chair. "Besides, you look too good not to dance."

Blake liked this side of Ollie. Laughing, she let him lead her to the dance floor.

She expected it to be awkward, but he smoothly pulled her into his arms. She settled one hand on his shoulder, the other in his hand, and let him sway her.

Around them, other guests were dancing, so she settled into his embrace and tried not to think about how perfect it felt to be there with him.

"See?" he said. "It's not so bad."

"Yeah, yeah. You were right," she teased. They danced for a while and Blake took in more of the crowd. Even on the dance floor, the conversation never ceased. No doubt, deals were being struck. Promises made. "Is being an actor as cutthroat as it seems?"

"You should probably ask Bran that question."

"I will, but you're in a unique position to observe. I remember how good you were at analyzing things. What's your take?"

Ollie hummed. "It depends. Mostly, it's just a matter of luck and being in the right place at the right time."

She understood that. More than she wanted to.

"And talent, of course," he added.

"So, why don't *you* use your own luck and jump in?"

"I have zero interest in acting."

She rolled her eyes. "You know exactly what I mean."

"Everyone is on my case today," he said, sighing heavily. "Can't we just enjoy...this?"

Smiling, he squeezed her a little tighter.

"We absolutely can, after you answer my question."

"I've only been out here a year. I don't want to jump the queue just because I have an advantage," he said, his gaze fixed over her head. She wanted his eyes back on her, but his answer didn't surprise her.

"I don't think anyone else in this room would have the same moral dilemma."

He snorted. "Perhaps not. But Bran has enough people trying to use him for this or that."

She could only imagine. It had been the same in college, from what she recalled. Back then, she saw Bran's popularity as obnoxious and entitled, had thought he acted as if the world owed him. Granting people favors, and flaunting his access and influence to get his way.

She was beginning to see it for what it was and not much had changed, except for the arena.

"I admit, I was surprised when you told me you and he were still friends. Downright shocked when I found you were working as his assistant."

"Does it change what you think of me?" Ollie stared intently into her eyes.

"Does it matter what I think?"

His jaw tightened as he looked away again. "More than you realize."

"Hey, it's a job. And you're very good at it, from what I've seen. It's not like you're—"

"Using him?"

She was taken aback by the hint of anger in his voice but, behind it, there was genuine fear.

Despite his many talents, Ollie had never seemed sure of himself. That he feared being judged by her, or anyone, shouldn't have been a surprise. But it was.

Back in Philly, he was always seeking Bran's approval, or so she had thought. Now she understood that it went much deeper.

"I think you're a rare person," she said, draping both arms around his shoulders. Slowly, Ollie wrapped his other arm around her waist and drew her closer.

"Rare?" he asked, dubious.

"Yep, unique. I still remember that short story you wrote in college. The one that won an award?"

His jaw dropped. "What? No, you don't."

"I do." She smiled, enjoying the way his hand felt splayed against her back. "There was one line that I still think about, from time to time. *To hesitate in love is to suffer the passage of time like a slow needle piercing the skin.*"

Ollie let out a short breath. "I can't believe you remember that. Though, it's probably the only line I ever wrote that I'm actually proud of."

"You should be proud, it's an evocative metaphor." It was a powerful sentiment, and it still spoke to her. Life was too short to hesitate. It was better to seize the opportunities that presented themselves, enjoy them and make the most of the brief moments.

"Come on," he said, stepping back as the song ended. He helped her off the dance floor, and they made their way back towards their table.

Blake tried to wrap her mind around how right it felt to have her hand in his.

Bran was at a nearby table when they arrived, and he gave Ollie a look that was part smug and part surprise.

"Finished schmoozing already?"

"For now," Bran replied, rising to his feet.

Beside him sat Valerie Saunders.

Bran offered Blake his seat. "You two looked good out there. Val, you know Ollie."

"Nice to see you again," Ollie said as he held out Blake's chair.

"And you," Val replied before turning to her. "You must be Blake Dillon."

She froze, hovering above her seat. "You know me?"

"Have you two met already?" Bran asked, eyeing Blake with something like suspicion.

"No, not yet," Val replied.

Blake remembered to sit down. She wasn't one to get starstruck, or so she had thought. She'd been an admirer of Val's for a while, ever since seeing her first film years ago. It had been inspiring to watch a beautiful Black woman in a leading role of a major motion picture that wasn't about trauma or struggle, but joy and hope. And had made her believe that anything was possible, that she could create a space for herself to shine, too.

She stuck out her hand. "It's such an honor to meet you."

Valerie Saunders was beautiful, with hair as dark as midnight and eyes the color of melted chocolate. Many of the women in the room appeared flawless, and Val was no exception, but her makeup, unlike others, was minimal. Her hair hung in loose waves above her bare shoulders, her simple black gown merely a showcase for her luminous, medium-brown skin.

The actor smiled, accepting the handshake. "It's nice to finally meet you. We have a mutual friend."

Blake glanced at Bran, who was watching the exchange with sharp interest.

"We do?"

"Yes," Val replied. "Deanna Lopez?"

"Oh, of course," Ollie said, touching his hand to his forehead. "How did I not put two and two together?"

"Who is Deanna Lopez?" Bran asked, looking thoroughly confused.

"Deanna runs the community center Adam and I told you about," Val replied before turning back to her. "I've been trying to get Bran to come volunteer."

Bran's shoulders, which had tensed, relaxed. "And I told you both I will, when time permits."

Val gave him a chastising look. "If you wait for that, you'll be a hundred years old. *Make* time."

"Yes, ma'am." He held up his hands in surrender.

"I didn't realize you volunteered with Play L.A.," she said to Val.

"It's a cause that's near to my heart, working with disadvantaged youth. Especially in the arts."

Bran tilted his head and crossed his arms as he spoke. "I had no idea you were helping out at the community center, Blake."

She glanced at Ollie, wondering why he hadn't mentioned running into her. "I'm working on a story."

"Yes," Val replied. "Deanna said you're looking into a predatory agency that's been targeting the kids."

"They lure them with promises of fame and cash, and then get them to sign contracts with horrible terms. Or worse."

"Worse?" Ollie asked.

"There's suggestion of trafficking. Drugs. I'm only beginning to get anywhere with the story."

"That's fucked up," Bran said, scowling. "Only assholes prey on kids."

"It's more common than you think," Ollie said, a note of something in his voice that she couldn't pinpoint.

"If you need anything, access or contacts, please reach out to me," Val offered. "Brandon has my information."

He nodded, still frowning. "Yeah, anything you need."

"I'll do that, thanks."

Val smiled brightly. "Bran tells me the three of you went to college together."

"We did." Blake accepted the glass of wine Ollie poured for her. "Though, I was a year behind."

"How long have you been in L.A.?"

"Not long." Realizing she hadn't eaten, she eyed the plate of the chocolate-covered strawberries at the center of the table. Ollie picked it up and brought it closer.

"Really?" Val glanced at Ollie and then back at her, a sly smile tugging at the corner of her mouth. "Not long?"

Bran snorted, but Val's gaze moved back and forth between her and Ollie, standing behind her.

"Long enough to gain Oliver's full interest," she said, before looking up at him, her eyes mischievous. "It's hard to come by, and I know it's not given easily."

His neck flushed as he glanced at Blake, a small smile playing on his lips. "I'm not sure what you're getting at, Val."

She laughed, and despite the fact that she was a mega star, Blake felt an almost instant camaraderie.

The lights flashed, signaling that the presentation part of the evening was about to begin.

"We should head back to our table," Ollie said.

"Stay. We have room." Val gestured to the empty seats to their left. "Two of my co-stars couldn't make it."

"Alright, thanks." Blake hadn't paid much attention to the agenda, and only just realized it was a launch party for a new independent film studio. The giant Azure Studios logo all over everything probably should have been a clue, but she had been too busy chatting with Val and people-watching.

"Is that Robert DeNiro?" she asked Ollie, keeping her voice low during the speech happening on stage.

He nodded.

"Oh, God... That's..." She nearly swallowed her tongue as Viola Davis was introduced onstage.

"Careful," Bran said, leaning close to her ear. "One might think you were actually having fun."

She rolled her eyes, but he was right. Maybe she was a little starstruck after all.

# 21

"How much did she have to drink?" Bran asked as Ollie helped Blake to her feet.

"It's not the wine," she protested, swaying in her heels. "I haven't eaten anything all day."

"That's not good." Ollie wrapped his arm firmly around her waist and was relieved when she proved to be steady on her feet. It wouldn't look good to have her drunk and stumbling around so many people. Around Bran. Too many reporters, some of which were probably her colleagues.

"No kidding," Bran said. "I'll tell Rory to bring the car to the side entrance, so we don't have to walk through that crowd. We've got food at the house, right?"

"I can whip up something."

"No, no. I drove here," she protested. "I'm fine. I should head back to my apartment anyway. I'll pick up something on my way home."

Bran met his gaze, eyebrow raised.

He nodded. "This isn't a negotiation. You're in no condition to drive."

She opened her mouth as if to protest.

An older man stopped in front of them. "Blake."

"Mr. Farrell."

He made a sound of disapproval. "Now, now. I told you to call me

Lowan."

"S-sorry, Lowan," she replied. Her words weren't as crisp as they usually were. She definitely wasn't herself.

"Lowan, have we met?" Plastering on his biggest Hollywood smile, Bran slid between them, his hand out.

The man frowned until recognition seemed to dawn on him. "Why, no. Brandon Cody," he said, shaking his hand. "Good to meet you."

A woman stepped out from behind him. "Bran is responsible for quite a bit of our revenue, thanks to his, uh, *colorful* social life."

His smile tightening, Bran shoved his hands into his pockets. "Well, you know what they say. You can't always believe what they print."

"Hello, Brandon."

"Sonja. I didn't know you were here."

"I see you've met the Editor-in-Chief at my local paper," Lowan said.

"I have," Bran responded coolly.

"Lowan, Blake is writing that feature on Bran for the Gazette."

Beside him, Ollie felt Blake rally to stand a little straighter.

"I am."

Lowan turned to Bran. "That's right. Sonja tells me you're giving us an exclusive." His gaze traveled from the arm Ollie had around Blake's waist to the protective stance Bran had taken in front of her, and back to Bran's face.

"I hope you're giving her all the access she needs," Sonja said.

The insinuation made Ollie want to throw Blake over his shoulder and get her the hell out of there. He forced himself to remain still.

Bran's smile turned lethal, and he took a step closer. "Of course. Blake has journalistic integrity. It's rare these days, and she's the only person I'd trust with my story."

Lowan narrowed his eyes as he looked between Bran and Sonja. "In that case, I can't wait to read the piece, Blake."

Ollie nudged her.

"I-I'm excited for you to read it."

Lowan clapped Bran on the arm. "Good to meet you, son."

"Later, Bran," Sonja called out as she took Lowan's arm and walked away.

Ollie saw Bran's hands ball into fists.

"That woman wouldn't know a moral code if it hit her in the face," Bran said.

"Let's get the hell out of here." Ollie guided Blake towards the exit.

The side door opened into an alley, which was thankfully empty.

"Where did you park?" He asked Blake.

She ran a hand over her forehead. "In the garage by the Gucci store."

"Where's your ticket?" Bran asked, taking her clutch from her.

"Hey! What are you doing?"

"Take her back to the house." Bran pulled the stub out of her bag and handed it back. "I'll drive her car."

"Or," he countered. "*You* ride back with her, and I'll drive her car."

Bran gave him a look he couldn't decipher.

"How about I drive myself?" she asked, taking the ticket back, her eyes flashing. "I'll be fine when I get some fries or something in me. Promise."

Ollie opened his mouth to protest, but Rory pulled up in the black SUV and jumped out to open the door. "What happened?"

Bran snatched the ticket out of Blake's hand. "Take these two back to the house. I'll be ten minutes behind you."

Frowning, Rory looked at Ollie.

"Do you work for him, or do you work for me?" Bran snapped.

Rory didn't blink. "That's an excellent question," he said, but opened the rear passenger door and offered his hand to Blake.

She stopped and looked at Bran. "Thanks for doing this."

"You're in good hands."

"Don't crash my car."

He grinned. "Promise."

Ollie was torn. He needed to get Blake home—*home* wasn't the right word, but whatever. He also didn't trust Bran to pick up the car and *not* pick up anyone else.

"Don't do anything stupid," he warned Bran, who's grin turned wolfish before he chuckled.

"Relax. I'm just getting her car. I'll be right behind you."

"Take this." Rory tossed him a baseball cap. "And give me your jacket." He handed him a hoodie.

Shrugging it on, Bran pulled the hat down and started walking down the alley.

Ollie sighed and gestured for Blake to get into the car. He got in after her and Rory closed the door.

Bran should have been his number one concern, but he couldn't be. Not at that moment.

Not when Blake needed him more.

"Let's get you fed."

Ten minutes into the drive, Blake was asleep, her head lolling against the window. Ollie couldn't stop looking at her. At the fine bones of her hands, the delicate curve of her eyebrows, or her full lips. The more time he spent with her, the harder it was to deny the attraction. It went far beyond anything physical. But then, it had always been that way.

They went over a pothole that jarred the car, and she made a sound of discomfort.

"That's it," he said to himself. He unbuckled his seatbelt and removed his jacket before unbuckling hers.

"Are we there?" she asked, half-asleep.

"Not yet. Come here." He guided her down until her head was on his thigh. "You should have room to lie down."

Once she curled up on the seat, he buckled her in as best he could and draped his jacket over her.

"Thank you. I'm not sure why I'm so out of it."

"Not eating and then drinking a couple hundred dollars' worth of champagne will do that to you."

"I only had two or three glasses."

"And?"

She turned her head, peering at him through one half-open eye. "Fifty bucks a pop?"

"For that vintage? At least."

"Sheesh," she said, returning to her original position which was, in retrospect, not an ideal place.

He was determined to keep this platonic. Not an easy task when she kept squirming against his leg.

"Didn't taste that fancy," she huffed as she finally settled into position.

Relieved, he stretched his arm along the back of the seat, denying the impulse to lay his hand on her back. But when she put her hand under her head—on his thigh—he gave in. She snuggled even closer at the contact. For a few minutes, the only sound in the car was the highway.

Ollie watched the rise and fall of his hand on Blake's back. He was so mesmerized by it, by the feel of her that close to him, he didn't realize his own eyes were heavy. The next thing he knew they were pulling up in front of the house.

When the car came to a stop, he brushed a few strands of hair from her face, unable to resist caressing her cheek lightly.

He realized he could stay like this forever, with her curled up against him, but he had to get out of the car before *he* was the one to do something stupid instead of Bran.

Rory killed the engine, and Ollie opened the door and carefully stepped out into the unusually cool night air. He unbuckled Blake's seatbelt and gently lifted her into his arms. Being careful to keep the jacket tight around her as he walked to the house.

"Hey," Rory said, opening the door. He lowered his voice when he saw Blake asleep in Ollie's arms. He arched an eyebrow. "Do I need to track him down?"

"He said he'd be a few minutes behind us," he replied, already walking to the couch in the great room. "We'll give him half an hour before we send out the cavalry."

"Meaning me?"

"Have you seen you, big guy?"

Rory grunted.

Setting Blake down, Ollie spread one of the throw blankets over her. She murmured something in her sleep, but he didn't know what it was. He gestured for Rory to follow him to the kitchen.

"Is she okay?"

"She's fine." Ollie tossed his jacket onto the back of a chair and went to the sink to wash his hands. "Tired, mostly. And the victim of good booze and not enough food."

Rory's lips twitched. "Bad combo."

"I'll let her sleep while I put together something." He opened the fridge to inspect the contents. "Hungry?"

"Nah, I'm all sorted. Ate one of those turkey wraps you made."

"They're good, right?"

"Better than the ones I'm used to, for sure."

"It's all in the seasoning." He grabbed the chicken breast he'd bought that morning and some fresh basil and set them on the counter before checking the cabinet for pine nuts. He could feel the other man's eyes on him.

"If you don't mind, I'll wait for Bran to return and then pop home to pick up my mail. I meant to earlier but I got sidetracked."

"That's fine." He washed the chicken before setting it on the cutting board. After cleaning his hands, he opened the cabinet to find the mortar and pestle set he'd spotted the other day. He poured some of the pine nuts in and began to grind them.

"Wouldn't that go faster in a blender?"

They both startled at the sound of Blake's voice.

"Jesus," Rory said. "You're a quiet one. I dinna hear ye comin.'"

She stared up at him. "Holy accent, Batman."

Rory rubbed the back of his neck. "Yeah, it gets a bit thicker when people scare the shit out of me."

She smiled. "Too freaking adorable."

A kernel of jealousy formed in Ollie's chest at the affection in her voice. "I bet that's the first time you've been called that."

The guy's face flushed a deep red. "Aye. I'm gonna go keep an eye out for Bran."

Clearly amused, she watched him retreat and then turned to Ollie, her eyes brighter than they'd been when they left the party.

"Are you making pesto?"

"Is that alright? It's late, but you need real food."

Her smile was soft. "It's totally unnecessary but I appreciate it."

"I think it's very necessary."

She bit her lip but didn't argue. "Can I help, at least?"

"Rinse and dry the basil?"

"Sure."

Blake washed her hands, and then the leaves, busying herself with the task.

The urge to reach out and touch her was almost impossible to quell. Despite his best efforts, his gaze kept sliding back to her. Damn, he was in so much trouble.

When she caught him watching her, he turned back to the counter and cleared his throat.

"Were you...uh...able to get anything useful out of the party tonight? I know you wanted to observe Bran in his world."

"A little," she replied, drying the leaves with a clean dish towel from the stack he kept by the sink. "He definitely knows how to turn it on and off, the movie star bit. I think he's a bit of an enigma."

"He's really not." He added the pine nuts to the bowl. "Once you get to know him, anyway." Then again, he thought, Bran didn't let people get that close.

He chopped some garlic, along with the basil, and blended the mixture with the pine nuts. As he poured in the olive oil, Blake inched closer. She took in a deep breath and then let it out with a sigh.

"That smells so good," she murmured. "How are you still single?"

He looked up. She was inches away, and he could feel the heat radiating from her body. His heart raced, the pulse thrumming hard and fast beneath his skin.

Shrugging, Ollie focused on the pesto. "It's not easy to form a connection when you keep a schedule like mine."

"I can understand that, but..."

"But?"

Blake bit her lip. "Bran doesn't seem to have problems finding...companionship."

Ollie snorted. "No, he does not." He stirred and tossed in a strong pinch of sea salt. "To be honest, I've never understood the whole casual sex thing."

"Really?" Her brows rose. "Same."

"Yeah?"

Her eyes were on him, her expression open and full of interest.

He wanted nothing more than to lean across the counter and kiss her, to feel her full lips pressed against his. But he couldn't. Shouldn't.

He cleared his throat. "It's nearly ready. I just need to sear the chicken."

"I could do that."

"No, I've got it. Do you want to change?"

Blake looked down at her dress. He had removed her shoes in the car, and she seemed surprised by what she was wearing.

"God, I totally do. I grabbed some clean clothes when I went home, but my bag is in my car. The only thing I have in the pool house is swimwear."

Ollie wouldn't mind her changing into that. At all. But he was a gentleman.

"Hang on." He washed and dried his hands before running to his room to grab her a t-shirt and a pair of his lounge pants. She'd drown in them, but she'd at least be more comfortable.

As he jogged back to the kitchen, he told himself it had nothing at all to do with wanting to see her in his clothes.

"Thanks." Blake took the shirt from him and held it up. "Really?"

"I get a lot of free merch."

She inspected the tee, one eyebrow raised. "I'm not sure how I feel about wearing a shirt with Bran's face on it."

Ollie snorted. "He's one of eleven people, and he's way in the back. You can pretend it's Regé-Jean Page, if it helps."

"Who?"

Shaking his head, he handed her the sleep pants. "Still stubbornly resistant to pop culture, I see. Go change so I can feed you."

"God, yes. I don't know why, but I'm starving." She started towards the powder room.

"That tends to happen when you subsist on trail mix snack packs and granola bars," he called after her.

"Stop snooping in my stuff," she called back.

He grinned.

Ollie was uncharacteristically giddy. He didn't remember the last time he'd smiled so much. He pulled the ten-inch skillet from the pot rack.

The house may have been pretentious, but it was well-appointed and didn't feel like a museum like so many others of its size and opulence. He wouldn't admit it to Bran, the price was still outrageous, but he could see the actor living there.

He was pouring olive oil into the hot pan when Blake returned.

"Your legs are obscenely long. I had to fold the cuffs three times to keep from tripping over them."

He turned to grin at her but felt it slide off his face, replaced by heat. He'd expected the clothing to be loose on her, baggy even, but she filled out the fabric in a way that had him forgetting his own name.

"Is that supposed to smoke like that?"

Or how to cook. "Dammit." H spun to the stove and removed the pan from the flame, turning down the heat.

"You must be tired, too."

"I'm tired every day," he said, sprinkling the chicken with sea salt. He ground some fresh black pepper over the flesh before gently placing it in the pan. It began to sizzle immediately.

"You're a man of many talents."

His chest warmed at the unexpected compliment. "Wait until you taste this to pass judgment."

"It smells divine. Are the plates in here?" She pointed to the cabinet above her head. He nodded, and she grabbed two. "Is the security guy still here?"

"I am, but I won't be joining you," Rory said strolling into the kitchen.

Ollie looked up, noting the frown on his face. "What?"

"You've been here for twenty-two minutes, and Bran was supposed to be behind you."

Had it been that long? "Shit." Ollie turned off the pan and wiped his hands.

"What's wrong?" Blake looked between the pair of them.

"Nothing. Probably," he added, taking out his phone. "Just Bran doing the opposite of what we agreed on." He opened up the app that allowed him to track the dude's location and enabled it. "You've got to be fucking kidding me."

"Where?" Rory asked.

"Silver Lake."

"What's in Silver Lake?" Blake asked.

"Send the address to my phone," Rory grabbed his keys from the island. "I'll go to him."

"Thanks," he said, hoping Bran was smart enough not to drag the press along with him to Val's house.

He turned back to the chicken to check the doneness. Satisfied, he set it on a clean cutting board to rest. "Do you want pasta with this? Or rice?"

"No, thanks. Maybe a salad?" Blake walked up next to him. "What, or should I ask *who* is in Silver Lake and why are you so freaked out that Bran went there?"

"I'm not freaked out," he argued, though he was. Only not for the reason Blake likely suspected. He looked at her, recognizing the journalistic instincts that had kicked in.

Whatever she saw in his eyes made her take a step back and fold her arms.

"Ollie, listen. I'm here to do a job, and that job is to write a feature on Bran. You promised me all-access."

"I know."

"So, who's in Silver Lake?"

"Val." Her brows arched sharply. "They're not... It's not what you're thinking."

"What am I thinking?" Her tone was challenging, and he hated the tension he saw on her face.

"I know...what your *editor* thinks, that Bran and Val are having some clandestine affair."

"I'm not my editor, or his boss, or hers," she said, raising her chin defiantly. "They're friends, and you say there's nothing more."

"There's more, but not in a romantic way. You saw them together tonight. Val is like a big sister to him. They've known each other forever."

"Then why all the cloak and dagger?"

"Because it's too easy to paint their relationship as something else," he said, shrugging. "Look, let me plate this up before it gets cold."

As soon as he said it, her stomach growled in agreement. She made a sound of surprise. "Well, that sounds like a plan."

Ollie rinsed some romaine and cherry tomatoes, slicing them up into a side dish. "Wine?"

"I think I've had enough for tonight."

"Oh, right." Ollie brought the plates through to the great room. "I thought we'd eat in here. More comfortable."

Blake followed him, emerging from the fridge with two bottles of sparkling water.

The patio doors were open, letting in a soft ocean breeze. The surf was a drumbeat in the distance, a steady rhythm of water breaking against rocks and shore.

They sat and ate the first few bites in silence, the only sounds the crashing waves below and Blake's occasional hums of pleasure.

"This is seriously good."

"Thanks."

After finishing half of her food, Blake put her fork down.

"That's all you're going to eat?"

"Just letting it settle." She watched him cut off a piece of chicken and bring it to his mouth.

"What?"

"Nothing." Blinking, she swallowed audibly and yawned.

"You're crashing. You should go to bed."

"I'm alright. I want to wait up for Bran and make sure my car is in one piece."

Chuckling, Ollie stood and held out his hand. "That could be hours yet. I'll wait up, you go sleep. You know you need it."

Reluctantly, she got to her feet. She was sluggish, and her fingers were a little cold. Without thinking, he took both of her hands between his and blew on her fingers to warm them.

Blake's eyes widened, and there was a moment where she seemed to hold her breath.

"Wh-what are you doing?" She sounded a little out of breath.

"Your hands are cold."

Her eyes softened. "Thanks. I hadn't noticed."

"It can happen, when you're tired. Now go get some rest. I'm sure you'll have plenty of time to yell at Bran tomorrow."

"I have a better idea, since you have to wait up anyway."

"Oh?"

"Let's watch a movie."

Okay, he was not expecting that but the idea definitely had its appeal. For one, it meant more time with Blake.

"It's been a while."

"Let's pick a classic, then. *Pride and Prejudice?*"

He groaned. "Jane Austen? When you said classic, I thought you meant *The Matrix* or *Lord of the Rings.*"

Her laugh was musical. "I'm going to go take off this makeup and, when I return, I expect popcorn and a flick. You can pick it, but make it good."

"Wow, no pressure," he said, laughing as he watched her dart across the patio to the pool house.

Ollie cleaned up after she left, checking his phone for updates from Rory. He was on the couch with a fresh bowl of popcorn and a bottle of sparkling water when a text came through.

**RORY: The wayward prince will be on his way back soon.**

**OLLIE: Thanks. Any lurkers?**

**RORY: None noted. I'll return at 8 a.m. Reach out if you need me sooner.**

**OLLIE: That's fine. See you then.**

He closed his eyes for a moment, the day catching up to him. He couldn't help but smile at the memory of dancing with Blake at the party, holding her close. Cooking for her.

Her cheek against his.

Her lips wrapped around the fork.

"Ols."

Bran's voice startled Ollie's eyes open.

"What?" Ollie said, rubbing his face. He was more tired than he realized.

"You sent Rory after me because Blake needed her stuff?" Bran asked, angry. "Also, since when do you have a tracker on my phone?"

"Since day one," he replied. He wasn't going to apologize for doing his fucking job. Sighing, he stood up. "You want to tell me what's really going on?"

"Val's going through something personal. I can't talk about it, but she needs a friend right now."

He nodded. "Fair enough."

"Popcorn for dinner?"

He glanced down at the coffee table. "No, we ate. I left something for you in the fridge."

"I'm not hungry." Bran squinted at him. "Are you...on a date right now?"

"What? No."

"You were clearly scrolling through movie choices before you conked out," he argued, hooking a thumb towards the screen. "There's popcorn. A little bubbly water. My dude, *you* are setting up for a late date night." He looked so proud, Ollie couldn't help but laugh.

"It's not a date, it's two friends hanging out."

"Hmmm."

Bran's expression turned pensive, and Ollie wondered what was going through his mind.

"It's so odd that she's here," Bran said finally.

"A little," he admitted. "You're welcome to join us."

"Oh-ho-ho, no." Hands in the air, he backed away. "I'm not about to play third wheel and crash your party. Besides, I'm not the best company."

"Why did you have go to Silver Lake tonight? You couldn't have waited until, I dunno. Daytime when it wouldn't look so shady?" He walked over to the kitchen to grab a couple of drinking glasses.

"Honestly? I went because I could." Bran's answer surprised Ollie.

"Because…you could."

"And I should be able to. Besides, I was in Blake's old beater— seriously, that car is a death trap—and I thought *no one would ever think to look for me in a piece of shit like this.*"

Ollie leaned against the island, exhaustion making his legs heavy. It wasn't that late, but his eyelids felt like they were made of lead. He wasn't sure he had the energy to stay awake for the film, despite the incredible company.

When the silence had stretched on for too long, he looked up and found Bran watching him.

"Was I supposed to say something?"

"This is the moment when you usually tell me I'm being reckless or childish."

"It's *your* life. I'm here to help you, not…" he ran out of steam. "I'm tired. I'm pretty sure Blake will want to sit down with you again tomorrow."

"Shit." Bran rubbed a hand over his face. "Noelia and I haven't even discussed what my talking points are."

"Listen to you. *Talking points.* This isn't a junket, it's Blake. Why are you so worried?"

"Because it's *Blake.*" The guy was practically whining. "You know me, man. I always put my foot in it when I talk to her. I can't *not* wind her up."

"Try."

"Help me."

"What am I supposed to do, stand in the bushes while she interviews you from her balcony?"

Bran snorted but then went very still. "That's actually not a bad idea."

"What isn't a bad idea? I don't think this place has a balcony."

"No, but you've coached me before. I need more of that," he said. And he was serious.

Ollie wanted to laugh.

"And you can be in the room, or somewhere close by. Somewhere we can see or hear each other. If I say something stupid, you can make the *I told you so* face, so I know I screwed up. I respond well to non-verbal cues, you know that. And if I do or say something stupid, you can interrupt with an *emergency.*"

"I...could do that, I guess" he said, trying not to think of all the ways this could backfire. "I'm sure Noelia will want to see the questions in advance. I'll alert her."

"Thanks. I need to be on my A game."

Blake had said she wanted the real man behind the celebrity. "I've got your back."

Bran let out a breath of relief. "Thanks, man. I owe you one."

"You owe me more than one," he said, shaking his head. "But I'll take it. Now, please go get some goddamned sleep."

"Sorry, sorry." Bran held up his hands. "I'll get out of your hair. Enjoy your not-a-date-night," he called over his shoulder as he walked away. "And don't forget to use protection."

He didn't see the finger Ollie saluted him with as he disappeared down the hall.

When Blake returned to the main house, she found Ollie sitting on the sectional in front of the soft glow of the television, his brow furrowed in concentration as he scrolled through a list of films.

She stopped in the open doorway, taking a moment to admire him. The night had turned cool, and he'd turned on the gas fireplace. The flames tipped his eyelashes in gold and cast a warm light over his angular features. She wanted to join him on the couch, snuggle up against him and watch whatever film he chose, but stayed put.

It was a dangerous knife edge they were dancing on now.

She closed the door softly behind her, and he looked over his shoulder. The way his gaze slid over her, from the messy bun atop her head, to the borrowed tee, and down to his sweatpants—so long she had to roll them up to keep from tripping herself—made her feel like she'd walked in with nothing on at all.

Blake wasn't sure anyone had ever looked at her that way, like they'd been offered a gift and didn't know how to receive it.

"I feel overdressed," he said, and she liked how rough it sounded. He cleared his throat. "Mind if I go get comfortable?"

"Please do." She walked around and curled up on the cushions, tucking her feet under. "I'll take over the search."

"Nothing too bloody," he requested.

"Not a fan of horror?"

"Horror's great. I'm not a fan of gore." He disappeared down the hall.

Blake yawned. She was beyond exhausted, but she wasn't about to pass up this opportunity. The last few days had passed by in a blur, with so much happening she was having trouble knowing where to focus.

Sonja clearly had an agenda that either Gideon knew about and didn't share or didn't know about and needed to. Then again, Brandon Peters-slash-Cody could want something from her that might be more than he'd let on. And then there was Ollie, who had been—at times—brazen with his interest, yet other times utterly shy and reserved.

She *liked* him a whole hell of a lot. More than that, she wanted him, which was the more dangerous development. And she didn't know if it was too fast, too soon, or a continuation of something they should have started years ago.

"Did you choose?" He returned, after what felt like seconds, wearing a grey Henley and navy sweats that hugged his thighs.

She realized she'd been sitting there, remote in hand, staring at the wall.

"How about *The Fifth Element*? I've seen it a hundred times, but it's a classic."

He grinned. "And, if we fall asleep, we won't miss anything. You're a genius."

"I have my moments."

They settled onto the sofa, a safe distance apart. It felt off, somehow, but Blake did her best to focus on the screen and not the way the dancing light cast animated shadows across the planes of his face.

The popcorn was salty, the sparkling water crisp and cool. Even the blanket Ollie had draped across her legs was perfectly soft and just the right weight for the temperature of the room.

It was all so fucking perfect, she wanted to scream. Or jump him.

"It's amazing how well this movie holds up," he said. "Considering its age."

"Right? It should be cheesy, but it's not."

"Ahead of its time."

She turned to him. "I never thought of it that way, but you're right. Questionable costume choices aside."

He gaped at her. "Are you blind? Ruby Rod's jumpsuits are the future of fashion."

On-screen, the character was strutting through the theater, his head framed in a ring of roses. "Okay, I take it back. I would totally rock that."

"Hell, I might, too, if I could pull it off." His grin was wide, and Blake found herself giggling.

Giggling. What had this guy sprinkled on the popcorn? This was fun. *He* was fun, and flirty, and witty, and...hot.

A wave of melancholy swept over her and she turned away from his sparkling eyes.

"What?"

She shook her head, unable to articulate why the thought of everything they'd missed—nights like these, and moments like this—had suddenly caught up to her.

"Hey." His hand was warm on her arm and she covered it with hers. "You want to call it a night?"

She squeezed his fingers. "No, I... No."

There was a beat before she felt him shifting closer. Before she knew it, Ollie's arm was around her.

His breath tickled her ear. "Is this alright?"

She nodded, not trusting her voice, and leaned into his warmth. He was solid and steady at her side, and she thought of what it might be like to have that all the time.

Could understand, suddenly, why Bran had called him to California.

Oliver Benjamin was a rock.

A sexy, brilliant, fiercely loyal pillar of everything good in a person. She felt cheated, having missed out on him for so many years.

"What is that accent?" he asked, pointing with his chin at Gary Oldman on the screen.

"No one knows," she replied, closing her eyes. She let her head drop back against his shoulder.

"You're exhausted."

"I'm okay." She opened her eyes and found him gazing down at her, his expression open and unguarded.

It was so easy to read everything on his face, the longing, the lust, and the sweet, careful hesitancy.

She looked back at him and let him see, too.

He let out a soft breath that she breathed in, her brain screaming *kiss me* even though she knew she needed to pull away.

"Blake..."

On screen, Plavalaguna began her operatic acrobatics, the music pouring through the speakers around them.

Ollie tilted his head, his brow knitting slightly. "I think...the universe is conspiring to get us to kiss."

She smiled. "I think you're right."

He searched her eyes. "Once wouldn't be so bad. Would it?"

"Not bad at all," she managed to say, her breath seesawing out of her lungs.

He cupped her cheek with a gentle hand and then held himself very still as she lifted her face to meet his.

"Just once." She brushed her lips over his.

At first, his only response was a quick intake of breath, but then he groaned and pressed his mouth against hers.

His lips were soft and warm, and she felt a familiar heat building up inside her. It had been too long since she'd been kissed like this, with such aching tenderness and hungry intensity.

She parted her lips, inviting him in, and he didn't hesitate. His tongue swept into her mouth, tasting her, teasing her, and she whimpered.

Turning her head, she broke away and tried to catch her breath.

"God..." Ollie's voice was hoarse with the same emotion and need she felt buzzing underneath her skin.

"Yeah," she replied, breathless as she met his eyes and was blown away by the desire she saw there.

Without thinking, she rose to her knees and straddled his legs.

His hands moved to her waist, guiding her even as he asked, "What are you doing?"

"No fucking clue," she replied before taking his face into her hands. She tasted the salty popcorn but, beyond that, it was only Oliver. She slid close and let him guide the kiss, drowning in the nearness of him, in the way his hands slid up and down her body—over her back, her ass, and her nape.

He wrapped an arm around her waist and hauled her close as she spread her thighs, the unmistakable feel of him hard and ready for her between her legs. Instinctively, she rocked against him and the sound he made drew an answering one from her.

Pleasure pooled at her center, threatening to spiral out beyond the point of no return.

She wanted him. Wanted him *inside* her, and that thought alone was enough to force her back.

She sat up and stared down into his wide eyes.

His grip on her was tight. It loosened as they both came back to themselves.

"Christ." He chuckled, running a hand over his face. "Once, my ass. It felt like we've been building up to that for years."

She smoothed her hands down his chest before letting them drop to her sides. Blake pointedly did *not* look at the bulge resting next to her inner thigh, nor the wet spot that had formed there, though it made her mouth water.

Her nipples were stiff and aching, poking at the infuriatingly soft fabric of his shirt, and she watched Ollie fight to avert his gaze from them.

His hands twitched on her waist, and his thighs were rock hard under her ass.

It felt as if they were standing on a precipice. Neither were prepared to leap, but they weren't ready to step back either.

Lifting her leg, Blake eased herself back to the sofa, settling against the arm. She stretched her legs along the cushion, surprised when Ollie stretched out alongside her.

He wrapped an arm around her legs and laid his head on her thigh, sighing contentedly.

"Comfy?"

"Hmmm, almost." He reached underneath himself and groaned.

It took a moment for her to realize his problem. A laugh bubbled up from her throat. "Oops."

"Yeah, oops." He laughed softly.

Without thinking, she lifted a hand to his hair, her fingers sifting through the strands the way she had wanted to do years ago. It was as thick and soft as she'd always imagined.

"It's almost impossible to resist you," he murmured against her leg. "And now that I know what your mouth tastes like, how it feels..."

"I know," she agreed.

"But it's worth it." He shifted and met her gaze. "You're worth the wait."

So was he, but it wouldn't be long. She could resist the look in his eyes and the way he licked his lips, as if he could still taste her.

They had waited years. What was a few more days?

Blake awoke with a mild headache. A triumph, considering the day and night she'd had. She was thirsty and levered herself into a sitting position, intending to go grab some water, when she spotted a bottle on the nightstand along with some ibuprofen.

*Ollie*, she thought and smiled.

After a quick trip to the *en suite* to pee and brush her teeth, she downed a couple of tablets and half a bottle of spring water. Then pulled out her laptop, relieved when it booted right up. It had been giving her fits, lately.

It was early, and she doubted anyone else was awake. Her thoughts swirled around the events of the last twenty-four hours, and she woke up thinking of everything Ollie had told her about Bran's relationship to Val and her history with Sam.

It was a lot. A quick web search had revealed the salacious details surrounding Sam and Val's very public courtship, as well as a frightening account of Sam's ex-wife and everything she put him through.

She had to be honest with herself. After Ollie had divulged the origin of Val's marriage to Sam, her opinion of Val had dimmed a little. Reading through article after article about how it really happened, she held Val in a new, somewhat shinier light.

It also drove home the point that Ollie had been making during dinner. Blake could see how the press, particularly Sonja and her ilk, would pounce on any hint of impropriety in the Saunders-Newman household. She also noted the disparity between the number of articles condemning Val for her alleged behavior compared to the ones about Sam, Most had painted him as a victim, trapped in a loveless marriage. Others portrayed Val as some kind of *exotic* seductress, using him to further her career. Blake couldn't help but to roll her eyes. The more things changed, the more they stayed the same.

Linking Bran and Val romantically might make it appear as if she were hitching her wagon to a brighter, younger star. And for Bran, it would look like he was using her status and position to bring legitimacy to a career that had, to date, been predominantly mindless action films.

She saw it all so clearly, now. The story had the potential for real damage no matter which way you looked at it.

An email popped into her inbox that had her frowning.

*From: N. Mokeyane*
*To: bdillion@lapostpress.org*
*Subject: Request for questions*
*Blake,*

*We request that you provide any questions you plan to ask Bran during the interview process in advance so that he will be better prepared to provide the answers you seek.*

*Please contact me immediately if you have any questions or concerns.*

*Yours truly,*
*Noelia Mokeyane*
*Creative Relations*

She opened a new document. After conversations she'd had with Ollie and Gideon, she'd expected something like this. Annoying as it was, it made sense that Noelia Mokeyane would want to pre-screen any further questions. After all, Bran's reputation was on the line, but so was Blake's.

She had to be careful, be sure to stay on-topic and keep him comfortable enough to let his guard down. He had matured, she knew that. How much remained to be seen. She typed out a few softball questions. *When did you know you wanted to be an actor? What drew you to your latest role? Where do you hope to see yourself in five years?* Then, she tossed in some more probing ones, considering each one carefully before sending off the email.

That task done, she got showered and dressed.

Entering the main house, she was surprised to find Hans in the kitchen. The island was covered in trays containing small clumps of oats, dried fruit, and nuts, and the air smelled of cinnamon.

"Is that...homemade granola?"

"Oh, hey, sunshine! Good morning. And yes, it is. Apple-walnut-cinnamon, slightly sweetened with monk fruit."

"What the hell is a monk fruit?" She scrunched up her nose.

"It's every Hollywood chef's secret weapon. Shhh." Winking, he held a finger over his lips.

She laughed. "Your secret is safe with me."

"They're out by the pool."

"Thanks, chef."

She snagged a piece of the warm granola, marveling at the flavor and crunch as she walked through the patio doors.

She found Ollie and Bran seated at the glass table, which was covered in papers again. When she got closer, she realized they were more scripts.

"Is this what breakfast looks like for movie stars?" she said, setting her laptop down in a clear spot.

It was pure coincidence that her chair was next to Ollie's.

His smile for her was soft. "I'm helping Bran narrow down a piece of bait."

Memories of last night's kisses sent a shiver through her, but she sat down and pulled the pitcher of orange juice towards her.

Ollie snuck a glance her way, a ghost of a grin playing on his lips as if he could see her thoughts.

"Bait for...?"

"Oscar bait," Bran said, pointing at one of the pages. "Take this one. A family medical drama set in an alternate universe."

She swore these people spoke a completely different language. "The academy has a type?"

"Oh, yeah, and it's got some strong female characters, which I like. It would be a chance to work with Val again."

He said it matter-of-factly, but she couldn't help but notice the way his eyes sparkled when he said her name. Not with longing or lust, but with...admiration. Pride.

"Well, that sounds great," she said, setting her notepad and pen on the table. She took the glass Ollie offered and poured some juice for herself. "I look forward to talking with you about your process."

He nodded, relaxing a bit. "Me too."

"I got the email from your publicist this morning, and sent over the questions, as requested."

Bran frowned. "Oh?" He looked at Ollie, or at least he turned his head that way. His sunglasses were so dark it was impossible to see his eyes, even in the bright morning sun.

"She emailed and let me know they were received, thanks. She hasn't had a chance to go over them yet," Ollie said.

She had been expecting that. "No worries. I can start with you."

"With me?" His brows rose. "What can I tell you that I haven't already?"

"Lots," she said, smiling at the panicked expression on his face. She took pity on him. "Okay, then. Bran, why Ollie?"

"Why Ollie, what?"

"Why did you hire someone with zero experience to work in such a pivotal position on your team?" she asked, her pen poised above her notebook.

Bran ran a hand over his hair and looked away, contemplative. "Because I've always been able to trust him," he finally said, quietly. "And I needed someone who would keep me grounded. Plus, he needed to be out here. In L.A."

"I did?" Ollie asked. "I mean, I probably do, but why do *you* think that?"

"Well, if you ever decide to pull the trigger and do something with the insane amount of talent you have."

Ollie's laugh was devoid of humor. "I keep telling you there's no need to spew sunshine all over me. I don't need you to butter me up to get me to stay."

Bran sat up and removed his glasses, his eyes narrowed as he stared at Ollie.

There was an uncomfortable stretch of silence and Blake held her breath, watching a silent exchange between the two men.

"I wish…" Bran let out a harsh breath before continuing. "I wish you could see you the way I do, man. You might realize how gifted you are."

Ollie appeared stunned, looking at him with wide eyes. He seemed both proud and embarrassed, like a student whose teacher had said something particularly kind about him.

She found herself smiling too, despite the oddity of someone like Brandon Peters dropping his guard in front of her.

It struck her then, that there was something special between these two, something that had nothing to do with the glitz and glamour of the movie business. They had an understanding, a level of trust between them that seemed almost palpable. Like brothers.

She cleared her throat. "Ollie, you've had to learn on the job."

"Yeah."

"What's been the most challenging thing about it?"

"Don't say me," Bran warned, but his tone had lightened.

"I thought this was about telling the whole truth," Ollie joked. "I suppose it's the schedule. It may not seem like it because you're here during a bit of down time."

"You call this week downtime?" Between their time on set and the event last night, she was exhausted. It had only been a few days.

Ollie pulled out his phone. "A week ago today, Bran had been on set for five hours already."

"Was that after the night we did twenty-three takes of the tank scene and I fell into bed at four in the morning?"

"That's the one," Ollie replied.

"You were on set until three and had to be back there," she calculated the math, "four hours later? Why not just crash in your trailer?"

"That's what I said!"

Bran shook his head. "If I slept on the lot every time I had a short night between calls, I'd never go home. Besides, there's always the chance the morning call will change and then you'll have stayed for nothing."

"That happen a lot?" she asked, taking notes.

"Depends on the project." Bran removed his sunglasses and tossed them on the table. His shoulders were tense, and she wondered what about this line of questioning was getting to him.

"Anyway, the schedule isn't just call sheets and red carpet stuff, it's..." Ollie let out a breath. "Meetings with studio execs, Bran's agent, his publicist, whom you've met. A stylist for a shoot or a designer for a fitting. It's working in his trainer, his nutritionist, and finding time for him to actually eat and work out."

"Who handles Bran's travel?"

"Me."

"What about his finances?"

"I take care of the everyday stuff, mortgage, phone bills, etcetera, and his financial advisor handles his accounts."

She had a hunch. "Who works with the financial advisor?"

"That would be Oliver," Bran said, looking at Ollie intently.

"And with all of that, when do you find time to do...you? Your entire life seems to revolve around his."

Ollie opened his mouth but then closed it. She could see the war raging behind his eyes. He wasn't happy with her at the moment, but she didn't particularly care.

She wanted them both to understand everything that Ollie had been sacrificing. It was also a good angle to lead into the story: best friends navigating the intricacies of the business together.

"I've been trying to get you to finish your script, *your* work," Bran said, his voice a little gravely. His laugh was self-deprecating. "Not sure how the fuck you're supposed to do that when you spend all of your time chasing after my dumb ass."

"Bran."

"No, man," he cut him off. "You know how much I love you but I've been a dick about this. I didn't realize..." He ran a rough hand down his face. "All that shit you're doing? The small stuff is assistant stuff, and it's beneath you. I shouldn't be telling you to pick up my fucking dry cleaning. And the rest of it? That's high level shit. Manager shit."

"You pay me as much as most managers make in this city," Ollie said, his voice calm. "And I don't *have* to pick up your dry cleaning."

"No, but I know why you do."

She sat back and let this scene play itself out, content to watch and take notes.

"You do it," Bran continued, turning to him, "because you're a good fucking dude. You do it because you're my best friend. You *do* it because you've always tried to make my life easy, even at the expense of your own. You've always bailed me out."

"You bailed me out first."

The look Bran gave him was somewhere between anger and sorrow. "I told you. You *never* have to make up for that. Or thank me for it."

Whatever *it* was had the two of them breathing hard and staring at each other in another silent conversation.

She closed her notebook and set down the pen. "If you don't want to tell me, I understand, but... I really want to know what happened that forged this incredible bond between you."

Both Ollie and Bran turned to her, equal expressions of surprise on their faces as if they'd forgotten she was there.

They exchanged a nervous glance.

Ollie took a deep breath. "Maybe another time."

Deflated, she nodded. "Sure."

Silence descended, thick and fast, and she realized that was all she was going to get from them for now.

Ollie poured himself a cup of coffee and held up the carafe, his brows raised.

"Sure, thanks." She watched as he poured for her and then went back to his work.

While things were quiet, she opened her messages and looked for the name that Micah had given to her, Yara Bujold. Launching a new tab in her browser, she searched the web for a contact, shocked by some of the results that came back.

*Pop star, missing and presumed dead, turns up in Philadelphia*

*Music mogul Marcus Kaine freed on bail, awaits trial on charges of assault and false imprisonment.*

"Jesus Christ."

"Something wrong?"

"No," she reassured Ollie. He seemed unconvinced. She checked the time. It was noon in Philly.

"Do you mind if I make a call? I can go inside, if it will bother either of you."

"Go ahead," Bran said.

Ollie gestured for her to continue.

The only number she found for Bujold was a home in the suburbs belonging to an older couple. Possibly related. There was also a notice of an open mic night at a bar that Yara hosted. Blake decided to call there first.

"Skinners," a guy answered after two rings.

"Hi, my name is Blake Dillion. I'm trying to reach Yara Bujold, I hope I'm pronouncing the last name right."

"Yara? Hang on." Blake heard his next words from a distance, as if he'd moved the phone away. "Hey, is Cam here? Someone's asking for Yara. Sounds like a lawyer or something."

Blake jotted down the name, Cam.

"This is Camden Skinner, who am I speaking with?"

"Mr. Skinner, my name is Blake Dillion. I'm with the Los Angeles Gazette and I'm trying to reach Yara Bujold about a story I'm working on."

"What story?" His tone was decidedly less than friendly.

Ollie turned a quizzical look her way and was listening intently.

"I'd prefer to talk about that with Ms. Bujold."

"She's my..." he hesitated. "We're together. You can talk to me."

As he spoke, Blake ran a quick search for Camden Skinner and came across a photo of him and Yara smiling behind a bar she assumed was inside Skinners.

"I understand," she replied quickly, happy to be dealing with a protective significant other rather than someone who merely despised her profession. "I'm writing a story about a company here in Los Angeles, Diamond Moon Enterprises, that has some shady dealing with minors wanting to break into the entertainment industry." She'd put it as delicately as she could.

There was a soft curse on the other end of the phone. "These people," Skinner said. "Yeah, Yara will definitely want to talk to you. Is there a number where she can reach you?"

"Of course!" she said, relieved. She gave Skinner her number. "She can call me anytime, I'm eager to move on this story."

"It's good that someone out there is paying attention to what's going on," he replied. "Yara will reach out to you."

"Thanks, Mr. Skinner."

"Not a problem. Have a good one."

Blake hung up, feeling like she'd moved a step closer to getting vital information on how these predators operated from someone who'd been in their clutches and escaped. She just hoped young Belinda wouldn't have to resort to faking her own death to get her life back the way Yara had.

"I didn't mean to eavesdrop," Ollie said.

"It's not like I'm sitting right next to you or anything." She winked and he visibly relaxed.

"You were talking to someone named Camden Skinner?"

She frowned. "Yeah, in Philadelphia. Why?"

He smiled and held up his finger. "One sec." He picked up his phone and tapped the screen a few times before bringing it to his ear. "Hey, Rory, are you on your way? No, nothing's wrong, but I may need you for something." He smiled at her. "Great. See you soon."

# 25

Ollie rarely thought about that night anymore, the one that changed everything. Beyond the shame and guilt it left behind, it had forged a bond between him and Bran he couldn't explain. Not in a way that would make sense to anyone.

When Blake asked about it, he'd half-expected Bran to tell her it was none of her business. But then he realized he'd never spoken the full truth about it either. Not to anyone, not since it happened. He'd never explained why or how he'd ended up floating face down in the pool in the basement of the university's athletics pavilion.

"I remember feeling completely useless," he said suddenly. He looked up and met her confused expression. "You asked how Bran and I got so close."

She nodded and sat back in her chair.

Across from him, Bran had lifted his head but Ollie didn't turn to look at him.

"Things at home had never been particularly great, but everything went sour my senior year in high school. By the time I got to college, I was a mess. Bran seemed to find it easy. He didn't need a transition period. Most of the kids I knew didn't, just me. And I struggled."

"A lot of people do," she said, her voice soft with compassion.

"I didn't know what I wanted to major in. I had no interest in anything or anyone. I had finally reached the point of wanting it all to just...stop." He looked up and caught her startled gaze. He wanted her to see it all, unwilling to hide this from her anymore. "And so, I decided maybe it would be better if...I just wasn't around anymore."

Her hand went to her mouth, her brow drawn down sharply over flashing eyes.

He recognized that look, the war between horror and rage. He'd seen it before.

"Ollie," she breathed quietly.

"I had a guy in my chem class who was always offering me stuff. You know me, I never... Anyway, I bought something from him. I don't even remember what it was."

"Quazepam," Bran supplied.

"Of course you'd remember." The joke landed like a brick, and he immediately regretted making it.

"Yeah, the name of the drug my best friend had pumped out of his stomach after I found him floating unconscious in a pool is not something I'm ever going to forget."

"I didn't go through with it," he argued. "I took one of the pills, but I thought of how my family would react. That I'd be even more of a burden on them by committing this...act...and they would hate me even more than they already did."

He turned to Blake. "I didn't go through with it because I didn't want to give them the satisfaction of proving them right."

"But you took one of the pills?" she asked, a tremor in her voice.

"And then, idiot that he is, he decided to go swimming."

"I didn't realize how potent they were. And since my tolerance for, well, anything has always been low, it hit me hard." He looked at Bran. "He found me like that."

"I'd been texting him because I'd locked myself out of our room," Bran said, his breaths coming short. "If I hadn't left my key in the room, I...I..."

"But you did. He did," she said, turning to him. "And...everything is okay now?"

Ollie knew what she meant. "The school wouldn't allow me to return unless I agreed to counseling, which I'm grateful for. I've been seeing someone ever since."

She smiled with obvious relief. "I'm glad. What about your family? They didn't want to keep you at home after that?"

"They don't know. I never told them."

"Still?" Bran seemed surprised.

"No. And since I wasn't a minor, they were never notified."

"How is that possible?"

"My mom was Ollie's emergency contact," Bran informed her.

Ollie watched her process that information, knowing she probably had no trouble putting the pieces together.

"I was in a very dark place," he said. "That night could have been a lot worse, but Bran found me." He swallowed around the lump in his throat, forever in awe of his own good fortune. "He pulled me out of the pool and called an ambulance. And here we are."

Blake's eyes had filled with unshed tears, but the corners of her lips tugged up in a gentle smile. "I'm *so* glad, Oliver." She turned to Bran as if seeing him in a new light. "I really get it now."

Ollie felt a swell of emotion within him. He nodded, blinking back the sudden tears that gathered in his eyes.

"What bends the bough doesn't always have to break it," Bran said.

She smiled. "You know, I didn't believe you'd watched it until now."

"Watched what?" Bran said, frowning.

"*I Am My Own Country*," she replied, and Ollie's heart jumped into his throat.

He turned to Bran and tried to catch his gaze.

"The film?" she added, blinking innocently.

"Oh! I totally forgot it was a quote from one of Ollie's boring old period flicks. God, no. I fall asleep within ten minutes of one of those. Wouldn't mind shooting one, though. The Academy loves them."

Her gaze swung to Ollie, full of mischief, and he had to bite the inside of his cheek to keep from laughing.

"You know," she said, gathering her things as she stood. "I think I'm going to go get some work done while you go over those questions. I'll see if Hans will let me take a bowl of that granola."

"Help yourself to whatever you like," Bran said, oblivious.

"Thank you."

Ollie watched her retreating form until she disappeared down the path and into the pool house.

"You're drooling again," Bran teased.

"Fuck," he swore, exhausted from the emotional rollercoaster he'd been on in the last few minutes. "You're an idiot."

"What's wrong? I thought that went fairly well, considering," Bran said. "Though you and I have a lot to discuss about your future in my employ."

That sent a fresh wave of panic racing through him, and he put his head in his hands. "I need a vacation."

"Dude, you're freaking out. Chill."

He looked up at him. "You don't even understand what just happened."

"You want to pump the breaks on the melodrama and fill me in?"

"I just...I can't believe I talked about that night. With her." He felt exposed, vulnerable in a way he hadn't felt in years.

Bran reached across the table and squeezed his hand. "I'm proud of you, for what it's worth."

"It's worth a lot." He squeezed back. "But I don't want you to think that night is the only reason I'm out here with you. I'm better with you around. You...you push me, too. Keep me from disappearing into the shadows."

"Hey, Bran said, getting to his feet. "My light shines enough for both of us, for now. Pretty soon, you'll start twinkling, too."

Blake didn't know whether to laugh, cry, or pack up her shit and go. Ollie confused her. One minute, he was sweet and funny and looking out for her, the next he was breaking her heart by opening up about a dark chapter in his past. He seemed to withdraw into himself as he spoke, and she'd never seen him like that before.

Then there was Bran who seemed to have no problems reaping the benefits of Ollie's gratitude. Whether he felt bad for that or not, acknowledged it or not, the fact was that he'd allowed it to go on. Ollie being at his beck and call.

However misguided, those two looked out for each other no matter what. She was glad Ollie had someone like that in his life, even if she felt he was being taken for granted.

She tossed her stuff on the bed, and there was a soft knock on the door.

Blake wasn't sure if it was wise to be alone with Ollie. Wasn't sure how she should even feel about last night, or this morning.

These two men had just sat there and explained that Ollie did everything for Bran. That would likely include coaxing the reluctant reporter to come to La Jolla and do this story on him.

She opened the door.

It wasn't Ollie.

"Can we talk?" Bran said.

If there had been any trace of the movie star about him, she probably would have told him she was busy. Instead, she stepped back and let him in.

He strolled through the French doors, his hands on his hips, and turned to face her. "I know I can't change what I said or did back at school, but I want you to know that I'm sorry. My actions hurt you and put you in a difficult position with the paper and with the Dean and, honestly, none of that crossed my mind. The only thing I was focused on at the time was playing with my team. Your article about the scholarships would have stopped that from happening."

"Would you do it again?" she asked. "If we were back in college now, would you sell me out so you could go play soccer?"

To his credit, he didn't answer right away. "Honestly, yes. I'd like to say no, but there was a lot of pressure on us to win the championship, and a lot of guys were dependent on that money to get their education. Ollie included."

She let that sink in. "Thanks for being honest."

He shrugged. "I try to be that all the time. It's just that people don't always like what they hear."

"Fair enough." She sat on the small sofa in the living area.

Bran took one of the armchairs. "I'm curious about something, though. The texts Ollie sent for me." His mouth curved into a half-smile. "What gave it away?"

"Ollie is... His brain works differently than yours, the way he communicates."

"He's different from anyone I know."

"Same," she admitted. "I wish he hadn't lied for you."

"As long as you recognize that he did it for me. He'd do anything for me."

"And you take full advantage of that."

Bran took a deep breath and let it out slowly. "You're right. And I'm going to work on that, but I came in here to... Look, Blake, I value his friendship just as much as he values mine. He's been loyal to me like no one else in my life, and I'm sorry if that's interfering with whatever might be happening between the two of you."

She startled. "The two of us?" Had Ollie said something? For some reason, the idea scattered her. She'd thought they'd agreed to keep whatever was happening under wraps for the time being.

His grin was slow. "I'm not blind. And I know him, probably better than anyone."

She felt her cheeks heat up.

"It's nothing, yet. We're just getting to know each other again."

He nodded. "Whatever happens between you, don't let my mistakes ruin it. He's an amazing guy, and he deserves to be happy."

"As a friend, you're the best he could have. But as his employer, you need to treat him better."

"I know. I am. I will," he promised. "Full disclosure, he's going to be coaching me on the answers to the questions you sent over. And on anything else you throw at me *on the record*. I'm not great at talking on the fly. I'll say something that...your readers might misconstrue."

"I won't misrepresent you."

"You'll try not to," he countered. "Truthfully, I don't trust your paper."

"Nor should you," she agreed.

"You understand my dilemma, then. Sonja is looking for anything she can legally print that will help her accomplish her goal."

"Which is?"

He spread his hands. "To ruin me, I suppose."

"What did you do to her that she has it out for you like this?"

He smiled, but there was no humor in it. "It's what I *didn't* do."

Bran held her gaze and, for a long moment, she wasn't sure what she was supposed to surmise from his words. And then it clicked.

"She wants to sleep with you?"

"I mean, who doesn't?" he joked, but only half-heartedly.

"I don't," she stated flatly. "God...Bran, that's..."

"Not as uncommon as you might think," he said. "Welcome to Tinseltown."

"Is everything rotten in this place?"

"Not everything." He relaxed into the chair. "A lot of people are doing a lot of good work, things to help the communities here and elsewhere."

"Like Play L.A."

He nodded. "And I need to get off my ass and get involved there. What's up with the other story you're working on? Is it for the Gazette?"

"I'm not sure if they'll run it," she confessed. "I'm not sure if I *want* them to. Sonja has already shot down my pitch."

"But you're invested in it?"

"It's too important not to be, and it's not dissimilar to what you were talking about with Sonja. People take advantage of young artists and actors, promising them work or exposure in return for favors."

"Favors." He snorted. "And someone's targeting the kids at the center?"

"At least five that I know of. I'm waiting to speak to someone back in Philly who may have an insight into the company."

"What's the name?"

"Diamond Moon."

Bran frowned. "I'm not familiar with it."

"I am." Rory stood in the doorway, Ollie behind him.

"I just got an email," Ollie said. "One of the kids in my writing group was just approached by them."

"They were?"

The two men walked inside.

"They want him to write lyrics for a group their putting together, but Deanna told Calvin he's too young to sign anything without parental consent."

"How old is he?" Blake asked.

"Fourteen."

"Fuck." Pulling out his phone, Rory dialed a number. "Hey Pierce, it's me. Can you find out more about a company called Diamond Moon? No, this is a hunch." After a minute of confirming the name, and imparting a sense of urgency, he hung up.

"Not that I don't love the help, but what do you know about Diamond Moon?" Blake asked.

"I don't, not yet," Rory replied. "I did some work with my cousins in Philadelphia for a bit. A while back, they had a case that dealt with a company that used similar tactics. I asked them to look into it. I should have something soon."

"That's great," Blake said, her head spinning at the sudden flurry of activity.

Bran stood. "Are we okay for now?"

"Yeah," she replied. "I'll schedule the photographer for the day after tomorrow if that works with your schedule."

"It's fine," Ollie replied.

"If you need me, I'm going to hit the gym." Bran stepped past a confused Ollie, giving him a pat on the shoulder before he pushed Rory out the door and closed it behind him.

Blake let out a surprised laugh. "He's not subtle."

Ollie squeezed the back of his neck. "That he is not." He turned to look at her, sheepish.

"Come sit." She patted the sofa beside her.

She expected him to keep to the other end and was pleased when he settled beside her. Their knees were inches apart and she wanted to close the gap and feel the heat of his golden skin against hers.

He wasn't shy, she realized. He simply navigated the world with a tremendous amount of respect for the people that he cared for. It was a revelation, knowing she was now one of them.

"I assume Bran didn't do or say anything stupid, since I didn't find him on the floor with your pen shoved into his eye."

She laughed. "That's...graphic. But, yeah. He actually apologized. For everything."

He held her eyes. "Again, I'm sorry, too. I think I'm so used to being his stand in that I let him... No." He stopped himself from saying whatever he'd been about to say. "This was on me. And I am sorry."

"I forgave you already. I don't think I realized—I mean, how could I have?—what you went through. Or what you mean to each other. I've never had that sort of bond with anyone."

"But you did," Ollie said. "You do. With your grandfather."

She smiled, emotions welling up inside at the thought of the many moments she shared with her granddad. "You're right, of course."

She could feel his eyes on her, but she studied the movement of the curtains, caught in the breeze coming through the window. "Did you know I had a massive crush on you back at school?"

Ollie made a choking sound that drew her gaze up to his.

"What?"

She smiled. "I had it so bad for a while, but you didn't see me that way. Or so I thought."

He was staring at her, his eyes dark with something she hadn't seen in them before. Something she wasn't sure she'd ever seen in him. "Blake..." Her name was a low husky word.

Her lips parted, remembering the feel of his on them. "Oliver."

His mouth curved into a soft smile. "We should probably—"

He stopped talking as Blake leaned in, ever so slowly and closed the distance between them.

She savored the softness of his lips and was thrilled when he pressed harder, a soft groan in the back of his throat. When she pulled away moments later, breathless and flushed, she couldn't stop staring at how red his lips were now. "Sorry," she said, not sorry in the least. "I...needed to do that."

He took a deep breath. "I'm sorry we stopped."

She shook her head, confused by her own actions. "I just wanted to remember what it was like to kiss you."

His dark-flecked eyes shimmered. "Was it as good as last night?"

She took a deep breath and met his gaze squarely. "It was even better, Oliver."

Lifting his hand, he curled it around her nape, tilting his head as he drew her close again. This time, his warm tongue pressed between her lips, teasing her own. He took his time, taking her apart like an expert until she was panting, her pulse like rapid fire beneath her skin.

She broke the kiss this time, needing air.

Ollie's smile was a mix of surprise and pleasure. "I would have done anything to be with you back then."

His words had an undercurrent of something serious that she sensed he hadn't meant to say out loud.

She arched a brow, considering him. "Anything?"

"You have no idea."

Oh, but she wanted to know. She wanted to tease it out of him with more kisses and find an excuse to get his hands on her.

Unfortunately, her phone rang. She cursed when she glanced over and saw who was calling.

"Sorry, I have to take this."

He rose slowly to his feet and turned away, but not before she caught the bulge denting the smooth line of his shorts. This was becoming a habit.

She flushed head to toe with unbanked heat. *Later.*

"I should, uh..." Ollie stopped at the door and looked at her. "To be continued?"

"It better be," she said picking up the call. "Hi, Gideon."

"Blake. Why did I just get a call from Yara Bujold asking me if you work here?"

Shit. "I can explain."

"Fuuuuuuuuuuck," Bran groaned looking down at his tablet.

Before Ollie could ask what the problem was, his phone began to ping. He opened his alerts and went ice cold.

**MYSTERY WOMAN ACCOMPANIES ACTOR BRANDON CODY HOME FROM INDUSTRY EVENT. THE PAIR HAVEN'T BEEN SEEN IN DAYS.**

**DID VAL SAUNDERS PLAY MATCHMAKER AT A RECENT EVENT AT THE BEVERLY WILSHIRE? ACCORDING TO REPORTS, SHE WAS SEEN INTRODUCING HIM TO A YOUNG ACTOR WHO LEFT THE PARTY DRAPED ALL OVER HIM. IS IT LOVE OR JUST ANOTHER HOOK UP?**

The photos were unmistakable—Blake with her arm around Bran's shoulders as he helped her to the car. Bran, Val, and Blake chatting at their table. Ollie was conspicuously cut out of both pics. He did recognize himself with Blake on the dance floor, though the shot had been cropped to cut out everything but his back and shoulder, with her hand there. Another dancer obscured any view of Ollie's hair or skin, which would have been a dead giveaway. This was deliberate.

"It's only a matter of time before other members of the press figure out who she is," Rory said, his phone to his ear.

"They know who she is," he replied, his stomach sinking with a sickening feeling. "They're just waiting for the right time to release the information."

Bran narrowed his eyes. "The interview?"

"The interview."

"What the fuck?" Bran said, knitting his fingers atop his head. "What did I do to Sonja that she would go to such lengths to discredit me? Blake is completely innocent in all of this."

"Bran, you're only crime was refusing to fuck someone who hadn't heard the word no in years."

Rory ran a hand across his mouth. "Okay, let me see if I've understood everything so far. The editor of the Gazette has a personal grudge against you, Bran, and she's using Blake and the interview as an excuse to dig up dirt?"

"She might be hoping Blake will find something juicy to use in the write-up, but there's no way Blake would do Sonja's dirty work."

"Agreed," Rory said, surprising him. Bran too, apparently. "What? I'm a decent judge of people, and she's a good sort."

"She is," Bran agreed.

"How do we stop her identity from being released? Her colleagues will drag her through the mud."

Bran looked down at his phone, buzzing in his hand. "It's Clark." Rather than put it on speaker, Bran walked to the edge of the pool and took the call privately.

"He alright?" Rory asked.

"None of us are at the moment." Ollie looked back towards the pool house. There wasn't any movement inside, and he wondered if Blake had seen the photos yet. Given how little time she spent on social media, it was unlikely.

Every cell in his body told him he needed to protect her and keep her out of harm's way. The problem was, she was in the thick of it. There was no keeping her away, and he knew she'd resent being kept out of the loop.

"I'm going to get Blake," he said.

"You think that's wise?"

"If we want to keep breathing," Ollie replied on his way over to the pool house.

He found Blake sitting on the floor in her bedroom, her back against the bed. Her laptop was open to TinselTalk news where the picture of her, Bran, and Val was on the front page.

"I thought I was going to get fired," she said without looking up.

"Would that be a blessing or a curse?" Ollie asked, easing down to sit by her side. The way her head automatically rested on his shoulder shouldn't have felt as natural as it did.

She gave a soft laugh. "That's the million-dollar question, isn't it?"

"What happened?"

She lifted her head and Ollie felt the loss of her heat like a blow.

"My editor, Gideon, is as confused as I am. He saw the photos and was about to tear me a new one but was instructed to tell *me* to, and I quote, keep up the good work." This time her laugh was brittle. "Fuck this job. Fuck that paper. Fuck it."

He was glad to see the fight in her. Blake had never been one to give in easily. "I have some other news that might cheer you up."

She turned to look at him. "Sonja's been arrested for having bad hair?"

He chuckled. "No, but Rory thinks there's a definite connection between that case he worked on in Philly a couple of years back and Diamond Moon."

"Really?" Her entire demeanor changed, the fire returning to her eyes.

"There you are."

Smiling, she paused. "*Rory* worked on a case in Philly. I can't believe I didn't put two and two together. Hang on." She pulled her laptop between her legs and opened up a file. "He couldn't be referring to Yara Bujold's case, could he?"

"I'm not sure but you can ask him. He's out on the patio with Bran."

She stared at the wall opposite them. "This is...wow. If Diamond Moon is connected to Yara's case, to Marcus Kaine, then this crosses state lines. We could be looking at federal crimes, here."

"Rory will be at your disposal," he promised.

"I can't afford to pay him."

"I can."

She was shaking her head before he could get the words out. "No, I can't allow you to do that."

"Allow? Blake..." He took her hand. "Am I wrong in thinking that there's something here?"

Her smile warmed him from the inside. "I hope so, but then I've kind of carried a torch for you for a long time."

Fuck, his heart had wings and was about to fly right out of his chest.

"Then, let me do this. It's not just about you, I care about the center. I work with those kids every week. I'm not going to sit by and let some fucking lowlife use their dreams against them. Not when I can do something to help protect them."

She pulled her bottom lip into her mouth as if she were trying to hold back words.

"What?"

Her eyes were half-lidded. "When this is all over, you and me are going to need some serious alone time," she said, her voice a bit raspy.

Ollie liked hearing how much he affected her. "What makes you think I can wait that long?"

Blake couldn't believe the wild swings of her luck. Photographed in the arms of a notorious Hollywood fuckboi—not that Bran had lived up to that rep. From what she'd observed, he was no more obnoxious than any other former-jock-turned-action star she'd known. Which was, admittedly, only him.

And now she had the first actionable lead on the people targeting the students at Play L.A.

"We need a game plan," Ollie said as the four of them—her, Ollie, Bran, and Rory—sat in Bran's office going through photos of Bran from the last few months.

Blake was shocked to see the ones allegedly lifted from his phone. "Those came from the Gazette?"

"Sonja sent them to me directly," Bran's agent, Clark, said over the speaker. He and Noelia had jumped on a call to try and mitigate the damage. Apparently, Sterling Studios was in a tizzy and Bran's new contract hung in the balance.

"And you think *she* had these photos of me, Bran, and Val snapped at the thing the other night? I'm not sure I buy that."

"That woman is capable of anything," Bran groused.

"To what end? I work for the Gazette," she argued. "It would only look bad for them. Right?"

"Except she's not bound by the same ethical standards that you are, Blake," Noelia said.

"Doesn't stop her from needing to sell ads." Clark added. "And, no offense to you, my dear, but my concern is Bran's contract with Sterling. You've been linked to Blake in these new photos. We can use that to our advantage, can't we?"

"Use...me?" She felt a pit forming in her stomach. Was she being played here?

Bran frowned down at the phone on the desk. "What are you proposing?"

"I'm not proposing anything," Clark replied, sounding a little defensive. "But you and Val have maintained you're just friends. And now we have photos of you with another attractive young woman, nameless for the moment, that *isn't* Val..."

The implication hung in the air and she felt cold, suddenly. She folded her arms around herself.

"You want Blake to be Bran's new flavor-of-the-month?" Noelia asked.

Bran's gaze snapped to hers, his forehead creased, but he remained silent.

"Not in the biblical sense," Clark said. "Unless, you know...but that's your business. I'm only wondering if we're missing a golden opportunity here. Assuming Blake is right, and the photos *aren't* from her paper, then the outlet that sent them doesn't know who she is."

"Those are a lot of variables," Rory said.

"Blake isn't here to solve Bran's image problems," Ollie said. "We'd be throwing her under the bus, once people figure out who she is. If they haven't already."

"By the time they do, her exclusive will have run and we can say the photos were misconstrued. That she accompanied Bran to the event as part of the story."

She could feel Ollie's eyes on her, but she watched Bran. Watched him consider Clark's idea.

He looked at her. "It's a big ask."

"It's fucking rich, that's what it is," Ollie said.

She reached out and found his hand, linking their fingers together and loving his instinct to come to her defense. Even if she didn't need it.

"Blake," Noelia began. "How certain are you it's not the Gazette behind those photos of the three of you?"

"Not one hundred percent," she admitted. "But we might have a card to play if we find out it was, something not even my boss knows."

"What's that?" Ollie asked.

She looked at him. "They don't know we went to school together. That I've known Bran for years."

Ollie's lips parted, his expression one of admiration and surprise. "Why didn't you tell them?"

She shrugged. "Call it a hunch. There was always something...weird to me about the way Sonja insisted I take this assignment. If it's her way of killing two birds with one stone, this might be our ace in the hole." She squeezed her eyes shut for a moment. "I'm mixing my metaphors."

"You always did," he teased.

"But the point stands. This is something we can use if the narrative gets away from us."

Ollie put his hands on her arms and turned her to face him. "Right now, you're just a woman in a photo. If we go with Clark's idea, and you're identified as a journalist before your article runs, it could ruin you."

"*Young reporter sleeps with movie star to land exclusive interview*," Rory said. "The headline writes itself."

"My reputation would be shot. No outlet would come near my story on Diamond Moon," she said as the gravity of the situation settled over her.

"We can't do this," Ollie said, looking past her. "Bran, tell me you're not seriously considering this."

"Ollie." She put a hand on his cheek and pulled his focus back to her. "The chances of me staying anonymous are slim to none, even if I don't have much of a presence online. That ship has sailed. What we *can* do is figure out a way to use this to our advantage." She turned back to the room. "All of us—Bran, the center, and the kids."

"And you?" Ollie asked.

The truth was, no matter how this played out, her name was going to suffer, whether it was in public or merely put on a list of "reporters never to hire."

"I need to go to the office tomorrow and talk to my boss, Gideon." She held up her hand to hold off Ollie's protest. "I'm not going to mention any of our suspicions about Sonja. I'll see if he brings it up. Gid isn't underhanded like this, at least I don't think he is. And he's pretty easy to read. I'll know."

"We need to schedule the photos," Bran said. "The sooner the better, so you can get your piece out quickly."

She nodded. "Agreed. I can call my photographer and move up the time. Here in La Jolla?"

"No," Bran and Ollie said in unison.

"I don't want this location known to anyone outside this group," Rory said. "I know we're not talking about a security issue, not yet anyway, but I'd feel better with something off the books until we identify the person who stole his data."

She rubbed her temples. "Why did I move to Los Angeles?"

"I ask myself that question every day," Ollie said.

"Okay," Noelia sighed. "I swear, Bran, I'm going to have silver hair because of you. Listen up. Stay the course. Blake, keep shadowing Bran and schedule the shoot. Bran, do...whatever it is you do."

He snorted. "Nice, Ellie."

"Oliver, how hard will it be to extend the rental at La Jolla?"

"Not hard at all. For how long?"

"Keep it open-ended if you can," she replied. "Rory, can you stick someone on Bran's house?"

"I've got a guy there already."

"Excellent. Clark, you and I can coordinate offline. I'll come by your office."

"What are you planning?" he asked.

"Whoever sent the photos wants a spectacle, but we're not going to give them one," Noelia said. "Blake, write the best damn actor spotlight that's ever been written. And Bran, this is still a big opportunity for you to show the public a different side."

Bran met Blake's gaze. "I can do that."

"You definitely can," she said giving him a smile.

"Alright," Noelia said. "We all have our roles. Let's put on a show."

Her hand in Ollie's, Blake was more than ready.

Blake had been on the call with Yara Bujold for an hour, listening to the harrowing ordeal of her accident and return from the dead. It sounded like something from true crime TV, complete with a romantic ending.

"You really showed up at Cam's pub with a gun?"

"And pointed it at me," Cam said over her shoulder. Behind Blake, Rory chuckled. "Shut it, cousin."

"I didn't say a word, *cousin*."

They were on a video call, the two of them moving about the kitchen of their home in Philadelphia as they prepared dinner. Blake couldn't deny that they made a handsome couple. Yara, famous for her violet-colored eyes and husky voice, had the kind of dark beauty that used to make Blake jealous as a teen.

As for Cam, his face matched the voice she'd heard on the phone when she called before. She'd been surprised to learn that Rory, who was from Ireland, was cousins with a pair of Scottish twins but the resemblance was undeniable. If the word strapping needed a photographic reference, these three men would do nicely.

"I'm sure Rory told you already, but whatever we can do to help bring down Diamond Moon, let us know," Cam said.

"I thought you left the Skinner Agency."

"Aye, I did, but I'll come out of retirement for this." Cam's expression was fierce.

"I occasionally freelance for them on the West Coast," Rory added. "This I'll do because those fuckers need to go down."

"Thank you both for all of your help," she said. "Yara, Cam, I'll be in touch."

There was a knock at the door before it opened, and Ollie poked his head inside. "I heard voices."

"We just finished with Yara and Camden."

"Get what you needed?" He pushed the door open and leaned in the doorway.

"Yeah, for now." Blake ran her hands through her hair. God knew what it looked like. She hadn't done much with it since the launch party two nights ago. Three? She was losing track of time.

"I'm going to head up to the city and do some digging," Rory said, crossing to the door. He gave Ollie a fist bump and squeezed by him.

"You people keep even stranger hours than I do."

Ollie smiled. "Again, this is tame. Hungry?"

She closed her laptop and got to her feet. She'd been sitting for too long and it felt good to stretch her limbs.

"Yes, but it's my turn to feed you. I'm no gourmet, but I can whip up omelets for everyone."

"I'm afraid it's just you and me," Ollie said, a grin tugging at the corner of his mouth.

"Where's Bran?"

"Bran has to do some work in post, and Rory is driving him."

She looked at the clock on the nightstand. "He's going to work? This late?"

"You seem to keep missing the part about his schedule—"

"It's unpredictable. No, I get it, but...shouldn't I have gone with him? I am supposed to be shadowing him."

He straightened. "Shit, I didn't even think about that. I can take you."

"No, no. It's fine."

"You were working, and I thought..." He shook his head. "Sorry."

"Nothing to be sorry for," she said walking towards him. "It means I get to show off my skills."

She expected him to laugh, move to the side, let her by, and follow her to the kitchen, but that's not what happened.

Instead, Ollie wrapped an arm around her waist, cupped her face in his free hand, and kissed her.

It wasn't anything like the careful, breathless kisses they'd shared thus far. Ollie was more assertive this time, his tongue probing gently but insistently, winding its way around hers.

Blake grabbed his shoulders to keep from toppling into him, her fingers gripping hard flesh, hot even under the cool cotton of his shirt.

Breaking the kiss, he dropped his head on her shoulder. His breath was hot against her skin, his whole frame vibrating as his grip on her tightened.

"You do things to me I can't begin to explain," he said, running his nose back and forth along the curve of her neck.

"T-the feeling is mutual." It surprised her how thick her tongue felt in her mouth. "Adrenaline. Shared history and the surprise of being in each other's lives again."

"That's not it." He lifted his head and rested his forehead against hers, both of them panting as the heat between their bodies rose.

Her heart thundered in her ears and when she looked up into Ollie's dark, heated gaze, her body responded in a way that it hadn't before. Not ever.

Her fingers tightened on his shoulders as he leaned in for another kiss.

His fingers sank into her hair as he pulled her in for an even deeper kiss. One hand on the small of her back, he bent and used his other hand to grip the bend of her knee. He lifted her, wrapping Blake's leg around his waist and turning until she was tilted back against the wall by the door. He nipped and kissed along her exposed collarbone, and along the arch of her neck.

"Oh, yes," she croaked, not caring how hoarse she sounded, how desperate. It was so good.

Ollie was breathing hard. When his teeth sunk into the soft flesh of her earlobe, Blake practically keened.

"Okay, alright," she said, panting like she'd run up a mountain. "No more worrying about this, about whatever it is that we're doing."

He sucked at the sensitive flesh behind her ear hard enough to leave a mark and drew back, his expression stormy.

"As long as you promise me—" he began.

"Later," she murmured, unwilling to let silly things like logic or reason get in the way this time. She pulled him in for another kiss.

She didn't want to think about what came after, not about the Gazette or Bran or even her career. Nothing else was possible until she got this craving out of her system. Be it for one night, or one millennium, she needed this. With Ollie. Right now.

For several minutes they stood there sharing slow, mind-melting kisses while the little voice in the back of her mind tried to warn her that she shouldn't allow it to go any further. Her body insisted she tell the voice to kindly fuck off.

"God...Blake...I want..."

The heaving rise and fall of Ollie's chest made her shiver.

He grabbed her thigh and raised it higher, pushing himself against the cotton-clad part between her thighs that was turning damp with need.

Blake could feel Ollie's erection pressing into her and she moaned, threading her fingers into his hair and claiming his mouth again. She couldn't get enough of kissing him.

Ollie groaned low in his throat, grinding slowly against her. "Fuck," he spat, setting her down and backing off suddenly.

Cool air rushed in where Blake had been burning up a moment before.

"Fuck." He ran both hands through his hair, his blue eyes dark with hunger. "Blake...I'm in real danger here. I don't know what you want. I don't want to...do anything you're not—"

Stepping forward, she lifted a hand to his lips and reached behind her to find the edge of the door. She pushed until it closed, and then felt for the lock, turning it.

Ollie's expression turned positively feral, and she bit her lip as she watched him.

"What I want is you," she said, making it as plain as she could. "What do you want?"

He huffed out a laugh, his hips giving a seemingly involuntary but unmistakable jerk forward.

"I think that's obvious."

"Tell me anyway," she said, impressed with her own ability to form complete sentences when her cells were screaming *fuck me, now, please.* "Consent is sexy."

A slow smile stretched his generous mouth. He reached down and took one of her hands in his. Mesmerized, she watched him bring it to his lips and press a soft kiss to the inside of her wrist.

Her pulse jumped, and he raised his dark focus to her mouth.

"I want you naked in my arms, on that bed, under me," he said, leaning in to run his lips along the curve of her jawline. "But I don't want to rush this with you. I've waited too many years to screw it up by taking things too fast."

Turning, she tilted her head, inviting him to follow. "You're just making up for lost time."

"Is that all right?"

"More than all right." Blake took his hand. "C'mon." She led him through the door and over to the bed, maneuvering him until the back of his legs hit the edge. Then she gave him a light push.

Ollie fell like a tree, landing on his back. He propped himself up on his elbow and watched from under hooded eyes as she undressed.

"Jesus..." he murmured softly.

She smiled. Only a few minutes ago she would have thought it impossible to focus on anything but her floundering career and the web the three of them had been caught up in, but that was then.

Now, she stripped down to her bra and underwear and then moved forward. She reached for his belt. "Is this okay?"

"Of course," he said, his voice raspy. "Everything. Anything you want. It's all okay."

Ollie held on to Blake's waist until she had managed his belt, then he reached up and pulled her down for another kiss. A giggle tried to push its way out of her at the absurdity of this situation, but she managed to stifle it, deftly unbuttoning his shorts and lowering the zipper.

"I'm going to die," he said.

"Don't die yet."

She slid her hands under the thin cotton of his t-shirt and pushed it up, revealing his quivering stomach. She loved that her touch did this to him.

He took the hint and managed to pull the shirt off, tossing it away as he lay back down to watch her. He shivered when Blake ran her nails lightly across his abdomen, the muscles in his stomach tensing.

His chest was surprisingly well-muscled, his shoulders broad and narrow at the same time. She ran her hand down his arm and traced her fingers along the strip of hair that led from his navel to where it vanished beneath the elastic hem of his underwear.

"I'm trying hard not to lose it here," he said, working to catch his breath.

"You're doing just fine." Hovering over him, on her hands and knees, she continued to explore.

She ran her fingertips along the curve of his arm and over the top of where his shoulder sloped up to his neck.

Ollie's gaze ricocheted from her face down to her body and back, like he couldn't believe what was happening and didn't know where to look. His nipples were stiff peaks when she dragged her fingertips over them, and he hissed.

"Blake," came the low warning.

"Oliver." She said, feeling powerful and sexy.

He ran warm hands up her thighs and cupped them, hitching her higher until they were eye-to-eye.

She looked down into that blue gaze and saw all of the desire surging within herself reflected back at her.

"What do *you* want, Blake Dillon?" he asked softly, his tongue darting out to wet his lips.

In response, she lowered herself to straddle him as she'd done before. The rough fabric of his shorts and the teeth of the open zipper against her needy center sending a shiver of pleasure up her spine. She wanted the feeling of flesh on flesh, was almost desperate for it.

Blake ground her hips in a slow circle and Ollie uttered something close to a cry, his face going slack.

"Oh, yes," he said. "Blake, yes."

She could feel him straining against the fabric of his briefs and couldn't resist sneaking a glance. But once she did, it was all she could think about.

Reaching down between them, she ran the backs of her fingers along his rigid length.

"I'm going to embarrass myself if you don't stop." He sounded pained.

"Condom?" she asked.

"Wallet." He started to turn, to reach his back pocket, and Blake slid to the side, taking the moment to gather herself.

This was wild. Reckless. But it was also Oliver, and she liked him. A lot. She always had, so this felt—as he'd said before—inevitable. That they'd see each other again, that they'd end up here.

The condom landed on the bed between them and Ollie flopped onto his back, breathing hard as he wiped a hand across his forehead. "You're going to kill me. I know it."

Chuckling, Blake lifted up on one elbow to look down at him. She let her gaze travel down the length of his torso and back to the spot that kept her interest.

She pulled the waistband of his shorts and underwear down and wrapped her hand firmly around his cock.

Ollie sucked in a quick breath, arching into her grip.

She slid her hand up and down, watching and feeling as he grew harder and hotter in her grasp. Glancing up at his face, her breath caught. The man was gorgeous, especially like this, already biting his lip as if to keep himself from begging for more.

"Is this what you've fantasized about?" she asked quietly.

His gaze burned into hers as lust twisted his features, leaving him looking slightly dazed. "Yes..." he rasped. "But... I need...to touch you."

Blake sat up, folding her legs under her, and reached behind to unclasp her bra. Ollie's hot, hooded gaze was like a caress against her bare skin.

"Gorgeous," he whispered.

She felt self-conscious and sexy all at once, his honest appreciation an aphrodisiac.

"Touch me," she replied with a whisper.

He sat up, moving slowly as if he were afraid she'd run away. She wasn't going anywhere.

He cupped one hand over her breast, grazing the nipple with his thumbs and she heard herself whimper.

"I never... I wasn't..." He paused, searching for words, and seemed frustrated when he didn't find just the right ones. "I didn't plan this. You," he said. "I was thinking about how we got here, running into you, Bran."

"You're thinking about Bran right now?" she teased.

Chuckling, he briefly closed his eyes. "No, trust me. Right now, I'm only thinking about what you'd taste like if I were to spread you out here and..." He ran a questing finger down her sternum.

It was her turn to shiver.

"Lie down," came the soft command, and she obeyed, moving the prickly condom square away from her sensitive back.

Ollie knelt between her legs, using his hands to gently spread her thighs further apart. He hooked his thumbs beneath the elastic at her hips and pulled.

She lifted to assist him, and then she was bare in every way.

"There was a pool party at Alpha Q the spring of my senior year, do you remember?" he asked, tracing a finger from her neck, down between her breasts, and south.

"Party?" She could barely remember her own name, much less a gathering that happened over five years ago.

"I got there late, and the first thing I saw when I walked around the back of the house was you in a bikini. Light blue with ruffles...here...and here."

He drew a finger across her chest and another across her waist.

She had a vague recollection of it, of a hot day in the sun and cold drinks with friends.

"I remember someone walking up to me but I couldn't tell you who it was or what they said," Ollie continued as his gaze traveled over her. "All I could see was you. And I wanted you so suddenly, and so urgently, that I walked away. Went straight to the bathroom and had to get off."

She froze, shocked by his confession. "Really?"

"I was so embarrassed," he said, his cheeks reddening even more. "I'm still embarrassed. I was so hung up on you, Blake. You made me stupid."

"You hid it well."

"Too well," he said, seeming to come back to the present. "But I would gladly do it all the same if it meant I could be here with you like this. Right now."

He shifted, and she found herself pulled forward on the bed, her legs splayed wide. He looked hungrily down between her legs as if he'd been presented with a lavish feast, his breathing becoming louder and deeper.

She gasped when he dragged a gentle finger through her folds. And then again when he touched her clit.

"Beautiful," he said, shaking his head as if he couldn't quite comprehend it.

Blake arched, the pleasure shocking in its intensity.

"I've thought about this the most," Ollie continued, his voice like whiskey, smooth and warm as he lowered his head to where she *needed* him the most. "About your hands in my hair and your legs over my shoulders as I sucked the honey right out of your body."

"Oliver," she cried out. She'd completely underestimated this man. This was Ollie, her nerdy, factoid-spouting friend from college who would recite Pablo Neruda by heart, who would give the shirt off his back to anyone who needed it, and run a five-mile loop every morning at oh-dark-thirty without fail. But he was also Oliver. The guy who'd danced with her amongst the stars and taken care of her when she wasn't feeling well. The guy who fed her and listened to her and made her feel things she hadn't thought possible.

"I love how you say my name," he murmured against her center.

She whimpered again as his tongue slid over her.

"What do you like?" he asked, looking up at her.

Shrugging, she answered, "Everything, if you're the one doing it."

His nostrils flared and he pressed a kiss to the inside of each knee.

Nothing had ever felt so good as his hands against her skin or his lips moving along the sensitive backs of her knees.

He helped her roll onto her side, layering kisses along her lower back and covering every inch of skin he had access to as he moved in front of her and helped position her leg over his shoulder. His fingers brushed through her crease before sliding around to curve over the swell of her ass.

He rested his head on her other thigh. All Blake could see when she looked down was the top of his head. All she could do when he finally put his mouth on her was slide her fingers into his hair and hold on for dear life.

# 29

Ollie needed to keep his head about him. Blake tasted like every fantasy he'd ever had rolled into one delicious, spicy cocktail and he was drunk on her already.

He suckled gently at her clit, delighting in every whimper and moan she made and craving the pinch of pain from her fingers tightening in his hair.

"Ride my tongue," he said, gratified when the muscles of her thigh tightened in his grip.

He was painfully hard. He wanted to roll her to her back and sink into her, but he was determined to hold out until she broke apart in his mouth.

He lapped at her with the flat of his tongue and pressed his thumb into her sex. Her body writhed and her soft cries filled the room. Slowly, with singular purpose, he circled her clit while slowly shifting his fingers to penetrate her.

Ollie's own release simmered not far beneath the surface, but he ignored his pulsing need, wanting to prolong this for as long as possible.

Her hips ground against his mouth, searching for what she needed, and he wanted to give it to her. Blake deserved only pleasure. She moved against him in undulating waves that made him groan.

He could feel her pleasure mounting as he locked one arm around her thigh.

"Ollie, I'm...I..." She began to tremble.

He lapped at her damp skin, urging her to let go. And then he felt it begin. He slid two fingers deep inside and sucked hard on her swollen clit as she spilled over, gasping his name.

She grabbed fists full of his hair as she cried out.

Slipping his fingers free of her, he brought her down slowly, kissing every delectable inch of skin between her thighs. He traced the delicate seam with his tongue and sucked gently at the swollen lips of her pussy, pleased at the hitch in Blake's breathing as she rode out the aftershocks.

Rolling her on her back, he lifted his head to look at her. She was gloriously splayed out over the bed, spent and smiling.

She stared up at him with wide eyes. "I think you broke me."

"I hope not, I need you." He rose up to lie beside her, one hand splayed across her belly because he couldn't *not* touch her. "That was so goddamned sexy," he confessed, suddenly aware of his cock pressing into her hip.

He could come like that, and it shocked him to realize it.

Blake glanced down at his erection and then back up to meet his eyes as she wrapped her hand around him and squeezed.

When she lifted her other hand, it held the condom.

"Put it on me," he commanded softly.

Without hesitating, she pushed him onto his back. Gone was her languid, post-orgasmic haze. Her expression was one of determination and mischief. Before Ollie could blink, she had ripped the packet open and sheathed his cock. Her thighs shook as she lifted herself up and then down over his erection. The movement sent waves of pleasure rushing through his body until all he could focus on was how good it felt to finally be inside her.

She started to ride him in earnest with slow rocking movements, working herself against him in a way that could only go untended for so long before something had to give.

"Shit," he muttered as she dropped forward to lay against his shoulder and he thrust up into her in an almost violent motion.

A jolt of white-hot energy shot through him, setting off an answering charge that left her quivering around him.

Breathing hard, Blake sat up and braced her hands on his thighs. His eyes focused on the place where their bodies were joined, and it took a moment before he could speak.

He hadn't stopped moving. The connection between them was so intense, he knew he'd never be able to look at her again without remembering the way she felt right then.

She rolled her hips, catching him just right, and every muscle in his body tightened excruciatingly.

"Blake," he moaned her name.

She hummed her pleasure, reaching a hand up to cup her breast. Heat began to radiate from her skin. Ollie knew it wouldn't take long. He had her right at the shimmering edge again, and that knowledge drove him onward.

Blake ground down against his hand as he found her clit and rubbed it in slow circles, all while his synapses began to misfire. Her hot little cries went straight to his head and pleasure rippled like ocean waves around his cock. It didn't take long before she shattered again.

He finally let go of his careful restraint, driving up into her and chasing his own release.

Shuddering, she lowered her mouth to his, kissing him and biting his lower lip as she spread her thighs wide.

The feel of her skin sliding against his, her breath hot in his mouth, it was too much and not enough. Ollie came with a shout, releasing hot into the condom in bright bursts of light and breath.

Her breathy, sweet laughter filled the room as she rose up and rocked against him again and again, milking every drop until he was shuddering hard beneath her.

Ollie had to close his eyes and re-center himself. He felt Blake move, felt her shift to the side, but he had no command over his own body.

"I can't remember my name," he said.

Warm skin enveloped his left side and he felt her place a soft kiss to his bicep. "Oliver."

"Mmmm," he hummed, smiling. "That's it." He rolled his head to the side and opened his eyes, taking in her loose curls and satisfied expression. "Hi."

"Hi," she said, softly, tracing small circles on his ribcage. "That was..."

He waited. "Any regrets?"

"What?" Her eyes met his. "No, none. You?"

"Only that I haven't taken you out properly," he paused, realizing he'd gotten ahead of himself. "If that's something you think you'd want."

Blake reached up to smooth the hair back from his forehead. "I like the idea of seeing where this goes," she said after a minute of silence.

"But we have to be realistic. Your work with Bran, it's hectic. And I have no idea where I'll end up after all of this. I might be out of a job. I might have to move back East."

The stab of pain that sliced through him at that thought made him draw a sharp breath, but she was right.

"We'll take it day by day," he said, hating that the real world was already threatening to keep them apart.

"Minute by minute." She cupped his jaw. "And in this minute, we're here. Together."

He leaned over to press a quick kiss to her lips. "Let me take care of this." He gestured to the bathroom and Blake disentangled herself. He could feel her eyes on him as he left the room.

Moving quickly, he cleaned up and returned to find her underneath the covers. He was suddenly unsure of himself. Did she want him to join her? Should he gather his things and go?

"I can hear you thinking all the way over here," Blake said. "Come."

He didn't need a second invitation.

His momentary trepidation vanished as he slid into bed beside her. It was late, and the sun was setting. He had the ridiculous impulse to scoop Blake up and carry her out to the patio to watch the sky change over the ocean. Then he remembered Bran and Rory were gone and wouldn't be back for hours.

"Are you sleepy?"

"Not particularly," she replied. "Just feel like a wet noodle. Why?"

Spying the coverall she'd worn over her swimsuit the other day, Ollie slipped out of bed and grabbed it. "Trust me?"

Sitting up, she smiled, confused. "Sure."

He tossed it to her and picked his shorts off the floor. After pulling them on, held out his hand when Blake came around the corner of the bed.

"Where are we going?" she asked.

"You'll see."

The house was quiet and dark when he popped into the kitchen. Ollie snagged a bowl of grapes he'd left on the island and brought them back to where he'd left Blake waiting for him by the pool.

The sky was already dipping into the deep golds of late afternoon.

"The view here is stunning," Blake said, staring out over the water, "I bet it's better at night."

He reached down, glancing at her to make sure she was okay with him taking her hand before he moved towards the pool. "I think the sunset is better."

"You're from out in the country. Of course you'd think that," she teased, but followed him over.

He set the bowl by the edge of the pool and helped Blake out of her coverall.

"What are you doing?" she asked, sounding alarmed. She looked beyond him into the house.

"They won't be back for hours," he assured her. "Trust me." He draped the garment across the closest lounger and then removed his shorts, tossing them alongside.

He took her hand in his and drew her towards the steps leading down into the water.

"If this is ice cold I'm going to murder you."

He laughed. "It's cool, but not freezing. I promise."

"You're asking for a lot of trust, buddy," she protested but followed him anyway.

The water was warm, as was the breeze, tinged with the scent of the ocean.

"Are we allowed to skinny dip out here?"

"It's private property. I don't think we'll be arrested," he turned back to face her, taking in the small smile on her lips and the way the setting sun made her skin glow.

He braced himself against the edge of the pool, facing out to take in the view, and Blake settled herself next to him. Ollie wanted to reach for her and realized, with a start, that it was allowed.

He curled his fingers around her hip, grateful when she squeezed into his side.

A few clouds drifted overhead, and the ocean stretched out before them like an endless possibility.

It was a stunning view, but that's not what made his chest ache with longing. He wanted this, more moments like this, with Blake.

"I have all of my grandfather's notebooks," she said as she looked out over the horizon. "Boxes and boxes of little green booklets, like the ones I use. He kept one for every assignment he ever did, more than one in most cases. There's a description of a sunset he experienced on the beach in Indonesia. It was about six months after a tsunami had wreaked havoc on the coastline. He said the ocean lay sleeping like a blue dragon, but that it only had to flick its tail and man would learn it wasn't tame. That it had never been tame."

He turned his head to watch her profile, burnished gold by the fading sun.

"We've been running around this past week trying to outmaneuver people, dealing with the misdeeds of man, and then you sit and look at this..." She shook her head.

"We don't need a flick of the dragon's tail to put things into perspective," he said.

Blake turned to him and smiled. "No. I guess we don't. Just a taste of his tongue."

This kiss happened because it had to, under the open sky. Free and sweet.

# 30

When Blake arrived at the Gazette, she half-expected the room to go quiet as she walked through and for every head to turn as she passed. It didn't, of course. The newsroom hummed along at its usual frenetic pace, and no one paid her any attention as she wound her way through the cubicles to Gideon's office.

"Come in and close the door, kiddo," he said when she knocked on his open door.

She took her usual seat, feeling a bit like she'd been called to the principal's office. She had planned to pop in later today anyway, so getting an email at six that morning was a surprise.

After spending a memorable afternoon with Ollie, she, Ollie and Bran had gone over the game plan once again at dinner. She wondered if this meeting with Gideon would help or hinder their plans.

Her boss eyed her from over the black, boxy rims of his glasses. "Is there something you need to tell me?"

"About?"

"You and Brandon Cody?"

Blake worked to keep her expression neutral. "Like what?"

Gideon removed his glasses and tossed them onto a stack of papers on his desk. "Dillon. Are you fucking him or not?"

"Wow, Gid. Don't censor yourself on my account," she said. "By the way, wouldn't this be considered an invasion of my privacy?"

"No, it would be considered a liability for your profession if you sleep with your subjects."

Fair point. She closed her mouth and tried a different tactic. She still wasn't sure if Gideon was entirely on her side.

"No. I'm not sleeping with Brandon Cody."

He let out a breath of what looked like relief, before nodding over and over. "Good. Okay. We have a different problem to deal with, then."

"Which is?"

Gideon leaned forward and folded his hands on the desk, looking as serious as she had ever seen him. "I think Sonja is planning to hang you out to dry." He opened a folder on his desktop and turned his monitor to give her a better view.

She only had to glance at the screen to know they were the shots of her, Val, and Bran at the gala.

"You don't look surprised," Gideon said, narrowing his eyes. "Or even that concerned. What the hell is going on? I feel like I'm missing the milk in my bowl of cereal."

Her lips twitched as she fought a smile. "That's...an interesting analogy."

He waved her off. "Something my mom used to say. Talk to me," he said, urgent and low. "I know I'm a dick of a boss sometimes, but I'm worried about you."

She searched his eyes and saw nothing but sincerity. "How did you get the photos?"

"One of the pool photographers came to me after Sonja paid him to take these, off the books." He opened another document on the screen. "And then I saw this in the approval queue for layout."

*The rumor mill is alive and spinning with news of a budding romance between cub reporter, Blake Dillon, and Hollywood superstar, Brandon Cody.*

*The pair have reportedly been spotted out on numerous occasions locking eyes and dancing intimately at a recent gala. But there's more to the story than just blissful new love—sources are saying that Dillon has been angling to score an exclusive interview with Cody for her résumé.*

*Could be their newfound relationship is much more transactional than it would appear at first glance. Whispers allude to Blake offering her affections in exchange for all-access to Cody's inner circle. What a way to get ahead.*

As she read the screen, Blake could feel Gid's eyes on her, but she couldn't swallow past the pain of her worst fear laid out in front of her.

She sat back, wondering if anything the group had planned could trump this. "When will it run?"

He frowned. "Why is she doing this to you? And why do I get the feeling you haven't been upfront with me about all of this?"

"I don't think it's about me," Blake said. "Or not *only* about me." She told him about Bran's history with Sonja.

"Jesus," he said, sitting back. "I think I need to look for a new job."

"I'm sorry you were dragged into this."

Gideon's eyes flashed with anger and hurt. "What? You think I want to work for a paper that would do something like this to anyone, much less one of its own?"

"I guess not."

"Look," he said. "I can't bury this, but maybe I can slow it down a day or two. Sonja is in New York meeting with corporate. Where are you on the Cody article?"

"I'm interviewing him this afternoon for the final piece. Stewart's going to meet me at the studio, where Bran is filming, to shoot the photos."

"That's great," he said, pulling up the production calendar. "Write like the wind and get it to me tonight. I'll make sure your article runs before this smear piece. It won't put everyone on your side, but it'll be a compelling counterargument to the picture she's painting."

"You sure you want to get involved?" She had to ask, knowing Sonja would be livid when she finds out he delayed her plans.

"There's a reason I saw the photos and the copy before they went to print," he replied. "Sonja isn't exactly beloved, here."

She stood up. "I need to run an errand before I head to the interview. Thank you, Gid, for everything."

"Send it to me tonight. If you don't, I can't do much more to help you, Blake."

"You'll have it." She started for the door but turned back. "Gid, after this? I think I'm done with this place."

Gid sighed. "Baby girl, you and me both."

Deanna was in her office when Blake arrived at Play L.A.

"Blake," she said, smiling warmly. "I was so excited to hear from you. You found something on Diamond Moon?"

"I'm following a lead, yeah." She looked around at the boxes. "Are you packing?"

The other woman looked up from the stack of files on her desk. "Yes...I'm leaving."

"What? Why?"

"I'm moving back East to be with my mom. She's not doing great."

"Oh, I'm so sorry to hear that," she replied. "I can't picture this place without you. Who'll take over when you're gone?"

"I've named a possible replacement, but it will be up to the board to confirm her. They'd be lucky to have her here. Inara has done great work in the field."

"I hope she's approved, then. But I bet the kids are sad to see you go."

"I haven't told them yet," Deanna said. "I have a little time. But listen, even if I'm on the other side of the country, these are still my kids. Keep me posted on your investigation. And if there's anything I can do to help, don't hesitate to reach out."

"Thanks, and I will." She paused. "Listen, I came by because..."

Deanna stopped what she was doing to look up. "Is something wrong?"

"I'm not sure. I saw Micah earlier this week. She reached out to give me some information, and she was... I dunno, she seemed stressed. Not afraid, but anxious. I just wondered if she was alright. I didn't see her out front."

Deanna sat in her chair. "Ah. Micah is a good kid, but she has a rough time of it at home. But don't worry, she's staying with her aunt in Bakersfield for a while."

"That'll be culture shock for her," Blake said, smiling.

Deanna laughed. "It sure will."

"I'm glad she could get away for a bit, though. Will you tell her I asked after her?"

"I'm sure she'd love to hear from you herself. I think you made quite an impression. She mentioned to me that she thought it might be cool to go into journalism."

"Really?" She was surprised. She'd thought Micah hated her profession.

"Really," Deanna assured her. "You should think about coming to teach here. We've never offered a class in journalism. I'm sure we have more than one budding news hound in our group."

"Oh, I don't know if I'm qualified to teach."

"The only qualification you need is experience and integrity, and you have both," she replied and this—this was why Blake couldn't let Sonja get away with smearing the Dillon name. It wasn't only about her, but her grandfather as well.

"I'm sure Ollie could twist your arm," Deanna added, with a knowing grin.

Blake tucked her hair behind her ear. "I don't know what you mean."

"I'm sure you don't." She winked.

After stopping at home for a couple of fresh notebooks and a change of clothes, Blake met Stewart at the visitor's lot near stage forty-six. He approached her as she pulled her car into the spot next to his pick-up.

"Someone's been making waves."

"Have I?" Blake grabbed her bag from the back seat and locked the doors. "I'm just doing the job I was assigned."

"And burning Sonja to the ground in the process," he said. He looked all too pleased.

She squinted up at him. "I told her I wasn't interested in the celebrity beat. Instead, she put me on a high-profile piece and then tried to dial up the drama. I'm working with her script."

"I believe that's called malicious compliance." He pulled his ballcap off, revealing a tangle of wavy hair, and wiped the sweat from his brow. Stewart's heather gray t-shirt was damp and stuck to his chest, and his jeans were stained with dirt and grass.

"I'm entitled to rewrites." Blake pointed at the logo on his shirt. "DeLillo Landscaping?"

"Photography doesn't always pay the bills. I have a change of clothes in my bag, if I can find a bathroom on the way."

They walked across the lot, dodging crews carrying set pieces and zippy golf carts transporting VIPs.

"Of course. We're a little early, and I think Bran is wrapping up a session in post."

Stewart side-eyed her. "*Bran*, is it?"

Blake nudged his shoulder. "Don't you start."

"I'm not, but it sounds very...familiar," he said, pointing over her head. "There's a restroom."

She followed him over to the one story, grey building. Before Stewart could head inside, she stopped him with a hand on his arm.

"Listen," she began. "I know we haven't worked together for very long, but I feel like we work well together. I may bitch about the type of work we do for the Gazette, but I respect your professionalism. I respect *you*."

He had been frowning, but his expression softened as she spoke.

"Thanks," he said gruffly before clearing his throat. " You have good instincts, and you're not a sensationalist. If I'm honest, I was a little surprised you wanted to work for an outlet like the Gazette. I'm familiar with Trent Dillon's work. Stellar journalist"

"Thank you. And *want* is a strong word," she said, pleased that he knew of her granddad.

He smiled. "I see. Well, you're better than most of the key-clackers in that office. I hope you land on your feet when the dust settles. And I respect you, too."

"Thanks, that means a lot."

Stewart hooked a thumb over his shoulder. "Be right back."

She leaned against the building and pulled out her phone.

**BLAKE: Hey. I'm on property, waiting for my photographer. Are we on schedule?**

**OLLIE: Yes, all set. Where are you, exactly?**

Blake looked around for a location reference.

**BLAKE: Outside the restroom across from stage 39. There's a giant flamingo leaning against the wall.**

**OLLIE: Stay put.**

Blake felt the grin pulling at her mouth as she tucked her phone away. It was ridiculous, the giddy excitement bubbling beneath her skin as she waited for Ollie to appear.

She couldn't say she felt like a teenager, because she'd skipped the kind of blushing, fumbling, awkward relationships her friends had in high school. In college, she dated infrequently, and only fell into one semi-serious relationship that was more study-partner-with-benefits than whirlwind romance.

But this thing with Oliver, it had the potential for something real. Scary as hell but real. The chemistry between them manifested in small things—a brush of hands across hips, the sweet warmth from his arm when he held her close, or the touch-and-go kisses that left her body tingling for more.

It would be easy to fall for someone like him, which was why she needed to get a grip on herself.

If things went to plan, she'd be out of a job by the end of the day. And then what?

It was difficult to think rational thoughts when the man in question was walking towards her with a shy grin on his kissable mouth and a bottle of water in his hands.

"I snuck away from the set," he said, handing her the tall, cold bottle.

"Oh my God, bless you for this." She was so thirsty. "How did you know?"

"You always forget to stay hydrated."

The condensation sluiced away in glistening drops as she stared down at it. She could feel his eyes on her as she lifted her head to drink. The cold felt like a kiss against her lips, and she shivered at the feeling of it sliding down her throat. She bit off a curse as the chill seeped down the front of her blouse and settled around her nipples.

It was impossible to miss the way Ollie's grin dissolved into something else, or the way he looked her over like she was a meal and he was contemplating where to start eating.

She lowered the bottle and raised her hand to wipe her mouth, but he reached forward. She froze as he swept his thumb across her lips, his gaze so hot and hungry she swayed involuntarily closer.

"Ahem," a voice to the right of them said.

Blake turned to find an amused Stewart, his gaze pinging between them.

"Stewart DeLillo." He held out his hand.

It took Ollie a moment to respond. "Oliver Benjamin." He nodded towards the camera bag. "You have everything you need?"

"I didn't bring lights, since you have your own setup planned."

They followed Ollie, passing rows of trailers and lot vehicles on their way to meet Bran.

"We're using a living room from one of the weeklies," Ollie said. "Bran wanted a neutral location, and this set is not in use this week."

When they reached stage forty-two, Ollie opened the door and ushered them inside. She felt his hand on the small of her back as she passed him and smiled to herself.

Bran was standing on the brightly lit living room set, Noelia talking at him animatedly while he nodded and frowned.

The scent of the food truck they'd walked by, the sharp odor of vinegar from the set dressing table, and the metallic smell of the light casings mixed with the disinfectant from the cleaning cart in the corner. But the set was beautiful, appointed with a sleek, contemporary style she might expect to find in the living area of a suburban home.

She walked over to the ivory sofa and matching armchairs. "This will do nicely."

"Certainly makes my job easier," Stewart said looking up at the lights. "I don't even think I need to adjust anything, but I'll take a few readings."

He set down his bags and removed a light meter.

"Will this work?" Ollie asked sounding unexpectedly nervous.

She gave him a smile and a half-shrug. "This is perfect. Whether our little scheme will work is a different story, but what other choice do we have?"

Ollie frowned. "I'm so sorry you were dragged into this."

"It's not your fault, or Bran's," she said. "Besides, if I hadn't been tasked with the story, we might never have..." She broke off, unsure how to finish that sentence.

Ollie gave her a look that said he understood anyway. He stepped closer. "Blake..."

"After," she said, cutting him off. "We'll figure it out after."

She gave his arm a squeeze and walked over to join Noelia and Bran by the faux window. Simulated daylight streamed through the gauzy curtain, flooding the floor with a warm glow.

"Good to see you again, Blake." Noelia said. "Thank you for agreeing to do this here."

"Thank *you* for agreeing to do it at all," she replied. "I know it's a risk."

"The only real risk is to you, my dear. Brandon might lose out in the short term, but he would eventually recover from any scandal." Noelia looked over her shoulder to where Bran sat in the makeup chair, a technician powdering his forehead.

She turned back to face Blake. "We women aren't afforded the luxury of flaws. If it weren't affecting Val the way it is, or you for that matter, I think Brandon would just power through. But he's a better man than I sometimes give him credit for." She paused. "Don't tell him I said that."

Blake grinned. "I won't."

"And if Brandon weren't going to do this on his own, I believe Oliver would disown him. And we both know our Bran would be lost without his Ollie."

"They're the very definition of brothers."

"Indeed. But I hope Oliver realizes someday soon that his life doesn't need to be tied so closely to Bran's."

This surprised Blake, and it must have shown on her face.

"Don't get me wrong, Oliver is a godsend when it comes to keeping Brandon in line," Noelia said. "But that's not his purpose in life."

"No, it isn't," she agreed.

"Blake," Stewart walked towards the two women. "I'm ready when you are. I set the recorder on the tripod just over there." He pointed at the end of the couch. "I can set up another, if you want to be in frame."

"No, the recording is more for reference than anything else," she replied. "Thanks."

"I'll get Brandon," Noelia said.

And Blake was left standing alone.

Ollie had gone to the door to greet Clark, Noelia was undoubtedly giving Brandon some last-minute instruction, and Stewart was checking his equipment.

She took a moment to breathe.

There was so much riding on this, but she couldn't think about that. She zeroed in on the interview itself. As a cub reporter, she'd been given the opportunity to conduct an interview that would be read by more people than anything she'd ever written in her life. The nerves in her stomach were a mixed bag—anxiety, anticipation, and apprehension— but she shoved them down as far as they could go and pulled out the green leather-bound book that contained her notes and questions. She stared at the worn leather. She had prepared for this moment her whole life. So, when Bran walked over and asked "Are you ready?"

Blake squared her shoulders and nodded. "Let's do this."

# 31

## No More Pictures, Please: the Trajectory of a Shooting Star by Blake Dillon for the L.A. Gazette

*Blake: Brandon, you have a history of being caught in compromising situations. Would it be fair to say this has shaped the public's perception of you?*

*Brandon: It definitely has, yes.*

*Blake: Do you think it's an accurate perception?*

*Brandon: (laughs) Of course not. It would be like judging a chef by the number of dishes he's burned.*

*Blake: An interesting analogy.*

*Brandon: A fairly accurate one.*

*Blake: Who would be the dish in this scenario, the women you've been associated with or you?*

*Brandon: I think it depends on who you ask.*

*Blake: I'm asking you.*

*Brandon: I think I'm caught up in the cogs of a well-oiled media rumor machine and a case of severely compromised journalistic ethics.*

*Blake: That's quite an accusation. Will you tell me who it's aimed towards? Certainly not me.*

*Brandon: No, not you.*

*Blake: Then who?*

Here, Cody pauses. Despite his reputation for being cavalier, some would say reckless, he chooses his words carefully.

*Brandon: Could I tell you a story?*

*Blake: Sure.*

*Brandon: Once upon a time, there was a young kid, twenty-one years old, who moved to Los Angeles with dreams of making it.*

*Blake: You could be describing hundreds, thousands of people.*

*Brandon: [smiling] Indeed. But this kid, he's completely green when it comes to how things work out here. He's from back East, a recent college graduate. Back home, he was a big deal. Athletic, popular, adored by his family and friends.*

*Blake: And his ego is smashed when he realizes he's moved to a town full of people just like him? Blake: All dreaming the same dream?*

*Brandon: Not quite. See, this kid was determined and a hard worker. He took any role they offered, played every part they asked him to. He didn't make one misstep. Except for one.*

*Blake: And that was?*

*Brandon: There was a reporter, very respected. They met at one of the kid's first press junkets. He only had a small part, but he made an impression on her. She told him he had "it—star quality. She told him she wanted to interview him individually, to give his profile a boost. Said it would be a big deal to have her interview him.*

*Blake: And he agreed?*

*Brandon: [another smile] Of course he did. Only, when he went to meet her it wasn't an interview she wanted.*

*Blake: What happened?*

Cody stays silent, and it's plain that he is having difficulty finding the right words.

*Blake: Do you want to stop?*

Cody's manager tries to intervene, as does his best friend-slash-assistant, but the actor waves them off.

*Brandon: The kid gets out of there, thank God. He literally runs out of the house and walks for a mile before he's able to catch a ride back to the studio apartment he shares with a budding director and another young actor.*

*Blake: And the reporter?*

*Brandon: She doesn't handle rejection well. And in the years that follow, she rises to prominence in her field and uses that position to exact her revenge on the young actor. On me.*

At this time, I feel the need to disclose my personal connection to Brandon Cody. He, his best friend and assistant—Oliver Benjamin—and I all attended the University of Philadelphia together. I've known Bran, off and on, for years. When I tell you that I believe with absolute conviction that he is telling me the truth, you may think that I am biased.

But like you, dear reader, I believed the gossip. Even after months of working in this industry, and seeing how photos are framed and often manipulated to support a narrative, I walked into this assignment with heavy prejudice. I believed the rumors, until I was at the center of one of them. To clarify, I am not romantically involved with Brandon Cody. And I did not trade sexual favors to gain access to him. The Editor-in-Chief of the Los Angeles Gazette personally assigned this story to me.

*Blake Dillon: Why are you telling the world about this now, after so many years? Aren't you afraid of reprisal? After all, if this person is as well-respected as you say, doesn't she have the power to discredit you?*

*Brandon Cody: She does. But my hope is that, by disclosing what happened...what is still happening...I can help the other people whose lives have been tainted by this poison. Valerie Saunders-Newman. Sara Hutchins. Desiree Stanley. And yourself. I hope that by opening up, I can shed some light into a few of the dark corners of this industry. Maybe others will come forward. Even if they don't, I couldn't let it go on.*

This time, when Blake walked into the office, heads did turn. She encountered a few looks of surprise, a few hostile stares, and more than one muttered jab as she made her way to Gideon's office.

She knocked on the partially open door, surprised when she pushed, and it hit a cardboard box on the floor. She wedged her way inside and found him filling another box on his desk.

"What's going on?"

Gideon looked up sharply. Fury coloring his expression, followed quickly by resolve and then, surprisingly, regret.

"Well, I'm not moving into the corner office, if that's what you thought."

She took in the blank walls where his framed degrees and front pages once hung. "She fired you?"

"She wants to see you as soon as you get in," he replied.

"Screw her," Blake spat, livid that a good man had gotten caught in the crossfire. "What are you going to do?"

Sighing, Gideon set the mug in his hands inside the box. "I'm going to look for another position, though I don't know who is actually hiring. Maybe I'll start a commune," he mused. "Or launch my own independent news website."

"That would be pretty kick-ass." She was trying to muster some enthusiasm. The truth was, they both knew how difficult it was to earn a living doing what they did.

"I didn't mean to cost you your job," she said, the pit in her stomach growing into a cavern.

Gideon met her gaze, his full of steely determination. "You didn't cost me anything, except maybe my complacency. I let Sonja bully me for too long. I'm sorry it took this for me to stand up for you."

Unthinking, she reached out and took his hand. "It may not have seemed like it, but I loved working for you, Boss."

He smiled. "You're my favorite pain-in-the-ass."

She let out a surprised laugh. "Ditto."

She found Sonja in her office. It was only the third time she'd ever stepped foot inside, and Blake found it as cold and imposing as the woman sitting behind the neatly pristine desk.

There were no stacks of paper and framed pictures covering every available surface. A single framed document hung on the wall, Sonja's degree. A spider plant sat in the window, and the desk held only her monitor, a mouse, and a cup with a few pens.

"I'll make this short," Sonja said without preamble. She didn't even bother to take her eyes off the monitor in front of her. "Clear out your desk. If you're not gone in fifteen minutes, security will be called to escort you out."

"You're not even going to deny it?" Blake asked,

Those cool gray eyes finally slid to her. "Deny what?"

She huffed out a bitter laugh. "Wow. You're really something."

"I am?" Sonja replied, her brows lifting. "Me? *You're* the one who got in bed with your subject and let him spew a bunch of bullshit in your *interview.*"

"I didn't sleep with Mr. Cody."

"*You're* the one who let him publicly defame the paper."

"How did he do that?" she asked. "Mr. Cody never mentioned the name of the paper or the editor who sexually harassed him."

Sonja's jaw snapped tight with an audible click. It was clear she wanted to say so much more, but she knew Blake was right. To say something would be an admission, or at least an acknowledgment that Bran's accusation was towards her.

"You're down to twelve minutes," Sonja said through a tight jaw.

Blake let her gaze travel over the woman behind the desk. "I find it odd that, instead of wanting to follow up on his story—which could be one of the biggest scandal's this town has seen—you're firing the person responsible for printing it."

"I was wondering the same thing," said a voice behind her.

Sonja's eyes went wide. She shot to her feet just as Blake turned to find Lowan Ferrell standing in the doorway.

"Lowan," Sonja said, her voice not quite as buttery smooth as she was going for. "I didn't know you were coming today. We're just finishing up. If you—"

"I'd like an answer to the young woman's question." Farrell's voice filled the room like treacle, slow and thick with a bitter edge.

The Editor-in-Chief of the Los Angeles Gazette closed her eyes and pressed her fingers against them as if fighting a migraine. When she remained silent, Farrell turned his steely gaze on Blake.

She fought not to take a step back.

"Ms. Dillon, I had a word with your editor a moment ago. He tells me you're working on a story about a targeted effort to prey on the students of a local community center by some sort of scout?"

Blake blinked in surprised. "Uh, yes. I've been working on it in my spare time. Sir," she added, belatedly.

Farrell frowned and turned to Sonja. "And you wouldn't give her the green light to pursue this for the paper?"

"Blake is our most junior correspondent," she replied. She seemed to have recovered some of her poise. "I didn't think it...appropriate to assign such an important story to a cub reporter."

"I see," said Farrell. "Who did you assign it to?"

Sonja frowned. "What?"

"You agree it's an important story," he said. "Who in the pool did you assign it to?"

"I..." She licked her lips. Swallowing, she said "No one, yet."

Farrell nodded. Turning back to Blake, he offered a small smile.

"Ms. Dillon, I want to congratulate you on such a thoughtful, provocative interview with Brandon Cody. It's already been picked up nationally."

"Th-thank you, Mr. Farrell." She glanced at Sonja whose hands had balled into fists.

"I'm moving you off of the celebrity beat," he continued. "You'll work in our investigative division, and I'd like you to continue your work on the other story. My sister-in-law served on the board of directors at Play L.A.—may she rest in peace. It holds a special place in our family."

"I had no idea, Mr. Farrell," she said, her head spinning.

"Lowan, you can't be serious," Sonja sputtered. "Blake isn't ready for—"

He turned to her. "Sonja, I think you have more important things to think about than whether my instincts about Ms. Dillon are unfounded." Shifting towards her, he squared his shoulders.

Out in the main room, Blake heard a commotion and had to move out of the way as a security guard stepped into the office.

"Please escort Ms. James off the premises," Farrell said.

"Lowan!" Sonja said, breathless. "You can't...I... My things..."

"We'll be sure to pack everything safely and have them delivered to you. And I'd advise you to retain counsel." Farrell put a hand on Blake's shoulder and guided her out of the room. They left a cursing, sputtering Sonja behind them.

In the main room, everyone looked as shell-shocked as Blake felt. She realized they were headed to Gideon's office.

When they arrived, Gid was standing by the window, both hands on his head.

He turned when he heard them come in. "Mr. Farrell. Blake." His eyes were saucers.

"Please. Lowan is fine." He released her and stepped aside. "Mr. Lopez. May I call you Gideon? How long have you been with us at the Gazette?"

"Uh, fifteen years, sir. Lowan. And yeah, Gideon is fine."

Lowan picked up the framed master's degree Gideon had thrown into one of the boxes. "I'm sure you have...a bad taste in your mouth from recent events, but I would consider it a personal favor if you would step into the role of Editor-in-Chief. It recently became vacant."

Gideon's wild gaze flicked to her and back to Lowan. "Chief? Me?"

"You don't think you're qualified?"

Gideon let out a startled laugh. "I am. It's just..." He shook his head. "The Gazette has a lot of untapped potential, but a reputation to clean up as well."

"I agree," Lowan said. He turned to Blake. "You'd be satisfied with this arrangement?"

"I'd be delighted, sir."

"Lowan."

"Lowan."

"And...I'm sorry for my behavior at the gala," he added. "The last time we spoke, I was...not myself."

"Apology accepted," she replied with a nod.

"Good, then. I'll leave you to it." Lowan moved to the door. "Gideon, will you need someone to help you move your things into your new office?"

Gideon grinned. "Nope, I'm good. Blake owes me a favor," he said, picking up a box and holding it out for her.

# 32

It was a good interview. As he read, Ollie's chest filled with pride for both Blake and Bran, as well as white hot anger towards Sonja fucking James.

"Why didn't you ever tell me?" He couldn't fathom the shame and embarrassment Bran had been carrying all this time.

Bran shrugged. His eyes were hidden behind his sunglasses, but Ollie knew his best friend too well. He could see the tension in his shoulders and in the corner of his mouth.

"It wouldn't have changed anything," Bran said at last.

"Wouldn't it have? Did Clark know? Noelia?"

"No." Bran shook his head. "Not the full story."

"Jesus."

They were back in La Jolla, out by the pool. The sun was high in the sky and the waves were lapping gently on the sand twenty feet below. He leaned against one of the posts that held up the pergola. Bran was sitting cross-legged on a lounger.

"I wish you had told me."

"I know."

"You've carried my secret but didn't trust me with yours."

Bran turned his head. "It wasn't like that. I..." He released a heavy breath. "I didn't want pity. Or for anyone to look at me like I was a victim. Or worse, a liar."

"A liar?"

"Look at me, Ols. And look at Sonja. Do you think anyone would believe I was afraid of her?"

"There's more than one way to have power over someone," Ollie said, sitting on the lounger next to his. Facing him, he put a hand on Bran's back. "And do you think you're the only person she's done this to?"

Bran's mouth dropped open. "Shit."

"Yeah."

"Sorry to interrupt." Rory walked out onto the patio. "I wondered if you were ready to head out?"

"Yeah," Bran replied, standing. "Blake said she'd meet us there?"

Ollie nodded. "She's been called to an emergency meeting at the Gazette. Maybe corporate didn't take too kindly to the interview, especially after it was picked up by the national news."

Blake had texted to say she was meeting with the publisher, a man he'd only met briefly at the gala. As far as Ollie was concerned, the interview was proof enough of Sonja's slander and the damage caused by gossip and innuendo. He wasn't sure the publisher and his cohorts would see it the same way.

Blake and Bran both deserved better.

Rory stood. "I'll be in the car."

"Thanks." When he was gone, Ollie turned to Bran and asked, "You sure you're up for this?"

"Not really."

The drive to Play L.A. was quiet, and he used the time to re-read the interview and scroll through social media. The response was largely positive, though there were a number of asinine comments that Ollie hoped Blake never saw.

He searched the Gazette for the article and photos about Val, Blake, and Bran, but there was nothing.

He thought about the events of the last few weeks.

Spending so much time with Blake, after not having seen her for years, suddenly felt like some sort of fever dream. He could almost convince himself he'd imagined the whole thing. But she'd been there, solid and real, in his arms. Under him.

He hadn't expected to grow as close as they had in such a short time, and he wondered if there was a way forward for them. If proximity and adrenaline had been the only thing bringing them together.

He had no clue what his next steps should be.

An email from Vincent Park sat in his inbox, marked unread. Taking him up on the offer to join the writer's room for *Blackbird* would mean leaving Bran's employ. Something Ollie had always planned to do. Eventually. Probably.

So, why did it feel like a betrayal?

"Are you still working for me because you want to or because you feel like you owe me?" Bran asked, making him wonder if Lorna mentioned something to him about the offer.

Ollie turned to face him, but not before he caught Rory's expression in the rearview mirror.

"Why are you asking me that?"

Bran shrugged again, but this time he didn't look away. "Because I don't want to lose you, but also because I don't want to be the reason you don't go for what you really want."

Ollie swallowed down the lump in his throat. "I don't feel obligated."

Bran let out a heavy breath then nodded. "Then you'll take the job?"

"What job?"

"Lorna asked why I wasn't letting you go do your own thing. Why I pressured you into staying." His smile was sad.

"I never told her that." The anger rose quick. "She didn't have the right to say that to you."

"She's not the only person to tell me how selfish I am, keeping you tethered to me. Noelia, Clark, even Blake, though she didn't have to say it out loud."

"It's not... You need someone in your corner who doesn't have an agenda. Someone who isn't looking to make a buck off of you or use you as a stepping stone to something else." Ollie said. "And, yes. I know I'm not working for free, but that's not why I'm here."

"Ols, in case you haven't noticed, I don't have many friends. I don't have an entourage. You're it." Bran shifted, bringing one knee up onto the seat between them. "I know it's not fair to you, but that's why I hold on so tightly. Of course, you should take the job—if you want it. *Of course*, you should do the thing you've always wanted to do and write."

"Bran—"

"I'm a selfish asshole. Ask Blake."

Ollie laughed softly. "I don't think she thinks of you that way anymore." He paused. "Well, that's not all she thinks of you. Anyone who does doesn't know you very well."

The car stopped at a red light, and he put his hand on Bran's shoulder. "You need more people in your corner. And you would have them if you trusted people. If you actually let them in." He flicked a glance at Rory, who nodded.

"Take the job," Bran said, his voice thick. "I'll figure things out on my own."

Ollie eyed him closely. "How about this? I'll take the job and transition out of my position as your executive assistant if you let me find you a manager. You need someone to handle your daily business, but I will be around to help you in any way you need. As your friend."

"You need a team," Rory said from the front. "Sorry to eavesdrop, but it blows my mind that you only have four people handling everything."

"I have an attorney, too," Bran argued.

Rory shook his head, pulling off with traffic as the light changed.

"Do you know people?" he asked.

"I know people." Rory nodded. "Good people."

"See?" he said, turning back to Bran. "Looks like I'm going to work with Lorna."

Bran smiled. "What about you and Blake?"

He sat back. "I'm not sure, there. This stuff with the Gazette..."

"She'll probably be out of job."

"There's nothing keeping her in L.A." It hurt to say it out loud, but it was the truth.

"There's you, idiot." Bran looked at him as if he'd lost his last remaining brain cell.

"We haven't talked... I mean, we're not... I don't know where we stand. There hasn't been time to...you know, sort it out."

"You'll have all kinds of free time now," Bran said, waggling his eyebrows. "I was thinking, by the way, I know you were talking of moving into the main house, but you should probably stay in the bungalow."

"You don't want it for your new manager?"

"Hell, no," Bran said, scowling. "They won't be *living* with me. Are you fucking kidding?"

"What the hell? You insisted *I* stay with you."

"Because you're my best friend, and I didn't want you saddled with trying to find a place you could afford."

He sat there stunned, his heart hurting. "Bran. Dude..."

"Yeah, yeah." he waved him off. "The free ride is over. I expect rent from now on."

Ollie cleared his throat. "Of course. Whatever you think is fair."

"Maybe you cook for me once or twice a week? I know the shit Hans makes is good for me, or whatever, but he can't throw down like you."

Smiling, Ollie nodded. "Deal."

"Thanks for coming," Deanna said, smiling at him. "And Mr. Cody, I wasn't expecting you. It's so nice to meet you. I'm a fan of your work."

Bran shook her hand, giving her one of his most charming smiles. "The pleasure is mine. I'm a huge admirer of the work you do here. Ollie and Val have been trying to get me involved and I hope to, schedule permitting."

Deanna waved them into the auditorium where several others milled about. Ollie spotted Blake over by one of the student's vision boards.

"Hey," he said walking up next to her. He was momentarily stunned by the smile she turned on him.

"Hey yourself." She nudged their shoulders together, her smile slipping into a worried frown. "Sorry I haven't been in touch. Everything is just so—"

Ollie held up a hand. "Blake, c'mon. You have a lot going on right now. I knew that. It's all good."

She exhaled a sigh of something like relief. "Did you read it?"

"I did."

"Did Bran?" She glanced over his shoulder.

"He did," he replied. "It was brilliant, Blake. Truly."

She turned back to the board, but he could see how much his approval meant to her in the way her cheeks reddened slightly. Fucking adorable.

Still, he couldn't help but worry.

"How did it go down at the paper?"

She took a quick breath. "Well, it seems the owner, Mr. Farrell, didn't take too kindly to the accusations."

"Shit." His heart sank into his stomach.

"Yep. He fired Sonja."

He squeezed his eyes shut. *Fuck.* This is what he'd been afraid of. He— "Wait, what?" He stared at her, wondering if he'd heard her wrong.

Fighting her grin, Blake turned to face him. "Sonja was fired. Marched right out of the office just like she'd threatened to do to me only minutes before," she said, a wicked gleam in her eye. "And, get this, Gideon is the new EIC."

"Your boss is now *the* boss?"

"Yep, but that's not the best part."

The best part was that Blake still had a job, he assumed. Which meant she'd be staying in Los Angeles.

"What's that?" He tried to temper his excitement.

"You're looking at the Gazette's newest investigative journalist."

He grabbed her shoulders as her entire face lit up. "What?"

Her smile was positively blinding, and he wanted to kiss her so badly.

"I know! Gideon told Mr. Farrell about the article I've been working on," she said. "Turns out, he has some emotional investment in the center, here. Anyway, he promoted Gideon and now I report to the head of IJ, Corinne Jensen."

"Blake, that's fantastic." He pulled her into a hug, trying hard not to crush her, overwhelmed on her behalf. "Trent will be so fucking proud of you," he whispered into her ear. "Are you going to call him? He may not understand, but he'll know."

She pulled back to look up at him, her eyes full of emotion. "Yeah. I hope so."

"God... I'm so..."

"What?" she asked, looping her arms around his waist.

"I'm glad you'll be in Los Angeles for a while."

She smiled. "Same."

They were gazing at each other, and he hoped she could see all the words he was too afraid to say.

"Ohhhh," a voice behind them said. "Ms. Dillon! Mr. Ollie! Y'all together?"

Blake grinned. "Micah, you know better than to ask personal questions."

"Yeah, but you're standing in the middle of the auditorium with your arms around each other."

"Kiss her, already," Bran said walking over to them.

Ollie did, but not because a chant of *kiss, kiss, kiss* broke out from the gathered adults and teens.

"Alright, everyone. Let's settle down." Chuckling, Deanna called the impromptu meeting to order.

He followed Blake to a row of chairs and took a seat next to her. There were members of the board in attendance, as well as a number of the volunteer instructors.

Val Saunders-Newman walked in, followed closely by her husband, Sam. The couple sat at the end of their row.

"Bran, hey." Sam clasped Bran's hand. "Glad to see you here."

"I wanted to meet with you all for two reasons," Deanna said. "One, to let those who haven't heard the news know that I will be leaving Play L.A. soon."

"We'll be sad to lose you," Val said.

"I'm sad to leave, but I'll stay in touch. I wanted you all to be aware of something I've been working on with Blake Dillon, a local journalist."

Blake waved.

"Is this about that agency targeting the kids?" a woman asked. Ollie didn't know her, but assumed she was with the board.

"Yes," Deanna replied. "Blake?"

"Hi, everyone. As Deanna said, I've been working on this story for a while, and it seems to be much bigger than what's been happening here are your center." She looked at Rory, who had been standing by the door. "Rory Skinner worked on a case at an agency in Philly that we think might be linked to this one."

"It was the Yara Bujold incident," Rory said. There was a series of gasps and murmurs.

"My God," Val said. "I remember that. Poor woman."

"If this is true," Deanna said, "then we need to get the police involved."

"The minute we do that, we run the risk of any potential witnesses or victims refusing to cooperate," Blake said.

"It's true," Micah agreed. "Some folks are scared to talk."

"I propose you let me continue to gather evidence and testimony, with the help of Rory here, and when we have everything, we'll take it to the police. This is going to take time and finesse," she added.

"Will this be before or after you publish your article?" This was from a guy in the back. He stood with his arms folded, his expression skeptical.

Blake took it in stride. "I'll hand everything over to the authorities the day the article is released. I'm afraid, if I turn it in prematurely, it won't get the attention it deserves, and we have a lot of puzzle pieces to fit together first."

"An article in a major newspaper would light a fire under the department to act, if they're reluctant," Deanna agreed.

This seemed to mollify the man in the back.

"What do we do in the meantime?" Val asked. "We can't just let them continue to target the kids."

"Absolutely not," Deanna said. "We also don't want to tip them off."

"I've already spoken to some of the others," Micah said. "Everybody knows that company is bad news. They're not the only ones sniffing around. A few of us older kids told the younger ones to come to us if someone starts promising stuff."

"And Micah will come to me," Deanna said. "Or, if not me, the new director."

"I hope they're as chill as you," Micah said warily.

"You're leaving big shoes to fill," Ollie told Deanna.

She smiled. "You'll all be in good hands."

After the meeting ended, he was standing outside with Blake, Bran, and Rory.

"I love the La Jolla house, but I'm looking forward to sleeping in my own bed," Bran said. "I'm gonna go pack up and head home."

"Oh," Ollie said, torn between staying with Blake and accompanying Bran back to the rental. "I suppose I should come along and help."

"Nope," Bran replied, slipping on his sunglasses. "You and Blake have somewhere to be."

"We do?" He looked at her but she appeared to be just as confused.

"You have your car here?" Bran asked her. When she nodded, he grinned.

"What's this about?" Ollie asked.

Instead of answering him, Bran turned to Rory. "We all set?"

Rory nodded. "All set."

"Excellent. Blake, do you mind driving this one home?" He hooked his thumb at Ollie.

She looked back and forth between Bran and Rory, stopping on Rory before a slow smile spread her full lips. "Not at all."

"What are you up to?" he asked his best friend.

"Me? Nothing. You two, hopefully...something."

Bran and Rory walked away, leaving him and Blake alone on the sidewalk.

"Any idea what that was all about?" he asked.

"Not a clue," she replied, pulling out her keys. Turning, she grinned. "But I can't wait to find out."

Blake drove up the winding road that led to Bran's Malibu home, the sun high in the sky. Bran had been more cryptic than usual when he insisted they head to the house without him.

When she'd been there the last time, she hadn't paid too much attention to her surroundings. She'd been too busy reeling from the fact that her new assignment was Brandon Peters, and his best friend from college—the most embarrassing crush she'd ever had on another human being—was Bran's assistant. She had missed how gorgeous the house was, a handsome two-story mansion, with large windows, a wide porch, and a sprawling backyard. The grounds were lush and green, and there was a large pool in the center of the property.

Behind it stood a sizeable bungalow which—they'd discovered when Ollie took her inside to change—had been filled with candles and flowers. There was music playing softly in the background in the entire pool area.

Blake wasn't sure what she had been expecting, but it certainly wasn't a romantic late afternoon rendezvous for two.

"Okay, I take back every awful thought I've ever had about him," she said, taking in the spread of fresh fruits and cheeses waiting for them in the outdoor kitchen. There were smoothies as well.

"Looks like he roped Hans into this little scheme," Ollie said, smiling.

They grabbed a couple of glasses of sparkling wine and sat on the edge of the pool, dipping their toes into the warm water.

Ollie draped his arm casually over her shoulders, and she felt a strange mixture of excitement and apprehension about this unexpected bit of privacy.

They hadn't been alone since that afternoon in La Jolla where they'd used a few stolen hours to make love and just...be together. The thought of many more days and nights like that sent a tiny thrill buzzing through her veins.

"You're smiling," he said before taking a sip from his glass.

"I feel good."

"Well, that's a relief."

He was still grinning when he took her glass and set them both down before turning to her.

She drew in a breath as he settled his mouth over hers. There was something incredibly tender in the way he seemed to hold himself back. He wasn't taunting or teasing, just following her lead.

The feeling he stirred in her was more than just desire—it was connection. Recognition. Something deeper and more primal than lust.

Not love, but a pathway to it. A freeway at that, if her racing heart was any indication.

"You're frowning," Ollie said against her mouth. Pulling away, he searched her eyes. "Is it too much?"

"Too much?"

His gaze swept the space around them, the lavish pool area, the food and wine, the...everything. Then his eyes met hers. "We can go slow," he said. "I know we kind of...back in La Jolla, we...but we don't have to now..." Laughing, he swore under his breath. "I guess what I'm trying to say is I want this with you. You're honestly the only person I've ever wanted *something* with beyond... This isn't coming out right."

"Oliver," she said hoping to head off his panic. "I want this, too. I want to see where it goes. What I *don't* want is to rush it. We have time, don't we?"

"We do."

"And I'm not going anywhere."

"Neither am I," he said, smiling.

Blake smiled back at him and then put her hands on the sides of his face. "I'm going to kiss you now."

The dark shadows that had settled across his features lifted as he pulled her into a fevered, possessive kiss. He always kissed her like he had been born to do only that, and she gave herself over to his desire.

Felt it in his touch, in every move he made, and she met each kiss with just as much hunger.

When they broke apart, they were both breathing heavily.

"I wonder," he said, gliding his thumb across her lower lip, "what you would say to going skinny-dipping again?"

"I think I might be persuaded to try that," she said with a grin. "What time will Bran be home?"

"Not until I text him," he said. "He's staying in La Jolla, at least for tonight. It was all a ruse." He pointed a thumb over his shoulder, gesturing to the spread Hans had set out. "Hungry?"

It was his way of slowing things down, she knew that. Ollie's way of showing her he wanted the same things she did—an adventure with no expectations and a future they both could figure out together.

This might be the first of many ways he would woo her, win her over, the way he might have when they were both back at school. If they'd had the courage to voice their desires.

"Not for food."

They stripped down to their underwear and waded into the water, settling by the edge where they'd set their glasses.

Overwhelmed by the wave of emotions that crashed over her, Blake found it hard to think about anything but his arms around her, his body against hers.

"How about we work up an appetite first?" she asked quietly before pulling him in for another long, heated kiss that left no more room for doubts.

Ollie groaned against her lips, pressing his body as close to hers as he could manage.

Blake didn't even care about the stucco and tile of the pool's surroundings pushing into her back as she pulled him close. She wound her arms around Ollie's neck, tilting her head to deepen the kiss.

Ollie's cock, hard and thick inside his boxer briefs, pressed against her belly.

She heard herself whimper when he used his thigh to nudge her legs apart. His lips traveled from her mouth, down her neck to nip at her collarbone before moving to her nipple.

She hadn't brought a swimsuit, and the lace of her bra seemed almost obscene with her pebbled nipple clearly visible through the thin fabric.

He made a pleased sound as his mouth closed over the stiff peak.

"God, I want to taste you so bad," he groaned, running his hands down her torso to grab her hips.

Her hands tightened where they'd landed on his shoulders. A moment later, Blake was airborne, lifted out of the water. Ollie had grabbed her waist and set her down on the ledge, using his broad shoulders to open her thighs.

She could only brace herself on her hands and stare down at his hungry eyes.

"Please say yes."

Were there other words in the English language? If so, she couldn't remember any. "Yes," she said in a thready, needy voice that sounded nothing like her own.

"You're right," he rasped as he deftly slid her underwear over her hips and down her legs. "Consent is so fucking sexy." The moment he dipped his head between her thighs, Blake knew Oliver Benjamin was going to be more than she had bargained for. Behind the shy glances and the quiet voice, behind the altruism and the fierce loyalty he showed to the people he loved was a man full of a kind of fire she had rarely seen, if ever.

It was an exquisite assault. Her breathing turned ragged as he laved his tongue over her clit. He took his time to explore her, alternating between long, lazy licks that made her thighs tremble and spearing his tongue inside her like he couldn't get enough.

He was expert at getting Blake to make sounds that would have mortified her had she been in control of her faculties. As it was, all she could do was writhe and moan broken versions of his name while she spiraled into oblivion.

"Yes," he said in a husky voice that made it impossible for her to catch her breath as the aftershocks came in waves.

She'd squeezed her eyes shut and opened them to stare up at the blue, southern California sky.

His gentle hands slid under her back and guided her upright until she was sitting on the edge of the pool. Dazed and dazzled.

Grinning, Ollie swam backwards until he stopped and stretched out, floating in the middle of the pool. His erection poked out of the water, proud and obscene.

"What happened to your underwear?"

"I had to take them off," he said, his voice drowsy. "The wet cotton was getting...uncomfortable."

Blake reached behind and unclasped her bra, dropping it on the patio before she slipped into the water and walked out to him. The water rose to just above her breasts, and she stopped when she reached him.

His eyes were closed but his lips were moving.

"What are you doing?"

"Counting backwards from one thousand."

She chuckled. "Why?"

"Because there are a million things I want to do with you and if I don't calm myself down, this will be over before it even starts."

Blake reached up and wrapped her hand around his cock. It was velvet and steel in her hand, slick with water and the essence of his arousal.

He gasped, sputtering. "Blake."

"Shhh," she said, soothing him and coaxing him to his back again. "Weren't we just talking about how we had time?"

"Yeah, but..." He moaned when she ran her thumb around the head of his cock.

"But?"

"Nothing," he said quickly, desperately. "Don't stop."

She let go long enough to slip between Ollie's legs. She carefully put them on her shoulders. "Open your arms wide."

He glanced down and seemed to understand because he obeyed, his breath coming in hard pants.

She was grateful this end of the pool was shallow and she was able to brace her feet on the bottom and keep him afloat. She leaned forward and kissed the head of his cock before taking him into her mouth.

"Fuck," he muttered.

Taking her time, she explored him with lips, teeth, and tongue. She loved being able to take over like this, to be in control without feeling like they were on borrowed time.

Instead of thinking about the future or the past, she focused on giving him pleasure, licking and nipping until his hips were straining in her hands.

"Blake."

Her name on his lips was followed by a burst of salty pre-come on her tongue and he moaned.

With a moan of her own, she leaned forward and slid her tongue along the vein running the length of his erection. Drawing back up to the head, she ran it around the crown and down again and again.

"Oh my God." He was panting now. Blake took his full length into her mouth. "*Blake.* Blaaaaake." It was a quiet warning, but she kept going, making sounds of encouragement.

She felt the moment his body seized up before a low growl bubbled up from his chest and he flooded her mouth.

Blake swallowed every drop and held onto Ollie's hips as he came down.

Eventually he righted himself, eyeing her like she was some sort of miracle he'd just discovered floating in the water.

"I didn't think..." he began. "I wasn't expecting you to..."

"Why don't we both throw our expectations out the window," she proposed.

His smile made her insides flutter. "I like the sound of that."

Ollie pulled her close and cupped her face in his hands. The kiss was slow, tentative.

"Let me feed you," he said.

*You just did*, she didn't reply, grinning to herself.

Wrapped in soft towels, they ate fruit, cheese, and fresh bread with fresh basil and thin slices of prosciutto. They talked about life in Philly versus life in California, about the things they liked and the things they missed.

As the sun set, Ollie lit the candles that had been placed all over the patio, and they sat at the table and talked some more. The entire time he kept a hand on her. Her arm, her leg, the back of her neck when he drew her in for a kiss.

They were using the time as they saw fit, not treating it as something they had in limited quantity.

"Will you show me some of your writing?" she asked after they'd been dancing by the pool for a while, her head on his shoulder. She wore one of his T-shirts, and it came down to her thighs.

Ollie was in a pair of basketball shorts and nothing else. She wished he could walk around like that all the time because...yum.

"I don't have anything finished," he said.

"So?"

Pulling back, he rubbed the back of his neck and she giggled.

"You really don't want me to read your stuff."

"It's not that," he said, hedging. "I do."

"But?"

She watched him wrestle with the idea before saying, "Yeah, okay. C'mon."

He led her into his bungalow where they sat on the overstuffed sofa. The windows were open to the breezes coming off the pool and the ocean beyond. It wasn't as upscale and modern as the one in La Jolla, but it had more personality. She liked it a lot.

Blake expected Ollie to pull out his laptop, but instead he brought out a large, spiral bound book. The cover was made of thick hide. When she opened it, she found the creamy ivory pages were unlined.

Ollie's handwriting was neat and fine. She gasped, running her fingers along the words without reading them.

"What?"

"Nothing," she said. "My grandfather writes like this."

He smiled. "Really?"

She nodded, Swallowing, she settled into the sofa and turned the page, focusing on the words and not the similarities.

*The first morning I woke and realized I'd stopped dreaming about her, it felt as if my mind had betrayed my heart. Like there had been a war for my senses and my soul was the battlefield. I, like so many soldiers returning home to a cool welcome, didn't know myself anymore. Who was I without her awareness of me? What fixed point in the sky was I to replace her with, just as elusive and unattainable and necessary as she had been? I didn't want to drift. I didn't want to fade. On the off chance that her light might touch me again, that I would be called up to serve in the army of her devotion, I remain at the ready. The wait is the appearance of movement when you're standing still and, in this, I am a master. I hope my dreams of her invade me anew.*

Blake didn't need to ask. She understood why he didn't want her to read this. When she turned, Ollie's eyes were on hers. Hope, fear, shame, and pride all swirling in his cobalt gaze.

She set the book down and took his hands in hers. His were shaking, so she brought his fingers to her mouth and kissed them, one by one.

His feverish gaze followed her movement. "I'm so glad it's you," he said, "here with me. That I've found this with you."

Blake pulled his right hand to her chest, over her heart. She didn't have the words, like he did, but found she didn't need them.

The crease in Ollie's brow, his beautiful brow, unfurled as he searched her eyes. His breath seemed to stutter out of him as the seconds passed.

She smiled, and he smiled.

She took a deep breath, and he did the same.

And when she released one hand to cup his cheek, Oliver Benjamin closed his eyes and whispered her name like it was the only word he knew.

# Epilogue

"Okay, everyone," Bran said. "Quiet down. My boy's show is coming on."

Ollie was too excited to be embarrassed. Bran had invited everyone over to watch the premiere of *Blackbird*, and it felt good to have the support of his closest friends.

He'd spent three months in his first writers' room, crafting the season arc for the new show. Genre television hadn't been on his radar, but he had found freedom in writing magical realism. Early buzz for the series was good, and he had high hopes the streaming numbers would be solid enough to earn them a renewal.

"Hey," Blake wrapped an arm around his waist and gave him a soft kiss on the cheek. "I know you're not nervous. You can't be. The pilot is a masterpiece, and the show only gets better from there."

"You're biased." He slid his arm around her back and pulled her close, grateful as always for her solid presence and unwavering confidence.

"I'm really not," she said, smiling up at him. "Aren't they already talking about renewing it?"

They were, based on the early buzz.

Around the room sat Bran, Noelia, Clark, Val and Sam, as well as a few friends Ollie had made at Play L.A.—Rudy and his partner, Tre, who were both in the cast of *We the People*.

Hans walked carefully into the media room with a tray of glasses. "Who wants a mojito?"

"I'll take one," Bran said. He took two, handing one to Lorna who sat beside him on one of the two-seaters.

Sam also took one.

"None for you, Val?"

Val smiled, glancing at Sam before she shook her head. "Um...I can't."

Bran grinned "Are you on some thirty-day cleanse or something?"

Val bit her bottom lip, drawing it into her mouth.

Both she and her husband looked like they were about to burst.

"Wait," Rudy said, scooting to the edge of the set he shared with Tre. His eyes lit up. "Val... You're not..."

"Holy hell," Bran said, getting to his feet. "Can I *finally* stop carrying this around?"

"Carrying what?" Blake asked.

"You're having a baby?" Ollie asked.

Val nodded vigorously, and Sam looked like he was about to hyperventilate, though he was smiling from ear to ear.

"We haven't made it public, yet." Sam was beaming.

"Yes, please don't say anything," Val added.

"Dammit, guys." Bran exhaled. "I've never had to keep a secret like that before."

"We have an interview set up with Melanie Cobb," Val told him. "You'll be off the hook soon."

"Wait." Blake eyed him. "Is this why you were spending so much time at Val's when Sam was out of the country?"

"It was," Val replied. "I had horrible morning sickness. It lasted all the damn time, and I was miserable. Bran was sweet enough to hang out when I was missing Sam."

"Thanks again for that, Bran." Sam lifted his glass in a toast.

Bran waved him off. "Just looking out for big sis."

"I'm so happy for you guys," Blake said. "That baby is going to be adorable."

"And spoiled rotten. I'm gonna be the best uncle." Bran was preening.

"Oh, God." Val laughed, shoving his shoulder. "We're going to have to have a talk, I think."

"Nooooo," Bran said. "I've had to carry this burden forever. It's my right to get the kid anything I want. Drums, one of those mini Jeeps...

uh...a baby boat. Do they make boats for babies?"

"Do we need to take out a restraining order?" Sam asked, chuckling as he pulled Val closer.

Ollie watched the exchange with a full heart, as Blake reached for his hand and squeezed.

Blake snuggled in close. "I'm so happy for them. They've been through a lot, and look at her. She's glowing."

He kissed her hair, unable to keep the smile from his face. He was in love with such a wonderful, kind woman. Struck by the sudden thought, the breath whooshed out of his lungs.

"Are you okay, babe?" She looked at him, concerned.

"Yeah," he replied, coughing a little. "Fine. Forgot how to drink liquids."

Loving her wasn't a surprise as much as it was a revelation. He had hovered in Blake's orbit in college.

After that, she'd become an ideal to him, one that he'd put firmly in the realm of impossibility until she appeared in his life again. And in the last few months, they had grown from impossibility to possibility to reality.

Now, she was his friend and lover, his rock and his champion. She was the woman he couldn't imagine life without. When she smiled at him, it made him feel like the luckiest man in the world.

It was too fucking early for him to picture the two of them like that, married with babies on the way. Way too early.

But the reality of her far outshone any fantasy he may have held about holding Blake's heart in his.

Blake pulled out her phone and frowned at the screen.

"Anything wrong?"

She shook her head. "No, it's from Rory. His cousin found a solid lead on the people behind Diamond Moon. Finally." She exhaled with apparent relief. Glancing up at him, Ollie could see the hope in her eyes. "We're going to drag these bastards into the light."

"I don't doubt it for a single second." He lowered his mouth to her ear. "You're amazing, Blake Tiana Dillon, and I'm crazy about you."

She was smiling when she lifted her head to look at him. Blake didn't say anything, but she didn't have to. It was all there in her eyes.

"Okay, gang, we're starting." Bran called out, rubbing his hands together.

The lights lowered, and Ollie pulled Blake down to sit with him, wrapping around her and resting his chin atop her head. She was warm and wonderful in his arms.

Bran's new assistant, Luca, slipped inside and took a seat in the back. "Sorry, I'm late," they said. "Just needed to drop off your dry cleaning."

"Thanks for that." Bran pointed to the sidebar in the back. "There's popcorn and mojitos."

"Nice."

"Shhhh," Lorna said. "You're going to miss the name cards."

As the show began, and the credits populated the screen, Ollie held his breath.

## WRITTEN BY OLIVER BENJAMIN

The screen froze and Bran started whooping, pumping his fist in the air.

Ollie laughed as the small group burst into applause. He held up his hand.

"Thank you, thank you. I appreciate it."

There was a swell of pride followed by a wave of nausea as he thought about how many people were going to see the show. Viewers and critics, people back home. His thoughts turned to the media tour he'd have to undertake. The thought of walking into a room full of people and fielding their questions made him nauseous. He didn't know how Bran, Val, Sam, and the others dealt with it.

He thought about how Bran handled himself. About how Blake was representative of most of the types of people he'd have to interact with. And he was only a writer, one of four on the show. Not the showrunner. Not the star.

He had this.

"Proud of you, man," Bran said, walking up to him.

He raised his glass and Bran followed suit.

"Can we watch the actual show, now? I had a hand in it, too," Lorna said.

Laughing, Bran took his seat and picked up the remote. "Alright. Ols, you ready?"

Smiling, he held Blake tighter, more prepared than ever to face whatever the future might bring.

"Yeah, man. Let's fucking go."

# Acknowledgements from the Author

A million thank yous to Liz Berry, Jillian Greenfield Stein, and M.J. Rose for welcoming me into the 1001 Dark Nights/Blue Box Press family. Also, thank you to my right hand, Ann R. Jones, for not laughing at all my wild ideas and for helping me bring some of them to fruition.

Writing a book is quite the undertaking, even in the best of times. 2022 was *not* the best of times, so thank you to my family and to my partner-in-crime, Mr. X, for helping me to find the silver lining in even the darkest of clouds.

# About Xio Axelrod

Xio Axelrod [she/her] is a *USA Today* bestselling author. She writes different flavors of contemporary fiction, romance, and what she likes to call, "strange, twisted tales."

A completely unapologetic, badge-wearing, fic-writing fangirl, Xio finds inspiration in everything around her. From her quirky neighbors to the lyrics of whatever song she currently has on repeat to the latest clips from her favorite TV series, *SKAM*, Xio weaves her passions into her books. (And if you're curious about *SKAM*, ask her about it. Just be prepared to settle in for the long haul.)

Xio grew up in the recording industry and began performing at a very young age. When she isn't working on the next story, she can be found behind a microphone in a studio, writing songs in her bedroom-turned-recording-booth, or occasionally performing under a different, not-so-secret name.

She lives in complete denial of the last five minutes of *Buffy* with one very patient, full-time, indoor husband, and two part-time, supremely pampered, outdoor cats.

Visit Xio Axelrod at https://xioaxelrod.com.

# Book Club/Reflection Questions

1. Blake looks up to her grandfather and hopes to follow in his footsteps. How difficult do you think it is for a young woman of color to advance in investigative journalism?

2. What do you think Blake and Oliver saw in each other during college that formed so strong a bond that it withstood the test of time and distance?

3. Ollie and Bran also have a special connection, with Bran often acting as a protector for young Ollie. How do you think that has manifested itself in their working relationship? Do you think their friendship would be as strong without the shared trauma of Ollie's history?

4. Blake investigates a shady entertainment company that preys on the underprivileged. Why might someone sign a contract with such an infamous organization? Is it the promise of fame or simply a chance to better their situation?

5. Ollie's love language is caring for people. He handles practically everything for Bran to make his life run smoothly and constantly feeds Blake and makes sure she's taking care of herself. What is your love language?

6. Blake doesn't hide that she loathes her current assignment on the celebrity beat. So why do you think she stayed at the Gazette rather than take a position at her grandfather's old paper?

7. Ollie is, in turn, both insecure and confident about his writing talent. What do you think feeds his insecurities?

8. Do you think Blake and Bran will come to be friends?

9. Do you think Ollie will ever finish his novel?

Sign up for the Blue Box Press/1001 Dark Nights Newsletter
and be entered to win a Tiffany Lock necklace.

There's a contest every quarter!

Go to www.thebluboxpress.com to subscribe.

As a bonus, all subscribers can download
FIVE FREE exclusive books!

# Discover 1001 Dark Nights Collection Ten

DRAGON LOVER by Donna Grant
A Dragon Kings Novella

KEEPING YOU by Aurora Rose Reynolds
An Until Him/Her Novella

HAPPILY EVER NEVER by Carrie Ann Ryan
A Montgomery Ink Legacy Novella

DESTINED FOR ME by Corinne Michaels
A Come Back for Me/Say You'll Stay Crossover

MADAM ALANA by Audrey Carlan
A Marriage Auction Novella

DIRTY FILTHY BILLIONAIRE by Laurelin Paige
A Dirty Universe Novella

HIDE AND SEEK by Laura Kaye
A Blasphemy Novella

TANGLED WITH YOU by J. Kenner
A Stark Security Novella

TEMPTED by Lexi Blake
A Masters and Mercenaries Novella

THE DANDELION DIARY by Devney Perry
A Maysen Jar Novella

CHERRY LANE by Kristen Proby
A Huckleberry Bay Novella

THE GRAVE ROBBER by Darynda Jones
A Charley Davidson Novella

CRY OF THE BANSHEE by Heather Graham
A Krewe of Hunters Novella

DARKEST NEED by Rachel Van Dyken
A Dark Ones Novella

CHRISTMAS IN CAPE MAY by Jennifer Probst
A Sunshine Sisters Novella

A VAMPIRE'S MATE by Rebecca Zanetti
A Dark Protectors/Rebels Novella

WHERE IT BEGINS by Helena Hunting
A Pucked Novella


*Also from Blue Box Press*

THE MARRIAGE AUCTION by Audrey Carlan
Season One, Volume One
Season One, Volume Two
Season One, Volume Three
Season One, Volume Four

THE JEWELER OF STOLEN DREAMS by M.J. Rose

SAPPHIRE STORM by Christopher Rice writing as C. Travis Rice
A Sapphire Cove Novel

ATLAS: THE STORY OF PA SALT by Lucinda Riley and Harry
Whittaker

LOVE ON THE BYLINE by Xio Axelrod
A Plays and Players Novel

A SOUL OF ASH AND BLOOD by Jennifer L. Armentrout
A Blood and Ash Novel

START US UP by Lexi Blake
A Park Avenue Promise Novel

FIGHTING THE PULL by Kristen Ashley
A River Rain Novel

A FIRE IN THE FLESH by Jennifer L. Armentrout
A Flesh and Fire Novel

VISIONS OF FLESH AND BLOOD by Jennifer L. Armentrout and
Rayvn Salvador
A Blood and Ash/Flesh and Fire Compendium

## On Behalf of Blue Box Press,

Liz Berry, M.J. Rose, and Jillian Stein would like to thank ~

Steve Berry
Doug Scofield
Benjamin Stein
Kim Guidroz
Tanaka Kangara
Stacey Tardif
Asha Hossain
Chris Graham
Jessica Saunders
Kate Boggs
Richard Blake
and Simon Lipskar

Printed in the USA
CPSIA information can be obtained
at www.ICGtesting.com
LVHW040717220823
755878LV00005B/25